D0960150

CANAAN'S GATE

CANAAN'S GATE

KATHRYN R. WALL

 MINOTAUR BOOKS NEW YORK

This is a work of fiction. All of the characters, organizations, and events portrayed in this novel are either products of the author's imagination or are used fictitiously.

CANAAN'S GATE. Copyright © 2010 by Kathryn R. Wall. All rights reserved. Printed in the United States of America. For information address St. Martin's Press, 175 Fifth Avenue, New York, N.Y. 10010.

www.minotaurbooks.com

Library of Congress Cataloging-in-Publication Data

Wall, Kathryn R.
  Canaan's gate / Kathryn R. Wall.—1st ed.
      p. cm.
    ISBN 978-0-312-60184-3
  1. Tanner, Bay (Fictitious character)—Fiction.   2. Women private investigators—Fiction.   3. Older people—Abuse of—Fiction.
4. Hilton Head Island (S.C.)—Fiction.   5. Domestic fiction.   I. Title.
    PS3623.A4424C36 2010
    813'.6—dc22

                                                        2009047483

First Edition: May 2010

10 9 8 7 6 5 4 3 2 1

To Norman.
For then. For now. Forever.

ACKNOWLEDGMENTS

My thanks to Regina Scarpa and Anne Gardner of Minotaur Books, as well as to my agent, Amy Rennert. Their advice was sound, and their support never wavered. Special thanks to my sister-in-law, the keen-eyed Dr. Barbara J. Everson, and to Loretta Healey, who provided an entrée into the hidden corners of Wexford Plantation.

And, as always, blessings on my husband and family. I couldn't do this without you.

CANAAN'S GATE

CHAPTER ONE

I'M AN ORPHAN."

Though I spoke the words aloud, there was no one in the office but me to hear them. I have no idea why the reality of it should have wormed its way into my head on that soft September afternoon. Maybe it was because I'd been watching sunlight slant through the half-closed blinds to send wavering lines of shadow dancing across the scarred surface of my father's old desk.

When I was a child, it had dominated his study in my family's antebellum home on St. Helena Island just off the coast of Beaufort. In later years, after a series of small but debilitating strokes had condemned Judge Talbot Simpson to a wheelchair, it had joined the other castoffs in the warren of attics above the third floor, its pride of place usurped by the utilitarian trappings of illness and infirmity. And death.

After the Judge's passing, I had it moved into the new offices of Simpson & Tanner, Inquiry Agents.

Orphan. I rolled the word around in my mind while my gaze traveled over the expanded space, fully twice the size of my former office. The addition of my husband to the staff had made the move to larger quarters necessary. Whether the sudden increase in our caseload was directly tied to the fact that Red had spent years in the local sheriff's department or whether it was simply that the exploding population of Hilton Head Island brought with it a corresponding increase in people with troubles, I couldn't have said. The fact was we were busier than ever.

I tried to bend my concentration to the files spread out across the Judge's massive mahogany desk, but my mind refused to cooperate. The faint smell of recent paint lingered in spite of my having thrown open all the windows on that warm Wednesday afternoon. My sole remaining partner, Erik Whiteside, had left right after lunch to track down information for a background check, and Red was at a meeting at his son Scotty's school over in Beaufort.

I smiled, remembering the call the night before from Red's ex-wife, Sarah. Scotty had gotten into a fight on the bus with another boy who'd apparently been taunting him about something. Though outweighed by twenty pounds, my stepson had given as good as he'd gotten. Red tried unsuccessfully to conceal his pride as he recounted the details of the battle. But the school had threatened suspension, so he was off to mend fences and promise swift retribution for any recurrence.

My gaze wandered again to the tangle of holly bushes spread beneath the loblolly pines just outside my window. We'd been lucky to find larger quarters in the same building just outside the gates of Indigo Run Plantation about halfway down the island. And I'd been able to keep this same calming view. Suddenly, I felt the urge to be out there, inhaling the sweet Lowcountry air, feeling the warmth of the sun on my face. I snatched up my keys, resurrected my sunglasses from the bottom of my bag, and locked the front door behind me.

With our hordes of summer tourists gone, the island had lapsed back into calm again, traffic on nearby Route 278 creating only a mild hum. I strolled aimlessly across the parking lot, stopping to listen to the sharp *rat-a-tat* of a woodpecker high up in one of the pines. I wandered down the drive and around the building, my face turned slightly upward to let the warmth soak into my skin.

It had been a hell of a year. My father's death had altered my life in a number of ways, as had my marriage to Red a few weeks later. It was a promise I'd made to the Judge that last day in the hospital, and I'd had no valid reason not to keep it. We'd been dancing around it almost from the day my first husband, Red's brother Rob, had been viciously murdered. My misgivings had been worn away by Red's unwavering pursuit and my own realization that I could care for him in a non-brotherly way. So far, it seemed to be working.

I waved to one of the partners of the public accounting firm that occupied the end unit of our building and flashed back to my own CPA days in Charleston. Rob and I had been a team, combining our expertise to help the state attorney general's office sever the financial head of the illegal drug business in South Carolina. I sighed at the memories of that idyllic time when Rob and I had loved and crusaded together.

History seemed to be repeating itself in any number of ways.

I swung back around and unlocked the office. Work would banish the megrims. The old favorite term of my late father's companion, Lavinia Smalls, had me grinning as I stepped into the reception area. She'd used it to describe this antsy, dissatisfied feeling of low spirits for as long as I could remember.

A quick glance showed the message light glowing brightly on the telephone next to Erik's laptop. I waited until I had pulled the heavy chair up behind my father's old desk before I dialed the answering service.

The female voice was pitched low as if afraid of being overheard. "Mrs. Tanner, if you're the one who used to be an accountant, please call me at this number."

I scratched it on a notepad. Local, but that's about all I could tell. I waited through a long pause.

"Just leave a message, and I'll call you back. It's important. I mean, I think there may be a crime involved. I'm not sure, and . . . Well, never mind that now. Please call me."

She didn't leave her name. Interesting.

I went through the rigmarole to save it. On my computer, I clicked onto Google and did a quick reverse-directory check of the number. Nothing. I tried a couple of the more sophisticated programs Erik had installed to assist us with the background checks we now did routinely for several county and local government agencies and nonprofit organizations. Vetting potential employees and volunteers had become a priority for such groups, and Simpson & Tanner was reaping the benefits. Again I came up empty.

I dialed the number the nervous woman had left. It was a generic answering service, the kind you can get in one of those package deals from the phone company. No name, just a repeat of the number. I told the electronic voice that I'd be in the office until approximately four thirty, then forced my attention back to the files still strewn across the desk. I told myself that vague feeling of unease and dissatisfaction that had sent me wandering the parking lot in the middle of the afternoon could be sublimated by hard work.

I'd been telling myself that a lot lately.

I barely managed to get my mind back on track when the phone rang.

"Simpson and Tanner, Inquiry Agents."

Erik would cringe if he heard me. He firmly believed that I should let the service pick up when he wasn't around to run interference for me.

"Is this Mrs. Tanner?"

"Yes?"

A short pause. "My name is . . . Well, that doesn't matter right now. And I don't have long to talk."

Calling from work, I told myself. I could hear a muted buzz of conversation in the background.

"Understood. Your message mentioned a crime," I said to spur her along.

"A *possible* crime. I just want to make sure . . . I mean, I don't want to get anyone in trouble. I could be completely wrong."

I waited a couple of beats, but she didn't continue. "Why aren't you talking to the sheriff?"

"I just said I'm not sure." The woman's voice had dropped to a hoarse whisper. She sounded afraid.

"Well, you're going to have to give me something concrete if I'm going to be able to help you." I listened again to the voices I could hear behind her and thought, *Retail store of some kind. Lots of coming and going, different people talking.* "Ma'am? Are you still there?"

"Look, maybe this was a bad idea. I'm probably wrong about all of it. It's just that they're such a nice old couple. I'd hate—" It sounded then as if she'd put her hand over the phone. I could just make out her muffled words: "I'll be right there."

When she came back to me, the woman's voice had dropped so low I could barely hear her. "Maybe I'll call you later. I don't know. I have to think about it." A pause. "I'm really sorry I bothered you."

The click in my ear told me I'd lost her.

Thanks to Erik's training I'd jotted down the caller ID number before she'd disconnected. Different from the first one she'd left me. I punched in the digits.

After three rings a chirpy voice said, "First Coast Bank of the Carolinas. This is Cindy. How may I direct your call?"

"Sorry, wrong number," I said and hung up the phone.

CHAPTER TWO

I CONSIGNED THE DOZEN OR MORE QUESTIONS RAT-
tling around in my head to their own mental compartment
and forced myself to concentrate on the work in front of me. But, in
spite of my good intentions, my mind kept swerving back to the hoarse
whisper on the telephone.

It had to be about money, of course. Something the woman had
run across in the course of business at the bank? I could understand her
reluctance to get into details, and the fear I'd heard in her voice was
probably tied to the fact that she could be putting her job at risk. Or
perhaps it was personal. Still, I wondered why she'd come to a private
agency when the sheriff was readily available. For free.

The opening of the outer door put an end to my pointless speculation.

"I'm back," my partner called as he stepped into the reception area.

"Hey, Erik. Have any luck?" I rose and stood in the doorway.

He settled his tall frame into the swivel chair behind his desk and
ran a hand through his blond hair. "Not much. Most of the people in
the neighboring apartments are new, and even the couple I managed to

talk to who might have been around when our guy lived there didn't have much to offer. He seemed to keep pretty much to himself."

"Sounds a little hinky," I said, and Erik shrugged.

"Maybe, maybe not. I'm not home enough to really know my neighbors, so they might say the same thing about me."

"Never. You're much too upstanding a citizen. It oozes out of you."

He grinned. "*Oozes*? Sounds disgusting."

"I meant it in the nicest possible way."

"Sure you did. Any calls? Anything I need to take care of?" He opened his laptop, and his fingers flew across the keyboard.

Erik Whiteside had dropped into my life in the middle of his own crisis, and our early, wary encounters had blossomed into a deep friendship. His computer skills had become legendary, and his contributions to the agency were invaluable. By working part time at an office supply store, he'd saved enough to buy his way into the business. I would have given him a partnership, but he'd insisted on earning it.

As I said, upstanding.

"We had one interesting phone call, a woman who said she might want us to investigate a possible crime."

"What kind?" Again his fingers beat on the keys, and I knew he was opening a client file. "What's her name?"

"I don't know, and she didn't say," I answered with a smile. "Very enigmatic conversation. I did use caller ID, and the number she was calling from was First Coast Bank."

"Embezzlement?"

"That was my first guess, but she didn't elaborate. She said she might call back, but I'm not putting any money on it. She sounded pretty stressed out."

"I'll label the file 'Madame X' just in case she gets her nerve up."

"Fine," I said, turning toward my office. "I'm almost finished up here. How about you?"

"I need to get this data entered and see if there's somewhere else to go on this guy applying for the teacher's aide position. If I can't nail a couple of concrete references down, I'm going to recommend they give him a pass."

"Sounds like a plan."

Twenty minutes later I finished collating the documents I'd been working on, transferred all the information to the computer, and signed out. I'd just slid open the bottom right-hand drawer and extracted my bag when the phone rang.

"Got it," Erik called from his desk.

I leaned back in my chair, some premonition telling me this was our girl. A moment later, my hunch was confirmed.

"The lady from the bank, I think," Erik said from the doorway. "At least she was whispering the way you described. I put her on hold. Line one."

"Did you get her name?"

"Nope," he said.

I nodded and picked up the receiver. "Bay Tanner."

"Mrs. Tanner? This is . . . my name is Cecelia. Cecelia Dobbs. We spoke earlier?"

"Yes, Ms. Dobbs. How can we help you?"

"I'd like to see you in person. Is that possible?"

I checked my watch. Red had said he'd be home sometime around five, and it was already after four.

She caught the hesitation. "I know you're located near Indigo Run. I could be there in just about five minutes."

I knew that was true because the bank at which she worked was just down the way on Beach City Road.

"Fine. I'll wait for you."

"Thank you. Thank you so much. I'll be right there."

I hung up and found Erik still lurking in the doorway. "She's on her way?"

"Yes. Can you stick around?"

"Sure. Stephanie's on deadline, so she'll be at the office until late."

Stephanie Wyler and Erik had been an item for a couple of years, and it felt as if the relationship might just be going somewhere. The daughter of my late partner, Ben Wyler, Stephanie worked for *Hilton Head Monthly,* a glossy local magazine.

"Good. By the way," I added, "you can delete 'Madame X.' Her name's Dobbs. Cecelia. We'll get the rest of her vitals when she gets here."

I retrieved a clean legal pad from the center drawer and loaded the cassette recorder with a fresh tape. Though Erik frequently argued for more sophisticated equipment, I felt most comfortable with the familiar standbys. There were some new tricks this old dog didn't feel like dealing with.

I'd just managed to get everything arranged to my satisfaction when the outer door opened. With the expanded space in the new office, I no longer had a clear sight line to the front door. I was standing next to the desk when Erik ushered in our prospective client.

Medium height and more than a few pounds overweight, Cecelia Dobbs clutched her out-of-season white straw handbag in front of her like a shield. Her brown hair shone glossily in the flickering rays of sunlight through the blinds, but the cut didn't suit her square face. She wore very little makeup; and her clothes, while obviously of good quality, were at least one size too small.

She hung in the doorway, her eyes darting from side to side as if she expected an attack from all directions at once. She jumped when Erik put his hand on her elbow and gently nudged her into my office.

"This is Bay Tanner," he said.

"Ms. Dobbs? I'm very glad to meet you. Won't you sit down?"

She scurried to the client chair and dropped into it, completely ignoring my outstretched hand. She blushed when I let it drop again to my side.

"Sorry," she mumbled, and red blotches appeared on both her cheeks.

"No problem," I said, returning to my own seat. "Now, how can we help you?"

Cecelia Dobbs glanced quickly over her shoulder at Erik.

"Would you prefer that we speak in private?" I asked. "Mr. Whiteside is a partner in the firm and will be fully informed of everything we discuss here, but he can wait outside if that would make you more comfortable."

"Oh, no! He can . . . I mean, that's okay if . . ."

She gave up, her voice trailing off into silence. The red splotches spread across her entire face.

"I'll be at my desk if you need me," Erik said, flashing a grin across the bowed head of our visitor before he tactfully retreated into the reception area. He didn't close the door.

I fiddled a little with the paraphernalia on my desk to give the poor girl a chance to regain her composure, but she didn't take the opportunity. After a few awkward moments, I said, "Does your problem concern the bank?"

Her head popped up as if a puppeteer had jerked invisible strings. "How do you know—? I mean, I never said anything about a bank."

"Caller ID. Modern technology can be a blessing or a curse, depending on how you look at it, don't you think?"

Cecelia Dobbs nodded. "I should have thought of that. I'm pretty tech-savvy. But this whole thing has me so upset."

"Why don't you just start at the—?"

"How much do you charge?" she blurted out.

I reached into the drawer and handed her a packet that contained a list of our services and their associated fees. It also included our standard contract.

"If you'd like to take a moment to look those over," I said, "I'll just step outside. Let me know when you're ready."

I made it about a third of the way out of my chair before she spoke.

"No, wait! That's okay. I was just wondering . . . you know. I can pay." She fumbled in the dirty straw bag and pulled out a checkbook. "How much do you need? Up front, I mean?"

I sat back down. "Look, Ms. Dobbs, why don't we do this? You can sign the contract and give me a dollar as a retainer. That will ensure you our confidentiality. Then, after you've told me your problem, we can both decide if we want to do business together. If so, we can work out the financial arrangements. If not, we'll just rip up the contract, and I'll give you your dollar back. How does that sound?"

A lot of the tension in her bunched-up shoulders relaxed. She dropped the checkbook back in her bag and pulled out a wallet. She handed me a crumpled single, and I gave her a pen and showed her where to sign. The transaction completed, she seemed to come to life.

"Thank you, Mrs. Tanner. I've never done anything like this before."

I smiled. "I understand. It can be pretty intimidating, I suppose. But I promise that we'll keep your secrets regardless of whether or not you decide to engage us." I waited a beat for her to settle more comfortably in the chair. "Now, as I was saying, why don't you start at the beginning?"

Cecelia Dobbs expelled a long breath. "I think someone at the bank is running a scam on some of our customers, and I'm afraid they're going to do something really bad."

I frowned at the last part of her statement. "Bad? Like what?"

The earnestness in her voice and on her face was hard to ignore.

"Like maybe someone could end up hurt. Or worse."

CHAPTER THREE

MY FIRST THOUGHT WAS THAT THE YOUNG WOMAN had been reading too many mystery novels or perhaps watching too many *Law & Order* reruns, two sins of which I would be forced to plead guilty myself. Still, she'd said it with a straight face and without a hint of melodrama.

"That's pretty serious," I said. "But let's back up a little. What exactly is your position at the bank?"

Cecelia Dobbs cleared her throat. "Well, I began as a part-time teller when I was in school and afterwards worked my way up to assistant manager of customer service, although when we have people off sick or on vacation, I fill in on the teller line." She looked away for a moment. "That's how I came to be aware of this . . . situation."

She seemed to run out of gas at that point, so I nudged her a little.

"You mean the scam?"

"Yes, ma'am. See, we have these customers. I helped them set up their accounts way back when they first came to the island, maybe six or seven years ago. Just a really nice old couple, sweet and . . . well, just *kind,* you know? Obviously devoted to each other. I'd watch them sometimes when they left the bank. He'd always go around and open the car door for her. A real gentleman."

Out of the corner of my eye I could see Erik, his head bent over his computer, typing quietly.

"They sound like wonderful people," I prodded.

"Yes. I'd guess they were in their early seventies then, so they must be close to eighty by now." She tugged at a ring with a small blue stone on the third finger of her right hand. It fit so snugly I couldn't believe she'd had it off in a long time. "She doesn't come in anymore. Just the husband. And the other woman."

Cecelia Dobbs looked up expectantly as if I might anticipate her next words. I almost felt as if I could.

"Some sort of caregiver?" I asked, and she nodded.

"Yes, exactly. I know it happens a lot around here. Some of these folks get too old to do for themselves, and they don't want to give up their homes to go into assisted living, so they hire a nurse or an aide, someone to look after things for them. We deal with the situation a lot at the bank. But this one . . ." She hesitated.

"Something struck you as not quite right about her?" I asked.

The jittery young woman looked directly at me for the first time. "I think she's stealing from them, but I can't prove it. I need someone to find out if I'm right so I can go to the police. Can you do that kind of thing?"

"We have some experience with financial cases. I think you already know I used to be an accountant. So, yes, we certainly have the expertise." I looked across her shoulder at Erik, and he nodded. I would never make a commitment to take on a client without his agreement.

"I . . . I don't make a lot of money." Cecelia's chin rose just a fraction. "But my dad's a doctor. A surgeon. He'll give me the money if I need it." The red stain inched across her cheeks again. "I live at home right now."

"Let's not worry about that just yet," I said, trying to ignore her obvious embarrassment. "What makes you suspicious of this caregiver? Do you know her name, by the way?"

The young woman nodded. "Yes. It's Blaine. Kendra Blaine." She paused. "She's probably in her late twenties, maybe early thirties. She lives in Hardeeville, but she stays a lot with the . . . the old couple."

"It seems you've done quite a bit of detective work on your own," I said, then smiled to take the sting out of my next question. "Is there some reason you're reluctant to give me the name of the supposed victims?"

Tension bunched in her shoulders. "This is bank business. I'm bound by confidentiality rules. If anyone found out I was blabbing about our clients' financial business with someone outside the bank, I could get fired."

"That's why you signed the contract and gave me the dollar, Ms. Dobbs. I can't reveal anything we talk about unless you give me permission."

Of course, there were other circumstances under which I might have to break her trust, but we didn't need to get into those at that point.

Cecelia glanced over her shoulder at the open doorway. "Does that mean . . . ?"

"Everyone that works for me or is associated in any legal way with the agency is bound by our agreement."

She drew a deep breath and nodded. "Okay. It's the Castlemains. Thomas and Rebecca." She paused as if expecting some reaction from me. "You don't recognize the name?"

It seemed vaguely familiar, but I couldn't place where or when I'd heard it. "Sorry," I said. "I take it you think I should."

"They're real big patrons of the arts. They donate huge amounts of money to just about every charity in the county." She seemed disappointed by my ignorance. "They have their names in the paper all the time."

I wasn't a big reader of the social pages, and my appreciation for the arts didn't extend much past an occasional play. Obviously, Cecelia Dobbs had a better handle on the activities of the upper echelons of island society than I did.

"Sorry," I said again. "Maybe you'd better fill me in." I flipped to a fresh page on the legal pad and waited.

Cecelia Dobbs's face turned grim. "Mr. Castlemain founded some sort of aeronautics company that's connected to the space industry," she said. "They're incredibly wealthy. At least that's what I read. My parents sort of know them, from charity events and stuff." Again her pause held just a touch of drama. "Best I can figure, Kendra Blaine has swindled them out of close to a million dollars."

The silence stretched out as I digested the bombshell Cecelia Dobbs had just dropped. "A million dollars?" I finally managed to croak out. "Are you sure? How is that possible?"

The woman drew a deep breath and leaned forward. "No, I'm not certain, or else I would have gone to my boss with it. Or the sheriff."

"So what first aroused your suspicions?" I kept my voice low and nonconfrontational, and Cecelia relaxed back into the chair.

"Usually the old folks end up giving the companion or nurse some sort of limited access to their finances. After they've had a chance to size up the person, you know? These aren't generally stupid people. They're not about to just hand over control of their money to some stranger. Sometimes their kids get involved, too. We've got several customers who set it up so a son or daughter has to countersign anything the caregiver does over a certain amount." She paused again.

"Would you like something to drink?" I asked.

"If you have some water . . ."

Before I could rise from my chair, Erik stepped into the office and lifted a bottle from the mini-fridge. She smiled when he passed it over to her, then cracked the top and sipped.

"Thanks. Anyway, more often than not the children aren't in the picture. They're back North or somewhere getting on with their own lives." She sighed. "I can't imagine leaving my mama and daddy to just . . . Well, never mind that. In this case, it took about six months before Mr. and Mrs. Castlemain felt comfortable with adding this Blaine woman as a signatory to some of their accounts."

"So what's she doing, writing checks to herself?" I asked.

"No, ma'am. That would be too obvious, too easy for anyone at the bank to catch. We're on the lookout for things like that. No, this is more like influence. At least that's what I think's been happening."

"Any idea how she's doing it?"

"She—the Blaine woman—she comes in with Mr. Castlemain, maybe twice a month. They're all chatty and friendly, and she's fussin' over him, helping him with the door and his cane and all. What first got me suspicious is that they usually wait to deal with one particular teller. She tries not to make it too obvious, but I've watched them. She always manages to stall long enough so she can have Dalton wait on them."

"So you think this Dalton is an accomplice?"

"He could be," Cecelia Dobbs said, "but I don't have any proof. He's a nice-looking guy. Could be Kendra Blaine just likes to flirt with him."

Her last statement brought the unattractive red flush back to her cheeks, and I wondered if maybe Cecelia wasn't above a little flirting with a handsome bank teller herself. The thought made me slightly embarrassed for her.

I cleared my throat. "So this Dalton, is he new?"

"Relatively," she said, her eyes dropping to stare at her hands clasped tightly in her lap. "Less than a year. No complaints, and he does have a way with the customers. Especially the women. I don't have access to the details of personnel evaluations, but I have wondered why he hasn't moved up the ladder in all that time. Good-looking guys like him usually don't stay tellers for long."

"So maybe someone else has noticed the same things you have. Possible?" I asked.

"Maybe. Anyway, I got suspicious a couple of months ago, and I've sort of made it my business to keep an eye on Mr. Castlemain and his . . . companion whenever they come in. I've made excuses to hang out by the teller line. There's nothing specific I can point to, nothing I could take to my bosses. It's just a feeling that . . . that Dalton and Kendra Blaine are *involved* in some way."

Her tone made the simple word sound dirty.

With a sigh, Cecelia Dobbs continued. "Here's the thing. Over the past few months, Mr. Castlemain has transferred over nine hundred thousand dollars out of his money market account to a company called Southern Preferred Investments. I've done as much checking as I can get away with. Without, you know, breaking any rules. I even tried Googling the company, but I couldn't find anything. But the transactions always take place when Blaine is with him, and they're always run through Dalton's window."

She watched my face for some reaction, but I didn't have one to give her. At first hearing, it sounded to me as if she'd concocted a dire scenario out of a few scattered bits of probably innocent coincidences. And maybe just a touch of jealousy for the attention the good-looking young teller was paying to someone other than Cecelia Dobbs? My hand hovered over the drawer with her dollar bill and contract inside.

But . . . there was the little matter of close to a million dollars. And some piece of scum who could be taking advantage of a nice old man.

I set my pen down on the desk. "I'll need to discuss this with my partner. I'm inclined to think we'll take your case, but it has to be a mutual decision. Are you ready to move forward?"

"Oh, yes. Thank you so much," Cecelia gushed as she reached into her bag to extract a single sheet of paper. "I've written down everything I know about the Castlemains, Kendra Blaine, and Dalton Chambers." She passed the paper across the desk. Her smile softened her face and made me realize how attractive she might be with a little care and attention.

"I'll look this over and give you our final decision tomorrow. Where can I reach you?"

The smile vanished. "You can't call me at the bank. Use my cell and leave a voice mail." She slid the paper back toward her side of the desk, took my pen, and scribbled a number across the bottom. "I'll check it every hour and call you back as soon as I can."

"That's fine. I promise we'll be very discreet." I waited a beat. "And we'll also require a reasonable retainer before we can actually begin work."

"No problem." Again she rooted in the dirty straw bag and emerged with a checkbook. "Just say how much you need."

I named a modest amount, enough to cover Erik's time in running down the players. "If we come up with something that requires more extended effort, I'll ask you for a full retainer."

I accepted the check and rose to indicate we were done.

Cecelia held out her hand. "Thank you so much," she said again. "I've been worrying about this for a long time. I feel a lot better now that someone professional thinks I'm not a complete nutcase."

I wasn't sure about that—yet—but I shook the wide, square hand. "You're welcome. I'll be in touch."

At the door, Cecelia Dobbs turned back. "You know, I'm pretty sure it's that Blaine woman who's behind all this. Dalton is probably just a . . . pawn or something." She hesitated. "I really don't want him to get hurt or anything."

"I understand."

She waved once and closed the door behind her.

Erik and I exchanged a look.

"A woman scorned?" he asked, and I laughed.

"Maybe. Or maybe she's a lot smarter than she looks."

Back in my office, I picked up the sheet of paper she'd left on the desk. Cecelia had given me the Castlemains' address and phone number. I didn't recognize the street name, but I'd have been willing to bet it had to be in one of the pricier plantations on the island, Wexford or Long Cove Club. I'd check that out later. I hadn't expected anything in the way of financial information. The girl had been adamant about not violating the bank's confidentiality policy if she could avoid it, and I certainly understood her concern. Blaine's address in Hardeeville didn't mean anything to me. I almost never had occasion to travel that way unless I was just passing through the outskirts on my way to I-95.

Dalton Chambers was another matter.

"Hey," I called through the open door, "isn't Compass Point in your condominium complex?"

A moment later Erik stood in the doorway. "Yeah. Why?"

"That's where this Chambers guys lives."

"No kidding. That's the high-rent district of Broad Creek Landing. Three bedrooms and a garage. Most of them are right on the water with great views. How does a bank teller afford that?"

"Good question. Maybe he's just renting."

He nodded. "Could be, but even then those things go for major bucks."

I gave him the number. "Swing by on your way home and check it out. See what kind of wheels he has, too, if you can."

"Sure. But wouldn't it be pretty stupid to be living way beyond your means if you were embezzling money? Why advertise it to everyone?"

"You're right, but criminals aren't always the brightest bulbs in the chandelier."

"Lucky for us," he said.

"We'll see," I murmured and did my best to shake off the brief, unexpected shiver of . . . *something* that skittered down my back.

CHAPTER FOUR

ED'S RESTORED BRONCO STOOD IN THE DRIVEWAY when I pulled up to my house on the beach in Port Royal Plantation a little after five thirty. *Our* house, I mentally corrected myself as I slid from the leather seat of my Jaguar. Rob and I had built it from our own plans when we lived in Charleston, using it as a week-end getaway whenever we could squeeze out the downtime. The bomb planted in his small government plane had ended all that in a fiery explosion that left my husband—my *first* husband—dead, and me with a series of scars, both emotional and physical, that had settled into dull throbs and the occasional flare-up of deep, searing pain.

Since Rob's murder several years ago and my subsequent marriage to his brother, it had again become an *ours* rather than a *mine*.

" 'Ob-la-di, Ob-la-da, life goes on,' " I murmured under my breath as I climbed the steps from the garage into the foyer. Red loved the Beatles.

"It's a friendly burglar," I called more loudly and dropped my bag on the console table just inside the front door.

"Out here."

I followed the voice through the great room and the French doors onto the wide deck that wrapped around three sides of the house. Red stood in front of the gas grill next to the screened-in area we often used as an outdoor dining room.

He turned and held out his arms, one gloved hand gripping a greasy pair of tongs. I stepped briefly into his embrace.

"Yuck, you're all sweaty," I said, pushing back on his chest.

"If you can't stand the heat, et cetera, et cetera," he said with a grin. "Preparing the perfect New York strip is a tricky business, my girl. Stand back and let the master work."

I flopped onto a chaise out of the drift of smoke that wafted up toward the clear evening sky. Out over the ocean, a deep V of Canada geese pointed directly south. From the beach just across the sheltering dune, I could hear children's squealing voices and the gentle *shush* of the waves curling onto the packed sand.

I laid my head against the cushion and felt some of the day's tension drain away. "Anything you want me to do?" I asked, my eyes drifting closed.

"Nope. Just relax for a while. The table's set, and potatoes are in the oven. I'm guessing about fifteen minutes."

"Don't burn mine," I said softly, the urge to drop off to sleep almost overpowering.

"Don't worry. I know you like yours just this side of mooing."

Red's voice seemed to be coming from a long distance . . .

"Hey!"

I jerked upright, disoriented for a moment to find myself on the deck. "Sorry. I must have dropped off." I swung my legs over the side of the chaise and rubbed my hands across my eyes. "I don't know what's the matter with me," I said, rising. "You want a beer with dinner?"

"Already on the table. And your sweet tea. But you can get the potatoes out if you want." He hesitated before saying, "You know, I wish you'd tell me why you haven't been sleeping lately. What's on your mind?"

I felt a flush creeping up my neck and turned back toward the house so he wouldn't see it. "Nothing," I said. "Just one of those things. It'll pass."

I left it there and headed for the kitchen.

The steak was perfect, red in the center and pink all around. I used the baked potato as an excuse to down about half a container of sour cream with a little butter on the side.

One day all this is going to come back to haunt you, I thought. *Or more likely your hips.* Still, I had always been a picky but hearty eater, and I seemed to burn it off. At least for now. With my mid-forties fast approaching, though, my luck could very shortly run out.

"So what happened at the school today?" I asked, mostly to shove aside the twinge that thinking about my biological clock always brought.

Red smiled. "I had a nice chat with the principal about Scotty's 'incident,' as she called it. Brought back some really uncomfortable memories, I can tell you."

"You spent a lot of time in the principal's office, did you? I'm shocked."

"Not a lot, no. But I had my moments."

"They didn't suspend him, did they?"

"No, but it was a near thing. I volunteered him for ten hours of community service and an apology to the boy whose nose he bloodied. She went for it, but he's on a short leash. One more time, and he'll get three days off."

"What did you say to him?" I asked.

Red had always been a strict, but loving father to his two kids, Scotty and Elinor, at least as far as I'd been able to observe. The fact that they'd morphed from my nephew and niece into my stepchildren was still taking some getting used to.

He laid his cutlery across his plate and leaned back in his chair. "I told him fighting is never the best solution to a problem." He tried hard to suppress a grin. "I also congratulated him on landing a right cross. Just the way I taught him."

"Talk about mixed messages."

"I know, but a boy has to learn how to defend himself. The other kid started it, and Scotty tried reason first. All the kids on the bus said pretty much the same thing, according to the principal." He paused. "And I grounded him from his video games for two weeks anyway. That hurt worse than the shiner he's got going."

In silent agreement we rose and began to clear the table. A few minutes later everything was put away, the dishwasher loaded, and we were back on the deck, stretched out side by side on the chaises. Twilight spread across the ocean as the sun sank over the mainland. A slight onshore breeze rustled the leaves of the live oaks and palmettos. I could feel myself getting drowsy again.

Red's voice drifted over to me. "So how was your day? Anything I should know about?"

I tamped down the brief flare of annoyance. Red had been a sergeant in the Beaufort County Sheriff's Office for many years, and we had crossed swords any number of times since I'd gotten into the private investigation business. His decision to quit had come as a surprise to me, but I'd been happy to see him relieved of the danger and stress that was a natural part of the job. I'd co-opted him into the agency, initially to help us on one specific case, but that part-time assignment had lengthened until it was the next best thing to permanent. He definitely had skills we could use, and his contacts on both sides of the law would no doubt prove invaluable. Still, we had our moments, being in each other's pockets, and every once in a while I had to wonder if it was actually going to work out.

In more ways than one, I'd been on my own a long time. Sharing, on many levels, took some getting used to.

"Just routine stuff," I said, stretching and turning onto my side to face him. "Except for just before I was ready to leave." I gave him the gist of Cecelia Dobbs and her suspicions. "I'm inclined to take it. I have some computer checking to do, and Erik will run down backgrounds on all the players, but I really don't like the idea of someone running scams on vulnerable old people."

For just a moment a vision of my late father flashed across my mind. He'd been anything but vulnerable, up until his last few weeks of life. Crusty and demanding, the retired attorney and judge had more than held his own into his eighties. I felt the tears rising and stamped them back down. I'd made a number of promises to him, and one of them had been no weeping. It was one of the most difficult to keep. We'd worked together on agency business, argued and carped at each other, and he'd never been able to keep himself from meddling in my life.

I missed him like hell.

I sat up suddenly. "I need to call Lavinia. I haven't talked to her in a few days."

Lavinia Smalls had been first our housekeeper, then my surrogate mother, and finally my late father's loving companion and caregiver. I owed her more than I could ever repay.

I started to rise, but Red's voice checked me.

"Wait a minute. What's my role in this case? What do you want me to do?"

I spoke without thinking. "Nothing right now. It's all computer work, and I want to check out the Castlemains with Bitsy Elliott. She's the expert on high society on the island."

I watched his face cloud over. "So, what? I should go fishing? Watch soaps? Hang around the office and make Starbucks runs?"

"Come on." I sat back down and leaned toward him. "You've been pretty busy the last few weeks, helping Erik run down some of these people we're checking out for the school system. It won't hurt you to back off a little."

"I don't want to back off. You're paying me a salary. I intend to earn it."

It was another one of the sticking points in our shaky alliance at the office. Erik and I were partners; Red, the hired help. At least that's how he categorized himself. I knew that he sometimes resented being married to a woman who was independently wealthy, but he'd known that going in. I wasn't about to apologize for having made some sound investments, both with my own earnings and with what I'd inherited. And having had the sense to get out before it all went bad. It wasn't as if I ever flung it in his face. Not intentionally, anyway.

"I'm sure there'll be plenty for you to do once we get into it," I said. I reached across and stroked his cheek with my hand. "Relax." I jumped up. "I'll call Lavinia and be right back. Bring you a beer?"

"Whatever," he mumbled as I headed inside.

I ignored his crankiness as I punched in the number of the house I'd grown up in. I wondered, not for the first time, how Lavinia could stand rattling around in the old place by herself. I had half expected her to go and live with her son and daughter-in-law, but so far she hadn't made any noises about moving. I had no idea what I'd do with the massive antebellum pile if its caretaker for more than forty years decided to abandon—

"Hello?"

"Hey, Lavinia. It's me."

"How nice. So you haven't forgotten me entirely."

As Lavinia's rebukes went, it was pretty mild. In fact, it was the sort of thing I would have expected from my late father—just a tip of the verbal dagger, inserted, but not twisted in too far. I let it go because I sort of deserved it.

"I'm sorry. It's been a little hectic around here. Is everything okay?"

The brief silence before she answered made me sit up straighter on the sofa where I'd stretched out to make the call. "Lavinia?"

"It's nothing, Bay, honey, really. I won't deny it's lonely here without your father. I keep expecting to hear that hum his wheelchair always made and the squeaks on the wood floor. I miss him so much."

I'd rarely seen Lavinia shed a tear, but I could hear them gathering in her voice.

"I know. What can I do?"

"I try to keep busy with the church and all, and I've been to Thad and Colletta's for dinner a few times. Isaiah almost never comes home anymore."

Lavinia's grandson had just entered his senior year of college; and, as with most young men his age, his life had become crowded with new friends and experiences. Her son and daughter-in-law, with an almost empty nest, might even be thinking about moving on themselves.

"Why don't you come and stay with us for a while? Maybe a change of—"

"No! Thank you, but I'm not some doddering old woman who needs looked after. I've been takin' care of this place since before you were born, and I'm not ready for the scrap pile just yet."

I smiled. That was more like the Lavinia who had badgered and molded me into a strong, independent woman. Just like her.

"You're always welcome. I hope you know that."

"Of course. Listen, honey, there's something I want to talk to you about."

"Shoot."

"It's about your sister."

The word made me swallow hard. For most of my forty-plus years I hadn't even known of Julia's existence. The circumstances of my finding her, coming so soon before the Judge's death, still seemed surreal. She and her caregiver, Elizabeth Shelly, lived in an old house, not unlike Presqu'isle, outside the small town of Jacksonboro on the road to Charleston.

"What about her?"

"Have you been in touch lately? I mean, with Miss Lizzie?"

"Not for a few days. Why?"

"She called here."

This time I swung my legs over the edge of the sofa and pressed the phone tight against my ear. "Is something wrong?"

"Now don't jump to your usual assumptions, Bay Tanner. I always said you just seem to expect the worst out of a situation. Hush up, and let a body get a word in edgewise."

"Yes, ma'am," I said, chastened. "I'm sorry."

"Miss Lizzie called because she just needed someone to chat with. You have to admit it must get lonely for her, too, stuck out there with Julia. Her being the way she is."

My half sister, the product of my father's relationship with his former lover, had psychological issues I didn't completely understand, problems that had kept her almost childlike for most of her adult life. My old college roommate and prominent Savannah psychologist Neddie Halloran had been working with Julia for several months.

"Is Julia making any progress? I mean, with Neddie?"

"Some. But it's not about your sister." She sighed. "Miss Lizzie is gettin' on, you know." Again that pause, loaded with meaning I felt certain I didn't want to examine. "She's worried about what will happen when she can't take care of Julia anymore."

The thought had crossed my mind as well, more than once. Lizzie Shelly had to be in her seventies, although she'd always struck me as sprightly for someone her age. But then, I'd thought my father would live forever, too.

"Is she ill?"

"Nothing specific. She was sort of feeling me out, I think."

"About what?" The idea sprang from nowhere into my head. "Does she want you to help her? With Julia, I mean?"

It might be a great solution all around, the two older women teaming up to care for Julia. Until she could look after herself. Neddie had made no promises, but she'd been hopeful that she could help my sister. Lost in my own tumbling thoughts, it took me a moment to realize she hadn't answered my question.

"Lavinia? What do you think she has in mind?"

"Well. She didn't say it in so many words, you understand. I mean, she didn't come right out and ask."

"Ask what?"

The words came out in a rush. "I think Miss Lizzie and Julia should come and live at Presqu'isle. With me."

CHAPTER
FIVE

I STARED AT THE EMPTY FIREPLACE, MY MIND AWHIRL with the possibilities.

"Bay? Are you still there?"

I jerked my attention back to the phone. "I think it's an excellent idea. Lord knows there's plenty of room. How do you feel about it?"

"It makes no never mind how *I* feel. It's your house."

My father had deeded Presqu'isle over to me on the occasion of my fortieth birthday, with the proviso that he and Lavinia would be tenants for life. His death hadn't changed that. Not that I needed some legal mumbo jumbo to tell me where my responsibilities lay.

"You can invite the whole damn neighborhood to live there if it makes you happy. You know that."

"Language," she snapped, and I felt a lot of the tension ease away.

"Sorry. I'm more worried about what that would entail. Julia hates being away from that old place in Jacksonboro. And she loves her animals. You up for having dogs and horses running around the property?"

I loved hearing her laugh again. "I guess the horses would have to go. No barn or anything. I can live with the dogs." Then her tone sobered. "I think their place might be falling down around their ears, to hear some of the things Miss Lizzie says need done. And it sounds as if there might not be a lot of money left."

My father had made no provision for Julia in his will, primarily because he'd had no idea where she was or even if she was still alive. I felt certain he would have done so had he been aware of her circumstances. After the estate was settled, I'd tried to offer my half sister her rightful share, but Miss Lizzie had firmly rebuffed me. For what were—to her—understandable reasons, she'd despised my father and refused to take a penny of his money.

I'd quietly set up a trust fund in Julia's name, to be used for her care in the event of Miss Lizzie's death. But I knew the older woman wouldn't touch it while she was still drawing breath.

"You know how she felt about Daddy," I said. "What makes you think she'd condescend to live in his house?"

"She doesn't think of it that way. She knows you own Presqu'isle." She paused a moment. "I think it's her age that worries her most. What would happen to Julia if Miss Lizzie got sick or fell down and broke a hip?"

I looked up as Red wandered in from outside, where night had fallen almost completely. Across the dune, I could see the lights of a freighter, far out on the ocean, plying slowly south toward Savannah.

"I'm in favor of it, Lavinia. You don't have to convince me. But it could mean a lot of extra work for you. I just want to be certain you're up for it."

"I'm fine, Bay Tanner, don't you worry about me. I just wanted to know how you felt about it, generally speaking."

"So, the ball's in your court. Why don't you have another talk with Miss Lizzie? Ask her right out if she wants them to come and live at Presqu'isle. I'm sure the state or the county would be thrilled to have that old rice plantation to preserve. She might be able to get a good price for it, even if it does need a lot of repair."

"I'll talk to her," Lavinia said. "You give Redmond my best, won't you?"

"Yes, ma'am," I said. "Keep me posted, okay?"

"Of course," she replied and hung up.

Lavinia has never been a great one for goodbyes.

I set down the phone and followed Red into the kitchen. I found him staring into the open refrigerator.

"We got any chocolate sauce?"

"I don't know," I said. "I don't remember seeing it on Dolores's list."

Dolores Santiago had nursed me back to health after the operations and skin grafts to repair the damage from the explosion of Rob's plane. She'd stayed on to be my part-time housekeeper, sometime cook, and dear friend. She came only twice a week now; and, between us, Red and I handled the culinary chores. One of the most important services she performed was the grocery shopping. I absolutely loathed the whole process.

"Here it is." He pulled the brown squeeze bottle from the door of the refrigerator. "Now if I can just find peanuts in the pantry we'll have sundaes."

"I'll look," I said, thankful that his good spirits seemed to have been restored. "Of course we'll need ice cream, too."

"Brilliant deduction, Sherlock," he said with a laugh.

We did indeed have an almost untouched carton of French vanilla. We busied ourselves with the preparations, moving silently around the kitchen. When bowls were heaping, we carried them back outside to the darkened deck. I stopped along the way and tucked my cell phone into the pocket of my shorts.

Red had lighted the citronella candles ranged along the railing, and the flickering light created a soothing ambiance. A while later, I scraped my spoon against the empty bowl and set it on the small wrought-iron table between us. I sighed and let my eyelids droop.

Red leaned back, his hands tucked behind his head. "This is how

I always pictured things. The two of us sitting somewhere like this, quiet, watching the stars come out on a warm, still evening." He reached across and captured my hand. "Happy?"

I could feel his head turn to look at me, but I didn't open my eyes. "Um-hmm," I murmured, the urge to sleep dragging at my consciousness.

"I love you."

"Um-hmm."

Somewhere above us, a bird whose song I didn't recognize trilled softly and was answered. Across the dune, a woman called to her dog.

"Bay? Are you asleep?"

I forced myself out of the half doze. "No. Just incredibly relaxed."

"How's Lavinia doing?"

"Fine. She misses Daddy."

"You do, too, I know. Is she going to stay on at Presqu'isle?"

I really didn't want to have this conversation, at least not at that particular moment. Presqu'isle, Lavinia, Julia—they were my responsibilities. I tried not to interfere in Red's dealings with his children. Or his ex-wife. Somehow he couldn't seem to grant me the same courtesy. I ordered myself to speak calmly.

"There are some issues, but I'll handle them. It's only a few months since Daddy died. Being alone will take some getting used to for Lavinia."

"I didn't much like it after Sarah and I got divorced. Coming home to an empty apartment basically sucks rocks."

That made me smile. "I know the feeling." I rubbed my hands across my face and forced myself awake. "I need to call Bitsy."

"Can't it wait until tomorrow?"

I picked up the sticky bowls and turned toward the French doors. "You just relax. It'll only take a moment. Aren't the Braves on TV?"

"West Coast. Game doesn't start until ten."

"Then just chill right there. I'll be back in a minute."

I rinsed out the bowls and spoons and added them to the dishwasher, then moved down the hall into the third bedroom, which Rob and I had converted into an office. I took a legal pad from the drawer and punched in the number of my oldest childhood friend from our days growing up on St. Helena. I listened to the rings, picturing her beautiful blue eyes widening in anticipation at the sound.

Elizabeth Quintard Elliott and I couldn't have been more different. My five-foot-ten-inch frame dwarfed her, and my dark chestnut hair stood out in stark contrast to her pale blond. We'd looked like polar opposites even when we were little. And appearance wasn't our only point of departure. I had been the hell-raiser, into and out of scrapes of one kind or another on a daily basis. Bitsy was the picture of perfect Southern girlhood—quiet, ladylike, obedient. She had quit college to marry the obnoxious Cal Elliott and have his babies, then take her rightful place in local society as the daughter of an aristocratic mother who could trace her French Huguenot ancestors back almost to the beginning of time. Bitsy's mother and mine had been friends and not-so-friendly competitors for the title of First Lady of Beaufort County society.

"Hello?"

"Hey, Bits. It's me."

"Bay, darlin', where have you been? It's been dog's years since we've talked. I was just thinkin' about you."

"Great minds," I said, smiling. Bitsy always had that effect on me. It was hard to be in a bad mood when engulfed in the glow of her natural exuberance.

"I was just sayin' to Big Cal that we need to have you and Red over for dinner. Wouldn't that be fun?"

I cringed and fumbled for some way out of answering. Red absolutely loathed Bitsy's big-mouthed husband, who never seemed to have much to contribute to any conversation that didn't involve his son's college football career or the success of his half-dozen used car lots scattered around the state.

"We'll see," I finally said. "We've been pretty busy with the agency."

"I haven't forgiven you for not inviting us to the wedding, you know. You didn't even let me have a tiny little hand in planning anything."

Bitsy's idea of the perfect ceremony would have included hundreds of guests, an acre of flowers, the sweeping grandeur of St. Helena Episcopal Church, and at least a dozen bridesmaids in some sort of hideous lavender gowns. I shuddered at the mere thought.

"We wanted to keep it just family. Because of the Judge. I know you understand."

"Of course I do, sugar." The long sigh told a different story. "I just wanted to be there for you."

"I know. Listen, I need to ask you something."

"Sure."

"In all your work with the arts council and the Junior League and all that, have you ever run across an old couple named Castlemain?"

"Becky and Thomas? Sure. Why do you ask?"

I smiled. I'd thought it might be a long shot that someone our age would have moved in the same circles as the elderly Castlemains. I should have known better than to underestimate Bitsy.

"Their name came up. What can you tell me about them?"

"Well, what exactly do you want to know? I mean, they're just the dearest people. And fabulously generous. They donated most of the money for that new wing of the arts center and pressured their friends into comin' up with the rest. They're big sponsors of Deep Well and Literacy Volunteers. Just about anything that's worthwhile on the island."

She paused for breath, and I jumped in.

"Have you ever met the woman who takes care of them?"

For an astonishing ten seconds, Bitsy remained silent.

"Bits? You still there?"

"You talkin' about Kendra Blaine?"

She said it as if the name tasted bad in her mouth.

"Yes. You know her?"

"Let's just say we've had a few . . . encounters."

"Spill."

"Why on earth would you be interested in that . . ." She drew a steadying breath. Her mother's strict upbringing would not have countenanced the use of epithets. "She's not a very nice person."

"Tell me everything you know."

"Why?"

"It might be important."

Again that long-suffering sigh. "Well, I'm sorry, but Kendra Blaine is just not worth wastin' breath on. She's a crude, nasty, arrogant woman. She's got Thomas completely flummoxed, but I think Becky has her number. Too bad the poor thing is too sick to do anything about it. My friend Lily Middleton, Becky's closest confidante, has been trying to convince their grandson to get rid of—"

"Whoa! Slow down. Rebecca Castlemain is ill?"

"Nothing specific. Poor old dear is over eighty, that's mostly what's wrong with her. Doesn't much leave that wonderful place of theirs in Wexford except to see her doctors, and not much of that anymore. Harley goes to the house most times."

"Harley Coffin?" My father's doctor. *Former* doctor. Patient privilege notwithstanding, maybe I could pry some information out of him.

"Right. There's a nurse comes in a few times a week, too. Miss High-and-Mighty Kendra Blaine wouldn't dirty her hands with changing bed linens or seein' to poor Becky's more intimate needs."

"What's she done—the Blaine woman, I mean—to get you so fired up?"

It usually took a lot to get Bitsy this riled. Something like being cruel to a child or kicking a dog.

"Oh, nothin' specific, I guess. It's just her attitude. She hangs on

Thomas like kudzu on a fence post. And the poor, silly man just laps it all up."

"What do you know about her?" I asked. "Specifically."

Bitsy sighed. "She's in her thirties is my guess, but she dresses and acts a lot younger. Not bad looking, if you like the blowsy type."

I laughed. Bitsy was one of the few people in the world who could use words like *flummoxed* and *blowsy* and get away with it.

"Big hair," she continued, "sort of like one of those Texas-cheerleader types. Bright red if you can imagine. Obviously fake. And lots of makeup slathered on. Even during the day."

I tried to feel properly shocked at Kendra Blaine's lack of taste. I never bothered with much besides mascara, sunscreen, and lip gloss, so I was a bad one to judge.

"You know anything about her background? Where she comes from? I heard she stays over in Hardeeville when she isn't with the Castlemains."

"This is another case, isn't it?" I could almost see Bitsy's deep blue eyes widen in excitement. "Oh, Bay, it is, isn't it? Is she stealin' the silver or whatever? It wouldn't surprise me one bit. Trailer trash, that's what that woman is. Might as well have it tattooed on her—"

"Bitsy!" I took a deep breath and let it out slowly. "Calm down. I'm simply gathering information, okay?"

Once before I'd tried to tap Bitsy's extensive knowledge of the up-per echelons of island society. She'd provided some useful information, but it hadn't kept Tracy Dumars from ending up dead in the trunk of her Mercedes. I should have remembered to tread a little more lightly.

"You mentioned something about a grandson. They have children?"

"Becky and Thomas? Sure. They have two sons living. Their old-est, a daughter, died of cancer a number of years back. Some sort of story going around about the boys, but I don't have all the details. They don't speak, way I hear it. Probably about money. Those kinds of family splits usually are, especially if you're in their tax bracket." She paused, and I could hear ice tinkling in a glass. "They're closest to a grandson, their daughter's boy. I think he might be something to do with the government. In Washington, I mean. At least he lives there. Now let me see, what was his name?"

I chewed on the end of a pencil and waited for my old friend to drag the information from her mental Rolodex.

"Oh, drat! I just can't dredge it up. I only met him briefly the one time, but I can tell you that he is drop-dead gorgeous. Let me call Becky or Lily and—"

"No! I absolutely forbid you to talk to the Castlemains or anyone else about this. Are we clear on that, Bitsy?"

"If you insist, honey," she said. "I know! I'll just check the guest list from the last fundraiser we had for the museum. That's when I met him."

"Okay," I said, "but be discreet. I may not even take the case. I don't need to remind you about the confidentiality issues, do I?"

"Don't be a goose." She paused, and her next words struck me as strangely ominous. "You have no idea the number of secrets I know. And about some pretty important people." Her tone brightened. "I'll call you back tomorrow."

"Thanks, I appreciate it. Hug the kids for me," I added and hung up.

I sat back in the chair and wished I hadn't given up smoking. Twice. I didn't like that remark about secrets. And important people.

I didn't like it at all.

CHAPTER
SIX

I FOUND RED SCRUNCHED DOWN ON THE SOFA IN THE great room, the baseball game blaring from the surround-sound speakers for the monstrous flat-screen TV he'd installed over the fireplace a couple of weeks before. I half expected him to have fallen asleep, but he reached out an arm for me when I walked into the room.

"Top of the second, two on, Chipper Jones is up. He needs to put one out right now. Break their hearts. I hate the Dodgers."

I flopped down beside him. "You hate everyone except the Braves."

"Cultural conditioning," he said, and I jerked my head to face him. "Hey, there's more to me than just a pretty face, you know," he added with a grin and kissed the end of my nose. "If my dad had been a Cleveland Indians fan, I'd probably be one, too."

We watched in silence for a few minutes while Chipper fouled off four consecutive pitches before finally striking out.

Red's long, drawn-out sigh said everything.

"Lavinia thinks Miss Lizzie wants to bring Julia to Presqu'isle," I said into the quiet when Red muted the commercial.

"To visit?"

"To live."

Red sat up straighter. "Really? How does she feel about it? Lavinia, I mean."

"I think she likes the idea. She's lonely. And you know she's always been happiest when she has someone to take care of. I'm afraid she's feeling useless on her own."

Red pulled me closer into the curve of his arm, and I let my head fall against his shoulder. The breeze through the screen of the open French door had turned chilly, and I snuggled into the warmth of his body.

"How about you?" he whispered against my hair.

"Me? I think it's a great idea. And that's partly selfish. It would be a lot easier to keep an eye on them on St. Helena than way out there in the boonies."

"So you're taking on the responsibility for them, too?"

Something in his tone set my teeth on edge. I pulled away to look into his face. "Of course. She's my sister."

"Half sister."

"So?"

He took a long time to answer. "When do *you* get to have a life?"

I felt myself stiffen, but I didn't want to argue. I made myself wait until I could speak calmly, without snapping. "I have a life, Red. *We* have a life. Together. Why should my caring for my sister be a threat to that?"

I felt his shoulders slump. "It isn't. I don't know what my problem is tonight." He turned to me and smiled. "Maybe it was sitting in the principal's office all afternoon. Bad vibes. I'm sorry."

"Me, too," I said.

The kiss was long and tender . . .

By the time we'd retrieved our clothes from the carpet and wandered hand in hand toward the bedroom, the Braves were losing ten to two, and neither one of us really gave a damn.

————

At 2:37, almost right on schedule lately, I found myself wide awake. I slipped out of the king-sized bed, pulled my old chenille robe around me, and tiptoed out into the hallway. I snugged the door closed on Red's soft snores and padded barefoot to the kitchen. I poured myself a glass of tea and carried it back into the office. I turned on the computer and sat staring off at nothing while it booted up.

For almost a full week now I had been coming out of what seemed to be a normal sleep sometime between two and three in the morning, as alert as if it had been seven or eight. I couldn't remember dreaming. There was nothing preying on my mind, as Red had suggested—at least nothing I could recognize or name. The business was flourishing. We'd finally reached the point where I didn't need to infuse cash every month from my own account to make payroll or cover the bills. Of course, the sadness of my father's death would be with me a long time, but that wrenching feeling of immediate loss had dulled a bit.

The glowing screen had come up on the desktop, but I still sat, my mind trying to wrap itself around what could be disturbing my sleep, night after night.

Red and I were good. We still carped at each other sometimes, just as we had done in the years following Rob's murder, but that was just our way. Red had alternately wooed me and pissed me off to the point of madness with his constant interference in my life and my business, while at the same time proving time and again that his feelings were real—and weren't going away. It had taken me a long time to overcome my own reluctance to become romantically involved with my late husband's younger brother, but the decision, when I was finally forced to make it, had been relatively easy. Besides that, I had financial security, more than most, and I was healthy as a horse. Lavinia would have told me to count my blessings and shut up.

I shook my head. Maybe it was just one of those cycles we all get into at one time or another. I'd get over it.

I signed on and checked my personal e-mail. A note from Neddie

asking me to call jolted me a little. Something to do with my sister
Julia? I scratched a reminder to get in touch with her first thing in the
morning. I smiled to myself. Technically, *later* in the morning. At least
after the sun came up.

I switched to Google and typed in *Southern Preferred Investments,* the
name of the company to which Cecelia Dobbs said Mr. Castlemain had
transferred almost a million dollars. Nothing. Well, with Google there's
always something, but not what I was looking for. I tried it again with
quotation marks, but the search yielded even fewer hits. I walked out to
the hallway and retrieved my bag, large enough to double as a briefcase,
and pulled out the notes I'd stuffed in there after my meeting with the
troubled bank employee. I double-checked the name. Southern Preferred Investments. Definitely plural.

Back in the office I tried it without the final *s* on the off chance
Cecelia had gotten it wrong. That yielded a Delaware company that
made me sit up a little straighter. It looked to be some sort of mutual
fund, licensed to do business in about six states, including South Carolina, Georgia, and Virginia. Nothing sinister, at least at first glance.
I had mutuals in my own reduced portfolio. It was even listed on
the stock exchange. So if Cecelia Dobbs had been mistaken, it could
mean that the company was completely legitimate, and she could quit
worrying.

I made myself a note to talk to my broker.

I jumped when the door across the hall opened. Red stood in his
underwear, his short hair standing almost straight up, his eyes scrunched
shut against the light.

"What are you doing?" His voice was raspy and heavy with sleep.

"Just playing around on the computer. I'm sorry if I woke you."

"I rolled over, and you weren't there. What's the matter?"

"Nothing. Go back to bed."

He shook himself and rubbed his hands over his face. "What time
is it?"

I glanced at the digital readout in the corner of the monitor. "Three thirty. Go back to sleep."

"You, too."

He turned and lumbered back into the bedroom. A moment later I heard the water running in the bathroom, followed shortly by his shuffle on the carpet. I waited. In a couple of minutes, his muffled snores once again drifted out into the stillness, and I moved back in front of the computer. I didn't want to risk the noise of the printer, so I made some notes on Southern Preferred Investment Group, logged off, and stretched out on the chaise in the corner of the office. I wrapped my robe more tightly around me and tried to work out just how much of Cecelia Dobbs's story had to do with concern for the elderly Castlemains and how much was engendered by her interest in a handsome bank teller who probably wouldn't give her the time of day.

As I finally drifted off to sleep, I was thinking that I needed to find out a lot more before Simpson & Tanner took on the case.

Red, Erik, and I arrived at the office almost simultaneously on Thursday morning. My husband and I drove separately since we often had to be out chasing things down at different times and in different directions. In the past, we'd been open three days a week, primarily because the level of business didn't warrant anything more. We'd recently expanded that to four days, closing on Fridays. If things were slack, it gave us all a long weekend. More often than not, though, we used the time for catching up on paperwork.

The message light on the phone indicated we'd had calls overnight, which was pretty unusual. I left Erik to check them, and Red followed me into my office. Although he had his own small space just off the reception area, we tended to congregate around the Judge's old desk.

We'd stopped for coffee and chai tea on our way in, and Red sank into the client chair, his hands clasped around the steaming paper cup, while I booted up my computer.

"What's on my dance card for today?" he asked.

Mindful of our conversation of the night before, I racked my brain for an assignment he wouldn't recognize as make-work. The only case remotely involving anything potentially criminal was Cecelia Dobbs's, and we hadn't even completely made the decision to take it on yet.

Erik interrupted my thoughts. "You'll want to hear this," he said, and his tone made my head snap up. "I'll put it on speaker."

Red and I both stood and followed him out. We ranged ourselves in front of his desk while he punched buttons on the phone.

"Mrs. Tanner? This is Cecelia. Cecelia Dobbs." She paused, and the quiver in her voice had us all looking at each other in alarm. The girl sounded as if she was on the verge of hysteria. We all heard her swallow hard before continuing.

"Okay, I know you're not in the office yet, but I just heard—" A sharp intake of breath. "My dad just told me that Mrs. Castlemain— she died last night. He got called in, and I don't know what—"

"Jesus," Red said softly under his breath, and our eyes met briefly.

Cecelia got control of herself and stumbled on. "They think it was her heart, but my dad said he knows her cardiologist, and he was really surprised because she'd just had a really good checkup, and everything looked fine." One more long, extended pause was followed by the statement I could bet we'd all been anticipating.

"You don't think they . . . *killed* her, do you? Oh, God, maybe this is all my fault."

CHAPTER
SEVEN

E STOOD IN SILENCE FOR A LONG MOMENT. CECELIA Dobbs's voice had simply trailed away, followed some time later by an audible click as she hung up the phone. Erik replaced the receiver in the cradle and sat down in his chair.

"That was creepy," I finally said to break the tension. I looked at the two men, who were both staring into space. "Hold on. We don't really think this was murder." I waited, but neither of them spoke. "Do we?"

"Of course not." Red shook himself and tried on a smile. "But you're right—it was kind of spooky. That's your client from yesterday?"

I nodded. "I thought right from the jump that she had a tendency to overdramatize things a bit." I turned toward Erik. "Didn't you?"

"Maybe a little," he said somberly. "But what if she was right about what's been going on? Can we come up with a scenario in which it would make sense for those two to bump off the old lady?"

I moved back into my office and picked up my cup of tea. The others followed, Erik dragging his desk chair behind him. The two men sat while I paced. I suddenly turned.

"I haven't told you about my conversation with Bitsy Elliott last night," I said, my mind racing. "She knows the Castlemains. She despises the Blaine woman, the caretaker, and believe me, it takes a lot to get on Bitsy's bad side." I conjured up her words. "She said that Blaine had Thomas completely . . . *flummoxed,* was the word she used, but that Becky had her number."

Red cleared his throat. "So you're proposing that this caretaker suddenly decided she needed to get rid of the old woman and somehow gave her a heart attack? On the very day your girl Dobbs comes to see you? That's stretching things a bit, even for you, Bay."

Red may have retired from the sheriff's office, but he hadn't lost that patronizing, snotty tone they'd taught him. Maybe there was actually a course they offered in offending private investigators. And wives.

"Thank you, *Sergeant,* for that insightful analysis. May I remind you that you're working for *us* now, not the cops? Try to stop thinking like one for a minute, okay?"

Erik squirmed in his seat, and I knew we'd embarrassed him. It was fine for us to snipe at each other on our own time, but my partner didn't need to be a captive—and reluctant—audience.

I ameliorated my tone and lowered my voice. "I'm not suggesting it happened that way. All I'm saying is this girl thinks it might have, and she's a lot more tuned in to the situation than we are." I sat and got a pen out of the center drawer. "Can you find out if there's any hint of suspicion at the sheriff's office? Or have you burned all your bridges?" I couldn't help adding while I jotted notes on the desk pad.

"I still have friends in low places," my husband said.

I could hear the smile in his voice even before I looked up. "Then hop on over there and pick some brains. Erik, see if you can track down Dr. Harley Coffin. He lives in Beaufort and doesn't practice much anymore, but Bitsy told me he used to look in on Rebecca Castlemain. I want to talk to him." I reached for the phone. "I'll call Bits and see if she's heard anything."

Red gave me a mock salute and rose. Erik said, "Okay," and followed him out.

A moment later my husband stuck his head back in the door. "There's going to be nothing to this, you know," he said. "You've got us all just spinning our wheels over some hysterical girl's wild imagination."

"I hope you're right," I said. And meant it.

I got Bitsy Elliott's voice mail, even on her cell. I wasn't surprised she was out and about at such an early hour. With three kids still living at home, I supposed she had any number of errands and things to take care of while they were in school. Still, I would have thought she'd have her cell turned on. I asked her to call me right away.

"Dr. Coffin's not picking up," Erik said from the doorway. "I left him a message to get back to you as soon as he gets in. Is there somewhere else I can try besides his house?"

"No, not really. Although, he does like to hang out at the bookstore, now that I think about it. You know, on Bay Street in Beaufort. The East Bay Book Emporium. He could be having coffee with some of the old-timers."

"I'll try it. But he's not going to tell you anything, is he? I mean, patient confidentiality and all that."

"Probably not. But he was one of the Judge's oldest friends. And mine. All I'm looking for is a little gossip, not a complete medical history."

"Understood." He moved toward his desk, then turned back. "You're not really thinking Cecelia Dobbs is right about this, are you?"

I took a moment before answering. "No, not really. But the timing looks a little fishy, don't you think? And Bitsy has a real thing about this Blaine woman. She's not usually wrong about people."

"It doesn't make Blaine a murderer, though, does it?"

"Absolutely not," I said firmly. "But let's just cover all the bases.

What concerns me is that the scam—if it is one—may just keep going on, regardless. And we have to decide if we're going to look into it or not. If there's the possibility of foul play in Rebecca Castlemain's death, we should probably run like hell in the other direction."

"Probably," Erik said, but something in his tone hinted that he didn't quite believe that any more than I did.

I fidgeted through most of the morning, my mind skittering around all over the place, while I tried to focus on preparing statements for our commercial and public entity clients. The latter required tons of extra paperwork and supporting documents aside from the simple accounting of services performed. I never wondered anymore why anything connected to the government was always ponderous, convoluted, and incredibly inefficient. One only had to look at the endless forms required for even the simplest task to get the picture of unfettered bureaucracy run amok.

A little before eleven, the phone rang. I strained to hear Erik's end of the conversation, but it was only a moment before he buzzed me. "Dr. Coffin on line one," he said.

"Thanks." I pushed the button. "Good morning, Harley."

"Mornin', Bay. How you holdin' up, honey?"

I smiled. Had the white-haired doctor been forty years younger, I would have called him on that *honey* business. But when someone has literally bounced you on his knee, familiarity was not only excusable but welcome.

"I'm fine. You keeping well?"

"Just tolerable. These old bones are getting mighty creaky, I can tell you. Takes me an hour every morning just to get my knees to cooperate."

That made me laugh. In the background, I could hear other conversations going on. "Are you at the bookstore?"

"Yup. Some of the boys and I meet up here for coffee on a fairly regular basis. Those of us who can manage to get upright, that is. We've turned into a bunch of old coots, honey, and that's a fact. Every damn one of us. Can't imagine how that happened."

"Life," I said, and the single word brought me to the sad reason for my call. "Harley, I understand you used to look after Rebecca Castlemain, over here in Wexford."

"Still do," he said, and my heart sank.

He didn't know. *Damn it!* I'd felt certain he would have been consulted—or at least notified—of the old woman's passing. Now I had to be the one to break the news.

"Harley, I'm really sorry, but someone told me that she passed away last night."

He didn't reply immediately. I felt my own heart racing a little too fast. Finally, he cleared his throat.

"Rebecca? Are you sure?"

That brought me up short. I really only had Cecelia Dobbs's word for it. Maybe I had unforgivably jumped the gun. But then I remembered that she had gotten it from her father, a surgeon at the hospital. Surely he wouldn't have made a mistake.

"The person who told me is . . . connected with the hospital. I understand she had a heart attack."

"I'm real sorry to hear that. She's . . . *was* a fine woman. I can't believe no one thought fit to notify me."

"Are you her doctor of record?" I asked, forcing myself to ignore the obvious pain in his shaky voice.

"No, I guess not officially, although I've been seeing her ever since they moved to Hilton Head. She had a whole slew of specialists over there. But I looked after her general well-being, minor ailments and such." He paused. "And we were friends."

"I'm sorry to be the bearer of sad news," I said. "I didn't even think that you wouldn't have been consulted."

"Should have been," he said with a little more steel in his tone. "Who said it was a heart attack? That the official cause of death? Far as I knew, woman's heart was as sound as yours. She had a lot of problems—diabetes, mostly—but I wouldn't have thought it would be her heart that carried her off."

"I don't know anything official. That's just what I heard."

Again there was a long pause. "Is that what you were callin' me about, Bay? To ask about Becky?"

He'd pretty much told me what I needed to know already. I couldn't disclose the real reason for my interest, so I fibbed a little.

"I thought you might be feeling low. It must be hard to lose a patient, especially one you've known for a long time."

I knew both our minds were filled with the image of my father in his last days.

"That was sweet of you, honey. You're a good girl."

I at least had the grace to blush before inspiration struck. "I also wanted to ask if you'd been over to Presqu'isle lately. I'm afraid Lavinia's a little lonely."

"Don't wonder, rattlin' around in that old place. I'll look in on her, see how she's getting on."

"Thanks, Harley. I'd appreciate it."

"And I'll certainly not let on that you suggested it. I know how prickly she'd get if she thought you were checking up on her." He chuckled. "I'll try and plan to get there about mealtime. Maybe she'll have some of those sweet potato biscuits in the oven."

I smiled. "I wouldn't doubt it. Even though she's just cooking for herself, she still makes enough for ten people. Why don't you call first? I guarantee you'll get invited to dinner."

"Should have thought of that myself. Gettin' to be an old fool. You take care, honey, hear?"

"I will. You, too. And I'm sorry about Mrs. Castlemain."

"Bye now." The phone clicked as he hung up.

I replaced the receiver and looked up to find Erik standing in the doorway. "Anything?" he asked.

I shrugged. "I'm not sure. Harley didn't know. About the death."

"That must have been hard. Any idea why he wasn't notified?"

"No. He said her heart was strong as mine. He was surprised about that being the cause of death."

"Still rumor at this point, though, isn't it?"

"True. But Cecelia's father is a surgeon. And she said he'd talked to Mrs. Castlemain's cardiologist. I don't think he'd get it wrong."

"So that's two doctors who were surprised by the heart attack."

I looked up and met his eyes, and I knew we were both thinking exactly the same thing.

CHAPTER EIGHT

RED'S ENTRANCE MADE ERIK TURN, AND THE MOMENT was lost.

Probably just as well, I thought. We had managed to keep ourselves out of anything really dangerous for quite some time. In the early days of the agency, it seemed as if everywhere we turned we were stumbling across violent death. And violent people. The respite had been welcome, and I'd almost convinced myself that nice, safe background checks would be enough to satisfy me. Besides, there'd been Kimmie Eastman, the teenager dying of leukemia, whose family we'd been hired to track down. That had been immensely gratifying. And, in one of those serendipitous things that make life so surprising, that case had brought me the one remaining member of my immediate family.

And that jolted me upright. I'd never called Neddie Halloran, the psychologist who was seeing Julia. The scowl on Red's face as he pulled up the client chair, however, made me shove that thought aside for the moment.

"What's up?" I asked. "You look seriously ticked off."

"It's a wonder you didn't strangle us all," he said, tossing a notebook onto the desk. "Was I ever that aggravating when I worked for the sheriff?"

I couldn't help it. I laughed. "Daily," I said, and he forced a smile. "I'm guessing you ran into the khaki wall of silence."

"Pretty much. Malik wasn't on duty, and Pedrovsky was prowling the halls. I did my best to keep out of her way."

Malik Graves and Red had formed a special bond during the business out at Sanctuary Hill, and Detective Lisa Pedrovsky was just a bitch on general principles, although she and I had some unpleasant history.

"Bottom line," he went on, "is that it wasn't an unattended death. Mrs. Castlemain must have still been breathing when they got her to the hospital. She was pronounced a few minutes later, so that's that. As long as a doctor was present, the sheriff's office isn't interested. Unless something weird pops up, it's just an old person conking off."

"Such respect for the dead," I said a little tersely.

"Sorry. Protective armor. Comes with the job. It'll take me a while to shake it off, I guess."

"I talked to Harley Coffin." I related the relevant parts of our conversation. "He seemed surprised at the diagnosis."

"He's not a heart specialist, is he?"

"No, but remember Cecelia said her father had talked to Mrs. Castlemain's cardiologist. He was puzzled, too."

"Unfortunately, stuff happens." Red shrugged and put his notebook back in his shirt pocket. "So what have you decided? Are you going to take this investment scam thing?"

"Erik?" I called. "Can you come in here a second?" When he stood in the doorway, I said, "What do you think about Cecelia Dobbs? Are we in or out?"

"I'd like to pursue it, at least for a while, see what shakes out. We could keep the expenses down so it doesn't cost Ms. Dobbs too much.

I'd feel better telling her there's nothing to it and be able to back that up. I don't think she's going to let it go." He paused. "Maybe we should talk to her again, though, see if she's still willing to pursue it. Mrs. Castlemain's death may have scared her off."

"Good point. Will you leave a message for her to call me?"

"Sure."

"Thanks." I looked at Red, who had slumped back in the chair. "What?"

"You really think it's a good idea to get involved in this? What if there *is* something fishy about the woman's death? What are you going to do about it?"

It was a fair question, and I gave it some thought. "I don't know, Red. I'm trying to separate the scam from the possibility of foul play. If there was any. The investment thing I feel comfortable tackling. I've even been working on a scenario that could get me on the inside. A little sting of my own." I smiled to counteract the frown on his face. "I'm a pretty attractive mark for something like this, financially speaking, but there are too many people who know my background. I'd never convince Blaine and Dalton that I was stupid enough to fall for their game. We'd need a proxy, someone who fits their profile." I waited a beat. "I was thinking about Miss Addie."

Adelaide Boyce Hammond was in her eighties but still bright and sharp. She had been one of my late mother's closest friends and lived in an upscale retirement community on the island. In fact, it had been Miss Addie who had first tapped my latent interest in butting into other people's troubles when she asked me to look into a real estate development scheme in which she'd invested most of the inheritance she'd received from her prominent, wealthy family. She could act like a dithering old lady when it suited her, but she was a true steel magnolia. Miss Addie would be perfect.

Red's face didn't change, but, "It might work," he said, surprising the hell out of me. "If she's willing."

"You really think so?"

"I think if you decide to take this case, you'll plow right ahead no matter what I think. I'm beginning to learn it's better to jump on your bandwagon than to get run over by it."

The boyish grin took most of the sting out of his words.

"Well, it's early times yet. I need to talk to Cecelia first."

"What are we doing for lunch?" he asked.

I looked at my watch. "I need to call Neddie," I said. "Give me about fifteen minutes."

He saluted and rose from the chair.

I lucked into reaching the office just as Neddie was finishing with her last morning patient. Carolann, her longtime receptionist, chatted with me for a few moments, offering her condolences on my father's death. I wondered how long it would be before it stopped hurting to talk about him.

"Hey, girl. I see you finally got my message."

"Hey, Neddie," I said. "Things have been a little crazy around here. Oops, sorry. I know you don't like that word. So how's Julia doing?"

Elizabeth Shelly, Julia's late mother's dearest friend and her official caretaker, had granted permission for Neddie to discuss my half sister's case with me.

"We're making some serious progress," the psychologist said. "Have you talked with her lately?"

"No. You said to keep my distance while she's in therapy. That she still didn't get the nature of our relationship. And because of . . . you know. The manner of her mother's death."

"I think we're past that."

"Really? How can you tell?"

I heard the note of triumph in her voice. "She came in on Tuesday in a pair of khaki pants and a nice cotton sweater. Yellow."

That brought a smile. Up until that time, my sister had refused to wear anything but red plaid shirts and jeans, the same type of clothes she'd had on the night her mother died.

"That is progress. What did Miss Lizzie have to say about it?"

"She said Julia asked if she had anything different to wear. Elizabeth whipped her right into Charleston for a shopping spree. I consider that a real breakthrough, and I wanted to share it with you."

"I'm so pleased. How's her demeanor?"

Julia and I were pretty close in age, but she came across, especially to strangers, as being very childlike. While it was endearing, I knew it was one of the symptoms of her illness, a form of PTSD that had been triggered by the witnessing of her mother's death.

"We're getting there. Untreated post-traumatic stress can do strange things to the brain, especially a child's. But I've great hope that we've turned a corner. I think you'll see a noticeable improvement in both her speech patterns and how she relates to those around her."

"So it would be okay to make contact? In person, I mean?"

"I think you should. I think it would do you both a world of good."

My old college roommate had been my lifesaver in the months following my first husband's murder. I trusted her—and her therapy skills—implicitly.

"Listen, while I've got you here, how do you feel about the possibility of their coming to stay at Presqu'isle? With Lavinia."

"A visit?"

"No, something maybe more permanent. Lavinia thinks they may be having money troubles. That old plantation must cost a fortune to maintain."

"And Lavinia is probably a little lonely."

"That, too."

Neddie paused, and I could almost see her running long, tapered fingers through her tangle of Irish-red curls. "I don't see any harm in

it, not on the face of things. It would be entirely up to them." Again
she halted. "But keep in mind that Julia has a routine and familiar surroundings she's comfortable with. Getting her into the car and over here
to Savannah was a major leap for her. It might be good to ease into it.
A visit for a few days to see how she adapts. Let's not push her too hard
too fast."

"You're the doctor. I'll talk to Lavinia about inviting them down.
We can see how it goes from there."

"That's fine. So how's married life treating you?"

"Good," I said.

"Really?"

I bristled. "What in the hell does that mean?"

"It means, Tanner, that *good* isn't exactly a ringing endorsement."

"Should I be giggling and going on about how great the sex is?"

Neddie laughed. "Well, I hope you found *that* out before you married the guy."

I forced myself to lighten up. "Savannah's world-famous child psychologist advocating premarital sex? I'm shocked."

"Don't try to change the subject." Her voice lost its bantering
tone. "You're sure everything's okay? With you and Red?"

"We're fine, Neddie. Worry about your own love life."

"Or lack thereof," she said with not a trace of humor. "I'm here if
you need to talk. Anytime."

"I know," I said, my own voice quavering a little. "I know that."

She sighed. "Okay. Give Red my best. And let me know when you
get that visit planned. I want to be prepared in case it causes Julia some
discomfort."

"Will do. Thanks."

I placed the phone gently back in its cradle and stared out into
the reception area. Sometimes Neddie's perception could be a curse
rather than a blessing. With a sigh, I turned my mind to the issue at

hand. There had been a lot of changes at Presqu'isle over the past few months, and I wondered if Lavinia was really ready for having two relative strangers move into the old antebellum mansion, for unfamiliar voices in the hallway and strange faces around the scarred oak table in the kitchen.

For that matter, I wondered if *I* was.

CHAPTER NINE

WE PUT THE "CLOSED" SIGN ON THE DOOR, AND THE three of us rode in my big Jaguar over to Applebee's. We always tried to avoid discussing client business anywhere out in public where we might be overheard, so I told them about Julia over our sandwiches. Both Erik and Red seemed enthusiastic about the idea of her and Miss Lizzie's coming to stay with Lavinia.

I appeared to be the only one with reservations, and I wasn't exactly sure why. It had seemed like a good idea the first time Lavinia proposed it. But, the more I considered it, the more possibilities for complication I could see. Rob had always told me I thought too much, had to analyze every situation as if it were a knotty accounting problem. Sometimes you just had to go with your gut, he used to say. I'd tried that over the years since his death, with decidedly mixed results, some of them bordering on disastrous.

Back at the office, we sat in the reception area and tossed around the idea of a sting operation, perhaps using Miss Addie as bait, to bring Kendra Blaine and Dalton Chambers out into the light. I needed a lot more information about them first, and Erik said he'd get back on that as soon as we finished our discussion.

"But we still don't know if we have a client or not," he said, crossing one long leg over the other knee. "Cecelia Dobbs hasn't called back."

"Good point. Try her again, will you?"

"Sure." He rose and picked up the phone.

"I've been thinking about this, and I'm not sure I like the idea of exposing Miss Hammond to these people." Red leaned forward in his chair. "If there's even a slim chance they had something to do with that woman's death, you could be putting her in a lot of danger."

"I know. On the other hand, if Bitsy was right and Rebecca was the only thing standing between them and the whole Castlemain fortune, Thomas could be on borrowed time as well."

"I left another message," Erik said a moment before the front door opened.

"I'm sorry. Am I interrupting something?"

Cecelia Dobbs looked even messier than the first time she'd stepped into the office. Her hair needed a good washing, and she hadn't even tried to brighten her sallow complexion with makeup. Her baggy T-shirt advertised a rock band I'd never heard of, and her jeans were just this side of grubby.

"Not at all," I said, rising. "Come in. Cecelia Dobbs, Red Tanner, my husband and one of our—" I stumbled over the word *employees.* "He works with us at the agency."

"Pleased to meet you, Ms. Dobbs." Red held out his hand, and she took it.

"Hi."

That unbecoming blush stained her pale cheeks.

"Let's go into my office," I said, shepherding her in front of me. "Red, will you join us?"

He brought in an extra chair and positioned it so that he could face both of us. He sat and folded his arms across his chest. Cecelia fumbled with setting her bag on the floor. When she looked up, I saw that she'd been crying.

"I'm sorry about Mrs. Castlemain," I said softly, "but I really don't think you have anything to feel bad about. She wasn't a young woman. These things happen. And even if—"

"Really?" Cecelia gulped twice before she got the rest of the words out. "So you don't think they killed her? Because I came here yesterday?"

Red spoke before I had a chance to. "I used to be with the sheriff's department. For a long time. I did a little checking after we got your message this morning, and there's no indication of foul play in the death of Mrs. Castlemain. There's no reason to blame yourself."

If he'd been closer, I would have kicked him. I settled for a pointed look I wasn't sure he even caught. "At least that's the preliminary finding," I said. I waited a moment, but the silence held. "Did you go in to work today?"

"No, ma'am. I just couldn't face— I mean, I kept thinking, what if they'd . . . I called in sick."

"I understand. I'm sure it was very upsetting for you. The question is, Ms. Dobbs, whether or not you want to pursue the matter we discussed yesterday." I reached into the right-hand drawer and removed the contract she'd signed, the crumpled dollar bill and her initial check paper-clipped to the top.

Cecelia jumped as if I'd just produced a tarantula. "I don't know," she said, her voice breathy. Her hands trembled, and she clasped them together in her lap. "What do you think?"

"I can't make that decision for you. We'll take your case, providing you agree to the terms and fees, but you have to be certain you're willing to go forward." I gave her a moment. "You're going to have to go back to work and carry on as if nothing has happened. You'll need to be our eyes and ears inside the bank, keep us up to date on what Blaine and Chambers are up to. Can you do that?"

"I don't know. It scares me."

"It has to be your decision." Red spoke softly, as he might to one of his kids who'd had a bad dream. "But we'll be right here every step of the way. We won't let anything bad happen to you, Cecelia."

The young woman blossomed under Red's steady gaze and reassuring voice. I bit my lower lip and ordered myself to be just as calm.

"My husband doesn't mean to imply that there might not be some danger involved. If these two are cold enough to scam old people out of their life savings, they aren't going to give up quietly. You'd have to be on your guard all the time not to give anything away. It could be very stressful for you."

I purposely kept from looking at Red, all my attention focused on our potential client. I could almost read her mind as the various possibilities flashed through her head and registered on her face. Cecelia would be a lousy liar. Maybe this was a bad idea all around.

"I'll do it," she said. Her shoulders straightened, and she lifted her head. "I've been such a coward about so many things. It's time I started acting like a grown-up."

I watched her beam under Red's approving smile.

"Good girl," he said, and once again I wished I could kick him in the shins.

It took only a few minutes to complete our business. Cecelia handed over the additional retainer check without batting an eye. I'd lowered the figure by about twenty-five percent, in deference to her circumstances, but I kept the hourly rate and expense reimbursement clauses intact. I felt sorry for her, but business is business.

We talked a while longer and agreed that Cecelia should stay home on Friday as well. That would give us time to gather more information and decide how best we could utilize her unique position inside the bank. It would also allow her a chance to get herself together before she had to confront Dalton Chambers. She assured us she could keep out of his way in the normal course of her job but that she'd be able to observe him more closely whenever it became necessary.

Half an hour after she'd walked in, Red ushered her out the door with reassurances that we'd be in touch over the weekend. I flipped open the recorder and carried the tape to Erik.

"I updated the file," he said. "I'll transcribe this and add it. I've also got some more information on the players. You ready for it?"

"Give us a minute," I said as Red edged up beside me.

I gripped his arm none too gently and walked him through my doorway. He dropped into his chair and held up a hand before I had a chance to open my mouth.

"Don't get all bent out of shape," he said quietly. "You know you wanted to take the case, and I think it's a good idea to see what we can come up with on those two slimebags. If we get anything solid, we can turn it over to the sheriff. There's no reason Cecelia or anyone else should be in any danger."

"You're making me so damned dizzy I'm about to throw up. How many times an hour do you plan on changing your mind? Is there a schedule I could follow so I don't get lost?"

He laughed, and I slapped my hand on the desk.

"It's not funny, Red. You've been lukewarm about this idea right from the jump, and suddenly you're pushing that poor girl into cooperating. What kind of game are you playing?"

His face lost the boyish grin that usually forced me to smile back. "It's a legitimate case for the agency to take on. She just needed a little nudge in the right direction."

"That's my call," I said as calmly as I could manage. "We've had this discussion before. Erik and I decide on what cases we'll accept." I sat down and let out a long breath. "I know it's awkward sometimes, Red, but that's the way it has to be. You knew all this up front, remember?"

"Of course I do. But I thought you wanted her to agree. I was just helping the situation along." He paused. "And it's the kind of thing I can sink my teeth into instead of being just your errand boy."

I knew that was the crux of the problem, but I didn't know how to fix it. I wanted my marriage to work, and I wanted Red to feel useful and a part of what Erik and I were trying to build. No one had said it would be easy.

"Okay, you've got a point. But please try not to jump all over an interview like that, all right? We need to be on the same page. Let's discuss things first before we get ourselves at cross-purposes again."

"Understood. So now what? You still think a sting is the right way to go?"

"I'm not sure. Erik said he had some more info on the players. Let's get his take."

I called him into my office, and he came bearing printouts. I knew he'd overheard most of what had gone on with Cecelia Dobbs and Red because I'd purposely left the door open.

"So what have you got?" I asked, slipping off my loafers and tucking one leg up under me on the chair. "Were you able to track them down?"

"Yes and no," he said.

Kendra Blaine didn't own any property, either in Beaufort or nearby Jasper County. She'd never been in the military, and there was no record of her ever having been involved in a lawsuit, either as complainant or defendant. She wasn't licensed as a nurse in any database Erik had been able to locate.

"One strange thing I did run across," he said, looking up from his notes. "She applied to become a police officer in a small town in the Upstate, and they ran a background check on her. I can't find any record that she ever got hired, so maybe the check kicked up some dirt." He glanced at Red. "Any chance you could find out what?"

"Maybe. But my best guess is that she had some sort of criminal record. Even if it was something minor, it could have been enough to keep her out of law enforcement."

"Even in a small town?" I asked.

"Everybody's jumpy about getting sued these days. I'd think if they had the capability to run the check, they'd be smart enough to steer clear if they found anything." He thought a moment. "Or it could be something entirely different, like budget cuts."

I filed that information away for future reference. "Anything else?"

"She owns a 2003 Honda that's paid for. That's about it."

"So no big displays of wealth. And you say she doesn't own property, so she must be renting. Smart. What about Chambers?"

Erik shuffled papers and smiled. "He's the interesting one. This guy seems to have sprung from nowhere. He owns that condo in Compass Point. Or at least he and the bank do."

"The one where he works?" Red asked.

Erik nodded. "Got a pretty good deal on it, too. The sales price, I mean. I know things have been dropping everywhere, but he just about stole this one. He bought it right before the bank was ready to foreclose on the previous owner. A short sale, I think they call it. Even then, it's quite a stretch on the salary of a bank teller."

"Did you check out his place last night?" I asked.

"Yeah, on my way home. There was a new Lexus in the driveway."

Red whistled. "What model?"

I frowned, but Erik ignored me. "The little sports job. Black. Fine-looking piece of machinery."

"Could we get back to business?"

Erik grinned. "Sorry. But here's the kicker with Chambers. I couldn't find any legitimate paper trail on him at all. No place of birth, education, previous employment. At least nothing that jibes with Cecelia's description of him. I found a couple of name matches, but they were for much older men, and one of them's dead."

"So how did he manage to land a job at a bank? They have to be paranoid about references, don't they?" I looked at Red.

"You'd think so," he said. "What's your best guess, Erik? Identity theft?"

"That would get my vote. Easy enough to do these days. Get a copy of a birth certificate for a few bucks in some small county clerk's office, and you're in business. But I'm still stumped as to why the bank would have hired him if they couldn't verify his background." He glanced at me. "Do you think Cecelia could get a look at his personnel file?"

I shrugged. "We could ask, but I don't think she'll be too receptive. She's jumpy enough as it is. It might not be a good idea to push her. Besides, if he's got something in his past he's gone to that much trouble to conceal, he flat-out lied on his job application. What are the chances of getting a criminal check run on him, Red?"

"Little and none. We . . . they've got no probable cause to look at him. If we come up with something shady, something we can prove, I'm sure I can get someone to take a run at it. Best bet would be fingerprints. Or at least a photo."

"The picture's easy enough to come by," Erik said and pulled his cell phone from his pocket. "I can just run over there right now. Won't take a second."

I looked at Red, and he shrugged. "No law against it. Might come in handy down the road."

I thought about it for a moment. "Okay, sure. Go for it. Wait!" I called as he rose from the chair. "I have another idea."

I fished my wallet out of my bag and handed him five twenties.

"What's this for?"

"Ask for a new hundred-dollar bill. And make sure Chambers puts it in one of those little white envelopes. We might have a chance to get a useable print off it, especially if it's brand-new."

"Good call."

"And remember, this is just a reconnoitering mission. Try not to

let him get too good a look at you. We might want to use you later on
if we go with the sting."

Erik nodded. "Gotcha. Back in a few."

I watched as he stopped to pull a baseball cap from the lower drawer
of his desk and settle it low on his forehead. He slid on wraparound
sunglasses and waved on his way out the door.

"Now what?" Red asked, slouching down in his chair.

I reached for the desk phone. "Now we get ready for a funeral."

CHAPTER TEN

ED PULLED OUT MY CHAIR UNDERNEATH THE MAS-sive head of Waldo the Moose at Jump & Phil's, our favorite local pub on the south end of the island. The doors were open to the soft evening breeze, and the outdoor patio was crowded, mostly with the smokers. They would normally have been hanging out at the bar, but the town had recently declared all our restaurants smokeless. Packed with golfers and tourists in the summer months, the room now held mostly locals and carried only a low hum of conversation.

"I love September," I said after we'd given our orders for burgers and fries. "It's almost as if you can hear the entire island breathe a huge sigh of relief."

Red smiled across the table at me. "Yeah, it's nice to have things a little quieter. We always felt the same way at the sheriff's office."

I sipped my sweet tea and leaned back. "Do you miss it?"

He knew exactly what I meant. "Sometimes." He twirled his sweating glass of beer in his hands and didn't look up. "But I guess it was the right decision."

"You guess?"

His concentration on the glass in front of him seemed to increase. "It's just taking me a lot longer to get adjusted to civilian life than I thought it would. You know, I went right out of the Marines and into law enforcement." He glanced down at his white polo shirt. "It feels funny to be out of a uniform."

I reached across and squeezed his hand. "I know. But I have to tell you it's a lot easier for me. Not just that we can plan dinner and not get interrupted by a call. I worried about you a lot."

He didn't squeeze back. "I might say the same thing."

We pulled our hands apart as the waitress set our plates in front of us.

"Thanks," I said, reaching for the ketchup bottle. "But you have to admit it's been pretty quiet at the agency. We're managing to make a nice profit with the computer work."

We busied ourselves preparing our burgers before Red swallowed his first bite and spoke.

"So I guess I could ask you the same question. Did you like running around the county chasing down bad guys? Do you miss it?"

I studied his face, but I couldn't read his eyes. "Truth time? Yes. A little."

We ate in silence, the ebb and flow of people and conversation a soothing backdrop. I glanced up occasionally at the TV in the corner tuned to *SportsCenter* on ESPN. Half an hour later, Red paid the check, and we wandered out, hand in hand, to the parking lot.

"So what's the deal with Mrs. Castlemain's funeral?" he asked as I climbed into the passenger seat of the Bronco.

I'd had a long conversation with Bitsy Elliott while Erik was out getting us a photo of Dalton Chambers. And hopefully his prints on the envelope he'd brought back sealed in a plastic bag. Bitsy had been shocked at Rebecca Castlemain's death, but the upper echelons of island society had rallied around the widower. There would be a memorial service at First Presbyterian on Friday evening, with the funeral on Monday. Bitsy was certain the grandson would be in attendance at both services.

"Nicholas Potter," she'd told me when I'd finally caught up with her. "That's the grandson. I found it on the museum benefit's guest list. I haven't talked to him myself, but Lily Middleton has been in touch."

"Is it private, or can I attend?" I'd asked.

"The memorial service is open for sure."

"I'll need introductions. Can you help?"

Bitsy had been eager. Maybe a little *too* eager? I'd shoved that thought aside and taken down the information.

"I assume Kendra Blaine will be there," I'd said and earned a snort of disgust from Bitsy.

"I can guarantee it." She'd paused. "And to be fair, Thomas will need the support. I'm afraid he's going to be completely lost without Becky. She handled the house, their finances, everything. I just wish he had someone more . . . trustworthy to look after him."

I'd hung up with the promise to see her on Friday evening.

"You don't have to go if you don't want to," I told Red as we stopped for the light at Palmetto Dunes. "I'm sure we'll have to sit with Bitsy and Cal, and I know you and he aren't exactly each other's biggest fans."

"Blowhard," he answered, accelerating down Route 278 when the light changed. "Man has no topic of conversation other than himself."

"I know. So I'll represent us, and you can stay home and watch baseball."

I glanced over when he didn't respond, but he stared straight ahead.

A few minutes later we made the turn into Port Royal Plantation and followed the meandering road back to our house beside the dune. It was another soft evening, and I suggested a walk on the beach before it got full dark. Hand in hand, we crossed the boardwalk and stepped onto the packed sand. The tide was out, and a muted glow of lights from the Westin Hotel down the way cast wavering shadows out into the calm ocean. Without discussion, we turned away from the more inhabited area and headed toward the narrow spit of rocks that jutted out into the water.

"You know, I'd be glad to go to the Castlemain services with you." Red's voice sounded loud in the hazy silence.

"I know you would. But you hate those things, and I might do better on my own."

I felt his hand stiffen in mine. "Why's that?"

"Because I want to stay under the radar as much as possible. Bitsy can pass me off as a mutual friend. And she can point out the players. There's bound to be someone there who knows you used to be a cop. I don't want to spook anybody."

"I see your point," he said, but his hand didn't relax its grip. "But there's just as likely to be people there who know you, too."

"I don't have much contact with the high rollers. I'll keep a low profile."

Red stopped and pulled me around to face him. His voice quavered. "I want to be part of your life, Bay. I don't like this feeling that you're shutting me out."

I looked him directly in the eyes, his face dimming now as the sun faded over the mainland. "You *are* a part of my life. We're married. We work together. How much closer can two people get?"

He kissed me then, a soft brushing of the lips, almost tentative, as if he wasn't sure of my reaction. When he leaned back, there was a profound sadness in his voice. "I just feel sometimes that you're drifting away. That I'm losing you."

I felt a hole open up in my chest, and for a moment I couldn't speak. I didn't want to analyze the emotions that squeezed my heart. I shook my head and forced a laugh.

"Don't be ridiculous! I'm right here."

I kissed him back, hard, and his arms came around me. We stood like that for a long time, and I hoped he couldn't feel the tremors washing through me. Finally, I slipped out of his embrace. We turned back and walked slowly, Red's arm draped across my shoulder. As we neared the boardwalk, he leaned down and whispered against my hair.

"I love you, Bay Tanner."

"I know," I murmured, but I wasn't sure if he heard me.

I wore the navy blue suit with matching low-heeled pumps, the outfit I seemed to drag out for every funeral. I met up with Bitsy and Cal outside the sprawling First Presbyterian Church after parking what seemed a mile away from the entrance. The lot was overflowing, and I had to admit that the size of the turnout surprised me.

Bitsy's black sheath fitted her size-four body as if it had been made to measure, which it probably had. Flickering rays of the waning sun glinted off her shining blond pageboy so that she seemed bathed in her own special halo of light. Beside her, Cal looked like an overstuffed bear. As I stepped up to them, he nodded once, then turned and disappeared inside the church.

"Hey, honey," Bitsy said and stretched on tiptoe to air-kiss me on the cheek. "Cal's gonna get us seats toward the back. That way we can see everyone that passes by."

"Good plan," I said, falling into step beside her. "But I want to stay under the radar if possible. I don't need to be introduced to everyone you know."

Bitsy's delightful laugh seemed out of place amid the somber sea of blacks and browns, underlain with the heavy organ music pouring out of the sanctuary. "That could take us the rest of the night and into tomorrow. I'll just point out the ones you need to know about."

Inside, Bitsy steered us through the wide doors and down the center aisle. A few rows in, I spotted Cal's massive head and shoulders. He slid over, and Bitsy and I slipped into the end of the pew.

"Thomas is already down front," Bitsy whispered in my ear. "The Blaine woman is with him. We won't be able to speak to them until after the service. But it'll be brief. This is mostly just a chance for folks to pay their respects. The funeral will be private."

I ducked my head closer to her. "How did they put this together so quickly? Mrs. Castlemain just died yesterday."

"I understand the arrangements had all been made ahead of time. Becky was very specific about what she wanted. Said she couldn't stand the idea of a bunch of strangers staring at her in an open coffin. The rest of it and the burial service will be just family."

Her words gave me a start. The Judge had said pretty much the same thing to me a few weeks before he passed away.

I watched the steady stream of latecomers trying to find seats. Most of the heads were gray, and many of the mourners shuffled slowly on arthritic knees and hips. A few leaned on canes and walkers. The three of us looked to be among the youngest members of the congregation. I wondered what I'd be like at eighty, always assuming I lived that long. I had the Judge's genes to help me along, but my mother had died in late middle age. Maybe it averaged out. I touched my right temple, where the strands of gray seemed to be gathering lately, and thought—

Bitsy's elbow in my side made me jump. "That's him!"

"That's who?" I whispered back.

"The grandson. Nick Potter. Just coming down the aisle."

Nicholas Potter was movie-star handsome, and he carried himself as if he knew it. I put his age at late thirties, although his smooth, tanned skin and thick dark hair made it hard to judge. I could have been off by a few years either way. The starched white shirt and pleated black pants hung nicely on his tall, slender frame. He carried his suit coat draped casually over one arm.

I watched him, along with just about everyone else in the sanctuary, as he took his time arriving at the front. He disappeared behind the sea of heads when he sat, presumably next to his grandfather. I wondered why he hadn't arrived with Mr. Castlemain. Maybe he enjoyed making an entrance.

"What does he do?" I said softly.

"I'm not sure," Bitsy murmured back as the pastor stepped up to the lectern high above us on the altar.

"Let us pray," he said in a beautiful, mellifluous baritone, and I bowed my head.

Somehow, the image of Nicholas Potter's striking face stayed firmly fixed behind my closed eyelids.

CHAPTER
ELEVEN

A S BITSY HAD PROMISED, THE SERVICE WAS OVER quickly. The highlight had been a brief, moving eulogy by one of Rebecca Castlemain's oldest friends. After a medley of hymns, sung by a woman in an amazingly clear mezzo-soprano, we received the benediction. The pastor invited us to share our memories of the late Rebecca Castlemain with the family and each other over coffee in the fellowship hall.

I wondered why Nicholas Potter had not been asked—or moved—to speak of his grandmother.

I caught a quick glimpse of an elderly man, slightly bent, leaning on Nick's arm as they made their way out a side door, and I hoped they were in fact sticking around for the more informal gathering. I also managed a fleeting look at the despised Kendra Blaine, whose flaming red hair—just as Bitsy had described it—stood out like a beacon against the mass of gray and white.

Not everyone stayed, and it was a much smaller group that clustered around the coffee urns and trays of cookies and pastries laid out on long tables against one wall. Cal immediately latched onto an acquaintance and drifted away. Bitsy and I hung back, surveying the assembly.

"Thomas is sitting down, over there by the door," she said. "With *her.*"

I followed her gaze to where Kendra Blaine hovered beside the old gentleman, his plentiful hair a soft white that caught the overhead lights. He wore a dark suit and an understated tie, and his lace-up black shoes shone. He seemed composed, his face fixed in a thoughtful expression, broken occasionally by a thin smile as someone stopped to offer condolences. I wasn't close enough to see his eyes clearly, but he had obviously steeled himself to suffer what must be an extremely painful occasion with stoicism.

I moved my attention to his caregiver. Kendra Blaine had a pretty face buried beneath too much makeup. Her recently dyed red hair had been gathered into a loose knot on the top of her head, and the obligatory black dress stretched tightly across her voluptuous figure. From a distance, the pearls looked real, a double strand she couldn't help fingering every few seconds as if to be certain they hadn't fallen off.

Kendra fussed over Thomas, smoothing his tie where it had become bunched up under his suit jacket. Something about the way she touched him made me uncomfortable. I searched for Nick Potter and found his gaze locked on his grandfather as mine had been. Though I couldn't be certain from so far away, I thought I saw him wince in distaste.

"I want to meet them," I said, taking Bitsy by the elbow and steering her in Thomas's direction. "Nothing about what I do. Say I met Rebecca at one of the fundraisers and wanted to pay my respects."

Bitsy frowned at me as if I were one of her children. "I know what to do," she said curtly. A moment later, we stood before Thomas Castlemain.

Bitsy took both his hands in hers and leaned over to brush her lips against his cheek. "I'm so sorry, Thomas. Becky was a wonderful woman. She'll be missed by everyone who loved her."

"You're very kind, my dear. Becky did so enjoy her work with you on the museum board. She always said, 'If you want to get a project off the ground, get Bitsy Elliott on your side.' She was very fond of you."

"Thank you. That means so much."

I'd been hanging back, studying the players, until Bitsy reached out a hand to me.

"I don't believe you know my friend, Mrs. Tanner. Thomas Castlemain."

"I'm very sorry for your loss, sir," I said softly.

"You knew my wife?"

"Only briefly. We did some charity work together. I understand why everyone admired her so much."

It was only a small lie, but it hurt me to tell it now that I was face-to-face with this kindly old man.

"Thank you. And this is Miss Blaine." He raised a hand in the woman's direction. "She looks after us."

"How do you do?" She had a nice voice, and her face held just the right amount of reserve and sadness, appropriate to the occasion.

I nodded. "Miss Blaine."

"I'd like you to meet my grandson, too," Thomas said, looking around the slowly emptying room. "As soon as he's free."

I spotted Nick Potter engaged in conversation with a tall, willowy blonde, elegantly turned out in unrelieved black. They stood close together, their heads averted, as if they didn't want to be overheard. Or maybe that was just my natural cynicism.

Bitsy touched my arm, and we moved off to the side as an older couple stepped up to speak to Thomas.

"Who's that with the grandson?" I asked softly, inclining my head toward the pair who still stood shoulder to shoulder in the center of the room.

"Oh, that's my friend Lily Middleton. She saw to all the arrangements."

I couldn't help staring, and I wasn't the only one in the room. His dark head bent slightly to her ash blond one made a striking contrast. Suddenly, Lily turned, glancing over her shoulder to catch me staring. I dropped my eyes, but not before Nick Potter slid his gaze in my direction as well.

"Shall I introduce you?" Becky whispered, and I shook my head.

"No. Thanks."

I looked away, embarrassed to have been caught spying, only to find myself face-to-face with Kendra Blaine. It took a moment for me to remember just what had brought me there in the first place.

I offered a sad smile. "It must be a difficult time for Mr. Castlemain," I said quietly.

She started, appearing surprised that she'd been spoken to. "Uh, yes. Yes it is. They were devoted to each other."

"He's fortunate to have you to look after him," I said, smiling.

"I do what I can," she said, dropping her eyes in a pretty good parody of humility. "I've been a caregiver almost my whole life."

"How rewarding," I answered, forcing any hint of sarcasm out of my voice. "Where did you receive your training?"

"Excuse me," she said and turned away. "I need to get Mr. Castlemain a glass of water. It's time for his medication."

I watched her cross to the table and pour from a clear pitcher. A moment later she returned to stand next to her employer. She fumbled in the small handbag she carried, retrieved a brown plastic container, and shook out two small white pills. She waited for an opening before stepping around in front of him. She held out her hand.

Thomas Castlemain, titan of industry and millionaire many times over, closed his eyes and dropped his jaw while the woman next to him laid the pills on his tongue. She held the glass to his lips, and he swallowed dutifully.

"Dear God."

I whirled to find Nick Potter standing beside me, his face wrinkled in disgust.

No one else seemed to have noticed the exchange, and I found myself almost blushing to have been a witness to this sweet man's humiliation. Before I had a chance to react, the handsome man beside me turned and held out his hand.

"I don't believe we've been introduced. I'm Nick Potter. Rebecca was my grandmother."

"Bay Tanner," I said, mesmerized by steely blue eyes that reminded me of another man in another time and place, a man best forgotten. "I'm sorry for your loss," I added. I took his offered hand, and he covered it with both of his. I wasn't counting, but it seemed to me he held it just a few seconds too long. Bitsy's nudge jerked me back to myself.

"This is Elizabeth Elliott," I said. "She and your grandmother worked together a great deal on charity affairs."

Nick Potter turned the same devastating smile on Bitsy. "We've met. Thank you so much for coming." His gaze moved back to me. "Both of you."

Kendra Blaine spoke from behind me. "Don't you think we should be getting your grandfather home, Nick?" Her tone sounded like the contented purring of a satiated cat when she said his name.

I felt him stiffen. "You can go on home, Miss Blaine. Your *own* home." The harshness of his words wasn't lost on any of us, nor was the edge to his voice. "I'll see to my grandfather."

"But, what about—?"

He cut her off mercilessly. "I've asked Mrs. Proffit to spend the next few days with us."

I could see how shocked Blaine was by this abrupt dismissal, and

I watched her try to control the anger that blazed from her eyes. She swallowed hard before she spoke.

"I think Mr. Castlemain would feel more comfortable with familiar people around him." She raised her chin. "At a time like this."

I glanced at Thomas Castlemain. He must be furious to be sitting right there being discussed as if he were an inanimate object to be batted back and forth between these two antagonists. But I found his face strangely slack. Although his eyes were open, it almost looked as if he'd fallen asleep.

"I believe I'm the best judge of what's good for Granddad," Nick said. "He needs to be with family now. Nurse Proffit always took excellent care of Grandma. I'm sure she'll be able to handle anything that comes up."

I could feel Kendra Blaine fuming, but I had to give her credit. She recognized when she was beaten. She pulled her shoulders back and gave her charge's grandson a dazzling smile. "I'll be back then, on Monday. To help with the funeral." She paused for effect. "Thomas will expect to see me there."

She held Nick's gaze for a long moment before turning to place a hand on the old man's cheek. "I'll see you in a couple of days," she said, and Thomas nodded absently. He seemed to have retreated somewhere the outside world couldn't reach.

Kendra Blaine nodded in Bitsy's and my direction and raised her chin. "Monday," she said to Nick Potter.

We watched her weave her way through the few remaining mourners, her head high, the mass of brilliant red hair piled on her head swaying in rhythm with her hips. More than a few heads turned to watch her exit.

"Bitch," Nicholas Potter said through clenched teeth to her retreating back.

The shock of the venom in his voice held us speechless. It was as if all the oxygen had been sucked out of the room. Then he made a conscious effort to relax his shoulders on a long exhale, and the tension level dropped a few degrees.

"My apologies, ladies," he said, the devastating smile back on his face. "Somehow that woman brings out the worst in me."

"I know exactly what you mean," Bitsy said, and I could sense her gearing up for a nice gossip about Kendra Blaine.

"We should be going," I interrupted, my hand firmly on Bitsy's arm. "It was nice to have met you, Mr. Potter, although I'm sorry it had to be under these circumstances."

"Please, it's Nick."

His long fingers reached out and squeezed my shoulder. Normally, I would have had to control the urge to jerk myself away. I'm usually not big on being handled, especially by people I've known for all of five minutes. His touch was almost intimate, though, and I could feel myself leaning toward him.

Bitsy's voice snapped me back to reality. "Ready, Bay?"

I stepped away and glanced at her. Only someone who'd known her as long as I had would have been able to detect the frost underlying the innocuous words.

"Thank you so much for being here, Mrs. Elliott. It meant a lot." His roving hand had transferred itself to Bitsy's arm and lingered there.

If my best friend had been an ice sculpture, she would have been reduced to a puddle on the floor. Her voice, when she spoke, had the breathless quality of a teenager confronted with her rock-star idol. "If there's anything I can do for you, anything at all, you'll be sure to call me, won't you, Nick?"

"Of course. You're too kind."

Embarrassed—for my own foolishness as well as Bitsy's—I turned my gaze away to Thomas Castlemain. He had slumped a little in the straight-backed chair, and I could have sworn he'd fallen asleep except that his eyes were still wide open. It gave me the creeps, and I stepped in front of him and leaned down.

"Mr. Castlemain? Are you all right?"

Nick Potter whirled and nearly knocked me out of the way. "This has all been too much for Granddad. I need to get him home."

"Can we help?" Bitsy, too, edged around me.

"No, thank you, Mrs. Elliott." The suave undertone had gone from his voice. He took his grandfather's arm and gently helped him out of the chair. Thomas barely responded, his posture sagging. Nick put a cane into his hand and guided him toward the main entrance.

"Why don't I stay with Thomas while you bring the car up?" Bitsy stationed herself on the other side of the old gentleman, and for a moment it looked as if the two of them would snap him apart like a Thanksgiving turkey wishbone.

"We'll be fine." Potter glanced once at me, but his eyes held an intensity that made my breath catch a little in my throat. "I hope our paths cross again, Bay. Soon."

Bitsy and I stood and watched them slowly shuffle across the room, Potter nodding to everyone as they passed. We waited until they'd disappeared before either of us spoke.

"What a charming man," Bitsy said in a breathless rush.

"And dangerous," I said quietly, but I didn't think she heard me.

CHAPTER TWELVE

I FOUND RED STRETCHED OUT ON THE SOFA. THE TV was on, but the sound had been muted. I tiptoed into the great room in case he'd fallen asleep, but he grinned and waved a half-empty bottle of beer in my direction. I set down my bag as he swung his feet to the floor and patted the cushion next to him. I kicked off my shoes and tucked my feet up under me. He drew me close and kissed me softly on the temple.

"You look as if it was a rough night. I should have been with you."

"I'm fine. Just tired."

I smiled then, thinking how things might have gone had Red been by my side when Nicholas Potter put his hands on me. It would have been more than embarrassing to have my husband deck the grandson of the woman whose death we'd gathered to mourn.

"Did you see the Blaine woman?"

I stretched. "I'll tell you all about it after I change. Will you get me a tea?"

"Sure."

I picked up my shoes and carried them into the bedroom. I stuffed the suit in the bag for dry cleaning, washed my face, and slid a long cotton nightgown over my head. Back in the great room I dropped onto the couch. I gulped down almost half the glass of tea in one long swallow.

"Ah, thanks. I don't know why I'm so thirsty."

Red gathered me to him, and I snuggled in. A moment later I jerked up with a start.

"Hey, that's football! I thought you were watching the Braves."

"Special Friday night college game. South Carolina and Wake Forest. We're kicking butt."

We watched in silence for a few minutes. When they broke for halftime, Red clicked it off.

"So what happened at the church?"

I gave him the basics. "Blaine is attractive, in a rough kind of way. She and the grandson seem to be at odds when it comes to Mr. Castlemain. It almost felt like a tug-of-war between them. She treats the old man as if he were completely senile, which he doesn't appear to be." I told him about the episode with the pills. "I don't know if they had anything to do with the change in his demeanor. It could be that he just ran out of gas. It's hard enough dealing with that kind of loss without having to smile and be pleasant to a whole gaggle of people for hours at a time."

Red hugged me harder. "You know, it amazes me how you put on this tough-girl face most of the time, and underneath you're . . ." He stumbled to a halt.

I pulled away to look at his face. "I'm what?"

"A pussycat. A pushover. Especially where old people are concerned."

I relaxed back into his arms. "Pussycats get kicked around. And pushovers get . . . well, pushed over. I was on my own for a long time, Red. I learned how to take care of myself." I paused for a beat. "Or at least how to give that impression."

"Don't I know it," he said, but I could hear a smile in his voice. "I've been on the receiving end of some of your 'impressions,' don't forget."

I laughed, happy to have our equilibrium restored. I'd known there would be awkward moments, times when our joint memories of Rob and our own stormy past would intrude on our new and sometimes fragile relationship. Before, there had always been the idea, lurking somewhere in the back of my head, that I could walk away if things got too difficult. Or painful. But I'd made a commitment, and I intended to honor it.

Stand by your man, I thought. *Tammy Wynette would be proud of me.*

Red reached for his beer and took a sip. "What's the grandson like?"

"Arrogant," I said without thinking. Then, "But to be fair, it probably wasn't the best venue to judge someone. He's understandably upset about his grandmother. And, as I said before, I don't think he and Kendra Blaine are on the best of terms."

"Maybe he's on the same wavelength as Cecelia Dobbs. He could have some idea that she's been stealing from his grandparents."

I sat up. "Could be." I thought about it for a moment. "But that wasn't the vibe I got from him. I think maybe it's more like Blaine may have made a play for him and been rebuffed. May still be trying, for that matter. There was an underlying tension there that was almost . . . sexual, I guess."

"Really? You got all that in just a few minutes of seeing them together?"

"It was pretty obvious. At least to me." I swung my legs out from under me and rose. I didn't want to get into a lengthy discussion about Nicholas Potter's sexual magnetism. "I'm going to call Bitsy, see what her take is on it."

Red flipped the television back on. "Hurry it up. The second half's about to start."

In the office, I fired up the computer while I waited for Bitsy to answer. Unfortunately, it was Cal who picked up the phone.

"Hey," I said. "Can I speak to Bits?"

"Who's calling?"

I forced myself to speak calmly. "It's Bay, Cal."

He didn't respond, but I heard his breath wheezing as he walked with the phone. The man seriously needed to lose about a hundred pounds.

"Hey, honey," Bitsy said. "I'm just getting ready for bed. What's up?"

"I just wanted your take on things tonight. What did you think about the interaction between Kendra and Potter?"

She didn't answer for a moment. When she did, there was pure venom in her voice. "That woman! Making a play for Nick right there at Becky's service! I thought it was absolutely shameful."

I didn't remind my friend that she'd been doing more than a little simpering and flirting with the handsome grandson herself. And I didn't want to deal with any pot-and-kettle comparisons, either. "Did you notice how she treats Mr. Castlemain? Almost as if he were some sort of idiot child?"

"I told you. She has him completely wrapped around her little finger. Did you hear Nick put her in her place? I wanted to kiss him for standing up to her like that."

I couldn't resist. "*Please.* You wanted to kiss him, period. I almost had to wipe the drool off your chin."

"Lydia Baynard Simpson Tanner! How can you say such a thing?"

"Come on, Bits, lighten up. I'm just teasing you." I sobered. "He's a good-looking guy, there's no denying that."

"I noticed you noticing," she said with a little bite in her voice.

I ignored it. "But don't you find his arrogance a bit off-putting?"

"I don't know what you mean. I thought he was a perfect gentleman."

"Okay. I didn't call to get you all riled up. So you're not invited to the funeral?"

"No. It's just going to be family. I don't know if the sons are coming or not. Lily Middleton says Nick notified them, but . . . I can't imagine they wouldn't show up for their own mother's funeral, but you know how these family feuds can be. So senseless."

I thought about all the lies and secrets in my own family and spared a little sympathy for Thomas Castlemain's sons. No one ever knew for sure about what went on behind closed doors. Maybe they had good reasons for being estranged. Or maybe not.

"Do you think Blaine will be there? She seemed pretty adamant about it."

Bitsy paused. "I'd bet on it. I don't think she wants to let herself get shuffled off to the side. Not her style at all."

Something had been nagging at me ever since I'd gotten back in my car at the church, something I'd heard that I'd meant to pursue, and suddenly it popped into my head.

"Do you know the nurse that looked after Mrs. Castlemain? I think Potter called her Mrs. Proffit?"

"Yes. Cady Proffit. She's a certified home-care provider, I think. Maybe she has a nursing degree, I'm not sure."

"I know her," I said. "Or at least I've met her. She's the woman who was looking after Kimmie Eastman when they sent her home from the hospital."

"She's very good. I know a couple of people who have used her for in-home care."

I wondered what the protocol was for nurses, confidentiality-wise. If she'd spent a lot of time in the Castlemain household, she might be a gold mine of information. I made myself a note to contact her, although I would wait until after the funeral.

"What?" I said, suddenly aware that Bitsy had been talking.

"I said is there anything else you want me to do?"

"No, Bits, thanks. I appreciate your help. If you hear anything you think might be useful, though, give me a call. And remember—"

"I know, I know. It's all confidential. Such a bore, but my absolutely perfect lips are sealed."

With a laugh, I said goodbye.

Back in the great room, Red had moved to the floor, stretched out with a pile of pillows behind his head. I dropped onto the sofa.

"Get anything useful?" he asked.

"Not really. I think Bitsy's judgment may have been a little overwhelmed by the dashing Mr. Potter."

He turned his head to stare up at me. "Good-looking?"

"Devastating," I said with a grin. "Think a dark-haired Robert Redford back in the days before his face started to sag."

Red laughed. "Should I be worried?"

I slid down beside him and hitched up the nightgown a little so I could drape a leg across his. "Not for a second," I said and kissed him.

I woke up with a start, awakened by something I couldn't get a handle on. I eased myself up in bed, careful not to disturb Red, and listened for several moments. The wind was quiet, and even the rolling of the ocean was silent behind the closed windows. I tried to recall if I'd been dreaming, but I couldn't pull anything up out of the daze. The clock read 3:16, a little past my usual waking hour lately, but still pretty much on schedule. I debated whether or not to get up, maybe make myself some decaffeinated tea. Instead, I wiggled back down under the sheet and tried to will myself back to sleep.

Beside me, Red mumbled and rolled over.

I concentrated on my breathing—long, slow inhales. I consciously relaxed each part of my body, starting with my toes. I pictured the beach at sunset, deserted, with the Atlantic rollers breaking rhythmically on the packed sand. But every time I felt myself drifting off, something jerked me back. As a last resort, I mentally began a recitation of "The Highwayman," the poem by Alfred Noyes I'd had to memorize for a presentation in my sophomore English class in high school. That almost always did the trick. But, by the time I'd run through it from start to finish—twice—I was even wider awake, and the numbers on the digital clock face had rolled over to 3:42.

With a sigh, I slid out of bed, slipped on my robe, and moved silently out into the hallway. I paused outside the door to the office, then turned toward the great room. I stood at the French doors and gazed out toward the ocean. A nearly full moon rode high in the sky, its thin light casting undulating shadows across the deck as the long branches of the live oak quivered in a light onshore breeze. I opened the door and stepped outside, the wood dew-damp and chilly on my bare feet. I propped my elbows on the railing and tried to remember when this inability to sleep through the night had begun.

I cast my mind back to all the life-altering changes that had occurred in the past few months: My discovery of a half sister I never knew existed. My marriage to Red. My father's death. The drudgery of dealing with all the paperwork involved in settling his estate. Lavinia's pain of loss and loneliness.

No wonder you can't sleep, I told myself, but somehow that didn't ring true. In the darkest recesses of my brain, a small voice was trying to get my attention, and my conscious mind wouldn't let it be heard. I had no idea what it was trying to tell me. I just knew for certain there was . . . *something* I needed to deal with, something I wasn't yet ready to face.

The screech of a barn owl, swooping to its prey, made me jerk upright. I wasn't certain if the shiver that made me grasp my arms and bolt for the door was fear or cold. Either way, I knew I needed the comfort of Red's solid, warm body.

Once inside, I dropped my robe and slid into bed beside my husband. I snuggled up against his back and warmed my chilled feet on his own. Sooner or later, I'd know what my subconscious was trying to tell me.

For better or for worse.

CHAPTER THIRTEEN

$\mathscr{I}$ SAT AT THE GLASS-TOPPED TABLE IN THE ALCOVE IN the kitchen, sipping my second cup of Earl Grey, the Saturday *Island Packet* spread out in front of me. I glanced up at the clock over the sink for about the hundredth time that morning, still cursing myself for having overslept. Whether Red had deliberately let me sleep in or had driven off in a huff without me, I'd have to wait a while longer to find out. He'd headed to Beaufort for Scotty's soccer game, leaving me to fuss about what kind of reception I'd get when they returned.

I folded the paper and tossed it onto the empty chair across from me a moment before I heard the low rumble of the Bronco pulling into the drive. I dropped my cup into the dishwasher, gave the tabletop a quick wipe, and trotted down the steps into the garage. I breathed a sigh of relief when all three of them tumbled out of the car, laughing.

In a moment I was surrounded.

"Aunt Bay, we won! And I scored the winning goal!" Scotty held up his hand, and we high-fived. Again I marveled at how tall he'd gotten.

"Awesome," I said.

Elinor pranced around us on the concrete apron. "And I yelled and yelled," she shouted. "I clapped so hard my hands hurt."

I gathered her to me and kissed the top of her head. Her mother had pulled her silky, light brown hair into twin ponytails that swished around her head as she bounced in excitement. "I bet you're the best cheerleader ever," I said.

"I'm going to be one for real when I'm bigger. When I go to middle school," she said, stepping out of my embrace. "Cheerleaders are always the coolest girls in the class, aren't they, Aunt Bay?"

I smiled down at her sweet, earnest face. "Not always, honey. But if that's what you really want to do, we'll see about getting you to a cheerleading camp next summer. Would you like that?"

"Absolutely positively," she gushed, hugging my legs again.

Over the top of her head, I saw Red frown.

"We'll see," he said. Then he ruffled his son's hair. "You guys hungry? How about if you go wash up and get changed, and we'll grab a pizza at Giuseppi's."

Amid a chorus of cheers, we herded them inside and toward the guest bedroom and bath. Both kids kept a supply of clothes there so there was never any necessity for them to drag suitcases with them. Occasionally, they brought along schoolbooks if they had work to finish up, but Sarah usually insisted that they get it all behind them by Friday evening. Once in a while Scotty might have a report to do, especially now that he was in middle school, but the previous Christmas I'd bought them a laptop to keep in their room, so they generally traveled pretty light.

We watched them scamper down the hallway, and Red draped an arm across my shoulder. "What time did you manage to drag yourself out of bed?" he asked, and his voice was tinged with laughter. I breathed a mental sigh of relief.

"A little after ten. You should have wakened me."

He followed me into our bedroom where I slipped my bare feet into Birkenstocks and ran a brush through my hair. Red stepped up behind me and wrapped his arms around my waist.

"I tried, but you weren't having any of it," he said, nuzzling my neck. "I broke out some of my best moves, too."

That made me laugh. "Sorry I missed it."

"You were up again in the night, weren't you?" he asked, his tone sobering.

"For a little while. But when I came back to bed, I dropped right off." I turned and put my arms around his neck. "You're always so warm."

We kissed softly.

"I need to be. Your damn feet were like ice," he said, holding me tighter. "What did you do, go wading in the ocean?"

"I just walked out on the deck. I—"

"Jeez, you guys. Come on."

Scotty stood in the doorway, his damp hair curling around a thin face that reminded me so much of his father's. And his late uncle's. Red and I jumped apart as if we were teenagers busted by our parents.

"Did we embarrass you, son?" Red asked with a grin. He kissed me again, briefly, and Scotty groaned. "Get used to it, boy."

"Yes," I added, taking Scotty by the shoulders and aiming him toward the great room. "It's one of our primary missions in life, you know. It's in the manual. We're required to embarrass you at least once a day."

Elinor came barreling along behind us, and we locked up and piled into the Bronco. The interior smelled like boy-sweat and old socks, so we opened all the windows to the warm autumn air.

"Daddy, can I have mushrooms on my pizza?" Elinor wheedled from the backseat. "And pepperoni?"

"You can have whatever you like, princess," her father answered, and the word sent a little shiver through me.

The Judge had called me *princess* when he was in one of his better moods. Not often, but I felt somehow protective of the title, as if it should have been reserved for me alone. I shook my head at my own silliness.

"What are you having, Aunt Bay?" Scotty asked.

"I'm with your sister," I said, smiling to myself. "Just don't anybody order any of those yucky fish on their pizza. I'll have to go sit at another table."

"Anchovies aren't that bad," Scotty offered with a grin. "Maybe I'll get some on mine, Aunt Bay."

Red and I had had a long discussion about what the children should call me after I officially became their stepmother. I'd told him to ask them what they felt comfortable with. So we'd sat them down and kicked it around for a while. At first they'd been reluctant to join in the conversation, but finally Scotty admitted that he'd feel funny if I was anything but "Aunt Bay." Elinor, heavily influenced by whatever position her idolized older brother took, nodded her agreement. So Aunt Bay it was and would remain. I continued to marvel at how well they'd both adapted to the idea that I was now married to their father. It was a blessing that the transition had gone so smoothly.

Our favorite pizza place next to the Mall at Shelter Cove was busy on that sunny September Saturday, but we managed to snag a table outside. Tiny sparrows and huge, ugly grackles hopped back and forth on the concrete, scrounging for crumbs and scraps earlier diners had let fall.

We'd just given our order when my cell phone rang. I fished it out of my purse and checked the caller ID. I didn't recognize the number. Under ordinary circumstances, I wouldn't take a call when the four of us were out together, but we had a new client in Cecelia Dobbs, and I knew the death of Rebecca Castlemain had hit her hard. Although I didn't hand out my private cell number to just anyone, I'd written it on the business card I'd given to Cecelia.

I stood and moved over close to the newspaper rack. "Bay Tanner."

"Good afternoon, Bay. I hope I'm not disturbing you."

"Who is this?"

"It's Nick. Nick Potter. We met last night?"

"Of course." I paused, not quite sure how to react. I glanced over at Red, but he was occupied with organizing drinks and straws. "How did you get this number?"

"I'm sorry. Is this a bad time?"

"I'm having lunch with my family." I didn't want to sound too rude, considering the strain he must be under. "Is there something I can do for you, Mr. Potter?"

"Nick, please," he said. "I know it's an imposition, but I wonder if I might talk with you. About a little problem we're having."

He paused, waiting for a response, but I let him hang. What was *this* all about?

"Bay?"

His constant use of my first name was beginning to irritate me, along with my own guilty memory of his hand on my shoulder. "Is this a business matter, Mr. Potter?"

"I know it's a terrible imposition, but Bitsy . . . Mrs. Elliott felt sure you'd be willing to help." Again he waited. "I'm only on the island for a few days."

A not-too-gentle reminder of his loss. Going for the sympathy vote, I guessed.

"I have office hours from Monday through Thursday, nine to five. I'd be happy to see you there." I kept my voice even.

"My grandmother's funeral is Monday," he said softly. "I need . . . I'd hoped to talk to you before then. It's important."

Damn Bitsy and her big mouth! She'd obviously given Potter my private number. I hoped to hell she hadn't let anything slip about my real reason for being at his grandmother's memorial service the night before. I cast another glance over my shoulder to find my husband frowning in my direction.

"I don't think that's possible," I said firmly. "I'm sorry, Mr. Potter, but I try not to let business interfere with my weekends unless it's an emergency."

When he spoke again, his soft tone had hardened into anger.

"Does attempted murder qualify as an emergency?"

CHAPTER
FOURTEEN

RED AND I WOULD HAVE A BLAZING ROW BEFORE THIS was all over. I could feel it in my bones.

In front of the kids, he'd been restrained, even pleasant, when I announced that I'd need to run over to the office for a little while after we got home. He didn't ask questions, but I could tell he was bursting to demand an explanation. And I understood his anger. Up to a point. We'd established an unspoken rule that nothing interfered with our time with the kids, and we'd managed to make it through the summer without anything popping up to disrupt our schedule. I didn't like it any better than he did, but sometimes it couldn't be helped. Maybe I expected too much, but I thought he might have cut me a little slack for a first offense.

Scotty and Elinor sensed the tension, but we all did our best to ignore it. We finished our pizzas, and Red let them wheedle ice cream cones out of him. I tried not to fidget, but it almost felt as if he was deliberately wasting time. Finally we climbed back into the Bronco and headed for home. Ten minutes later, the kids were racing down the hall to change for the beach. Red and I avoided looking at each other as

I slipped into slacks and a cotton sweater more appropriate for the office than shorts and a tank top.

"How long do you think you'll be?" he asked, and I could hear the effort it took to keep his tone neutral.

"I don't know, Red. I'll make it as quick as possible."

"I had Dolores stock up on hamburger and hot dogs. I thought we'd cook out on the deck tonight."

I leaned in and kissed him lightly on the lips. "That sounds great. I'll be here long before then."

"The kids'll be disappointed you're not going to the beach with us."

"They'll be fine," I said through clenched teeth. Red had been playing the *kids* card quite a bit lately, and I resented it. "You guys have fun." I gathered up my bag and slung it over my shoulder. "See you in a bit."

I didn't wait for a response. I slid into the Jaguar and gunned it out of the garage. I tried to put Red's possessiveness out of my head and concentrate on what the hell kind of game Nick Potter was playing.

He was waiting for me in the parking lot, his lean body resting against the side of a black SUV. I could have guessed that would be Potter's choice for transportation: big, flashy, and macho. His tanned face was partially hidden by sunglasses, and his pressed jeans and white shirt with the cuffs rolled up made him look rakish, as if he'd seen one too many James Bond movies. He wore Top-Siders—with no socks, of course.

Straight out of a GQ *ad,* I thought. *And he knows it.*

I pulled in and cut the engine. Before I even got the key out of the ignition he was opening my door. Just as he had at his grandmother's memorial service the night before, Nicholas Potter was crowding me. I stared up into his face, waiting for him to get the message that his easy charm wasn't going to work again. Although I couldn't see his eyes through the shades, I thought they'd probably be twinkling to match his smile. He waited a moment before stepping back.

"Thanks for coming, Bay," he said.

I slammed the car door a little harder than necessary. "I don't have much time, Mr. Potter. Let's make this quick."

I unlocked the door to the office and preceded him inside. Without looking back to see if he was following, I marched into my office and around the desk. I didn't invite him to sit, but he took the client chair and crossed one long leg over a knee. I picked up the Dobbs file, which I'd left on my desk the night before, and slid it into the center drawer. I pulled out a contract package, a legal pad, and the tape recorder. I didn't look up until I had everything arranged precisely on the desktop, then leaned back in the chair and folded my hands in front of me.

"So. How can I help you?"

He slid the glasses off and tucked them into the breast pocket of his shirt. "You could start by calling me Nick."

"This is a business transaction, Mr. Potter. You're in my office. Let's keep things professional."

He shrugged, and I had the distinct feeling that he was laughing at me. A handsome man, especially one who came from money, probably believed that every woman he met was preparing to swoon at his feet. And maybe they did. I'd just decided not to be one of them.

"As you wish." He leaned forward. "You met Kendra Blaine, my father's . . . companion. What did you think of her?"

"I thought she obviously has a great deal of influence over your grandfather. And frankly I was a little put off by how she treats him. How old is Mr. Castlemain?"

Potter finally realized that charm wasn't going to work. His face sobered. "I completely agree with your assessment, Mrs. Tanner."

I would have smiled if not for the seriousness of the discussion. *Round one to me.*

"And Granddad's just turned seventy-nine."

"What's his general health?"

Nick Potter waved his hand. "Oh, pretty good, I think. He doesn't complain about any ailments." He paused. "He is getting a little forgetful. I noticed it especially this trip, but that could be because of . . . you know, my grandmother."

I found myself warming to him as he spoke. The brash assurance had given way to what I perceived to be genuine affection when he spoke of Thomas. And real pain at losing Rebecca. I felt myself relaxing. I waited for him to continue.

"The thing is, Kendra treats him like a three-year-old. You saw that?"

I nodded. "That routine with the pills was definitely a little creepy. Do you know what she was giving him?"

"Blood pressure medication, she told me, but she keeps the bottle with her. I haven't had a chance to check it out."

"Do you know who his doctor is? He might be persuaded to tell you."

Potter shook his head. "Living in D.C., I don't get down here as often as I should. Besides, I've always felt that Granddad and Grandma could take care of themselves. They had someone keeping an eye on them, so I guess I didn't pay as close attention as I should have." He glanced away for a moment. "It was always my mother who looked after them."

I remembered Bitsy's telling me that Nick's mother had died of cancer. I waited, but he didn't seem to have anything else to say.

"On the phone, you asked if I considered attempted murder an emergency. What's that all about?"

He seemed to shake himself, and the old charm machine cranked back up. "I may have overstated that a little bit."

"It's what got me down here on a Saturday afternoon while my husband and stepchildren are stretched out on the beach. Are you tell-ing me it was a ploy?"

When he didn't answer right away, I whipped open the drawers and began tossing things back into them. I should have known better than to trust this snake oil salesman. I'd been genuinely concerned, especially coming on the heels of Cecelia Dobbs's suspicion that her visit to my office might have precipitated Rebecca Castlemain's sudden death. Then Potter had come along, implying that Thomas might be in danger. I didn't know what his game was, but I was definitely sitting it out.

"Bay, wait! Mrs. Tanner."

I stopped and looked at him. "What?"

"Please," he said. "Just hold on a second. I'm seriously worried about my grandfather. I don't like Kendra's control over him, and it makes me wonder about my grandmother's death. I know it sounds like a bad made-for-TV movie, but I'm worried. And I know I'm handling this all like a complete jerk. I really do want your help."

I closed the drawer quietly and studied his face. You'd think some-one that looked like he did would be used to it, but my scrutiny made him uncomfortable. He could only hold my gaze for a few seconds before his eyes slid away toward the window.

I spoke softly. "If you seriously believe Kendra Blaine might somehow have had a hand in your grandmother's death, you need to be sitting in the sheriff's office."

He was shaking his head before I'd even finished the sentence. "No! I mean, I have no proof of anything. It's just a . . . a feeling." He paused and made sure he had my full attention. "Did you notice the pearls she was wearing last night?"

"Yes. They looked real."

"They are. They belonged to my grandmother."

He had my full attention now. "You're sure?"

"Yes. The clasp is unique. Granddad had it designed especially for

her on their fiftieth wedding anniversary. We had a big celebration."
His snort made him suddenly seem more ordinary. More like the rest
of us mortals. "Even my uncles and their broods showed up. Anyway,
they were all complaining that the necklace must have cost more than
the GDP of some small countries."

I wanted to ask about the family split, but I didn't want to get sidetracked. "Do you mind if I record this?" I nodded toward the little machine. "It saves me from having to take notes."

He nodded, and I switched on the cassette recorder. I quickly
noted the date and time and the names of the participants.

"Okay, back up a little. Kendra Blaine, your grandparents' paid
companion, was wearing a very expensive piece of jewelry that belonged
to your late grandmother. Do you think it's possible Thomas gave it to
her?"

"Why would he? I mean, he has daughters-in-law and grand-
daughters. Rebecca's things should rightfully go to them."

I glanced quickly at Potter's left hand. Bare. So no female heir on
his end of things. Maybe.

"But if Thomas was her sole beneficiary, they'd be his to do with
as he pleases, no?"

Nick Potter looked angry. "Of course. But, my God, she isn't even
in the ground yet. And my grandmother left a will. Knowing her, it
will be specific about making sure where the things she cared about
end up. I can guarantee you she didn't intend that woman to have her
jewelry."

He had a point. Mention of the burial had triggered something
else in my head. "Did they perform an autopsy?"

The word disturbed him. Most of us have seen enough episodes of
CSI and other cop shows to know what an autopsy entails. The mental
images gave me the creeps, and I hadn't even met the deceased woman.

"I don't know. Would they do it as a matter of course? I mean, she
died in the hospital. They told me it was heart failure."

I toyed with whether or not to tell him about Cecelia Dobbs's father and Rebecca's cardiologist and their surprise at the supposed cause of death. And Harley Coffin's, too. I decided that I couldn't violate her confidentiality without her permission. I hedged. "If the death is attended by a physician, I don't think it's required. But I believe you could request one. Or, probably Thomas could."

I wasn't at all sure of my facts, but I knew I could find out. Then it occurred to me that the body might already have been released to the funeral home. Once embalming began— I swallowed hard against the thought.

"If you have serious doubts about how your grandmother died, you should contact someone official. And right now. Before her body is released. An autopsy is the only way to determine if there was anything fishy about it."

Potter was having as hard a time with the subject as I was—maybe more. I found myself warming to him once again. "I think it's already too late. I spent the morning with Granddad arranging things with the funeral home. She's . . ." He gulped. "She's already there. We took her clothes and things over."

"I'm sorry. This must be very painful for you and your grandfather." When he didn't respond, I said, "So I guess that's that."

"But there's still Granddad."

"True. So why don't you just fire the Blaine woman? It sounds as if you have confidence in the nurse you mentioned. Maybe she'd take over your grandfather's care and running the house until you find a permanent replacement."

"Cady Proffit? She might. But I don't have any authority to fire anybody. And Granddad likes Kendra. I'm not his guardian. He can do whatever he wants."

My mind flashed back to the arguments I'd had with Lavinia when my father had insisted he wouldn't have the surgery that might have prolonged his life. The heart surgeon had persuaded her that having him declared incompetent would open the door for one of us to override his stubbornness. Since I'd held his medical power of attorney, it had been up to me to see that his wishes were carried out. It had nearly broken my heart, but I'd done what Daddy asked. I wasn't certain that Lavinia had yet entirely forgiven me for it.

"Do you think he's . . . still capable of making those kinds of decisions?"

Nick Potter took the question seriously. "I don't know. But right now, I can guarantee you he's not going to fire Blaine. We had a little bit of a row this morning when he realized I'd told her to stay away for a few days."

It seemed as if the discussion had come full circle. "So let me sum this up. You have a vague suspicion that your grandparents' caregiver may have—and continues to wield—influence over them, and you're concerned that she might even have hastened Rebecca's death. You also suspect that she might have stolen a valuable piece of jewelry. But you have no proof, and you have no authority to override Thomas's wishes. And there's no chance of an autopsy to prove or disprove your theory." I clicked off the recorder. "I don't see how I can help you."

"I want you to find out everything you can about Kendra Blaine. I need some ammunition to take to Granddad. And I want you to look into their finances. There'll have to be some sort of accounting to settle the estate, won't there? Bitsy said you're really good at that kind of thing. I need a way to get Blaine out of the house."

He paused for dramatic effect, and it worked.

"Even if we can't prove she had something to do with my grandmother's death, I want to make damn sure she doesn't have a chance to hurt Granddad. Will you help me?"

I told myself it wasn't the steel blue eyes, the ones that reminded me so much of Alain Darnay's, but I found myself nodding yes.

CHAPTER
FIFTEEN

"WE'VE ALREADY GOT A CLIENT!"

Though Red spoke sharply, he'd kept his voice down in deference to the kids. They'd hauled themselves off to bed a little less than an hour before, everything they'd managed to cram into the day making their eyelids droop only shortly after nine o'clock. Their father and I sat on the deck in the darkness, side by side on the chaises, the only light provided by a citronella candle and a moon now almost completely full.

"He understands that," I said evenly.

"You told him about Cecelia Dobbs?"

I held the sigh of exasperation and let it out slowly. "Not in so many words. I told him we might have a conflict of interest and that I'd have to check out a couple of things before we finalized any agreement."

Red set his glass of iced tea on the table between us and tucked his hands behind his head. He never drank, not even a beer, when Scotty and Elinor were in the house. "I just don't see why you want to complicate everything."

"It's not a complication. Think about it. We have two different sources—independent of each other—voicing the same concerns. It

makes a much stronger case for the possibility that Blaine and this
Dalton Chambers maybe had something to do with Rebecca Castlemain's death. If you were still with the sheriff's office, wouldn't that
make you sit up and take notice?"

He didn't answer for a few moments, and I used the time to remind myself that this was my *husband* I was talking to. The days of
Red's and my butting heads should be a thing of the past. We needed
to work this out—together—and not get tangled up in arguing at cross-
purposes the way we used to. We were on the same team. In more ways
than one.

"You're right. If both Dobbs and Potter had come to us with these
suspicions, we'd have given the totality of it more weight than we would
have separately. The fact remains that the body has been released for
burial, there was no autopsy performed, and any chance of determining
if foul play was involved in her death is going into the ground with her
on Monday. End of story."

"I can't believe you're just willing to shrug your shoulders and say
oh well. We're talking about a possible murder here."

"*Possible* being the operative word. The woman was nearly eighty
and not in perfect health. If nothing set off alarm bells for the hospital,
it's probably just what it seems—a heart attack in an elderly woman
whose body couldn't fight back. Regrettable, but it happens. Blaine
may be a thief, and by all accounts she's not the flower of delicate
Southern womanhood, but that doesn't make her a murderer. Con art-
ists like her, if that's in fact what she is, don't generally resort to violence. They use their brains. And their charm." He paused and looked
across the gap between us. "I know you're trying to do right by our client, but let's stick to the facts and leave speculation to the scriptwriters.
Nailing her for fraud will be a big enough challenge."

I welcomed the softer tone in his voice, and I felt my shoulders
relax a little. "You're probably right. But there's still Thomas."

"Okay, then let's think this through," he said, sitting up and swinging his legs over the side of the chaise. He rested his elbows on his knees and let his hands dangle down between them.

It made me smile, so familiar was the gesture, and I knew we'd stepped out of the quicksand of our bickering and onto the firmer ground of reasoned discussion. I waited for him to continue.

"Cecelia Dobbs suspects Blaine and Chambers of stealing from the Castlemains. And she was the first one to suggest that they might have had a hand in Rebecca's death. There's nothing concrete to prove or disprove that part of her theory, so we have to let it go. Potter apparently pussyfooted around the same subject without actually coming out and accusing the caregiver of murdering Rebecca. Right?"

"Right. He has suspicions, but they're pretty much based on the fact that she's wielded a lot of influence over his grandparents, especially Thomas. And that she was wearing the pearls last night. But he realizes, too, that accusing her of harming Rebecca is pretty much a lost cause at this point. He's more concerned now with his grandfather. He has a bad feeling that she'll worm as much money out of the old man as she can, then get him to change his will. That would certainly give her a motive to knock him off." I sighed. "Nick himself said it sounded like a bad melodrama, but I think he's sincerely afraid for Thomas."

Red's face suddenly appeared in the glow of the candle as his head snapped up. "Nick? We're on a first-name basis now?"

The moment I laughed I knew it was a mistake.

"Am I amusing you?" my husband asked through clenched teeth.

I reached across the short space between us and grabbed one of his hands. "Come on, Red, for God's sake! Am I getting all bent out of shape because you refer to Cecelia Dobbs by her first name? If we're going to be working with the guy, I'm not going to go on calling him Mr. Potter. That would be silly." I squeezed his fingers to emphasize my point. "Although, I find it flattering that you think you have anything to be jealous about."

He jerked his hand away. "I'm not jealous! And no one would look twice at the Dobbs girl anyway."

The casual nastiness of the remark ticked me off. It was so typically . . . *male*. Red was usually above all that. Or so I thought.

"We're getting sidetracked again," I said, more calmly than I felt. "We've got Cecelia on the inside of the bank where the fraud may be taking place and *Nick*"—I deliberately emphasized the word—"inside the family. Plus, there's Cady Proffit. Remember her from the Eastman case? She and I seemed to be on the same page back then. If she can be persuaded to talk, that's three people working for us in places we wouldn't normally have a prayer of cracking. I'm thinking it won't take long to get the information we need, one way or the other. If Cecelia agrees, we could wrap this up in a nice neat package and dump it on the sheriff's desk in a few days."

"That's the goal? Gift wrap it for the sheriff?"

"Of course. Isn't that what Cecelia Dobbs asked us to do right from the beginning? Find enough proof to get the authorities to investigate? The same goes for Nick. He doesn't expect us to be judge and jury. It's not a hit."

That made him laugh out loud. "I'm certainly glad to hear *that*." This time it was his hand that reached out for mine. "And you couldn't contact the Dobbs woman?"

I squeezed back. "I left a message on her cell phone. I hesitated to call her parents' house since she's been so paranoid about no one's finding out she's hired us."

Red stood and pulled me up with him. "Then I guess we just have to wait until she calls us back." He drew me into his arms. "What shall we do in the meantime?"

"Oh, we'll think of something," I said a moment before his lips found mine.

Our Sundays had a routine that I'd come to look forward to. We ate breakfast together, all four of us, before Red dropped the kids off at the children's service at the Methodist church on Pope Avenue. He spent that hour at Java Joe's or Starbucks, reading the paper until it was time to pick them up. Of course, it would have set a much better example if we had actually accompanied them to the service, but neither one of us was enough of a hypocrite. They understood that we were adhering to their mother's wishes, neither promoting nor discouraging attendance on our own behalf. So far the questions had been few, and they'd fallen into the rhythm of it without much protest.

I took the *Island Packet* with me out onto the deck where the wind off the ocean helped ameliorate our sudden return to cloying humidity and temperatures soaring into the high eighties. By October, hopefully, we'd be cooler and drier. I stopped at the article about our slower than usual hurricane season. The middle of September was the height of the danger for those of us who lived in coastal areas, but so far we hadn't even had a close call. Most of the activity seemed to be in the Gulf of Mexico, except for one little disjointed blob meandering around near the Bahamas. I sent up a silent prayer of thanks to whoever might be listening, not unmindful that I was wishing ill fortune on others at the same time. I flashed back to my one experience with the might and destruction of a tropical cyclone as it roared across the flat, vulnerable sands of Anegada in the British Virgin Islands. I never wanted to experience that level of terror again, ever.

I sipped at my cooling cup of tea and stretched. For the first time in weeks, I'd slept the entire night through. I had no idea why, but there was no sense tempting fate. Even so, I felt my eyes growing heavy a moment before the bleating of the cell phone next to me jerked me awake. I flipped it open.

"Hello?"

"Mrs. Tanner, it's Cecelia Dobbs. I just picked up your message. I'm really sorry, but I was out to dinner with my parents last night, and Daddy made me shut it off. He hates when a meal gets interrupted even though he's got his pager on all the time." She paused for breath. "I forgot to turn it back on until I came out of church this morning."

"That's okay," I said, laying the paper aside. "I'm glad you called."

"Did something happen?"

Apparently I wouldn't be able to pause for breath before Cecelia felt the need to fill the empty air with words.

"I need to discuss something with you, and you're going to have to understand that I can't divulge any details. This person deserves the same level of confidentiality that I've promised you, so I'm limited as to what I can say. Do you understand?"

"Sure. It's something about the Castlemains, then?"

I stood and walked to the edge of the deck where I could rest my free arm on the railing. The morning sun sent glints of reflected sunlight off the water almost directly into my eyes, and I turned slightly away. "Here's the situation. Someone else has approached the agency about the situation with Kendra Blaine and Thomas Castlemain, although from a slightly different perspective. Even so, this person shares your concerns with Blaine's influence and with Thomas's safety."

I paused a moment in case she wanted to jump in, but she stayed silent.

"So, based on this person's connection to the family, it seems to me that joining forces would give us the best opportunity to gather the evidence you need to approach the authorities. I need your permission to disclose your name." I heard her gasp and hurried on. "Or, if you're uncomfortable with that, at least the specifics of your concern and its origins."

She was quiet a long time. "I don't know," she finally said. "You really think this is a good idea?"

"I do," I said without hesitation. "The more angles we have from which to approach the problem, the more likely we are to arrive at a good outcome. This other client has already given me permission to give you—" I almost said *his* but caught myself just in time. "To reveal their identity to you if I think it will help you feel more comfortable. But it has to be a quid pro quo." I didn't know if it would matter or not, but I added, "And this would also spread the expense out so that you wouldn't be carrying the entire burden alone."

Again the usually voluble Cecelia Dobbs held her tongue. I walked back over to the chaise and stretched out again just as I heard the rumble of the Bronco's engine in the drive.

"You can think about it and get back to me," I said, "but I'd like to have an answer by tomorrow morning. For reasons I can't explain right now, it's important that we get moving on this as soon as possible."

"Okay," she said and left it there.

The woman could be irritating, but I spoke evenly. "Okay you'll think about it, or okay you agree to the terms?"

"I'll think about it. I'm not real comfortable with anyone else knowing about me."

I stifled my exasperation. "That's certainly your privilege. When do you think you'll have a decision for me?"

"Can't you just tell whoever this is about the scam and leave me out of it?"

It would complicate things immensely, but she had a right to her anonymity. "If that's how you want it."

"Yes. I'm okay with you working for both of us, but I don't want them to know who I am."

"Fine. Let me get the ball rolling, and I'll talk to you later this evening. Will that be all right? If I call your cell?" I kept my voice low-key, but the frustration settled into a hard knot in my chest.

"Yes, ma'am. Daddy and Mummy are going out with friends on their boat, and they probably won't be back until late." She sighed. "I'll be here all day."

Poor girl, I thought. *Why didn't her damn parents take her with them?* What I said was, "Great. We'll also need to map out a strategy for how you should deal with Dalton Chambers. I don't want to spook him. You be thinking about that, too, okay? We'll put our heads together tonight."

"Okay," she said, and I sensed a little less enthusiasm than she'd expressed that first day in the office. "Talk to you later."

Just as I punched the phone off, the kids came charging through the French doors onto the deck. They looked so grown up, Scotty in dress pants and shirt and Elinor in an adorable blue sundress trimmed in ruffles.

"Can we go to the beach for a little while, Aunt Bay? Pleeeeease?" She drew the word out as if it had four syllables.

I glanced up at Red. "Time?" I asked him.

He smiled. "Sure." He made a show of glancing at his watch. "But only if you can be changed into your bathing suits in four minutes flat."

They nearly knocked him over on their way back into the house.

"And that means all your stuff hung up and put away, too!" he hollered after them.

I moved my legs over, and he sat down next to me. His kiss tasted like coffee, and I reached up to wind my arms around his neck.

"You're a good father," I said against the soft skin of his cleanly shaved face.

"Thanks." He leaned back. "You're not doing so bad as the wicked stepmother, either."

"I need to change, too," I said and wriggled away from him. "We can grab lunch on the way to Beaufort. That'll save some time."

We were due to have the kids back at Sarah's at two o'clock.

Red followed me inside and down the hallway. "Cecelia called," I said over my shoulder as I yanked one of my bathing suits from the drawer and headed for the bathroom. "She's in. Sort of."

My husband swatted me on the butt as I passed. "Good," he said. "Let's drop off the kids and go catch us some bad guys."

CHAPTER
SIXTEEN

*A*FTER SHARING CHICKEN SANDWICHES AND MILK-
shakes with the kids on the way back to Beaufort, neither of
us was very hungry, so I threw together a salad for dinner, and we ate
it out on the deck. The humidity hadn't abated with the approach of
evening, and we headed back inside to the air-conditioning as soon as
we'd finished.

In the kitchen, Red picked up the threads of our conversation,
interrupted while we carried our plates to the sink. "I just think we
could have spared a few minutes to run over there since we were so close.
Lavinia would have been glad to see us."

I rinsed and stacked the dishes, my back turned to my husband so
he couldn't see the effort it took to control the tears. How could I explain to him how painful it was for me to step inside the house where
I'd grown up and not find my father waiting for me? And even harder
than that was facing Lavinia Smalls, a woman who had been both
friend and mother to me through all the erratic years of my childhood.
She'd changed in the months since my father's death, the loss of their
special relationship having left a void nothing could ever fill. Two different women might have taken solace in each other's company, a relief

from the burden of grief in the sharing of it. Lavinia and I hadn't found that place yet. Rather, confronting each other brought our joint loss more sharply into focus.

"Honey?" Red stood behind me, his hands on my shoulders. "You okay?"

I sniffed as softly as I could and forced the tremor out of my voice. "Fine. Did you wrap the garlic bread in foil?"

He stepped back, and I could tell he'd been hurt by my refusal to share the pain with him, but old habits die hard.

"Well, you need to talk to her about Julia and Miss Lizzie. Didn't your pal Neddie say she thought it might be a good idea for the three of them to have a go at sharing Presqu'isle?"

Firmer ground. I rinsed my hands and reached for a dishtowel. "Yes, she did. And you're right. I'll give her a call later on."

We wandered back down into the great room and curled up on the couch. September Sundays brought us both baseball and football from which to choose, and Red used the remote to scan through several of the sports channels he had programmed into the new flatscreen. He settled on pro football and stretched his legs onto the coffee table. Though I'm generally as interested in the games as my husband, I couldn't bring myself to focus, and I got up after a few minutes and stretched.

"I have a couple of calls to make. Want a beer before I get started?"

Red looked at me for a long moment before replying. "I'll get one later. You sure you're okay? You've been awfully quiet this evening."

I forced a smile. "Plotting," I said over my shoulder. "I won't be long."

I debated about whom to call first and decided on Lavinia. I hadn't really given a lot of thought as to how to deal with the Castlemain/Dobbs/Potter issue, and I wanted to have a clear plan of action in my mind before I spoke with Cecelia. I scribbled a couple of notes on the desk pad in the office while I waited for Lavinia to pick up.

Her voice sounded breathless when she finally said hello.

"It's me," I said. "Were you far away?"

"I just got in from evening church. Glory dropped me off."

"Sorry I made you run. You could have let the machine pick up and called me back."

There was a short silence before she answered. "I need to talk to you about that. Tally . . . Your father's voice is still on there, tellin' folks what to do. It gives me a turn every time I hear it." Again she paused, gathering herself. "I don't know how to get it off."

"I can do that. Next time I'm by, I'll take care of it."

"Thank you, Bay. Did you call just to chat?"

"No, ma'am. I want to talk to you about Miss Lizzie and Julia. I had a long conversation with Neddie the other day, and she thinks it's a good idea for them to come to Presqu'isle. But she suggested a sort of trial run, maybe a couple of weeks just at first. To see how Julia adapts." When she didn't answer right away, I added, "You still want them to come, don't you?"

"I've been thinkin' on it. It would be good for the child to see how her daddy lived. It's her birthright, too."

Though Presqu'isle had come to us through my mother's family, I didn't see any reason to point that out. And I sensed an unspoken *but* beneath her words. "You don't sound as enthusiastic as you did a few days ago. What's changed?"

I could hear her moving around, probably setting her purse on the console table in the wide center hall where the main phone had sat for as long as I could remember. A delicately carved chair sat next to it, and I could picture Lavinia settling herself onto it. She had been such a mainstay of my life, from my earliest recollections of myself in the old mansion, but she had aged along with the house. She often commented lately that her bones were as creaky as the heart pine boards that swelled and contracted with the heat and humidity of the island. Maybe that was the cause of her misgivings. Maybe her heart was telling her it was the right thing to do, but her body was protesting at the extra work it would entail.

"This is entirely up to you," I said when she didn't answer my question. "If it's going to be too much, just say so." An idea struck. "Maybe I could hire someone to help them out at Covenant Hall. I'll bet Ellis Brawley next door would do it. Or maybe he'd know someone who'd be willing to do odd jobs and help keep the place in repair. I'd be happy to pay for it."

"It's not about money, Bay. Not everything is, you know."

I slumped in my chair, shocked at the severity of her voice. And the not so subtle accusation.

"What does that mean?"

She took a long time answering, and I plainly heard the soft exhalation of her breath, as if she were forcing herself to relax.

"I'm sorry, honey. That was unkind. And unnecessary. I know you always try to do what's right."

Try? I thought to myself. Where had I fallen short this time?

"The truth is," she went on before I could muster a defense, "that I'm just a little leery of Miss Lizzie. She has a mighty strong personality, and she's used to doin' things in her own way. I don't know how we'd deal together, being cooped up with one another all the time."

The same thought had crossed my mind. Both women had spent a lifetime ordering the lives and daily routines of those they'd chosen to watch over. At Presqu'isle, Lavinia would naturally feel the right to be in charge. I shrugged. If it came to pass, they'd just have to work it out between them.

"It's up to you," I said stiffly, the sting of her earlier words still fresh.

"Child, don't be cross with me. Sometimes things just pop out of my mouth before I can call them back. You know I wouldn't ever hurt you on purpose."

I did know that. Still . . . "I didn't mean to offend anyone by offering to pay for help for Lizzie and Julia. It's just that you said you thought they were having money troubles."

"You're right. And I know your heart's in the right place." She paused. "I miss seeing you, is all. And so does Julia. Writin' a check can't make up for being around, honey. That's what I meant."

Red's words came back to me. He was right. We should have stopped on St. Helena after we dropped the kids off in Beaufort.

"I'm sorry. It's just that . . ." I swallowed the easy lie about work and responsibilities. "It's hard for me. To be there without Daddy."

And the moment I said the words I realized how selfish it was. Lavinia had to face that emptiness every single moment of every day.

"I know. I know. It's all right." Her soft voice absolved me, as it had so many times in the past. "You come when you can." She cleared her throat, and I could almost see her straightening her shoulders. "I'll talk to Lizzie and see how she feels about comin' to stay. I'll let you know what she says."

"Good. You call me if you need help. With anything."

"I will, honey. Say hello to Redmond for me, won't you?"

"Yes, ma'am," I said and hung up.

Cecelia Dobbs's cell phone rolled over to voice mail. I left a message and spent the next half hour mapping out a strategy I thought she could live with in dealing with Dalton Chambers on a daily basis at the bank. I hoped she'd be able to pull it off, but her timidity made me doubt her ability to sustain the charade that she was totally ignorant of his possible involvement with Kendra Blaine and the Castlemains. I tried her phone once more before shutting down the computer and joining Red on the sofa.

"What's the score?" I asked, although I hadn't paid enough atten-tion earlier to know who was playing.

"Tied," he said, gathering me against his side, "just starting the fourth quarter."

"You were right," I said, and he looked down at me.

"I frequently am," he said with a grin, "although there are folks who don't always appreciate that."

I kissed him lightly on the chin. "Guilty as charged. Lavinia misses us. We need to make an effort to get over there soon."

"Whenever you say." He pulled me closer. "I know it hurts you, love, but you can't avoid it forever."

We slouched in silence, our bare feet propped up on the coffee table, our eyes on the controlled violence of the football game, but our thoughts—at least *mine*—drifting to other times and other places. Other people. I might even have drifted off when the sharp ring of the landline jerked me upright.

"I'll get it," I said, pushing myself to my feet. "It's probably Cecelia Dobbs. I left her a couple of messages."

I shook my head to clear the cobwebs out as I climbed the three steps into the kitchen.

"Hello?"

"Is this the Tanner residence?"

I didn't recognize the deep male voice. The drawl left no doubt that this was no displaced Yankee invader but a true Southerner.

"Yes, it is. This is Bay."

"Ma'am, I wonder if I might speak to your husband."

I glanced down into the great room where Red had turned to stare up at me. I couldn't read the expression on his face, but he looked . . . *anxious* was the word that popped into my head. I motioned to him.

"May I ask who's calling?"

"Ma'am, I believe he'll want to speak to me. Could you just put him on, please?"

Red had already risen as I carried the portable phone down the steps. We met in the middle, and I pressed the mouthpiece end of the handset against my chest.

"It's for you," I whispered. "He won't say who it is."

Red nearly snatched it out of my hand. "That's okay. I'll take it."

I relinquished my grip. I opened my mouth to ask, but my husband turned away and marched down the hallway, the phone to his ear, his voice too low for me to catch the words. He paused in front of the entrance to the office, and our eyes locked for a moment before he stepped inside.

And closed the door firmly behind him.

I waited for nearly an hour.

The game had ended, and I scanned through the myriad movie channels that had come with the cable package, settling on an old black-and-white from the forties. My gaze kept jumping from the screen to the hallway, and it took me a moment to recognize one of my old favorites: Joan Crawford and Ann Blyth in *Mildred Pierce.* I always wondered why Joan as Mildred should have been so surprised that her daughter had turned into such a conniving, scheming little bitch. Mama hadn't been above stomping on people in her rise to fortune, and the apple didn't usually fall far—

"Sorry that took so long."

Red stood at the end of the sofa, his hands thrust into the pockets of his shorts. He didn't look at me when he spoke, but rather stared at his tanned bare feet, dark against the white carpet, as if he found them endlessly fascinating.

I muted the television. "Who was that?"

He didn't answer right away. Instead he turned toward the kitchen. "You want anything? I'm going to get a beer."

I stayed where I was, refusing to chase him down. One thing I'd learned about the Tanner men: They couldn't be wheedled or bullied into spilling their secrets. Like his late brother—and my own father, for that matter—Red would talk when he was damn good and ready. And not before.

I forced myself not to look at him when he padded back in and set his beer on a coaster on the side table. He sat down and took my hand in his.

"What kind of bad news is it?" I asked.

"It's not bad. At least I hope you won't think so."

"You don't look like someone who just won the lottery."

He smiled. "You know I've been feeling restless for a while now."

I tucked my legs up under me, pulled my hand away, and crossed my arms protectively over my chest. I could already tell this wasn't going to be a conversation I was going to be pleased with.

"No, actually, I didn't. I thought you were settling into the agency—and our marriage—quite comfortably. I guess I was wrong."

"Honey, don't say things like that. I love being married to you. I love *you*." He cupped my cheek with his hand, and I felt my stomach drop. In spite of his tender words, I had a strong feeling that I really wasn't going to like what came next.

He faltered a little before he said, "It's just . . . Well, the truth is I miss law enforcement. I told you that the other night. I didn't think I would, but now that it's been a while, I guess the old juices have started flowing again."

"Just tell me, Red. Let's get it out there so we can discuss whatever it is." I had an idea now of what might be coming, but I wanted him to say it out loud.

He reached out and pulled me to him, his chin resting on the top of my head.

So he doesn't have to look me in the eye when he tells me, I thought.

"The thing is, I've been talking to this guy. Someone I met at one of the training seminars I used to go to in Columbia."

He paused, but I'd already decided I wasn't going to help him out. I waited. Finally, he said, all in a rush, "They want me to be the assistant chief of police. In Walterboro."

I jerked away and stared into his face. I'd convinced myself that he wanted back into the sheriff's department. In Beaufort. I could live with that.

"Walterboro? That's like an hour and a half drive from here. Why would you want to take on that kind of commute? It would be an absolute nightmare in the summer."

"You're not surprised I want to go back to work? I mean, you know, for someone else?"

"No," I said softly. "I know it's been difficult for you. I thought maybe you were coming around, but I guess I can understand that you might want more . . . autonomy." A nice way of saying my husband just couldn't stand working for me. I brushed aside how much that hurt.

"You're not angry?" he asked.

"A little. That you didn't talk to me about it right from the start more than anything else. I take it you really want to do this?"

Again he tucked my head under his chin. "Yes, I do. But there's something else."

"What?" I murmured against his chest. The worst was over, I thought, now that his dissatisfaction was out in the open.

The words took a moment to register.

"We have to move there. To Walterboro."

CHAPTER SEVENTEEN

"NO! ABSOLUTELY NOT! I CANNOT *BELIEVE* YOU EXpect me to do that!"

I had exploded off the sofa and taken up position in front of the French doors. I had an overwhelming urge to bolt outside, sprint across the dune, and pound down the beach until I was too exhausted to go on. I could feel the anger like a giant fist in the center of my chest, swelling, cutting off my breath.

"For God's sake, calm down, honey. Jesus, you'd think I just asked you to kill somebody."

I forced myself not to shout. "I don't recall that you *asked* me anything. It sounds to me as if it's a done deal."

Red stretched out his hand in supplication. "Come back here and sit down. Let's discuss this like rational people."

I stayed where I was. "The time for discussion was when you first got this job offer. How long have you known about it?"

He dropped his arm. "A couple of weeks. At first they were just feeling me out. It didn't get serious until the last council meeting on Thursday." He held my gaze. "Joe just called to say they wanted me. Officially."

"Joe who?" It was irrelevant, really, but I found myself floundering around for something to say, my mind unable to grasp this . . . I couldn't find a word. *Betrayal* sounded too harsh, and yet . . .

"Joe Pickens. He's the acting chief. The former chief took a job up in Greenville and left almost right away. They've been hunting for someone to help Joe when he moves up." He spoke calmly and rationally, his gaze darting up at me every once in a while. "Someone younger. He's nearly sixty." He paused, and this time he looked directly at me. "In a few years, I can probably be running the whole show. If I do a good job."

The room had grown darker as this unbelievable rearrangement of my life was being spelled out, and the glow of the mammoth TV screen over the fireplace cast flickering shadows on the carpet. But I didn't have to see my husband's face. I could hear the longing in his voice, and suddenly I felt my arms go slack. I took a few deep breaths and walked back over to the sofa. I sat down at the far end and tried to order my thoughts.

"I understand, Red. Really, I do. It's a tremendous opportunity, and you must be flattered. It's a big step up."

He leaned toward me but wisely made no move to take my hand or pull me into his arms. "That's it exactly. I should have been a lieutenant by now. I earned it, and I still don't get why I was passed over."

"Lisa Pedrovsky," I said, remembering the barely concealed animosity that crackled from the detective's hard eyes every time we encountered each other. I'd always hoped her hatred of me hadn't spilled over onto her professional relationship with Red, but I was convinced it had. So it was at least partly my fault.

"No, it wasn't just her. Anyway, that's ancient history. Joe said no one on their force who was really interested in moving up to assistant chief was qualified, so they had to go outside. There were a couple of other candidates, but I think the interview went really well. That may have decided things in my favor."

I felt myself stiffen. "When did this interview take place?"

He heard the anger in my voice. "I know I probably should have told you, honey, but there wasn't really anything to tell. If I didn't get the job, I didn't see any sense in getting you all upset for nothing."

"Lies of omission still count. Where did I think you were when you were really up in Walterboro plotting to totally disrupt our lives?"

"Trying to make things right with Scotty's principal." He held up a hand to cut me off. "That wasn't a lie. I did go there and work things out, just like I told you. Except it didn't take all afternoon. I went on up to Walterboro. After."

We could run around in circles forever over the trivialities. Red's deceit hurt. No getting around that. It was the last thing I would have expected from him. Both he and Rob had always been the straightest of straight arrows, and the lie sat heavily on my heart. Still, there were more important things to deal with at the moment. I forced myself to speak calmly.

"I'm not moving to Walterboro. My life is here. My house. The agency. Presqu'isle."

"You'd actually be closer to Lavinia than you are now. And Julia. Covenant Hall is just down the road from there, and you could—"

"Listen to me, Red. I know this is a great opportunity for you. I'm proud that they want you, and I understand how much you want to accept. But you can't ask me to give up everything I've worked for, everything I've built over the last twenty years. Just toss it away and start all over again. It's not fair, and you know it. That's why you've been skulking around behind my back. You knew—"

"Hold it!" His booming voice filled the great room. "You need to back off a little, Bay. I'm willing to take some crap about this, but don't push it too far. You're always telling me that you run your business how you see fit, that it's not my place to interfere. Well, that's fine. But just keep in mind that what's sauce for the goose is . . . whatever the hell the rest of that is. You can't have it both ways. You can't live your life and mine, too."

"Is that what you think I'm doing? Living your life for you?" My teeth were clenched so tightly together I could barely get the words out.

Red ran a hand through his hair, the gesture that always reminded me so much of Rob. I could feel the tears gathering in my throat. Intense anger always makes me cry.

"No. I'm sorry. I didn't mean that." He sighed, and I watched his shoulders slump. "I just didn't expect you to react like this."

I tried to match his tone. "What did you think I'd say, Red? I mean, really? Didn't you give a thought to how this would sound, coming out of left field? If I'd had some warning . . . I don't know, maybe if we'd just talked about the possibilities first." I let out a long breath. "Why can't you commute up to Walterboro? At least at first. What if we throw everything away down here, and you find out you hate the job? Then where would we be?"

"Honey, I've thought about that. But the town regulations require that the chief and his assistant live in the jurisdiction." He paused. "I guess I could get a place up there and come home on weekends."

A Bible passage popped into my head, a remnant of the quotation game the Judge and I used to play, with points awarded for being able to cite author and source.

" 'Whither thou goest, I will go; and where thou lodgest, I will lodge,' " I said softly. "The book of Ruth."

"Come here." Red pulled me into his arms, and I went without resistance. "I love you, honey. I want you to be happy. Isn't there some compromise we can work out here? I don't want to go back to living by myself, even for a few days a week. But I'm willing to give it a try."

I felt the tears dripping down my cheeks and onto his shirt. I didn't want to fight. And I didn't want him to go. But what other choice was there?

"You're sure this is what you really want?" I murmured into his chest. "You could be a partner in the agency. Equal with Erik and me. You'd have a lot more freedom, and—"

"Shush," he said, patting my trembling shoulders. "Let's not worry about it anymore tonight. I have until Wednesday to give them my answer. We'll sleep on it and talk again tomorrow, okay?"

I stretched my legs out and let myself slump against him. I could hear the steady beating of his heart and feel the rise and fall of his chest. Why did things have to change? Why couldn't we just go on as we—?

The ringing phone made me jerk.

"Let it go." Red tightened his arms around me. "Let the machine get it."

I sighed deeply and wriggled free. "It might be Cecelia. I need to talk to her before she goes to work tomorrow."

In the kitchen, I grabbed a tissue out of the box and wiped my nose before reaching for the handset. I cleared my throat and picked up.

"Is this Bay Tanner?"

I didn't recognize the voice. Male. Assertive.

"Yes."

"This is Dr. Emerson Dobbs."

It took me a moment. Cecelia's father. The surgeon.

"Yes, sir. How can I help you?"

"Have you seen my daughter?"

The alarm bells set up a clanging in the back of my head. "No, sir, I haven't."

I'd thought Cecelia wanted to keep our relationship confidential. In fact, she'd been pretty adamant about it. So why would her father come looking for her here? For that matter, why was he looking for her at all?

"What business do you have with Cecelia?" he asked, and his tone was decidedly not friendly. "I found your business card in her room. You're a private investigator."

He said it as if I should be ashamed of myself. *He* was the one who should be ashamed for rifling through his daughter's private papers.

"Yes, I am. And my business with your daughter is confidential. I'm sorry, sir, but that's our agreement."

"I'm her father, and I have a right to know what's going on."

"I understand, Dr. Dobbs, but I'm afraid I can't help you."

"I want to know where Cecelia is, and I want to know now!"

I kept my voice even. "I talked with her earlier today. And we made arrangements to speak again this evening. In fact, I left two voice mails for her, but she hasn't called me back. Why are you concerned, if I may ask, sir?" I glanced at the clock over the sink. "It's barely ten thirty." *And she's a grown woman,* I wanted to add but refrained from doing so.

"Cecelia doesn't go out. And especially not on nights when she has to be up for work the next day." I could hear the anger being over-ridden by fear. "I'm concerned about her."

"Any particular reason?" I asked, my own stomach beginning to sink. "I mean, did she take her handbag and her cell phone with her?"

A number of scenarios involving Dalton Chambers, Kendra Blaine, and the late Rebecca Castlemain struggled for attention, but I squashed them all like bugs. Cecelia Dobbs was timid, but she wasn't helpless. Not completely, anyway. If she'd decided to go out to Starbucks or a club or whatever, there was no reason for any of us to jump to the con-clusion that she was in trouble of some kind. No reason at all.

There was a momentary pause while Dr. Dobbs spoke to someone else in the room. "Her mother says yes. Her purse and her phone aren't here. But it's very unlike her not to leave a note or some sort of expla-nation. Cecelia is a very responsible girl."

Maybe that's her trouble, I thought. What I said was, "I wouldn't worry, sir. There isn't anything that relates to our business together that could put her in any danger. I'm sure she'll be in touch soon."

I said goodbye and stood for a moment staring at the wall over the built-in desk, hoping that I knew what the hell I was talking about.

CHAPTER EIGHTEEN

J DIDN'T WAKE UP IN THE MIDDLE OF THE NIGHT FOR the simple reason that I never went to sleep.

Red coaxed and fussed at me until nearly midnight when he finally threw up his hands in frustration and left me curled in a corner of the sofa, my gaze fastened on the blackness outside the French doors. Eventually, I scooted down to stretch out on the cushions, a few pillows tucked behind my head and the afghan pulled across my bare legs, my cell phone clutched in one hand. Periodically I flipped it open to make certain I hadn't nodded off and missed Cecelia's call, but the hours drifted by with no word from my client. Or her father.

I'd left a couple of more messages, but I knew it was an exercise in futility. She'd either pick them up or she wouldn't, regardless of how much I jammed her mailbox. To take my mind off the insidious possibilities that kept crowding into my head, I tried to figure out how to text. Somewhere in the back of my mind I had the notion that maybe I could reach Cecelia that way, but the process eluded me. Lord knew I'd seen ten-year-olds with their tiny thumbs flying across the keyboards of their phones, but I couldn't seem to find the right combination to make the system work for me. Another thing I should ask Erik about, I supposed. Or Scotty.

I jerked myself back from any conscious thought of Red's bombshell about Walterboro. Time enough to worry about that.

The sun had just begun to streak the sky out over the ocean with a soft, warm glow when the notes of my cell phone startled me out of a half doze. I jerked and dropped it on the carpet, scrambling in the dim light to find it before the noise woke Red. I could feel my heart pounding in my chest when my fingers finally wrapped around it.

"Cecelia?" I said breathlessly.

"So you haven't heard from her, either." Dr. Dobbs's voice had lost its stern air of command. He sounded tired. And afraid.

"No, sir, I haven't. You've had no word at all?"

"None. I've been out most of the night looking for her."

I shuddered. There was no longer any way to suppress the fears I'd been holding in check during the long, dark hours. Still, there was a chance that Cecelia was fine, maybe spending the night with a friend or perhaps engaging in a small act of rebellion against her tyrannical father. It seemed unlike her, but what did I really know? We'd spent less than a couple of hours in each other's company, so who was I to second-guess the man who'd spent a lifetime caring for her?

"Sir, I think—," I began, but he cut me off.

"You need to tell me what's going on, Ms. Tanner. What business did my daughter have with you?"

I bit back the angry words that jumped into my head and let my breath out slowly. He had a right to question me. I just wasn't sure what—or how much—to tell him. Maybe I should suggest calling the sheriff. I knew an adult wouldn't be considered officially missing until after at least forty-eight hours, but maybe Red could nudge them to move a little faster. I'd been telling myself that Cecelia's disappearance— if it could be classified as such at this point—had nothing to do with our business, but that self-serving deception would probably have to be abandoned. What other reason could there be?

My brain was muddled with lack of sleep, and my lungs ached for a hit of nicotine. It amazed me how, in times of stress, I still felt the longing for a cigarette, even though it had been a couple of years since I'd quit. I flung off the afghan and walked up into the kitchen, my head whirling with how to answer this man who obviously feared for his daughter's safety.

"Dr. Dobbs, I have an agreement with Cecelia to keep the details of our discussions confidential. I'd need a compelling reason to violate that trust. How old is your daughter?"

I could hear his breath coming in short bursts, and I steeled myself for a tirade. He surprised me.

"She's twenty-six. But Cecelia is in many ways very naïve. She has little experience of the world outside our circle of friends and family. She would never intentionally cause her mother this kind of grief." He paused. "I know my daughter, Ms. Tanner. Something's happened to her. I can feel it."

I had no answer for that.

"Then call the sheriff and report her missing." I ran the cold water in the sink and used my free hand to splash some across the back of my neck. "Make certain you have all the details and a recent photo. And the information on her car—make, model, color, license number. They'll try to put you off, but be insistent. I'll contact my partner. We'll gather all the information we have about the matter Cecelia hired us to investigate. Where and when can we meet?"

The doctor was obviously a man used to making quick decisions. "I'll go in person to the sheriff's satellite office off Pope Avenue. I have no idea how long that will take. Millie—my wife—will wait here in case my daughter comes home or calls. Where is your office located?"

I gave him the details, and we set a meeting for nine o'clock. I hung up and stood for a long moment, leaning against the kitchen counter trying to quiet the fear gripping my chest. It would be okay, I told my-self. It had to be.

I hit the speed-dial for Erik's number as I filled a mug and thrust it into the microwave. It took him a long time to answer.

"Bay?" he mumbled. "What's wrong?"

"Cecelia Dobbs is missing." I pulled down the box of tea bags and dunked one into the steaming water. "Her father's been out all night looking for her, and she's not returning anyone's calls to her cell."

"You think it's related to the case?" His voice had cleared, and he sounded fully awake and alert. "Chambers and Blaine?"

"I don't know, but her father has no clue what else it could be. Can you check and see if Chambers' car is in his driveway?"

I took a moment to sip the scalding tea, feeling the warmth spread through my bloodstream along with the caffeine I so desperately needed.

"Let me pull on some clothes. I'll call you right back."

"Hurry," I said and hung up.

"Honey? Who are you talking to?"

I looked up to see Red standing at the foot of the kitchen steps, his hair tangled, and his eyes still heavy with sleep.

"Make yourself some coffee," I said. "I'm going to get dressed." I touched his cheek gently as I passed by on my way to the bedroom. "We've got trouble."

By the time I'd pulled on a pair of slacks and a cotton shirt, Erik was back.

"The Lexus is in the driveway," he said when I answered my cell. "I checked the hood, and it wasn't warm, so it probably hasn't been out, at least for a while. Tell me what's going on."

I filled him in on everything that had transpired, backing up to include the memorial service for Rebecca Castlemain, my first encounter with her grandson Nicholas Potter, and his insistence on hiring us to investigate Kendra Blaine.

"So Cecelia agreed to a joint effort with Potter?" he asked.

Red slipped back into the room, coffee in hand, and sat next to me on the bed.

"Erik," I mouthed before answering my partner's question. "Yes, although I didn't reveal his identity to her, and she didn't want him to know hers. It was going to be complicated as it was, but now . . ." I let the thought trail off.

"So how could the case have anything to do with her disappearance, if that's what it is? I mean, no one but us knew anything about it, and we sure as hell didn't tell anyone."

"I know. That's what's bugging me, too. But you know how I feel about coincidences, and it doesn't make sense that something like this would happen so soon after she came to us, and there not be some connection."

"You said we're meeting the father at nine?"

"Yes."

"Then let's get over there as soon as possible and hash this whole thing out. We need to have some answers ready when he gets there."

"Agreed. We'll be there in half an hour."

"Me, too."

I flipped the phone closed and looked at my husband. "Cecelia Dobbs is still missing."

"Oh, honey. I'm sorry."

His arm came around me, and I let myself slump against his shoulder. In as concise a manner as I could manage, I gave him the details. When I'd finished, he squeezed me once and stood. He set his cup on the nightstand and headed for the bathroom.

"They won't take the missing persons case at this stage of the game," he said over his shoulder. "Too soon." He disappeared, and his voice faded.

"Do we tell them about Dalton Chambers and Kendra Blaine?" I called after him.

"First, let's deal with the father. Then we'll see." He stuck his head around the doorway. "It could be that this has nothing to do with the agency. We don't have enough information at this point to make that judgment."

His calm helped to steady my own frayed nerves, and I found myself relaxing my tense shoulders. Just a little.

"Is that what you really think, or are you just trying to make me feel better?"

Again his voice came from far away, just barely discernible over the sound of running water.

"Suck it up and get a move on, honey," he hollered. "We've got work to do."

In spite of the fear still rumbling around in my stomach, I smiled.

CHAPTER
NINETEEN

*R*ED AND I HIT STARBUCKS ON OUR WAY IN TO THE office. We'd just arranged everything on my desk, including a variety of pastries, when Erik stepped through the door.

"Great minds," he said, saluting us with his own cardboard container of coffee as he pulled his chair around to join us.

I retrieved the file I'd carried home with me in my briefcase and laid it alongside the tape recorder. I hadn't taken the time on Saturday to transcribe my conversation with Nicholas Potter, and my scribbled notes were illegible to anyone but me. I distributed our makeshift breakfast before I leaned back in my chair.

"So. A quick synopsis. Cecelia Dobbs came to us with concerns about the financial dealings of Thomas and Rebecca Castlemain, especially those in which their caregiver, Kendra Blaine, and one of First Coast's tellers, Dalton Chambers, were involved. Before we could begin our investigation, Rebecca Castlemain died, ostensibly of heart failure, but there seems to be some question about that from her doctors and others who knew her. Unfortunately, there was no autopsy performed, and her body has already been released for burial." I paused to glance at the date and time readout on the desk phone. "In just a few hours, as a matter of fact."

I waited, but neither of the men spoke. "Okay. My observations of Blaine on Friday night led me to suspect that Cecelia may have been right about the amount of influence Thomas's caregiver exerts over him. His grandson voiced similar concern. He attempted to engage us to investigate on his behalf, especially after the Blaine woman showed up at the memorial service wearing his grandmother's very expensive pearls. I contacted Cecelia, who agreed to a joint venture so long as we protected her anonymity. We agreed to speak again last night, but she never returned my calls. Her father says she was gone when he and his wife returned from their boating trip, and she hasn't been seen or heard from since. Dr. Dobbs is right now at the sheriff's office to report her officially missing."

Red nodded at me, then glanced at Erik. "Anything to add or amend?"

"No. That's how I remember it, except for the parts I wasn't involved in. Cecelia didn't give you any kind of hint that something was wrong when you talked to her?"

"Not at all," I said. "She was nervous about going in to the bank today and having to deal with Chambers, but I told her we'd work out a game plan that she felt comfortable with." I thought a moment. "If anything, I'd say she felt relieved that someone else—Potter, I mean—shared her concerns about Thomas. I think she was glad to spread the responsibility around."

"And nothing about any plans to go out?" Red looked pensive, his gaze fixed on a spot on the wall beyond my right shoulder. "Or meeting anyone for dinner or anything like that?"

"Nothing. She mentioned that her parents were out with friends on their boat, and I remember thinking that they should have taken her with them instead of leaving her sitting alone in the house. But she said absolutely nothing about how she planned to spend the rest of the day."

"So somewhere between the time you talked to her—which was when, by the way?" Red asked.

"While the kids were in church. I was hanging up just about the time you all got back."

"And what time were you supposed to call her?"

"We just said later that evening. No specific time. But she did say she'd be there all day. I just remembered."

Erik jumped in. "So she definitely had no plans."

Red nodded. "Exactly. So sometime between say eleven in the morning and when you tried her after dinner, things changed." He paused, again studying the wall behind me. "Either someone dropped in, or she got a call."

"She might have gone out to dinner," I offered. "Maybe she didn't want to eat by herself at home, although from the sound of things she was probably used to it."

"We need her cell records. And the house landline. See if she made or received any calls in the afternoon." Red looked at Erik. "Can you do that?"

Erik didn't answer, but his gaze slid to mine.

"Let's wait on that," I said, "until we talk to her father. He could request the records, at least for his home phone, couldn't he?"

"And keep us on the right side of the law," Red replied, a smile twitching at the corners of his mouth. He turned again to my partner. "But if push came to shove, you could do it?"

"Probably."

I swigged down the last of my tea and tossed the container into the wastebasket. I checked the time. "We've got a little over an hour before Dr. Dobbs shows up, so here's the game plan. Erik, would you transcribe the Potter tape from Saturday?"

"On it," he said and pulled the chair back over to his desk.

"I'll get my own notes typed up and added to the file. Red, will you head down to the sheriff's office and see what kind of reception Dobbs is getting? If Malik is on duty, see if you can squeeze any information out of him. I'm thinking they might do a cursory search for her car, maybe just as part of the regular patrol routine. Possible?"

"Probable." He, too, rose. "Even if it's not an official missing person's case, they'll likely send out a local BOLO on the car. If it's on the island, it shouldn't be that tough to find."

"Great. Just make sure you're back here by nine. I'd like to present a united front to Cecelia's father. Wait," I added as he turned to go. "Both of you. Are we in agreement that we give him everything we've got?"

"Except Potter," Red answered before Erik could speak. "I think you have to protect his confidentiality at this point. He's got no connection to the Dobbs girl, so bringing him in would just muddy the waters."

"Agreed," Erik said from his desk, "although I'm still damned if I can figure out a scenario that would explain how Blaine or Chambers could get wind of Cecelia's hiring us and get spooked enough to . . ." His voice faltered. "To maybe do something about it."

His words brought that sinking feeling of dread clutching at my chest again. "Let's not borrow trouble until we hear what the doctor has to say."

My husband read the fear on my face and violated our unspoken protocol by stepping around the desk to kiss me softly on the lips.

"Try not to think the worst. It's early times yet," he said before making for the door.

I bit down hard on my lip as I watched him disappear out into the clear, bright morning.

At precisely 8:58, Dr. Emerson Dobbs stepped through the door into the reception area. Erik greeted him and guided him into my office where Red and I had already taken up our positions, side by side. We both rose as the doctor entered.

"Emerson Dobbs," he said, extending his hand to Red first. "Didn't I see you at the sheriff's office just a little while ago?"

"I used to work there," Red replied. "This is Bay Tanner, the owner."

If the situation hadn't been so serious, I would have smiled. Dobbs and I shook and took our seats. Over the doctor's shoulder, I saw Erik wheel his chair around to the doorway, his laptop resting on his knees.

"What kind of reception did you get?" I asked. "From the sheriff."

"Very cooperative, very understanding. They'll have their deputies keep an eye out for Cecelia's car while they're patrolling around the county. By tomorrow, if she doesn't—" He cleared his throat. "If she hasn't returned home, they'll initiate a full search, send her information out to other jurisdictions."

"That's about all they can do at this point." Red spoke softly. "Just keep in mind that it's a relatively small department with lots of square miles to cover. I hate to say it, but since there's no indication of foul play, it won't be a priority." He glanced at me. "Bay and Erik and I want to help in any way we can."

Some of the sadness left Dobbs's eyes. "You can help by telling me how my daughter got mixed up with a private investigator in the first place."

His hands were slim and long-fingered, almost delicate, which I supposed was an asset for a surgeon. He ran them through his thick, dark brown hair, only slightly tinged with gray at the temples. The blue of his Ralph Lauren polo shirt nearly matched his eyes. Red and I exchanged a look, and he nodded.

So I summarized Cecelia's concerns with the situation at the bank as succinctly as I could. As we'd agreed, I left out any mention of Nicholas Potter and the pearls. It took a surprisingly short amount of time. During the recitation, Dr. Dobbs neither spoke nor moved his gaze away from my face.

"I don't understand," he said when I'd finished my brief summation.

"What isn't clear, sir?" I asked.

"Why Cecelia would involve herself in this way with something she should have taken directly to her superiors. Why on earth did she think this was the proper course of action?"

Since I'd asked myself exactly the same questions, I didn't take offense. "I'm convinced she felt she wouldn't be believed. Besides, there was no concrete evidence that might spur either bank officials or the authorities to investigate. She hired us to get that evidence. Or be able to assure her that none existed."

"And have you?" Some of the bark was back in the tone of his voice.

"We'd only come to an agreement on Thursday," I said. "I did attend Mrs. Castlemain's memorial service on Friday evening. I met Kendra Blaine and had a chance to observe her relationship with Thomas Castlemain. I must say I came away feeling that your daughter's concerns about undue influence had merit."

His grunt raised the hackles on the back of my neck. Part disbelief, part derision, it sounded exactly like the kind of noise my mother used to make when I'd failed to use the proper fork or said something particularly inappropriate during one of her mind-numbing teas or some other equally boring social gathering she forced me to attend. I bit the inside of my cheek to keep from snapping back at him. The poor man was worried about his daughter. He had some slack coming. But his next words drove all my good intentions out the window.

"Cecelia is a child. She has no idea about the way adults interact." He leaned back in the chair and crossed one long leg over the other. "I can't believe you allowed yourself to take her seriously."

I itched to slap the smug smile from his face. No wonder the poor girl had the self-confidence of a rabbit. This was exactly what my mother had done to me: the constant harping about my shortcomings—too tall, too gangly, too much the tomboy, no social graces. Fortunately for me, the Judge had counterbalanced all her criticism with an appreciation of my quick mind and quirky sense of humor, both of which he nourished at every opportunity. I wondered if Cecelia's mother had provided that kind of support for her daughter. Or was she, too, in thrall to her husband's overbearing personality and ego?

I made certain to wipe any hint of what I was feeling out of my voice. "Your daughter seemed to me to be a reasonably intelligent, competent young woman. She stated her case with precision." I glanced around the room. "She convinced all of us of her sincerity and the probable accuracy of her observations." I thought just a moment before I added, as much for my benefit as for Cecelia's, "Perhaps you underestimate her."

Again Emerson Dobbs surprised me. Instead of telling me I didn't really know a damned thing about his daughter, he slumped back in his chair, all his bluster gone.

"Perhaps you're right," he said softly. "Perhaps I've never really given her a chance to prove herself."

He sighed, and I swore there were tears pooling in his eyes when he lifted them to mine.

"Please," he said. "We have to find her."

CHAPTER TWENTY

AFTER HE'D GONE, WITH OUR ASSURANCES THAT we'd do everything we could, the three of us sat quietly around my desk, now littered with pastry crumbs, dregs congealing in the bottoms of coffee cups.

"I'm not quite sure what to make of him." Red stretched out his long legs and folded his hands in his lap.

"I know what you mean," Erik said. "He seems to run hot and cold."

"Like Jerrold Eastman." Red looked at me. "Remember how he acted when we were trying to find a bone marrow donor for his daughter? I never knew from one minute to the next whether he cared about saving her or not."

"Maybe it's the doctor thing," I said, "although Eastman had a lot of other issues scrambling up his thinking. You have to be supremely self-confident to take other people's lives in your hands and think you can pull them through. Maybe they can't just turn that ego off, even when they want to."

"Maybe," Red conceded. "Well. What's our next move?"

I jumped at the last word, memories of our heated conversation of the night before lurking just offstage in my mind. I glanced around my new office, spacious and decorated in an understated way that suddenly reminded me of how my father had arranged his study. Could I give all this up and follow my husband to Walterboro? Could I sever the ties Rob and I had created when we'd built the house in Port Royal Plantation all those years ago? What about Erik? He had a say in this as well. If I were nearly two hours away, most of the day-to-day running of the agency would fall on his shoulders. Was it fair to ask—?

"Bay?" Red's voice cut through my jumbled thoughts.

"Sorry." I squared my shoulders and banished my personal worries to a far corner of my mind. "I don't know what we can do to help locate Cecelia. The sheriff is far better equipped than we are to mount that kind of search." I turned to Erik. "How long do you think it will take for Dr. Dobbs to get those readouts on calls in and out of his house on Sunday?"

"Hard to say. There'll be a lot of red tape to untangle. The phone company isn't just going to hand them over without a lot of paperwork to protect themselves. Ditto with the cell provider, although we're lucky it's his account she's using. At least we can be certain of getting them. Eventually."

"Would the sheriff have any better luck?" I asked Red. "Providing they think it's worth the effort?"

He shook his head. "Protocols will be even more stringent for them. They'll probably have to get a subpoena first, and that will require probable cause. She won't be officially missing—" He looked at his watch. "—for at least another thirty hours or so."

I couldn't just sit there waiting for something to happen. "Let's divvy up the island and go looking for her car. We'll start in the most likely places and fan out from there." I held out the papers on which the doctor had listed all his daughter's vitals, including a recent photo. "Erik, make some copies of these, please. One for each of us."

"Right." He rose and left the room.

"You think that's the best use of our time?" Red asked.

"If you have a better suggestion, I'm open to hearing it."

The sharp ring of the phone made us both jump. I beat Red to the receiver.

"Simpson and Tanner, Inquiry Agents."

The line crackled, the underlying noise interrupted by short bursts of silence, like hiccups.

"Hello?" I said.

I waited a moment before hanging up, my hand reaching for a pen to scratch the caller ID number on the desk pad from force of habit. It wasn't one I recognized.

"Wrong number?" Red asked.

"Nobody there. Could have been a cell cutting out, either from low batteries or moving out of range. If it was for us, they'll call back."

Erik returned with the copies, and I spread a map of the island out on my desk. We spent a few minutes discussing the likely places a twenty-six-year-old young woman might go for fun or even just for a quick bite to eat on a Sunday night in September. We added in the parking lot of the bank on Beach City Road, although none of us could figure why she might have gone there. Surely someone on her relatively low rung of the ladder didn't have a key.

I could tell Red didn't share my enthusiasm for the hunt, but I knew there was nothing to be accomplished by sitting around the office stewing about it. Nicholas Potter had said he'd be in touch with me after the funeral and the gathering at his grandparents' house following the burial service. He'd decided to stay on for a few extra days, and he wanted to hear how I'd resolved the potential conflict between his and Cecelia's interests. But we'd made no specific appointment, and he had my private cell number, probably thanks to Bitsy Elliott. I made a mental note to chew her out next time we spoke.

"Let's meet at Market Street around twelve thirty and compare notes," I said, gathering the remains of our breakfast and depositing it in the wastebasket.

"Right," Erik said. "That way Red can run over and see if the sheriff is getting any results. We can all stay in touch by cell if we find anything."

"Good enough." I slung my bag over my shoulder. "Let's roll."

I'd been mistaken in thinking that finding one particular vehicle on a relatively small island would be a simple matter. Even without the summer tourists, the level of activity on the roadways and in the parking lots was just this side of frenetic. I'd taken the middle, which encompassed a huge chunk of real estate, including the Mall at Shelter Cove, the adjacent harbor, several public beach accesses, Port Royal Plaza, and the Pineland Station shopping area, not to mention the huge Marriott and Hilton hotels and several sprawling condominium complexes.

My plan was to end up at the bank before reconnecting with Red and Erik on the south end. But, as I wove in and out of lines of parked cars, ignoring the out-of-state plates, it didn't take long for me to realize that I'd set us a nearly impossible task. Added to that was the fact that Cecelia's silver-gray Toyota Camry had to be the most popular make and model on the planet.

I'd covered less than a third of my assigned territory when it became apparent I'd never finish on time. I swung out onto Mathews Drive, crossed Route 278, and turned at Beach City Road. A few moments later I pulled into First Coast Bank of the Carolinas, nestled in the trees not far from the airport. It took only a minute to cruise by the parked vehicles and eliminate any of them from consideration. On impulse, I swung into a vacant space and cut the engine. No sense wasting an opportunity to get a look at the second of our chief suspects.

The cool air hit me as I stepped inside. It was a small branch, the tellers lined up against a back wall comprised mostly of windows to accommodate the drive-up lanes. Only three people manned their stations, and it didn't take a detective to pick out Dalton Chambers. Besides being the only man in the group, his dark good looks radiated sex appeal all the way across the room. Tall—over six feet, I guessed— with wide shoulders that looked as if he might pump a little iron, he wasn't classically handsome, not like Nicholas Potter. But he had that same . . . *something*. Hard to define, but—like art—you knew it when you saw it. He glanced up, and our eyes met briefly. He smiled, and I understood immediately why both Kendra Blaine and Cecelia Dobbs might easily have fallen under his spell.

"Welcome to First Coast."

I whirled at the voice at my elbow. A young black woman had risen from a desk set just inside the door.

"Good morning," I replied.

"How may we help you today?" She wore a smart navy blue suit over a crisp white blouse and looked the picture of efficiency and trustworthiness. Perfect first impression.

I let my gaze wander once again to where Chambers dealt with a gray-haired woman whose birdlike laugh could be easily heard all the way across the lobby. The guy was good, no doubt about it. I put on my professional face.

"I'd like to speak with someone in Customer Service."

The girl's smile wavered. "Is there some problem, ma'am?"

"Just a few questions. I've been speaking with a Miss Dobbs on the phone. Is she in?"

"No, I'm sorry, she's not. I'm sure Mr. Kramer, her supervisor, would be glad to assist you, but I'm afraid he's already gone to lunch." She moved back behind the desk. "I can have him call you, if you like. Or I'd be happy to make an appointment for you for later today, if that's convenient."

This woman knew her stuff. I stole a quick peek at her name tag. If I ever decided to expand the office and hire a full-time receptionist, I'd definitely keep Sharese Thomason in mind.

"Thanks, but I have another engagement. Do you expect Miss Dobbs any time soon?"

"I really couldn't say. I believe she's ill. At least she didn't come in to work today."

"You've been very helpful, Ms. Thomason. It's nothing urgent. I'll just stop in again another time."

With a final glance over my shoulder at Dalton Chambers, I pushed open the heavy glass door.

I was only a little disconcerted to find he'd been staring directly at me.

We took a table outdoors under the canopy that shaded a portion of Market Street Café's alfresco dining area. The small Greek restaurant in the heart of the Coligny shopping area was jammed with a lunchtime crowd composed mostly of locals who worked nearby, with a smattering of visitors thrown in. Our fall tourist season attracted mostly golfers and retirees, the families with children having settled back into the routine of school and endless activities. Both Scotty and Elinor were involved in so much extracurricular stuff, from soccer to ballet, it made any connection with them during the week nearly impossible to arrange.

"Nothing," Erik said, twirling his straw around in a tall glass of sweet tea. "But I didn't begin to cover everything. Didn't even make a dent, if you want the truth."

"Me neither." Red nursed a Coke. "I guess I never really paid attention to how many places there are around here to park a car."

I smiled as the waiter set our plates in front of us. I'd considered a Caesar salad, then decided on a cheesesteak. I thought a lot better with red meat in my system. "I gave up and stopped in at the bank." I took a huge bite, dripping with cheese and mushrooms, and wiped my mouth with my napkin. "Dalton Chambers and I had a little staring contest across the lobby. I wonder what made him home in on me. I wasn't the least bit obvious, just a couple of quick glances in his direction." I smiled. "Which, considering the amount of sex appeal he radiates, couldn't have been an unusual occurrence for him."

Red set down his hamburger sub and laid a hand on my forearm. "From what Cecelia told you about the guy, I'm not surprised. You're a fine-looking woman, Mrs. Tanner. I've noticed other men . . . noticing."

Erik laughed, and I ducked my head. Bitsy had said something similar about my own reaction to Nicholas Potter. Not that she was one to talk.

"Knock it off, Red. What I mean is that it was almost as if he knew who I was and why I was there. I know that's not possible, but it was sort of creepy."

"I think Red's probably right," Erik said. "I mean, no offense, but you do sort of stand out in a crowd."

That brought a smile. "Thank you, sir. It probably has more to do with the fact that I'm taller than just about any other woman in a group."

For a while, growing up, I'd been self-conscious as I stretched out to my final five feet, ten inches, towering over all the boys until I got to college. The Judge had forced me to stand up straight and take pride in my stature. Poor Mama, desperate to turn me into her ideal of a soft flower of Southern womanhood, harbored visions of chopping me off at the knees. In more ways than one.

We finished our meal in relative silence, all three of us lost in our own thoughts. When iced tea and Coke glasses had been replenished, I sat back in my chair.

"So now what? Do we resume the search?"

Erik spoke first. "I'm game. I don't know where else to go on this until we get those phone records." He looked at his watch. "What say we give it another couple of hours?"

"Red?"

"Hmm?" His gaze had fastened again on some spot over my shoulder.

"You think it's a good idea to keep looking for the car?"

"I guess. I'll walk over to the sheriff's office and see if they've had any luck, although I assume we would have heard from Dr. Dobbs if he'd gotten word." He pushed his chair away from the table. "I'll be right back."

I watched my husband weave his way toward the back of the plaza and head in the direction of Lagoon Road. It would take him only a few minutes to check in with his former colleagues. I leaned toward Erik.

"I need to ask you about something."

"Shoot."

I gathered my thoughts for a moment. "How would you feel if Red and I moved off the island? I mean, if a lot of the day-to-day running of the office fell on your shoulders?"

A frown creased the skin between his clear eyes. "Why would you do that?"

I lowered my voice and scooted my chair in a little closer. "Red's had a job offer with the police department in Walterboro, but he needs to live in the jurisdiction."

In the distance, I could hear sirens along Pope Avenue, and my head snapped in that direction. With so many of our older structures being made of wood, fire was something we feared almost as much as the threat of hurricanes. It sounded as if more than one engine had responded, along with an ambulance, and I searched the sky for telltale smoke. Around me, I noticed others doing the same. I jerked back around when Erik spoke.

"You're serious about this?"

"I don't know. Maybe. Red really wants to take the job."

"How do you feel about it?"

"Ambivalent. I don't want to stand in his way, but the idea of giving up everything I've worked for here is a little . . . daunting."

"I could do it. I mean, I feel pretty confident now. You're not talking about getting out altogether, are you?"

The sirens continued to howl, but I still couldn't tell where they might be headed.

"No, of course not. Actually, we considered that he could stay up there most of the week and come home on weekends if he has to. Neither one of us is thrilled about the idea of living like that, but it could be done. In that case, I guess my question's moot."

"The only thing I'd need would be someone to watch the office while I'm out. A receptionist who could do some of the paperwork and computer stuff would be ideal."

The figure of Sharese Thomason, the efficient young woman I'd just encountered in the lobby of First Coast, popped immediately into my head. "That could be arranged. Actually, I might have someone in mind."

The shriek was suddenly cut off, which meant the emergency vehicles had arrived at their destination. I hoped it was just a false alarm.

Erik cleared his throat loudly, and I turned back to see a blush rising along the strong line of his jaw. "I, uh, might have someone, too."

"Really? Who's that?"

He swallowed and let his eyes drift up to meet mine. "Stephanie."

The mention of my late partner Ben Wyler's daughter brought the usual wave of guilt washing over me. "You think she'd be interested? Isn't she happy at the magazine?"

It took him a long time to answer. "Yes, but it would be great if we could work together. And it wouldn't be full time. At least not at first, right?"

I shrugged. "I guess not, but it could work into that if the business continues to grow the way it has been. I'm just surprised. Red and I should be a good example of how sticky things can get when you work closely with someone you . . ." I groped for the appropriate word. "With someone you care about."

He didn't answer. I glanced up to see my husband striding back along the walkway.

"Don't say anything to Red yet. We haven't made a firm decision one way or the other. Just think about it."

Red was almost to the table when Erik mumbled something I didn't quite catch. At least I hoped I'd misunderstood.

"What?" My head whipped back in his direction. "What did you say?"

He looked me straight in the eye. "I said Stephanie and I are getting married."

CHAPTER
TWENTY-ONE

*I*T SURPRISED ME, THE NUMBER OF CARS IN THE PARK-
ing lot of the Marriott Hotel inside Palmetto Dunes on a
Monday afternoon in mid-September. Judging by the abundance of
Ohio and Pennsylvania and Michigan license plates, most of them did
not belong to employees.

Once again I cruised up and down the lanes, forcing myself to concentrate on the six digits of Cecelia Dobbs's plate number. But Erik's
bombshell kept running around in my head, like a tape caught in a
continuous loop.

Married! And to Stephanie Wyler. Somehow I couldn't wrap my
brain around it.

Red had forestalled any reply I might have made, which was probably a good thing, by reporting the sheriff had no new information on
Cecelia's vehicle. I'd paid the check with the company credit card and
allowed Erik to return to the search without so much as a word of con-
gratulation. I felt myself coloring. That was unforgivable. Regardless of
how confused I'd been by his sudden announcement, I should have said
something.

I came to the end of the last row of parked cars and pulled back into the entrance driveway. I'd make it up to him. I'd have them both to dinner and organize a celebration of some sort. I knew Stephanie's sister lived outside New York City, and her mother had remarried, a man from Arizona, so Erik and Stephanie would probably have to make all the arrangements themselves. Red and I would help. Maybe they could even be married from Presqu'isle, as Red and I had been. The setting was perfect, especially in the spring when the azaleas were in full bloom. Just a few people, and—

I brought myself up short. God, I sounded just like Bitsy Elliott! Before you knew it, I'd be picking out hideous bridesmaids' dresses. I swung right at the traffic light and headed back toward the office, determined to keep my nose out of the wedding plans. In spite of my misgivings, they were consenting adults who surely knew their own minds. I decided just to be happy for them and generally butt out unless they asked for my help or advice.

Easier, however, said than done, I warned myself as I slipped into the heavy outflow of traffic moving toward the mainland.

Neither Erik's Expedition nor Red's Bronco sat in the parking lot in front of the office, so I let myself in, grateful for the blast of air-conditioning. The outside air hung heavy and still, laden with humidity, the kind that made breathing difficult with the slightest exertion. Thank God October, with its milder temperatures, was only a couple of weeks away.

We had three messages, none of them pertinent to our search for Cecelia Dobbs, but all holding the promise of new paying customers. I made notes and had just hung up from arranging appointments with two of the organizations when the front door swung open.

Red looked tired and discouraged. On impulse, I rose and met him in the doorway to my office. I wrapped my arms around his neck and kissed him—hard. When I leaned back, I saw that he was smiling widely.

"What was that for?" he asked, running his hands up and down my back. "Not that I'm complaining, mind you." He kissed me back, and I felt myself responding in a way entirely inappropriate for the setting. When he finally stepped away, I found my knees more than a little wobbly.

"I could clear off the top of your desk, although it might be a little uncomfortable. And there's always the carpet."

I shook my head and laughed. "Wouldn't that make a nice scene for Erik to walk in on."

"We could lock the door from the inside." He stroked my cheek with the back of his hand, and I forced myself to move back to my chair.

"Tempting, but probably not a good idea." I exhaled slowly. "Sit down a minute."

His face immediately sobered, and I knew he was preparing for bad news.

"Erik and Stephanie are getting married."

He looked more than a little relieved. "Really? That's terrific! It's about time."

I sat down behind the desk. "You think so?"

"Absolutely. She's a wonderful girl, and it's obvious they're crazy about each other. When?"

"He didn't say." I felt myself blushing. "I wasn't exactly enthusiastic. I feel bad about that."

My husband reached across the wide expanse of desk and took my hand. "You have to get over the idea that Ben dying was somehow your fault."

"It was. I didn't trust him, and he came into that situation at the marina completely blind. If I had just—"

Red squeezed my hand tightly. "I was there, too, remember? Wyler did exactly what he wanted to do. You couldn't have changed a thing about how it went down." He waited a beat, then added, "Stephanie doesn't blame you at all. In fact, she doesn't understand why you keep her at arm's length. You need to let it go, honey."

I eased my hand out of his. "I'm trying. I take it you didn't have any better luck than I did," I said, determined to change the subject. "With Cecelia's car."

"Nothing," he said. "It was a long shot anyway."

"So now what do we do?"

"I think we have to leave it to the sheriff. By tomorrow, they'll be looking for her in earnest. Providing, of course, that she doesn't just come waltzing back home on her own. That's what usually happens in these kinds of cases. Maybe she got cold feet about dealing with Dalton Chambers at work and just took off for a couple of days. Stranger things have happened."

We both looked up at the sound of the outer door closing. I could tell by the slump of Erik's shoulders when he'd crossed the reception area that he hadn't been any more successful than we had. He paused to flick his laptop on before joining us in my office.

"Anybody got a Plan B?" he asked.

"We were just discussing that. Red thinks we have to sit tight until tomorrow."

Erik reached around Red and pulled a cold can of Coke out of the fridge. "I thought maybe I'd take her picture around to a couple of the bars and night spots this evening. It's usually a different crowd than during the day. Different staff, too."

"I'm not sure what good it will do, but I guess it can't hurt." I handed him the message slips I'd filled out along with the notes I'd made from my callbacks. "It's not as if we don't have other things to worry about. The one from the women's shelter in Beaufort looks interesting."

Erik took the papers and scanned them. "You're right. It's different, but I'm sure we can handle it." He glanced up at me. "If you're okay with it."

"What're you talking about?" Red's voice held just a hint of an edge.

"The shelter for battered women has had a rash of break-in attempts. The local police have put it down to just kids or druggies look-ing for loose cash or something to pawn, but the director thinks it's one or more violent husbands or ex-boyfriends trying to get to their clients. They don't exactly advertise their locations in the yellow pages, and she's concerned they may have been compromised."

"What does she want you to do about it?" Red asked.

"A lot of their referrals and requests for help come by e-mail," Erik said, consulting my notes again. "She thinks maybe that's how some-one is finding them. She wants us to check out their computers. She also has a list of possible suspects the cops are ignoring, men who are still actively threatening her clients. She wants them checked out, too."

Red's frown telegraphed his feelings on the subject. I forestalled what I knew would be his chief objection. "It doesn't have to be dan-gerous. The first step is to sit down with the director and hear what she has to say. We're just in the preliminary stages here. Chill out."

I almost added that, if my husband took the job in Walterboro, he would have even less to say about how I handled my business. Wisely, I kept that disloyal thought to myself.

"I'll get started on setting things up with her, unless you have something else you want me to do," Erik said.

I thought about our abbreviated conversation at lunch. "Use your own judgment," I said, making sure he caught my meaning. If it came to pass that I would be leaving a lot of the decision-making in his hands, he might as well get his feet wet.

He nodded and retreated to his desk.

Red made a point of looking at his watch. "You about ready to knock off?"

"I have a couple of things to clear up. You go ahead. I'll be home in an hour or so."

He rose and stretched. "What do you want to do about dinner?"

"Surprise me," I said, disappointed that he didn't smile back. "We can go out if you want. Whatever."

"Have you given any thought to what we talked about last night?" my husband asked, glancing over his shoulder in the direction of Erik's desk.

"Yes, I have. But let's wait until I get home, okay?"

"Sure." He pulled his sunglasses out of his breast pocket and slipped them on. "See you around five."

"Okay. Later."

I turned to the files stacked on my desk. Out in the reception area, I heard Red say good night to Erik. The top folder had Nicholas Potter's name, and it suddenly occurred to me that he hadn't called. His grandmother's funeral had been set for ten that morning, with burial immediately following. The gathering afterward was to be a luncheon at the Castlemain home in Wexford Plantation on the southern end of the island. At just coming up on four o'clock, that should have ended long before. I got my cell from my handbag and checked for missed messages, but there were none. I shrugged and slid his file off to the side.

Cecelia Dobbs's was next, and I opened it to study the printed information Erik had transcribed from her taped interview and my notes. I wasn't sure what I was looking for—some hint of where she might have gone and why, I guessed. On impulse, I tried her cell number again, but got the same "out-of-service" message I'd been receiving for the past few hours. Where in the hell was the girl? If she'd just decided to take off, why hadn't she left some word with her parents? As controlling as her doctor father had seemed, she'd surely know he wouldn't take her disappearance lightly. So did that mean she hadn't left under her own power?

I played with that possibility for a few minutes but again came up empty. I couldn't imagine a single reason for her to have been a victim of foul play, at least not anything that related to the current case. Maybe she had a secret boyfriend, and they'd run off to get married or something. Parents, especially of twenty-somethings, didn't necessarily know every last detail of their children's lives.

Thank God, I thought, smiling to myself. If the Judge had ever discovered some of the escapades I'd— The slam of the outer door made me jump.

I heard Erik say, "Red? What's the matter?" a moment before my husband appeared in my doorway. My heart hammered in my chest at the look on his face, his cheeks drained of all color.

"Red? What is it?"

"Sit down," he said tersely, striding around the desk to take hold of my arms and lower me into my chair.

"What?"

He perched on the edge of the desk. Erik stood just behind him, his own face creased in apprehension.

"Remember the sirens? While we were at lunch?"

I nodded, not quite able to speak.

"On Pope Avenue, back behind the miniature golf place. In between there and the old Smokehouse restaurant, there's a lagoon. You can't see it from the street."

He paused, whether for effect or because he had trouble finding the right words, I couldn't tell.

I drew in a long breath, remembering a story in the *Island Packet* a couple of months before. About a homeless man who'd— Red opened his mouth to continue, but I cut him off.

"A body?" I asked, and, slowly, my husband nodded.

CHAPTER
TWENTY-TWO

J HADN'T REALIZED I WAS CRYING UNTIL RED REACHED across and wiped away a solitary tear coursing down my cheek.

"Is it Cecelia?" I whispered.

"They don't know that for certain, honey." He sighed. "But definitely female. Caucasian. And about the right age."

"But why?"

Red and Erik glanced at each other, but I didn't expect an answer. It was a rhetorical question, one that might take weeks or months to answer. Or eternity.

"First things first." Red's hand again caressed my face, and I could see my own pain reflected in his eyes. "Malik called me from the station. He didn't have a lot of details, but he thought we should know. In case."

Erik cleared his throat, and I could tell the possibility that our client's body might just have been pulled out of the water had deeply affected him as well. "What's the procedure?" he asked.

"The scene will be secured and the body transported to the coroner's." Red checked his watch. "I'd guess it's been cleared by now. Let me go over there and see what I can find out."

I reached for my bag. "I'm coming, too."

"No!" Red and Erik spoke almost simultaneously.

Red plunged ahead. "They're not going to let you within a hundred yards of a crime scene, Bay. You know better than that. Let me scout around, see who's heading up the case. Some of the guys may be willing to share."

I knew he was right. I dropped my purse back into the drawer and sat down. "What if it's Lisa Pedrovsky? She's the most likely to have caught the call, and she isn't going to tell you a damned thing. She'd love an excuse to toss you in the can for interfering in an ongoing investigation."

"We'll cross that bridge if we come to it." Red moved toward the door. "You go on home. I'll meet you there or call when I have something to report."

Part of me wanted to fight him on it, but I didn't have the strength. I wasn't sure I could bear the mental images running around in my head: A stagnant lagoon, algae choking its placid waters, overhanging branches trailing across its surface. A young woman floating facedown in the muck, perhaps an alligator slithering into— My head snapped up.

"Was she—? Was the . . . body recognizable?"

Red saw the horror on my face. "I don't know, honey. That's what I'm going to find out. But if it is Cecelia, she couldn't have been in there too long. I'm guessing she'll be pretty much—" He swallowed and let out a little puff of air. "Pretty much intact. Don't think the worst." He clapped Erik on the shoulder. "Make sure she gets home all right, okay?"

"I'll be fine," I said, forcefully banishing the hideous pictures from my head. "Go. Let me know as soon as you find out anything for certain."

He nodded once and headed for the door.

Erik dropped into the client chair and ran a hand over his face. "Jesus! That's the last thing I expected."

"It was always a possibility," I said softly. "None of us wanted to say it out loud, but we were all thinking it, weren't we? I mean, what other explanation could there be? Even I didn't think Cecelia was the kind of girl just to run off without a word to anyone." I sighed and leaned back in my chair. "Her parents had to have something like this in the back of their minds, too."

"I guess so. But we're jumping to some big conclusions here, aren't we? It might not even be her. Didn't I read about them finding some homeless guy drowned in one of those lagoons a while back?"

"I saw that, too. But it's just too much of a coincidence. I'd love to be wrong, but I'm afraid I'm not. It's Cecelia." I tapped my chest in the vicinity of my heart. "I can feel it."

We sat in silence, each of us with our own thoughts. I knew that, sooner rather than later, we'd have to begin trying to piece together what could have happened. I told myself that nothing we had done could have precipitated Cecelia's murder, that the hard knot of guilt I felt forming just below my breastbone was undeserved and pointless. It didn't help. As I had after Ben Wyler's death, I began a mental rundown of every interaction, every word of my conversations with Cecelia Dobbs and everyone else connected with the case. Somewhere, we'd screwed up. *I'd* screwed up. Unless every instinct I'd had about the girl had been wrong, the only possible motive for someone to want her dead had been her association with me and my agency. Nothing else made sense.

"It might have been suicide."

Erik's voice startled me out of the wash of guilt threatening to swamp me.

"Why?"

"I don't know. It could have absolutely nothing to do with the stuff at the bank or Mrs. Castlemain or any of it. We don't . . . didn't really know that much about her. Her personal life and all that." He paused, and I looked up. "I know what you're thinking, but it's not your fault. Or the agency's."

"Maybe."

"Let's get out of here," Erik said, rising. "Why don't I drive you home? You and Red can pick up your car later."

"Thanks, but I'm good. I don't want to be stuck without wheels in case . . ." I didn't know how to finish the sentence. "I'll be fine."

Erik had learned over the years not to argue with me once I'd made up my mind. Along with my height, I'd inherited my stubbornness from the Judge, the original immovable object.

"You'll keep me informed?"

"Of course. As soon as I hear anything."

I gathered my things together while Erik shut down his computer and set the phones. We walked out together into the late-afternoon sun. Next to the Jaguar, he hesitated, and I reached over to squeeze his arm.

"I'll be fine," I repeated. "And by the way, I never congratulated you on your engagement. I'm really happy for you, Erik. And Stephanie. I'd like to help in any way I can with the wedding plans. Red, too. I know her family's not going to be able to, so please let us act in their stead."

His smile helped to banish some of the new lines from his usually boyish face. "Thanks. That means a lot. To both of us." He sighed, and the light went out of his eyes. "We'll worry about all that once we get past this . . ." His voice trailed off.

"I know. I'll call you as soon as I hear anything."

We climbed into our respective vehicles and headed out into the evening traffic. Though he usually took the Cross Island Parkway, I found the image of his hulking Expedition firmly in my rearview mirror all the way down Route 278 until I turned left at the entrance to Port Royal Plantation. I gave him a brief wave as he sped by me toward the south end of the island, and some of the calm I'd been feeling for the past few minutes followed in his wake.

The thought of food made me literally nauseous as I trudged up the three steps into the kitchen. I poured myself a glass of tea from the pitcher in the refrigerator and carried it with me out onto the deck. At times like this, I could almost understand the lure of alcohol and its ability to numb the senses. Nicotine could have that effect as well, at least on me. If there'd been a cigarette anywhere in the house, I would have been tumbling off that particular wagon in a heartbeat.

The air still dripped with humidity as I stretched out on a chaise, but the wind was blowing onshore, ruffling branches high up in the live oaks and the fronds of the palmettos closer to the ground. I kicked off my shoes, set the cell phone on my stomach, and let my eyes drift closed. Slowly, painstakingly, I reviewed my interactions since the first anonymous phone message Cecelia Dobbs had left on the machine at the office. I forced out the gut-wrenching images that kept trying to worm their way into my head, concentrating instead on my conduct over the past few days. I tried to be brutally honest with myself; but, at the end of it all, I couldn't come up with a single instance in which I had inadvertently revealed either Cecelia's name or given up enough information that would have enabled someone to home in on her as our new client.

Red. Erik. Me. And Dr. Dobbs. We were the only ones who had the complete story. In the course of getting the investigation up and running, I'd spoken to very few people who might even remotely have been able to make the connection: Dr. Harley Coffin. Bitsy Elliott. Nicholas Potter. Kendra Blaine, although she had no idea I had any interest in her or her partner, Dalton Chambers. He'd seen me that morning at the bank, but again, how could he know anything about me or why I was there? We hadn't even exchanged a word. Besides, that was only a few hours before the body had been discovered, and he'd been at work in full view of his colleagues and who knew how many customers.

So. Logic decreed that we hadn't put Cecelia at risk. Nowhere could I find even a hint that we'd compromised her confidentiality or inadvertently let slip anything that could have put her in jeopardy. Erik was right. It had to be something else, some facet of her life about which we were completely unaware. Maybe even something that could have led to suicide.

A coincidence. I opened my eyes at the squawk of a jay just above my head. In my mind, I heard the Judge's voice, stern and commanding: *Bullshit, darlin'. You don't believe in them any more than I did. Look again. You'll find it.*

I picked up my glass off the wrought-iron table and began a reexamination of the facts. A moment later, the cell phone chimed. I snatched it up, splashing tea all over my sweater.

"Red?"

"You okay, honey?" My husband's calm voice slowed my racing heart.

"Just sitting here on the deck thinking. What did you find out?"

"I'm just pulling in at the security gate. I wanted to make sure you were home. I'll be there in a minute."

"Tell me now."

"It can wait until—"

"God damn it, Red, just say it. It's Cecelia, isn't it?"

The pause was short, followed by a deep sigh.

"Yes," he said, and I slapped the phone closed.

CHAPTER
TWENTY-THREE

WE DEMOLISHED AN ENTIRE BOX OF WHEAT THINS and the last of a bag of pretzels that had gone stale and called that dinner. Red had joined me on the deck, a bottle of beer in his hand and the snacks in another, about ten minutes after I'd hung up on him.

He'd leaned over to plant a soft kiss on my forehead before settling himself beside me on the other chaise. For a long time, neither of us spoke.

"I should call Erik," I finally said, reaching for my phone.

"It can wait." Red took a long swallow of beer. "The initial assumption is suicide."

I felt his gaze drift my way, waiting to gauge my reaction, but I didn't meet his eyes. "Why?"

"Because there were no signs of trauma—no apparent bruises, no wounds. The preliminary coroner's guess is that she drowned. He'll have to wait until the autopsy to determine if there's water in her lungs, but . . ." His voice trailed off.

I steeled myself to ask the next obvious question. I'd shed my tears for Cecelia Dobbs, and I needed to be done with all that. "The body was intact then?"

Red waited a long time to answer. "Mostly." He turned his head in my direction, and I could feel his stare against the side of my face. "And don't ask me for any more particulars, okay? Let's just leave it at that."

So some of the creatures that lurked and slithered in the depths of the lagoon had been at work. I shuddered. Red was right. I didn't need to know the details. I forced my mind back to the enigma of why Cecelia might have taken her own life. And in that specific way. I sat up and wrapped my arms around my knees.

"How far off the beaten path is this lagoon? You said you can't see it from the street?"

"No. It's sort of in between the bike path and the parking lot for the beach."

"Who found the body?"

Red set his bottle of beer on the table between us and swung his legs over the side of the chaise. "Why don't you just let it go, honey? We may never know what drove the poor girl to do what she did."

I felt his hand begin to make slow, calming circles on my back, and I shrugged him off. "I'm not a child, Red. Did she leave a note?"

He sighed and rose. He crossed the deck and rested his elbows on the railing. The soft light of the fading sun burnished his face and arms. "No. After the doctor made the formal identification, they sent Pedrovsky and a couple of the guys over to their house. They checked her computer and her room. Nothing."

"What about her purse? Cell phone? IPod?" I waited, but his silence was my answer. "More importantly, where's her car?"

He turned and leaned back against the railing. "I know where you're going with this. That's the kicker. Malik says they haven't found the Toyota yet."

"That doesn't make any sense. How did she get there?"

"She could have left it almost anywhere and walked. Even though it's past tourist season, there's still a lot of cars on the island. As we found out today. Give them time. It'll turn up."

I closed my eyes and let the facts percolate for a moment. It didn't take long. "Cecelia didn't kill herself. There isn't one thing you've told me that points to that. What's wrong with Pedrovsky? She losing her touch? I may detest the woman, but she's not stupid."

"I said it was a preliminary finding. When you don't see any knife wounds or bullet holes in a body, you can't just jump to the conclusion that it was murder."

"But look at the evidence! No note. Her missing car. The fact that no one can come up with any reasonable explanation for why she'd take her own life." I paused. "I'm assuming her parents couldn't shed any light on that?"

"No, they couldn't." Red walked back over and sat down on the edge of the chaise. "You're right, honey. All that's being taken into consideration. It's only been a few hours since they found her body. Let's wait and see how things shake out."

"Who found her?" I asked again. That awful feeling of despair that had numbed my brain was beginning to dissipate. I wished I had paper and pen to take some notes.

"Some poor guy out walking his dog. The pup took off into the trees, and he waded in after it. Guy's in his seventies. Almost had a heart attack when he saw the . . . remains."

I swallowed down the last of my lukewarm iced tea. "But think about this. From the way you describe the place, it sounds nasty. Why would Cecelia pick a place like that when she's got the whole damn ocean? I mean, if I was going to drown myself, I sure wouldn't do it in some slimy lagoon. You wait until the middle of the night when there's no one around, and you just walk out into the Atlantic and keep on going. Clean and probably quick." I jumped up. "I want to see where it happened."

Red reached for my hand. "It's almost dark, honey. Give it a rest." He squeezed my fingers and stood beside me. "We have our own business to deal with. I have to give Joe Pickens up in Walterboro an answer, and we haven't had much of a chance to talk things over."

I knew he was right, but I couldn't think about that. Not then. I wasn't about to let Detective Lisa Pedrovsky make her life easier by stamping SUICIDE on Cecelia's file and letting it go at that. Even if—somehow—I had been the inadvertent cause of the young woman's death, her family deserved to know the truth. I reached for the phone.

"Bay—"

I raised a hand to cut him off.

"Erik. Me. It was Cecelia," I said when my partner picked up.

Behind me, I heard my husband slam the French door on his way into the house.

As it turned out, Red drove me to the crime scene, but it wasn't a pleasant ride. Neither of us spoke until we were nearly at the turnoff to the parking area. Yellow tape was still strung across the trees, and a cruiser sat sideways in front of the only access to the lagoon.

"Stay here." Red turned off the Bronco's ignition and pushed the door open. "Let me see who it is."

I undid my lap belt and leaned over the seat to rummage around in the back. I knew Red kept a flashlight back there, but I couldn't put my hands on it. The last, soft glow of twilight couldn't penetrate the roof of overhanging branches from the trees that lined the end of the parking lot, and I knew it would be even darker back by the lagoon itself. Assuming, of course, that the deputy left to guard the crime scene would let me get that far.

A moment later, I saw Red step toward the car and motion me forward.

"I need your flashlight," I said, moving around to the back of the Bronco.

"Forget it. Come here."

I swallowed a retort to the command in his voice and walked the short distance to where he stood beside the sheriff's cruiser.

"Ted, this is my wife, Bay Tanner. Deputy Miles."

He was tall and young and nice looking. He shook my hand firmly.

"Nice to meet you, ma'am." Even in the dim light, I could see him color. "I mean, except for the circumstances and all."

"You, too, Deputy," I said. "Red's told you about my connection to Cecelia Dobbs?"

He nodded. "Yes, ma'am. I'm sorry."

"We can't cross the taped perimeter, but you can see just about everything from here." Red held out his hand. "Do you mind, Ted?"

The deputy handed over the flashlight stuck in his belt. Red snapped it on as we moved around to the rear of the cruiser. He played it slowly across the tangle of brush and bracken, the light reflecting dimly off the layer of algae on the placid water. Only a crushed beer can and a wide swath of glistening mud where the body had been dragged onto the shore gave any evidence that humans had set foot in the area in decades.

I tried not to shiver, but the breeze off the ocean and the fading sunlight combined with the eeriness of the place to raise goose bumps along my arms. A picture of Cecelia Dobbs, her hands fidgeting with her old straw handbag, her face reddening in confusion and embarrassment as she sat in my office cemented my conclusion: No way would someone like her have walked willingly, probably in the dead of night, into this wild tangle of mud and weeds and slimy water. No way.

Beside me, Red spoke. "Enough?"

"Yes." I turned to Deputy Miles. "And thank you, Officer. I appreciate it."

"No problem, ma'am," he replied in his soft, Lowcountry drawl. "Just between us, though, okay?"

"We were never here," I said, and he nodded.

I walked back toward the Bronco, eager to get home and put all my swirling thoughts on paper. I'd get Erik involved as well. I knew once he heard the particulars of the location, he'd agree with me: It was nothing but a dump site. How long it would take Pedrovsky to figure that out, I had no idea. In the meantime, Erik and I would pursue our own investigation into Cecelia Dobbs's murder.

Red slid into the driver's seat beside me but didn't start the car. I looked over at him to find his gaze locked on me. "You're not going to let this go, are you?"

"If Pedrovsky rules it a homicide, I'll cooperate with her all I can. If she tries to sweep it under the rug, then, no, I'm not letting it go."

His smile warmed me. "I didn't think so." He cranked the engine. "But there's nothing more we can do about it tonight." He backed around and headed onto South Forest Beach Drive. "You hungry?"

"Ravenous. What's still open?"

"Most everything, I guess," he said, maneuvering into the roundabout. "Pizza or burgers?"

"Your call," I said and reached across the space between the bucket seats to lay my hand on his thigh.

"Burgers it is," he said, his smile widening.

I let my head fall against the back of the seat, comforted that I had my husband back on my side. There was still the matter of where we were going to live to be discussed, and I'd just about made up my mind to give him his chance at this new career when my cell phone chimed. I reached into my bag and pulled it out. The caller ID read PRIVATE NUMBER. I hesitated a moment before answering.

"Bay Tanner."

"This is Detective Lisa Pedrovsky, *Mrs.* Tanner."

I didn't imagine her snide emphasis on my title. *Here we go,* I thought. I took a deep breath and looked over to find Red's eyes flick toward me. I held his gaze for a moment before I replied, "Yes, Detective?"

"I want to talk to you. About the Dobbs girl. Where are you?"

Red turned onto New Orleans Road and pulled into the empty lot of the new Compass Rose Park the town had completed the previous year. He shoved the gearshift into Park and stretched out his hand.

"Let me talk to her," he whispered, and I shook my head.

"I'd be happy to help in your investigation into Cecelia's—" The hesitation was intentional. "—death," I finished. "Within the bounds of my confidentiality agreement, of course."

"She's dead. Those bets are off."

Pedrovsky had the finesse of a bull moose. "I'll have my attorney call you for an appointment," I said calmly.

"You don't need a lawyer." Her voice had softened as she realized, once again, that she didn't intimidate me. "I just have some loose ends to wrap up, and I thought you might want to help the family."

"I'll get back to you," I said and flipped the phone closed. I looked at Red. "She wants to 'interview' me. More like an interrogation, judging by past experience."

"The attorney line was good." Red started the car and moved back onto the nearly deserted street. "That probably pissed her off."

"Good," I said with a half smile. "She's talking about wrapping up loose ends. That says to me she's decided it's a suicide."

"What is it you're so fond of saying? You know, from *Gone with the Wind*?"

" 'Tomorrow is another day'?"

"That's it." Again he captured my hand. "Let's get some food and then sleep on it. Things will look different tomorrow."

It was a nice sentiment, but I seriously doubted if he was right. In spite of Scarlett's best hopes, things almost never worked out that way. For either one of us.

CHAPTER
TWENTY-FOUR

ACTUALLY, IT DIDN'T TAKE THAT LONG FOR THINGS to go downhill.

Stuffed with a Big Mac, large fries, and a vanilla milkshake, I felt more like myself than I had all day when Red and I climbed the steps into the house a little after nine thirty. By habit, I checked the answering machine and found three messages waiting for me. Sandwiched in between two increasingly strident commands from Detective Lisa Pedrovsky that I needed to call her immediately, Lavinia's soft voice was an island of calm. At least at first.

"Hey, honey," she began. "I guess you and Redmond must be out to a late dinner. I just wanted to let you know that I've talked to Miz Shelly, and she and your sister are comin' up tomorrow to spend a few days. We're going to see how Julia does away from home. I think you need to be here. They'll be arrivin' around noon, so I want you to come for lunch. Redmond is welcome, too, of course." She'd paused, and the tenor of her voice changed, reminding me of the stern woman who had ordered our lives for more than forty years at Presqu'isle. "Don't let me down."

"Damn it," I muttered under my breath, but Red heard as he climbed the steps behind me.

"What's the matter?"

I told him about Lavinia's message and my command performance at Presqu'isle.

"I thought that's what you wanted."

"It is," I answered, pulling open the door to the refrigerator and removing the pitcher of iced tea. "I guess. But the timing couldn't be worse. I've got Pedrovsky on my butt, and there's a million things to do on Cecelia's cases." I poured a glass of tea, added ice, and stood staring off into the darkness outside the kitchen window.

"Cases?" Red had moved up behind me to place his hands gently on my shoulders, and his breath ruffled the hair behind my ear. "Plural?"

I turned so I could look him squarely in the face. "Yes. I'm going to pursue Chambers and Blaine and their scam." I paused. "And I'm going to find out what really happened to Cecelia. She didn't kill herself. I know she didn't."

I could see that Red wanted to argue. But I also detected that shift in his eyes that told me he'd realized the futility of trying to talk me out of it. Instead, he took my hand and led me down into the great room. We hadn't turned on the lights in there, and the soft glow of the moon cast the room in its own twilight. I set my glass on the side table and curled up next to my husband on the sofa.

"You know you're letting yourself in for a lot of heartache." He still held my hand, and his thumb absently stroked the skin on the backs of my fingers. "I'm worried about you."

I snuggled closer. "Don't be. I've learned a lot over the past few years. From the Judge." I smiled into the darkness. "And from you. I'll do this by the book—no unnecessary chances, no running off half-cocked. Promise."

He didn't respond right away. With the French doors and all the windows closed, the silence was almost complete. Only our breathing, almost in synch, stirred the warm air. "I guess this means we're not moving to Walterboro," my husband finally said, his tone even, his disappointment almost concealed.

"*I'm* not moving. At least not yet." I pulled away and leaned back so he could see my face. "But I want you to take the job. We'll find you an apartment or something up there and see how it goes."

Again he was silent for a long time. "Are you sure?"

I nestled back into the circle of his arm. "Yes. Positive. You deserve this chance, and I'm not standing in your way. When do you have to start?"

"Not until the first of October, officially, but I'll need to go up there and get oriented. Joe said he wanted me the last week of the month so he can brief me, and I can get to know the guys a little."

I sighed, quietly. *That's how it always is,* I thought. *Everything at once.* What I said aloud was, "Then we'll need to get on that. Why don't you come with me to St. Helena tomorrow? We'll get Miss Lizzie and Julia settled, then we can run up to Walterboro and find you a place to live. Maybe even a house. There's bound to be a lot of them empty with the housing market the way it is. And there's enough stuff in the attics at Presqu'isle to furnish a dozen places."

Red squeezed me then and kissed the side of my forehead. "I don't like the idea of living apart from you."

"I'm not crazy about it, either. But I think it's the best solution. For now. Don't you?"

"I guess. You going to be okay with this Dobbs thing?"

I didn't remind my husband that I'd survived Rob's assassination, been shot at, actually *shot* once, and solved a lot of cases, all on my own. It wasn't what he wanted to hear. Instead, I said, "You'll be close by if I need help. And I've got Erik."

"You sure?" he asked again.

I sat up and reached for my glass. "Go call this Joe guy and tell him you're in." I rose and took my cell phone from my pocket. "I need to talk to Erik."

Red stood and hugged me, hard. "We'll make this work, honey. I promise."

"I know," I said absently, my mind already on what needed to be done to get the wheels of justice rolling for Thomas and Rebecca Castlemain. And for Cecelia Dobbs.

When Erik answered, I could hear a lot of noise in the background: raised voices, laughter, and some sports announcer screaming, "That's outta here!"

"Sorry, Bay, I can barely hear you. I'm going outside," he said.

I waited as the pandemonium faded. A moment later, he was back. "Bay?"

"I'm here."

"That's better. Pretty raucous crowd in there."

"Where are you?"

"At a bar. My third one tonight."

It came back to me then, his stated intention to see if anyone remembered seeing Cecelia Dobbs on Sunday night. I'd thought it a long shot at the time and still did, but Erik knew the places the younger crowd liked to congregate much better than I did. I still couldn't see Cecelia as a bar crawler, but I'd been wrong before. Still . . .

"What's the point? I mean . . . now," I asked.

"I guess I just needed to do something. You know."

"Yes, I do. Any luck?"

He sighed. "No, not yet. That picture of her the doctor gave us isn't that great. A couple of the bartenders thought they might have seen her, but no one could say for certain. Or even when. I guess I'm just spinning my wheels."

"Maybe not." I told him then about my visit to the crime scene and why it had cemented my conviction that our client had not killed herself. And about Detective Lisa Pedrovsky's badgering phone calls.

"She really doesn't like you," Erik said, his voice light despite the seriousness of the situation.

"It's mutual. But I'm convinced she's going for suicide, and that's just ridiculous. If you saw that slimy hole, you'd understand. Cecelia was scared of her own shadow. There's no way she voluntarily walked into those creepy woods and lay down in that muck in the dead of night. No way."

Behind me, Red walked back into the great room and joined me on the couch. His smile seemed out of place in light of Erik's and my conversation, but I grinned back when he made the *okay* sign with his thumb and index finger.

"So what do you want me to do?"

I jumped at Erik's voice in my ear. "Keep looking for the car. It hasn't turned up yet, and that may be the best way to convince Pedrovsky that this wasn't a suicide. Tomorrow we'll brainstorm a plan for both the death and the scam investigations. I'm going to deposit Cecelia's checks on my way in so we have a solid case for being involved."

"What about the detective?"

I smiled in the darkness. "I'll handle Pedrovsky."

"See you tomorrow," my partner said and hung up.

I flipped my phone closed and set it on the table. "So what did Joe Pickens have to say?" I asked.

Red reached behind him to turn on one of the lamps on the sofa table. "It was pretty ego-pumping," my husband said with a smile. "I think they really want me."

"Of course they do. Why wouldn't they? And there won't be any damned Lisa Pedrovsky slinking around trying to undermine you at every turn." I put my arms around his neck. "I'm very proud of you, Red."

"Thanks, honey." He actually blushed. "Joe says he knows of a couple of places for rent that are in town and really nice. One of them even comes furnished. He gave me the name of the guy who's handling them. I thought we could call tomorrow and set up an appointment."

"Great," I said, my mind already moving away to the issue of Cecelia Dobbs. I wondered if maybe I should quit avoiding Pedrovsky and take the opportunity to pick her brain. I'd have to be careful to keep what I knew to myself, but I'd been down that road with her before and come out all right. Or maybe I should call Alexandra Finch. The attorney and I had met when she represented Billy Dumars as the chief suspect in the murder of his wife, Tracy. The brusque lawyer and I had bonded almost immediately. Whenever I'd had a need for legal advice in the intervening months, I'd called Alex or her associate, Claudia Darling.

I glanced at the clock on the mantel. At just past ten thirty, I didn't have the nerve to disturb her at home. Tomorrow would be soon enough.

"Have you heard anything I've said in the last five minutes?" Red's voice had lost its excitement and sounded harsh in the quiet of the evening.

"Sorry. I was thinking about Cecelia." I shook my head lightly to clear it. "What did you say?"

Red swallowed his exasperation, perhaps afraid to tip the delicate balance of my cooperation with his plans. "I asked if you thought you might be able to come up to Walterboro some weekends. That way the kids could get used to my new place, wherever it turns out to be."

Scotty and Elinor! I had completely dismissed how this whole thing might affect them. And Sarah. How would she feel about her children traipsing around the Lowcountry from house to house?

"Did you discuss it with them at all? Or Sarah?" I asked.

"Only generally. The kids are fine. They don't care where we go. They'll miss the beach, but it won't be every week. We'll come down here most of the time."

"And your ex-wife?"

I knew from the look on his face that he didn't want to talk about it, but I had a right to know. I'd come to love both of Red's kids in a way I hadn't thought possible just a few months before. I didn't want them in the middle of some power play between their divorced parents.

"She'll come around," was all he said, and I knew we were in for some battles.

"Red—"

"Come on, it's been a long day. Let's get some sleep."

I let him pull me up, then switched off the lamp. Arms around each other, we walked down the hallway toward our bedroom. Just inside the door, Red stopped and turned me to face him.

"Thank you, honey. I know this isn't the best solution, but we'll make it work. I promise."

I kissed him then and pushed all my doubts into one of those mental compartments I was so fond of. I closed my eyes, and suddenly the face of Cecelia Dobbs, blotchy and frightened, filled my inner vision, only to be replaced almost immediately by the nearly blank, childlike image of my sister Julia.

My priorities, at least for the foreseeable future, had already been decided.

CHAPTER
TWENTY-FIVE

ERIK BEAT US TO THE OFFICE NEXT MORNING EVEN THOUGH I pushed through the door at one minute before nine o'clock. The ever-present coffee sat in its cardboard container on a corner of the desk, and his laptop was fired up and running.

"Aren't you the early bird," I said. Red followed and mumbled, "Good morning."

"Hey, you two. I woke up early, so I figured I might as well get some work done. If we're going to concentrate on Cecelia Dobbs, I wanted to make sure all our other clients were up to date."

"Thanks. Come on in when you reach a stopping point." I walked into my office and around to my chair. Red set his drink on the desk.

"I'm going down to the station and see what's happening," he said, slouching in the client chair. "Or do you have something else I should be doing?"

"Hang on a minute until Erik—"

I cut myself off when he appeared in the doorway, dragging his chair behind him. I waited for him to get settled in.

"Okay, here's the plan. First, I'm going to call Pedrovsky and set up a meet. I need to know which way the wind is blowing. But I'm going to talk to Alex Finch first and see if she thinks she needs to be present. We're walking a fine line here. I put Cecelia's checks in the bank, but our client is dead. That puts our confidentiality agreement with her on shaky ground. I'll see what Alex has to say about it, but I'm going to try to stonewall on why Cecelia hired us for as long as I can."

I looked across at the men and didn't hear any objections, so I pressed on.

"That's assuming the sheriff and the coroner are looking at her death as a suicide. If they come to the same conclusion I have—that she was murdered—then all bets are off. We'll have no choice but to cooperate."

"What about the scam?" Erik asked.

"That's a different story. I never heard from Nicholas Potter, the Castlemains' grandson, yesterday, which is kind of strange." I looked at the notes I'd made during my now almost habitual wakefulness in the middle of the night. I tapped the file I'd left on my desk the day before. "I'll call him and see what's happening. Regardless of whether or not he's gotten cold feet, we're going ahead with the assumption that Cecelia's concerns had merit. Erik, let's get all the information we have on Dalton Chambers and Kendra Blaine collated into one report, as concise as possible. Just the salient points. Then get back to digging into Chambers' past. See if you can scare up any photos of the 'real' guys by that name that you ran across. And get a printout of the picture you took at the bank the other day."

"Got it," Erik said, rising. "I just need to prepare our recommendation to the school district for your signature and get that in the mail. We should be clear for a couple of days to concentrate on this." He paused. "What about the problems at the women's shelter? You want to let that ride?"

I cursed under my breath. It had completely slipped my mind. "What do you think?"

"If it's computer related, I can handle it on my own." His chin rose just a fraction. "If that's okay with you."

"Go with it," I said, the decision to step back into a supporting role much easier than I had expected. "You've got the contact info. Let me know what you need."

He chewed on the corner of his mouth to keep a smile from breaking out. "I'll take care of it," he said on his way out to his desk.

Red stood, too. "I'll get over to the substation and see what's happening. Malik's working days now, so I should be able to sweat some details out of him."

I frowned. "Don't put his job in jeopardy."

To my surprise, Red grinned. "I'm thinking of stealing him away once I get organized up there. He lives just outside of Yemassee. Walterboro would be a much shorter commute for him."

I smiled back. "And you look like such a nice Southern boy. I had no idea you could be so sneaky."

He waved on his way across the reception area. "I'll call you," he said over his shoulder.

My tea had gone lukewarm, but I drank it down anyway. The caffeine was more important than the temperature. I wondered for a moment how much longer these bouts of insomnia were going to last. We were into the second week, and I wasn't certain how much longer my middle-aged body would be able to hold out before rebelling at the abuse.

I stifled a yawn and punched in my attorney's number. I'd expected to have to leave a message, but she surprised me by being at her desk.

"Bay! Good to hear from you. Unless you're in trouble, of course." More than a few pounds overweight when I'd first met her, Alex had been on a punishing diet and exercise regimen for months. I hadn't seen her in person for a while, and I wondered if she'd been as successful at beating her body into shape as she was at beating her opponents in court.

"Maybe I'm just calling to invite you to lunch," I said.

"No way. Neither one of us has time for all that social networking nonsense. What's up?"

I gave her a condensed version of the events of the past few days. She was shocked to learn of my connection to Cecelia Dobbs's death.

"I saw it in the paper this morning, just a brief notice about a body's having been found over on Pope Avenue, but no name. God! I sort of know her parents," she said, her voice hushed and a little gravelly. Her laugh held no humor. "Met them at some shindig or other. Sometimes there's just no avoiding those social things." She paused to clear her throat. "They must be devastated."

I blushed then, because I hadn't really given much thought to how this whole nightmare must be affecting Dr. Dobbs and his wife. "He came to us to help find her," I said, feeling a lump rise in my chest. "I never really expected it to turn out like this."

"So what do you need from me?" Alex was back to business. "Hate to rush you, but I'm due in court over in Beaufort at eleven."

I explained my desire to sit down with Detective Lisa Pedrovsky and my concerns about where I stood, legally.

"Stick to your guns about not revealing the nature of Cecelia's concerns. Unless and until it becomes a murder investigation. If the old bat gives you any grief—or starts on one of her rants about arresting you for obstruction—call Claudia. She'll be here all day, and she can also reach me by text if it's an emergency."

"Thanks, Alex. I think I'll be okay, but I wanted some backup just in case."

"Call if you need us," she said and hung up before I could finish saying goodbye.

Before I lost my nerve, I contacted the sheriff's office and left a message for Pedrovsky requesting a meet. Next, I flipped open the file on my desk and punched in the number for the Castlemain home in Wexford. It was answered on the second ring. Kendra Blaine identi-fied herself, and I hung up. I had no desire to alert one of our suspects that I was in touch with Nicholas Potter. I cursed myself for not try-ing his cell first. If the house phone had caller ID, Blaine could back-track me without too much trouble. That's what came of operating on four hours' sleep, I told myself. I crossed to the mini-refrigerator and took out a Diet Coke. The more caffeine, the better.

Back behind the desk, I tried Potter's cell phone. It rang four times before going to voice mail. I left my callback numbers, although he already had them. I sat back, wondering if he'd still be as fired up about pursuing the Blaine woman as he'd been over the weekend. He'd buried his grandmother on Monday. Maybe he just wanted to forget about it and get back to his life in D.C.

"Erik?" I called, and a moment later he stood in the doorway. "Did I ask you to run a check on Nicholas Potter, the Castlemains' grandson?"

"Nope. I transcribed the notes you cleaned up. And the tape. You can access it on your computer now."

"But I didn't ask for a background?"

"Not that I recall. It was pretty hectic around here, though. Yes-terday, I mean."

I nodded. "Do you have time to get something in the works?"

"How deep do you want to go?"

I thought about it for a moment. "Just cursory for the time being. DOB, school, work history. Just see if anything weird pops up. I'm waiting for him to call me back."

"I should be able to get started on it in an hour or so. That work?"

"Sure. Sorry to dump everything on you, but I have some other calls to make."

"No problem."

I turned back to the list I'd made in the early hours of the morning. I added a couple of notes, glancing up at the silent phone. Now that I'd decided to duke it out with Lisa Pedrovsky, I wanted to get it over with. I sipped from the bottle of Coke and leaned back in my chair, my eyes growing heavy in the quiet of the September morning. I could feel myself slipping, the hand holding the drink sinking slowly toward the floor. I jerked myself awake. Tonight I'd take something, one of those over-the-counter things that combined aspirin or Tylenol with some sort of sleeping pill. I couldn't go on like this. Sooner or later, my fatigue would make me do something stupid. Or careless. Cecelia Dobbs and Rebecca Castlemain deserved my having *all* my wits about me, not just half of them.

As I reached for the phone to call my broker, it rang under my hand. I jerked back and heard Erik pick up. A moment later, he stood in front of my desk.

"Detective Pedrovsky. Line one. Are you in?"

"I'll take it," I said. I waited until he'd returned to his desk before rubbing the still cold bottle across my cheeks and forehead. I set it down, took a calming breath, and reached for the receiver.

"You said you wanted to meet, Detective."

"And good morning to you, too, Mrs. Tanner."

"Let's cut the crap, shall we? I'm available now. How soon can you be here?"

"I'd prefer you to come down to the substation."

"Not going to happen. Unless I'm under arrest?"

She laughed. "Of course not, Mrs. Tanner. We're merely asking for your cooperation with our investigation into the death of Cecelia Dobbs."

"Then I repeat: How soon can you be here?"

I knew the fake pleasantness couldn't last.

"Ten minutes," she said and slammed down the phone.

I drew a deep breath and rose from my chair. I passed Erik's desk on my way to the restroom at the far end of the reception area.

"Pedrovsky's on her way," I said. "Will you put another chair in my office? She usually brings reinforcements. Or an audience, I've never decided which."

I stepped inside the bathroom and wet a paper towel with cold water. I wiped my face, careful not to smear my mascara. I'd need all my defenses for the coming encounter. I washed my hands and smoothed the creases from my light cotton blazer. I pinched some color into my cheeks before turning from the damning mirror.

"In for a penny," I muttered to myself on the way back to my office.

CHAPTER TWENTY-SIX

DETECTIVE LISA PEDROVSKY SURPRISED ME, ON A couple of counts. First, she came alone. Second, she'd changed her look since the last time we'd done battle. Although she strode into the offices of Simpson & Tanner, Inquiry Agents, as if she owned the place, she'd let her formerly close-cropped blond hair grow out a little. It curled around her chin and softened her square face. She'd also exchanged her customary crisp white blouse and navy slacks that had looked almost like a uniform for pleated khakis and a pale yellow sweater that made the green of her eyes stand out. She almost lulled me into complacency with her smile and proffered hand. Almost. Until she opened her mouth.

"So. Here we are again," she said, pulling up one of the chairs. "I seem to spend a lot of my time talking to you about dead people."

"Maybe if you were better at your job, there wouldn't be so many of them," I snapped back.

That shut her up for a second. But the detective and I had been around this barn before, and I knew it wouldn't last. I wondered if she'd come alone so she wouldn't have to treat me with the sort of restraint and respect she'd be forced to grant a member of the public if she had a colleague or subordinate as a witness. She pulled a notebook from her bag and flipped it open.

"Cecelia Dobbs. Her father said she hired you to investigate some supposed irregularities at the bank. I need details."

I felt as if someone had poked me with a sharp object. I had to control the urge to let my breath out in a rush. So much for keeping the details from the cops. I'd completely forgotten that Dr. Dobbs had been fully informed of his daughter's concerns and might have, in the course of being questioned about Cecelia, offered up her connection to the agency. I fumbled around in my head for a Plan B, but the fog of insomnia had slowed my thought processes to a crawl. So I stalled.

"How does that have any bearing on her death?"

"You tell me. The doctor couldn't remember any names, but I'm sure you can supply those." She held her pen poised over the notepad as if she expected me to begin rattling off information.

"But I heard you think the girl killed herself." I leaned back in my chair and steepled my fingers under my chin. It was a delaying tactic, and someone as savvy and experienced as Pedrovsky would recognize that in a heartbeat. This certainly wasn't going the way I'd planned.

The detective looked up. "There's been no official ruling, so I'm not at liberty to discuss it." Her eyes, dark with tamped-down emotion, stared into mine. "You know that, *Mrs.* Tanner."

I could feel a headache beginning just behind my eyes, but I refrained from giving any indication. Pedrovsky was like a stalking lioness: Show the first sign of fear or weakness, and she'd pounce for the kill.

"What bugs you about my title, Detective? I was Mrs. Tanner before I married Red." It struck me then that I had no idea if she'd ever had a husband. Maybe that was it. I smiled. "You can just call me Bay if you like. Since we seem to be destined to spend so much time together, it might be nice."

That ticked her off, as I'd intended it should. "I don't want to be your pal, Tanner. In fact, I want to spend as little time in your presence as possible." Her own smile was wolfish. "If so many of your clients didn't end up dead, we might be able to avoid each other altogether."

Score one for the opposing team. I let out a long sigh and rubbed my hand across my forehead. I didn't have the energy or the mental sharpness for this kind of battle of wits. Not that morning.

"Just explain to me why you're so convinced Cecelia killed herself. If she wanted to drown herself, why would she choose a slimy, shallow lagoon when she had the whole ocean to work with?" I asked, giving voice to my thoughts of the night before. "And where's her car? Have you located it yet? Or a note?" I felt better being on the attack. "Was there water in her lungs?"

Pedrovsky shifted her weight in the chair. "You apparently still don't understand how this works, Tanner. I ask, you answer. Everything points to suicide. We're just covering all the bases." She waited a beat. "And if I were you, I wouldn't be so eager to have this ruled a homicide. If they determine she was murdered, you might become much more interesting to the sheriff."

I decided I'd had enough of our sparring. "Here's the bottom line, Detective. My attorney advises that I don't need to divulge confidential information unless and until this is declared a murder investigation. I think it should be, but that's neither here nor there. You're obviously convinced you're dealing with a suicide, and that makes my cooperation voluntary." I stood, towering over her. "And I don't choose to cooperate. Have a nice day."

We held each other's gaze for a long moment before she rose from the chair. "You know, I thought at one time we might work together. You're not without some talent at investigation, although you get it wrong more often than you get it right. You're not the typical sleazy PI." She put her notebook and pen back in the big leather bag that doubled as a briefcase. "But you've got a lousy attitude, Tanner. And you get people killed."

I opened my mouth to defend myself, but she was already moving toward the door. "Detective, wait." I swallowed some of my self-righteous pride and spoke softly. "That's not fair, and you know it."

She stopped and turned. "Isn't it? Would you like me to give you the body count?"

I felt my shoulders droop. "Look, I accept some responsibility for Ben's death. Part of it was his own fault for charging in without all the facts, for wanting to be the hero. But I played a role, too. I'll have to live with that."

Some of the color drained from her cheeks, but she didn't speak. Still, I could tell my words had struck home.

"I know you cared about him." I lowered my voice even farther. "I'm sorry."

I don't know what I expected, but I felt better for having said the words. Out loud. And to Lisa Pedrovsky.

We stared at each other a long time before she said, "Thanks for that. I'll be in touch."

And with that she was gone.

My cell phone rang just as the Jaguar coasted down the ramp off Route 278 toward Beaufort.

"Probably Lavinia," I said, reaching for my bag. "Beating me up for being late."

"I'll tell her it was my fault. She always liked me better than you."

I punched Red gently on the arm and flipped the phone open.

We'd left his Bronco in the parking lot at the office. He loved driving the Jag and always tended to speed when he had its umpteen horses under his control. I supposed he planned on using his former connection to the sheriff's department to get him off the hook for any tickets. I had insisted on taking my car because, unlike Red's beloved restored vehicle, my air conditioner actually worked.

"Hello," I said without checking caller ID.

"Bay, it's Nick. I got your message."

I glanced sideways at my husband. "Yes. Thanks for calling me back. I was a little surprised not to have heard from you yesterday. How did everything go?"

"Fine, I guess. For a funeral. It was understated and elegant, just the way Grandma would have wanted. Simple."

He didn't offer any explanation for his not having been in touch as promised, but I could understand why he might not have been in the mood for business.

"I'm sorry again for your loss. I wish I could have known Mrs. Castlemain."

"She was a pistol," Nick said with a hint of amusement. "I could always wrap my mother around my little finger, but Grandma didn't stand for any nonsense. Not from any of us."

I could feel Red's eyes glance my way, one eyebrow raised in question. I mouthed *Nick Potter,* and he nodded. Aloud, I said, "There have been some developments in the case that we should discuss."

"How about I buy you lunch? You could come to the club here in Wexford. They do a wonderful sea bass."

"Sorry. I'm on my way to Beaufort on another matter. How about this evening? Are you free?"

Red's scowl could have been picked up on radar.

"Dinner is even better. We could have drinks at seven and—"

"I'm afraid that's out of the question. Can you meet me at the office . . ." I checked my watch and did some mental calculations. ". . . say around eight? That is if you're still interested in pursuing the matter."

It didn't hurt my ego any that he sounded disappointed. "I suppose that will work. And yes, after everything that went on yesterday, I think it's imperative that we pursue the investigation. Kendra has firmly ensconced herself at Canaan's Gate, and it looks like it might take dynamite to get her out of there."

"Canaan's Gate?"

"Oh, that's what my grandparents call their house in Wexford. And actually the one they had in Virginia before that. Hang on."

He must have covered the mouthpiece with his hand, and I could hear mumbled voices in the background.

"You're meeting this Potter guy tonight?" Red's tone was peevish. "We've got an appointment with the real estate guy at four. I don't want to have to rush through looking for—"

I cut him off with an upraised hand when Nick Potter came back on the line.

"Sorry about that. My uncles and cousins are organizing something for this evening." He snorted. "All of a sudden we're one big, happy family. Something to do with the will, no doubt. Can we make it a little later? Say nine?"

"That will actually be better for me, too. Nine at the office. I'll see you then."

"I'll bring the wine," he said and was gone before I could offer a protest.

I slid the phone onto the console under the dash. I looked at my husband, but neither of us spoke as we glided into the sweeping turn past the place where the information center for Grayton's Race had once stood. I never navigated this stretch of Route 170 without a shiver at the terrible memories the place evoked.

"Why couldn't you just discuss this over the phone?" Red's voice sounded stilted, not quite angry, but definitely headed in that direction.

"Because I have a lot to dump on the man, and I'd rather do it in person. I need to tell him about Cecelia."

"Why? Her death doesn't concern him."

I twisted my head around on my neck, trying to work out the

tension of a sleep-interrupted night and the low-grade headache. "It's all connected somehow. I just haven't figured it out yet." I sighed and closed my eyes. "Let's not talk about it now, okay? Let me rest for a few minutes."

"Sure," I think he said about two seconds before I fell down a long, dark corridor.

"We're here, Bay. Wake up."

I forced my reluctant eyes open to find myself staring at the split staircase that led to the wide front verandah of Presqu'isle. The overhanging live oak cast swaying shadows across the circular gravel driveway. I stretched and yawned.

"Nice little catnap," my husband said, and I smiled at him.

"Sorry."

"No problem."

We pushed open our doors, and I realized we'd pulled in behind a huge boat of a car, an old station wagon with fake wood paneling on its sides.

"Oh, my God, look at this!" Red bounded forward, his eyes alight with wonder. "It's a Country Squire. Mid-eighties, I think. It's perfect! Even the paneling hasn't faded."

I stood in the open door of the Jaguar watching my husband run his hand over the finish on the old wagon, rattling off statistics that meant absolutely nothing to me. Cars had never been my thing. You got in, they started, you went on your way. Not that I didn't enjoy my convertibles, especially the Z-3 that had ended up at the bottom of a pond out in the middle of nowhere. I smiled to myself. Lately, I'd gone more for comfort than rakish styling. Bottom line, the big Jaguar made me feel safe. Cocooned. A function of age, I told myself. My sports car days were behind me.

I turned at the sound of Lavinia's voice above us.

"Do I have to come down there and drag the two of you in here? Frogmore stew isn't edible stone cold. Besides, we have guests."

"Yes, ma'am," I said automatically. "Come on, Red."

He pulled himself away from the old car and reached for my hand. I raised a finger and ran it across his chin.

"What?"

"Just wiping off the drool," I said, and he laughed.

"It's a beauty," he said as we mounted the sixteen steps, side by side. "I'll bet Miss Lizzie bought it new. She must keep it under cover all the time."

"I'm sure you'll find out."

Lavinia had left the front door open and stomped back into the house. We stepped into the wide foyer, and I set my bag on the floor next to the console table as I'd been doing for decades. Entering my childhood home, bathed now in the soft light filtering in through the long side windows that flanked the door, always brought back a flood of memories. I swallowed the lump that rose unbidden in my throat as I glanced down the short hallway that led to my father's study. I hadn't been in there since his death except to retrieve the will and his other papers from his files. I had no idea if Lavinia had cleared it out, had someone remove the sickroom equipment that had defined its purpose over the last few years of the Judge's life. Or maybe, like me, she had been unable to bring herself to alter any of it. Perhaps she'd left it, a shrine to the man she had loved, mostly in secret, for the better part of forty years.

"Bay Tanner, I swear you are gettin' on my last nerve, girl. Get yourself in here."

The hoarse whisper came just a few inches from my ear, and I jumped. Lavinia spun on her heel and marched away down the long hallway toward the kitchen. I had a moment to be thankful that she hadn't spread us out around the huge mahogany table in the austere formal dining room before I reached for Red's hand.

"Don't worry, honey. It'll be fine."

I relaxed a little under his loving smile, squared my shoulders, and took the first step toward the unknown—a relationship with my long-lost sister.

CHAPTER
TWENTY-SEVEN

HEY BOTH LOOKED UP WHEN WE WALKED INTO THE kitchen. Elizabeth Shelly—Miss Lizzie—turned her lined face, devoid of expression, and nodded once. Julia Garrett-Simpson, my half sister, bounded out of her chair and flung her arms around my neck. I was so startled it took me a moment to return her exuberant hug.

"Hi, Bay," she said. "I'm so glad to see you."

"You, too." I set her back a little from me and studied her face.

She'd lost that almost vacant, childish look, especially in her eyes, a sort of bluish gray that sparkled now as they'd never done before in our few encounters. Her face, similar in many ways to my own, was still unlined, as if the failure of her mind to mature past her early years had somehow translated to her skin. But the gray streaks in her long dark hair told a different story.

"You look wonderful," I said, meaning it.

"I have new clothes." She did a pirouette in the middle of the kitchen floor. "Do you like them?"

The soft rose color of her cotton sweater complemented her tanned face and arms, and her jeans were stylish and pressed to a sharp crease.

I smiled at her sparkly sandals. I'd never seen her in anything but bare feet or tennis shoes.

"They're terrific."

She took my hand and pulled me into the chair beside her. I looked for Red, who stood a little awkwardly, not quite sure of his place in this reunion.

Lavinia pulled out a chair. "If you'll sit here, Redmond." She turned toward the stove. "I'll have this on the table in two shakes."

My husband seated himself and smiled all around. "It's good to see both of you."

Lizzie Shelly nodded and unbent enough to grant him one of her rare, fleeting smiles. "We're pleased to be here, Sergeant."

"Oh, not anymore. I'm a civilian now." He glanced my way, and I nodded. "At least for a while."

"What's this?" Lavinia began placing heaping bowls in front of each of us. "You're going back to the sheriff's?"

The steam from the shrimp, sausage, and corn on the cob in its spicy broth made my stomach rumble. Aside from the basics of this favorite Lowcountry dish, Lavinia had added her own special touches—mussels and huge chunks of lobster. Before joining us, she put a heaping basket of sweet potato biscuits in the center of the table.

As Red explained his new job opportunity, I watched my sister out of the corner of my eye. She in turn watched Miss Lizzie, imitating her by placing her napkin in her lap and picking up the soup spoon from beside her bowl. She seemed afraid of making a mistake, and I wondered if her caretaker had given her strict instructions on how to behave. If Julia had to spend her time here worrying about her table manners, it was going to be a long, uncomfortable visit.

"Do you like mussels, Julia?" I asked.

"I don't know," she said softly. "Is that these black things that look like butterflies?"

I smiled. "What a good description. Yes. See this little fork?" I lifted mine from the table. "You just pick up the mussel and scoop out the meat."

I demonstrated, and my sister giggled. Lavinia had left an empty bowl in the middle of the table, and I tossed in the shell. It rattled against the china, and Julia laughed louder. Just for good measure, I licked the dribbles of juice from my fingers.

"Let me," my sister said, and I smiled when she tossed the shell in beside mine. "Mmm, it tastes like the ocean. I like it."

That seemed to break the ice, and we all bent over our bowls. If we had been eating outside, the picnic table would have been spread with newspapers. The broth would have been served in separate bowls, and the seafood, sausage, and corn would have been drained and dumped in the middle of the table for everyone to help himself. I guessed that might have been what Lavinia originally had in mind, except that it was just too bloody hot for it on this steamy September afternoon.

As the bowl filled with shells and discarded corn cobs, very little conversation interrupted our concentration. Red kept his head down, no doubt aware of the uneasy undercurrent floating through the room. Lavinia did her best to inject a question or observation here and there, but it was painfully obvious that none of us was completely comfortable. I buttered my third sweet potato biscuit and decided it was time to get the ball rolling.

"So where did you get your new things, Julia? I love the color of your sweater."

My sister beamed. "Do you? Really?" She glanced at the closed face of Miss Lizzie. "We went to Charleston. It's a wonderful place. So many buildings. And they have horses that pull big buggies around with tourists in them." Her smile wavered a little. "I wanted to ride in one, but we didn't have time."

"You have your own horses, Julia." Lizzie said it softly, but with a look that reflected her annoyance at the implied criticism.

"I never saw your horses," I said. "What color are they?"

I glanced across at Lavinia, who had risen to begin clearing the table. Lizzie pushed back her chair. I saw Lavinia open her mouth to protest, and I shook my head. She nodded, and the two older women carried empty bowls and silver to the sink. I turned back to my sister.

"Well, Rusty, he's kind of reddish brown. Like his name. And Sally is mostly white. She likes apples, but Rusty always wants a carrot. I carry them in my pockets when I go to visit them."

"Do you ride?" I asked.

"No." The single word came from Elizabeth Shelly. "Not anymore. They're just old plow horses, put out to pasture."

I wanted to tell her to butt out, but it would have been rude. And probably unsuccessful. Julia had been her sole concern for a long time, and she wasn't about to let anyone else muscle in on her territory. Perhaps this whole thing had been a bad idea. I looked over to see Julia's head drooping, like a puppy who'd been swatted for peeing on the rug. I felt Red's hand on my arm, a gentle pat of encouragement. He glanced over his shoulder and made a shooing motion. A moment later he said, "So, Ms. Shelly. I understand Covenant Hall has a really interesting history. Was it really one of the places where the secession was planned?"

I smiled my appreciation, grabbed Julia's hand, and dragged her out of the chair. "Come on," I whispered, "let's go explore."

She looked startled for a moment before her lovely smile lit her eyes. She nodded once, and we bolted from the kitchen.

"And this was my room," I said, pushing open the door to my childhood haven. Nothing much changed at Presqu'isle, primarily because maintaining tradition had been my mother's principal reason for being. The same furniture—four-poster bed, whitewashed oak desk and dresser, even the same goose-down duvet—stood as it had when I'd last abandoned it for college. Sleeping over on nights when it was too late to make the long drive back to Hilton Head had always engendered ghosts and memories, most of which I'd spent my adulthood trying to suppress. Julia's presence somehow sent them all skittering into the far corners of the room.

"It's pretty," my sister said. She sat on the bed and ran her hand over the duvet. "I like it."

"You can sleep here if you want. While you're visiting."

"I think we're supposed to be in the same room," she said. "In case I get scared."

I joined her on the bed, kicking off my shoes and tucking my feet up under me.

Julia hesitated, then sloughed off her sandals and imitated my semi-lotus position.

"But why would you be scared? Lavinia stays here all the time. There's nothing to be afraid of."

She thought about that for a moment. "Miss Lizzie says it's always scary to be away from what you're used to. In a strange place." She sighed. "It's safe at home."

I resisted the urge to bolt down the stairs and give Miss Lizzie a good shaking. "Maybe sometimes. But this isn't a strange place. This is where I grew up, and nothing bad happened to me." It was a lie, but one offered up in a good cause. "You can just scootch down under the covers like I used to do and pretend you're anywhere you like. And Lavinia and Miss Lizzie will be right across the hall."

We fell into a comfortable silence for a few minutes. I wanted to let my sister get accustomed to the room. Somehow it had become very important to me that she spend her visit sleeping here. There was a symmetry to it that appealed to me. The curtains had been drawn against the afternoon glare, and it seemed once again the haven I had always thought it as a child. I forced myself not to jump when Julia's hand reached for mine.

"Miss Lizzie says you're my sister."

It wasn't exactly a question, but I could tell the idea still puzzled her.

"That's right. We both had the same father, but different . . ." I wasn't sure introducing the word *mothers* into the conversation was a good idea, but I couldn't figure out how to backtrack now that I'd begun. "We had different mothers," I finished softly.

"My mother died." She said it without any evidence of emotion.

I squeezed her fingers, wrapped tightly with mine. "I know. I'm sorry. Mine did, too."

"And my father. Miss Lizzie says he wasn't a very nice man."

I forced myself to speak calmly. "That's not exactly true. He was my father, too, and I loved him a lot. You would have liked him."

I waited, not quite prepared to answer all her questions but knowing I'd give it my best shot to be as truthful as I could be. There had already been more than enough innuendo and supposition. Neddie had told me not to try and pussyfoot around the tough answers. I drew in a deep breath and exhaled slowly.

"Do you have horses? Or dogs? I love dogs." Julia disentangled her fingers from mine and bounded off the bed. She rushed to the window and pulled back the curtains. "Oh, look, Bay! You can see the water from here. Is that the ocean? Is it warm? Can we swim? Miss Lizzie doesn't like me to swim, but she taught me how. I brought my new bathing suit, just in case."

I joined her at the window. "It's called St. Helena Sound." I pointed east. "The ocean's out that way. It's not too good for swimming here because of all the reeds and marsh grass. You'll have to come to my house . . . my other house. It's right on the ocean, and we can go swimming whenever we want."

"I'd like that. Dr. Halloran says I should start trying new things. She says I'm making progress."

It was said with a mixture of pride and a little undercurrent of fear. I squeezed her shoulder, and she smiled.

"I can tell. We'll see if Miss Lizzie will come to visit me while you're here, and I promise we'll go swimming in the ocean."

"I like having a sister," Julia said, hugging me back.

"Me, too."

I swallowed down the tears a moment before Lavinia's voice floated up the stairs. "Bay? Julia? Are you up there?"

"Coming," I called.

Once again we locked hands, and I could have sworn my sister's smile looked as conspiratorial as my own as we headed down the hallway.

CHAPTER
TWENTY-EIGHT

*T*HE DRIVE TO WALTERBORO TOOK LONGER THAN usual. Red had decided to take the back roads instead of the interstate, and we found ourselves stuck behind a school bus for mile after mile with no opportunity to pass. My husband grumbled and tapped his fingers on the steering wheel, but I decided to sit back and relax. Bugging him about it would only make his temper worse.

I closed my eyes, remembering our parting from Julia and Miss Lizzie. We'd come downstairs to find the table in the kitchen once again laid out, this time with slices of warm apple pie and mounds of vanilla ice cream on dessert plates. Julia squealed in delight and would have attacked hers if Lizzie hadn't restrained her with a firm hand on her arm. I wondered at the time if that wasn't part of Julia's problem, that she hadn't been allowed to express herself or act in anything other than the manner proscribed by her caretaker. Stuck out in the middle of nowhere at Covenant Hall, she'd probably never had much chance to interact with other adults on a social level. It seemed to me she'd be better off just finding her own way. Or I could be way off base. I'd have to ask Neddie about that.

"I'm going to sleep in Bay's room. In my sister's room," Julia had announced between bites of pie. "I like it there."

"That's fine," Lavinia said, but Lizzie cut her off.

"I thought we'd be sharing a room," she said. "Julia is bound to be nervous in a new environment."

"I'll just hide under the covers if I get scared," Julia said. "Like Bay used to do."

I'd avoided looking at Lavinia, who more than once had found me standing beside her bed in the middle of the night back in the days when my parents had been going at it hammer and tong. She'd always flicked aside the sheets and welcomed me in, spooning my small body against the warmth of her own. I hadn't told Julia that part. Maybe I should have.

"You'll be right across the hall, Miz Shelly. I'm sure it will be fine."

Lizzie frowned but kept silent. The first battle lines had been drawn, and I wondered how many more there'd be before things got ironed out.

I stretched and sighed. Not directly my problem, and it might be better for all concerned if I just butted out of the whole thing. If the three women had any chance of making a go of sharing the huge antebellum mansion, they'd have to work it out for themselves.

I had to admit they'd made a striking picture, the three of them standing on the verandah of Presqu'isle to wave us off. It might have been my imagination, but I thought Julia looked a little sad at my going.

We rolled into town just before four o'clock and found the real estate office on the main street. Gary Wheeler was young and eager, and he chattered nonstop the entire way to the first property. It was so close to downtown that we walked, and I noticed that the streets were fairly deserted. Several storefronts were boarded up, and I began to have se-

rious misgivings about what kind of place he was showing us. Until
he stopped in front of the gracious old home surrounded by a wrought-
iron fence. Azalea bushes lined the short walk to the wide front verandah, and the freshly painted siding carried up to the third floor.

"It's beautiful," I said. "But surely this isn't the place. I mean, we
only need an apartment."

"Yes, ma'am, that's what Chief Pickens said. This here's the old
Amiston place, been around since before the War. A couple from At-
lanta bought it and redid the whole thing, right down to modern
plumbing and electric. They even have it wired for cable."

"Is it a B and B?" I asked, thinking Red might do well in a place
like that.

"No, ma'am. They set it up in apartments. Four altogether. Two of
them have a full kitchen, and two just have a microwave and small refrigerator. Most of the tenants take breakfast together. It's mostly re-
tired folks. You know, those who can still look after themselves but
don't want to be ramblin' around in a big old house of their own."

Red glanced my way, and I grinned. "Ready for the home yet,
dear?" I asked, and he laughed.

"Maybe. It could be an ideal situation. Can we see inside?"

"Of course. Mrs. Trimble, the owner, is expecting us."

It turned out to be a perfect choice, and we didn't bother looking at any
of the other offerings. The apartment was on the second floor, in the
back, which meant none of the street noise would penetrate. Besides,
the windows looked out on a lovely garden, Maddy Trimble's pride and
joy, or so she announced.

"Everything grows so much better here than it does up in At-
lanta," she said in response to our praise for the neatly laid out islands
of flowering shrubs and annuals. The shade of two large oaks protected
the oasis and shielded it from view of the neighbors. I could almost

picture myself curled up in the hammock set along the back fence, reading and dozing away a summer afternoon.

"Now, this only has minimal kitchen amenities," the trim, sixty-ish woman said with a warm smile, "but you do have a private bath. And I serve a full breakfast every morning in the dining room. It's buffet style, so you can come and go as necessary for your job. The others—that would be Mr. Pratt and Mrs. Mulrooney—are both re-tired. The other unit on this floor is vacant, too, just at the moment."

Her voice had gone softer, and I wondered if both of the second-floor tenants had perhaps gone on to the big boarding house in the sky.

"I have a waiting list, you understand," Mrs. Trimble added, "but I told Chief Pickens I'd make an exception for his new assistant." She smiled at my husband. "Can't say I object to having a law enforcement officer on the premises. Just in case."

"What do you think?" Red asked as we made our way down the wide staircase, its oak banisters gleaming in the afternoon sun blazing through floor-to-ceiling windows flanking the solid front door.

"I think it's perfect. The only problem will be the kids. I think you're going to have to come back to the island on weekends. There's no room here for them to sleep."

Mrs. Trimble stopped and turned back to us. "Oh, I'm afraid we can't have children. My lady and gentleman are very used to the quiet. I hope you understand."

"That could be a problem," Red began, but I interrupted him.

"We could all meet at Presqu'isle. There's plenty of room, and it would be fun for all of us to be together. Julia will love the kids."

For some reason it had become important for me to be able to picture my husband in these gentle surroundings rather than in some cookie-cutter, sterile apartment. But it was his decision more than mine, so I'd waited for him to take the lead.

"I'll take it," he said, "providing we can do a six-month lease." His eyes found mine. "I'll need to have some flexibility in case . . . things don't work out."

"Of course, Mr. Tanner," the older lady said with a smile. "You won't have to bring anything with you but your personal belongings. All the linens and kitchen supplies are already included."

We'd spent about half an hour doing paperwork. I'd written the check for the deposit and first month's rent. Outside on the sidewalk again, we'd thanked Gary Wheeler and sent him on his way, that day's commission having been earned rather easily, I thought.

All the way home, we talked about what Red would need to take with him, how the problem of his visitation with the kids would be handled, and pulled into the driveway at a little past seven laden with optimism and Chinese takeout. I still had my doubts about how this new job and our living apart was going to play out, but the smile on Red's face and his obvious anticipation did a lot to push my misgivings to the back of my mind.

"So I'm thinking just one suitcase should hold everything," he said, laying his chopsticks across the rim of his plate. I'd never mastered the awkward utensils, but Red was a pro.

"You'll be in uniform all day," I said, "so that should work. You'll be eating out every night, but Walterboro doesn't look like a coat-and-tie kind of town. Polo shirts and shorts should get you by most of the time."

I glanced at the clock over the sink as we carried our used dishes to the counter. "I need to get cleaned up a little," I said over my shoulder. "I'm meeting Nick Potter at nine."

"I'll go with you."

Red's tone of voice made the hackles rise on the back of my neck, and I forced myself to speak calmly. "There's no need. I shouldn't be more than an hour."

He pulled open the door of the dishwasher and began loading it. "Is there some reason you don't want me there?"

I bit back the flood of annoyance. "No. But since you're about to hit the road for another job, I think I need to handle this on my own. I've done it a few times before, in case you've forgotten."

"I don't like you out running around at night all by yourself. Especially with some guy you don't know a damned thing about."

"Get used to it," I said, forcing myself to smile. "I'm not going to crawl into bed and pull the covers up over my head just because you're going to be out of town all week." The image reminded me of my conversation with Julia earlier in the day, and I wondered how the three women were getting along on their own.

I considered holding the rest of that thought but decided it needed to be said. I turned and wrapped my arms around my husband's neck. "Don't start getting overprotective on me, Red. I was doing this a long time before we got together, and I managed to survive."

"Barely." He hugged me back, hard. "I don't know what I'd do if anything happened to you."

"Nothing's going to happen," I said, resting my head against his shoulder. "Trust me a little, okay?"

"Famous last words," he said, with only a trace of humor.

I kissed him soundly and disengaged myself. "I need to get cleaned up." I turned and trotted down the three steps. "I'll be home before you know it," I called over my shoulder, peeling off my sweater as I made my way down the hall to the bathroom.

Back in the kitchen, I could hear my husband muttering to himself and thought it was probably good that I couldn't understand a word of it.

Twilight still lingered when I drove into the empty parking lot of the low building that housed our office. The glowing clock on the dash read 8:56. I pulled into a space right in front of the door and cut the engine. As I reached for my bag in the seat next to me, my cell rang.

"Bay Tanner."

I cringed a little when I heard Red's voice. "Hey, honey."

I told myself he wasn't checking up on me. "What's up?"

"What did you do with those papers from Mrs. Trimble? The lease and all that."

"They're on the desk in the kitchen. Why?"

"I just wanted to check a couple of things."

Right, I said to myself. "Okay. Talk to you later."

"Potter there yet?"

I bit my lower lip. "No. He may be running a little late. He said something about a family get-together with his uncles and cousins. I'll get some paperwork done while I'm waiting."

I grabbed my bag and slid out of the car as I spoke. The *beep* indicating the doors had been locked sounded unnaturally loud in the quiet darkness.

"Make sure you lock the door behind you," my husband said.

"I'll be back soon," I replied and disconnected.

I shook my head as I dropped the phone back into my bag and fumbled for the office key on my ring. Maybe it was good that Red would be spending time away from home, I thought. I didn't deal well with being checked up on or being smothered with concern, no matter how loving the intent. Our relationship might actually benefit from a little distance.

I inserted the key in the lock and pushed the door open. My hand felt for the light switch and found it a split second before something crashed into the back of my head, and I fell, facedown, onto the carpeted floor.

CHAPTER
TWENTY-NINE

I COULD HAVE BEEN OUT FOR A MINUTE OR AN HOUR. The first thing I noticed, besides the ache in the back of my head, was that it was dark. I knew I'd turned on the lights a moment before the attack, but they were off now. I lay sprawled in the middle of the carpet in the reception area. Gingerly, I rolled onto my side, then levered myself into a sitting position. The room swam around me for a moment, but my head cleared enough that I didn't sink back onto the floor. I took a deep breath and felt through the tangle of my hair to the small lump. It was painful, but my hand came away clean. No blood.

I scooted over closer to Erik's desk and used it to pull myself to my feet. I edged back toward the door—closed, I suddenly realized—and flipped on the lights. The stab of brightness made me wince. With trembling fingers, I turned the lock. Using the desk again for support, I shuffled around and sank into Erik's chair.

What in the hell just happened? The question rattled around in my pounding head as I checked myself for other injuries. I registered, dimly, that my knees hurt, and I pulled up the legs of my trousers to find brush burns. I'd been dragged across the carpet at some point while I'd been out, probably to get my feet out of the doorway. Nothing serious. I touched the knot on my head again, thankful that it didn't feel as if it was getting any bigger.

I needed aspirin. My bag lay across the room, its contents scattered, more as if it had spilled during my fall than that someone had rifled— I gasped at the sudden realization that, although my personal property had escaped, the office itself hadn't been so fortunate. The carpet was littered with paper, the drawers of Erik's desk yanked out, and their contents strewn across the floor.

I levered myself upright and slid my feet slowly in front of me. I didn't want to risk bending over, so I stooped and gathered everything back into my bag. As I slipped the Seecamp I now carried as a matter of routine into my pocket, it dawned on me to wonder if I was actually alone. I froze, my finger curling around the trigger of the small gun, and waited. I held my breath but heard nothing above the pounding of my own heart. Satisfied that my attacker had gotten what he came for and fled, I moved on to the restroom.

In the mirror, my dazed eyes stared back at me. I splashed cold water on my face, found the bottle of Excedrin in my bag and a paper cup in the small cabinet next to the sink, and downed three tablets.

The sharp rap on the outer door made my head snap up and sent a fresh wave of dizziness washing over me. A moment later, I heard the voice.

"Bay? It's me. Nick Potter. Are you in there?"

I patted my pocket, reassured by the small bulge of the gun, and moved slowly across the carpet.

"Bay?" he called again.

I twisted the lock and pulled open the door.

His gaze traveled quickly from my disheveled appearance to the storm of paper littering the floor of the office, and the bright smile died on his handsome face. "God Almighty, what happened?"

I felt his strong hands on my shoulders as he pulled me toward him, and I stumbled a little. In an instant, his arms were around me, supporting my weight. For just a few seconds, I relaxed in the feeling of warmth and safety and told myself it was relief that made my heart pound in my chest. Reluctantly, I finally wriggled free.

"Come in and close the door," I said. It sounded firm and steady inside my head, but I could hear the raspy squeak of the words when I said them aloud.

"Sit," Nick Potter said, guiding me to Erik's chair. He perched on the corner of the desk, his eyes grave with concern. He held my left hand in both of his, and I didn't pull away. "What the hell happened? Are you all right?"

"Someone attacked me just when I opened the door." My voice had gained some confidence, now that I wasn't alone. "I woke up a few minutes ago to find the place had been ransacked."

"Wait here." Nick released his grasp, then turned and made for my office. He flipped on the light.

From my vantage point in the reception area, I could see that my own desk and files had been similarly trashed.

"Did you leave your computer on?" Nick called.

"No. I always shut it down." I forced myself to my feet, grateful that the spinning sensation had subsided. I walked steadily into my office, my steps scattering papers in their wake.

The computer screen glowed with a list of files running in long columns across its face.

"Looks like someone may have been downloading stuff. I don't know enough about it to tell."

"Me either." I gazed stupidly at the screen, my muddled mind unable to grasp the significance of what lay in front of me.

"We need the cops." Nick reached for the phone.

"No! Wait!"

He hesitated, his steely blue eyes boring into mine. "What?"

"I need to speak to my husband first. I don't want him to hear about this from anyone else."

Nick Potter shrugged and moved his hand away from the phone. "Your call. But we should wait outside, shouldn't we? So we don't mess up any evidence?"

My brain was obviously still not firing on all cylinders. "You're right. I'll use my cell."

Nick tucked my arm up under his and guided me toward the door. It felt too comforting for me to pull away, and again I found myself leaning against him. Outside, he took the key from my icy fingers and locked the office behind us.

His huge SUV sat next to the Jaguar, and he led me toward it. I needed his help to climb up into the high interior, and I had to wait while he moved a slim bottle wrapped in a brown paper bag before I could sink into the wide leather seat. Apparently, he hadn't been kidding about bringing the wine. It took me a moment to fumble my cell phone out of my bag. Nick joined me as I hit the speed-dial for my home number.

Red answered on the second ring. "Bay? You on your way home?"

In as few words as possible, I told him about the attack and the desecration of my office. He said only three words: "Call the sheriff."

He didn't have to tell me that he was on his way.

In the few minutes we had, I tried to bring Nicholas Potter up to date on Cecelia Dobbs's supposed suicide and what that might mean for the investigation into Kendra Blaine, but he didn't seem interested.

"That can wait. Maybe we should go to the emergency room," he said, his hand hovering over the key in the ignition.

"We have to wait for the sheriff. Besides, I'm fine." I managed a smile as my hand again traced the lump on the back of my head. "Well, I will be when this damn headache goes away."

"You could have a concussion. Or a subdural hematoma." He blushed a little at my raised eyebrows. "Okay, maybe too many episodes of *ER* and *Grey's Anatomy.*"

"I'm a *Law and Order* junkie myself," I said. My head jerked around at the sudden stab of flashing red lights behind us. "Looks like the cavalry has arrived."

I'd been running a silent prayer inside my head that it wouldn't be Detective Lisa Pedrovsky who climbed out of the second, unmarked car that roared into the parking lot behind the cruisers. Someone must have been listening, because it was a man I didn't recognize, his sharply pressed dress shirt a blaze of white in the darkness. I had a moment to register that he looked too young to be a detective when the door next to me was suddenly jerked open.

"Bay!"

I hadn't seen Red's Bronco pull into the lot. My husband scooped me up and into his arms as easily as if I were one of his kids. I clung back for a few seconds before easing out of his grasp.

"I'm fine, Red. Just a bump on the head. But they trashed the office."

"Screw the office! We need to get you to a doctor."

I stepped farther back and rested my hands on his shoulders. "Take a breath. I'm okay. Let's not make a scene in front of them." I inclined my head in the direction of the knot of deputies surrounding the guy in civilian clothes. He caught my eye and moved toward us.

"Mrs. Tanner? I'm Detective Michael Raleigh. Are you injured? Oh, hey, Sergeant," he added when Red turned.

"Mike." They shook hands.

"A bump on the head that knocked me out for a little while."

"Any idea how long?" The detective whipped out a notebook and pen from the breast pocket of his shirt.

I looked back at Nick Potter, who had been sitting unnoticed in the driver's seat of the Expedition. "What time did you get here, Nick?"

Beside me, I felt Red stiffen, but he kept quiet.

"A little before nine thirty. I could kick myself for being late. If I'd shown up on time, I might have been able to—"

I cut him off. "I walked in at almost exactly nine o'clock, and I'd been conscious for a few minutes before Mr. Potter arrived. So, twenty minutes? Maybe less."

"You have the key?" Mike Raleigh asked.

I handed over my ring. "The silver one with the square edges."

He in turn passed it to one of the deputies. "Check it out. Make sure the interior's secure."

I watched the deputy unholster his sidearm. Behind him, his partner did the same. No one spoke as they pushed open the door and pierced the darkness inside with their powerful Maglites. I held my breath, although I knew the place was empty, until one of them called, "All clear, Detective."

"If you'd come this way, Mrs. Tanner." Raleigh led me toward his unmarked car.

I was pleased to find myself feeling steady on my feet, but Red kept a tight hold on my arm nonetheless. Behind me, I heard the door of the Expedition slam shut.

Raleigh turned back. "Mr. . . . ?"

"Potter. Nicholas Potter."

"If you'd wait there, sir, I'll be back to take your statement in a moment."

"No problem."

I looked over my shoulder to see Nick stretch his long frame against the front of the SUV.

"Now, Mrs. Tanner. Can you tell me exactly what happened?"

I recited the details of my attack. It took less than a minute. Red ran his hand along my arm as I talked, and I found myself wishing he'd back off a little. I didn't have time to examine why his hovering presence was getting on my nerves.

"And you didn't see anyone? Hear anything before you were struck?"

I forced myself to concentrate on those few seconds just before the lights went out, both literally and figuratively. "No, I'm sorry. I can't think where he could have been hiding." We all turned to look at the front of the building. "It had to have been behind that crape myrtle. There wasn't another car in the parking lot, and I would have heard someone running across the blacktop. It was dead quiet."

"We'll check it for footprints, but it's been pretty dry the last few days. Okay, so what's missing from inside?"

The thought of going through every piece of paper we'd ever accumulated over the years Simpson & Tanner had been in operation made me shudder. I didn't pull away this time when Red threw his arm around my shoulder.

"It's going to take a long time to figure that out. It's a total mess in there. He . . . they booted up my computer. It was running when Nick got here."

"Did they access any files?" Raleigh asked.

"I don't know. Everything's passworded. My partner—" I jumped at the realization. "Erik will be able to tell if anything's been tampered with." I reached in my pocket for my cell phone and suddenly realized that the Seecamp was nestled there beside it. "Uh, Detective, I should tell you that I'm armed. I'm going to reach in and remove my pistol."

I did it slowly and deliberately, and I could feel the tension in the detective until I had offered it to him, butt first. The small gun almost disappeared in his large hand.

"Thank you, Mrs. Tanner." He turned and reached through the open window of the unmarked to lay it on the front seat. "You were saying about your partner?"

This time I pulled out the cell phone. "Erik Whiteside. He's the computer expert. He should be here."

"Call him. Tell him to park over there." He pointed to the far side of the lot. "Excuse me then, ma'am. I want to take a look around inside. If you'll wait here?"

It was a question, but I knew he wasn't giving me options. I rubbed my hands across my eyes and leaned against my husband.

"You want to sit down, honey?"

"I'm okay," I said for what felt like the millionth time that night. "Let me call Erik."

"I'll do that." Red took the phone from my hand and began punching numbers.

I moved a little away, out of the glare from the outside security lights. *Not much security,* I thought. My gaze wandered to the open door of my office. Inside, I could see some of the papers lifting in the breeze that had sprung up in the warm autumn night. I caught movement and shifted my attention to Nick Potter, leaning casually against his SUV. Beside me, I heard Red relaying the details of the break-in to Erik.

Nick turned his head, and our eyes met. It felt as if he was trying to convey some message, but my fuzzy brain couldn't begin to interpret it. I glanced again at Red and realized that was probably a good thing.

CHAPTER THIRTY

$\mathcal{B}$Y THE TIME THE FINGERPRINT GUYS AND WHAT seemed like the entire Beaufort County Sheriff's Office finally left us alone, it was well past midnight, and I felt as if I might just collapse onto the surface of the Judge's old desk and sleep for a week.

Photographs had been taken, so Red and Erik and I had gathered up all the scattered papers and stacked them in neat piles on the tops of the filing cabinets. It would take days to sort through everything, and none of us had the energy even to think about it. Nick Potter had offered to help, but Detective Mike Raleigh had asked him to come down to the substation. Erik and I had been printed for our PI license, and Red's would naturally be on file. They needed to eliminate Nick's.

I didn't hold out much hope that it would prove helpful. A lot of people were in and out of our offices, and there was no way to account for all the prints they might have left. They did take my keyboard and mouse since it was obvious someone had used them to try and access our files. Luckily, Erik kept spares in the small storage closet next to the restroom. Once we'd managed to clean up most of the gray print dust, he began downloading software onto my hard drive. He guaranteed that, once everything was installed, he could tell which—if any—of the files had been accessed or copied.

Red and I left him to it.

We carried Diet Cokes out into the reception area. A quick check of Red's small cubicle with its desk barren of anything but a phone and a gooseneck lamp showed the intruder had left it pretty much alone. It must have been immediately obvious that there were no files or anything else worth rifling. I sat down in the swivel chair while my husband slid one hip onto the edge of the desk.

"We should go home, honey," he said, concern heavy in his voice. "You look like something the cat dragged in."

It was an old, familiar expression of Lavinia's, and it made me smile. "Thank you, Red. I feel so much better for knowing that."

"Any idea who it might have been? Or what he was looking for?"

"No." I ran both hands through my tangled mass of hair and gently massaged my scalp. The headache hadn't yielded to the aspirin, and I wondered if I could safely pop a few more. "Cecelia's death, maybe. But it isn't generally known that I think she was murdered. I haven't exactly taken out an ad in the *Packet*. You. Erik. And Pedrovsky, of course. She might have broadcast my suspicions, but I have no idea why. Or to whom, other than around the sheriff's office."

"How about the Blaine woman? Or Chambers?"

I thought about my phone call to the Castlemain home earlier in the day, the call Kendra Blaine had answered. The idea that I might have brought this on myself by virtue of my own carelessness made me angry.

"I suppose it's possible," I said, unwilling at that point to share my blunder. "But what would be the motive? I mean, even if one of them found every scrap of paper and computer file relating to the investigation, that wouldn't stop me. I've still got my brain, scrambled though it is right now. And Erik's. And yours, for that matter. I mean, what would they have hoped to accomplish? Trashing the office and stealing files wouldn't solve anything. For them, I mean."

Red sipped from his Coke, one leg swinging back and forth as he thought about it. "Then there's Potter," he said, not looking at me.

"What about him?"

"He showed up pretty conveniently after it was all over."

"Red, get over this thing you have about Nick, okay? He showed up because we had an appointment. Quit trying to make something sinister out of it." I sighed and forced myself to stand. "Let's go grab Erik and get the hell out of here. I'm about ready to drop."

I let him take my hand and lead me back toward my office. We found my partner hunched over my computer, his fingers flying across the new keyboard.

"Hey," I said, and he looked up. "Let's call it a day. We can get back at this after a good night's sleep, what do you say?"

"You guys go ahead. I've got the scanning program up and running. I want to monitor it for a while."

"I don't like leaving you here alone," I said. "What if they come back?"

"Why would they?" Red interrupted. "They had plenty of time while you were unconscious. Besides, if they hadn't gotten what they wanted, they wouldn't have left."

It sounded logical, but I wasn't thinking. My reactions were pure gut instinct driven by anger and fear. I could hear my voice trembling on the edge of tears.

"I don't care. I'm not leaving Erik here alone."

"Okay, how about this?" Red stroked the fingers of the hand he held tightly. "I'll take you home and come back until Erik's finished."

My partner shook his head. "That's okay. You're probably right. The program will run without me, and it's going to take a couple of hours. I'll go home."

The relief made my knees wobble a little. "Good. That's good."

We waited while he gathered up his disks and typed a few lines into my computer. I paused outside, surveying the now bare carpet for a moment before I turned off the lights. On the surface, everything looked back to normal, but I knew it wasn't. It would be a long time before I walked back into my office without flinching in anticipation of another blow to the back of my head. The place had been violated, and the aura of it would linger.

"Leave the Jag." Red spoke softly. "We'll drive in together tomorrow."

I wanted to protest, but I knew I probably shouldn't be driving after a crack on the head. "All right. Erik, did you get any sense of what they were after?"

"Not yet." In the glow of the outside light, I could see his head had dropped, and he wouldn't look at me directly.

"What? You've found something, haven't you?"

"No! I mean . . . There's something I should probably tell you. It may not have anything to do with this, but then again . . ."

I waited. Beside me, I could feel that Red's body had tensed.

"You know who might have done this?" my husband asked. "Or why?"

Erik spoke softly. "This afternoon, after you guys left for Presqu'isle, I talked to the woman at the shelter."

I didn't have to fake my confusion. "And?"

"I went over there and met with her." His chin came up. "You told me to take the case and run with it."

I leaned against the front fender of the Jaguar. "Yes, I did. So why are you being defensive about it? Did something happen?"

"Not exactly. She didn't want to take me to the actual shelter until after we'd had a chance to talk, so I met her at the Fig Tree. We had Cokes and talked. She seemed pretty jumpy, looking around all the time as if she was afraid of being overheard."

"Doesn't sound like much so far," Red interrupted, and I shushed him.

"Go on, Erik."

"Well, she gave me some names. Of some of the husbands and boyfriends she thinks might be responsible for the trouble at the shelter. She slid the paper over to me under her napkin." His smile dispelled some of my anxiety. "It felt like something out of a James Bond movie."

My brain had been on autopilot for the last few hours, but it hadn't completely deserted me. "And you brought that paper back with you. Is it still here? Did you find it in the mess?"

He reached into his back pocket and pulled it out. "I didn't come back to the office afterward. I checked for messages from my cell. Stephanie and I had plans, and I was worried I was going to be late."

"So you didn't open a file or transcribe anything to the computer."

"Right. If this had anything to do with the shelter, whoever broke in was disappointed."

"It's not your fault, Erik," I said, "even if it was someone who figured out what was going on from your meeting today." I tried to swallow the yawn, but it sneaked out anyway. "Besides, I don't think that can have been it. It's too soon for someone to have figured out the connection and be worried enough about it to break into the office." Something niggled at the back of my brain, but almost immediately the phantom thought slithered away. I sighed. "Let's all get some sleep and tackle this in the morning."

"I should have told you about the meeting," Erik said.

"You would have. Go home and quit blaming yourself. It probably has absolutely nothing to do with the shelter."

I could see his relief washing the tension from his shoulders.

"See you tomorrow. I'll try to get here early and check on the program."

"Good night," I said and let Red lead me to the Bronco.

Once strapped in, I fought all the way home to keep my eyes open. Ten minutes after we walked in the door, I had fallen into a deep but troubled sleep. I dreamed of a blizzard of luminescent paper floating through the deserted office.

And a single pair of gleaming eyes staring straight at me out of the darkness.

CHAPTER
THIRTY-ONE

*I*N SPITE OF EVERYTHING, I CAME WIDE AWAKE AT seven thirty. Beside me, Red grumbled and rolled over, gathering me into his arms. For a few minutes I let the warmth and comfort of his body hold me there in our bed, the memory of the night before safely held at bay by the rhythmic rise and fall of his chest against my cheek. I hadn't wakened in the early hours to roam the house as I'd been doing for the past couple of weeks. Perhaps whatever had been plaguing my unconscious mind had been resolved in some way I wasn't aware of.

Or maybe getting conked on the head had driven it even deeper.

I eased out of my husband's embrace and swung my feet onto the carpeted floor.

"Where you going?"

I turned back. "To the shower. I suggest you do the same."

"Uh-huh," he mumbled and rolled back over.

I smiled to myself while the steaming spray of the shower and the bright sunshine cascading through the skylight chased away some of the terror of the night before. Half an hour later, dressed and fortified with tea and peanut butter, I felt ready to tackle the morning. The headache had receded to manageable proportions. Red joined me in the kitchen and poured coffee from the pot I'd made him.

"Thanks," he said, waving the cup in my direction. "You doing okay?"

"Fine. You want some breakfast?"

"No thanks. We'll swing by McDonald's on the way in and grab a couple of Egg McMuffins."

"It's your stomach," I said, flipping the morning paper to the sheriff's report. "Nothing in here about the break-in."

Red slurped coffee, leaning against the counter. "Too soon. Besides, it's not technically a break-in. You unlocked the door."

I didn't dignify that with an answer. I was relieved to find my husband a little less inclined to fuss over me, hovering as if he was afraid I'd disappear.

"You ready? I want to see what Erik's program turned up. If anything."

Red set his cup in the sink and turned off the coffeemaker. "Let's rock and roll."

Because of the number of offices located in our building just outside Indigo Run, the parking lot was generally close to full. That morning, however, we pulled in to find not a single available space. A quick scan of the vehicles told me that at least one of the interlopers belonged to the sheriff. The sparkling white Crown Victoria with its lack of frills screamed unmarked cop car. Red had to squeeze the Bronco in among the trees.

We stepped inside to find the reception area looking as if we were throwing a party. Detective Mike Raleigh chatted with Erik. In the far corner, Lisa Pedrovsky pointedly ignored Gabby Henson, who was firing questions at her a mile a minute. I almost turned around and walked back out, but Red's hand on my elbow propelled me into the melee.

Conversation ground to a halt at our entrance. Gabby was the first to pounce.

"Bay! Did you see your attacker? Was anything stolen? Whose chain have you rattled enough to make them come after you this time?"

"Back off," Detective Lisa Pedrovsky said, interposing her body between Gabby's and mine. "This is an official interrogation, not open to the press. You'll have to leave."

Mike Raleigh looked at his feet, clearly uncomfortable with his colleague's gruff treatment of the reporter. He obviously didn't know Gabby.

"This is private property, Detective. You have no more right to be here than I do. It's Bay's call."

Her eager eyes found mine, almost daring me to throw her out. I ignored the unspoken challenge—ignored everyone in fact—and picked my way through the crowd to my office. Erik followed, and I shut the door. Outside I could hear Red trying to calm the natives, assuring them that I just needed a few minutes with my partner. Pedrovsky's strident voice trumped everyone else's with her demands that I get my butt back out there this minute. Apparently the truce I'd thought we'd struck had already been torn up and tossed away.

I dumped my bag on the desk and collapsed into the chair. "When did all this start?" I asked.

Erik remained standing. "They were waiting for me when I showed up around eight thirty. I didn't know if I should call and warn you, but they didn't give me a chance."

I glanced at my computer screen, now staring blankly back at me. I gestured at it. "You find anything?"

"No. I mean, none of the files were accessed or downloaded. I think whoever it was didn't have the knowledge to get any farther than they did. The passwords probably defeated them. Or maybe they heard you coming around and got scared and ran. All I can say for certain is that nothing was compromised."

"That's good." My gaze strayed to the piles of paper on the file cabinets. "But we still don't know about those."

"True. Listen, I hope it was okay, but I asked Stephanie to come in and help us sort through everything. She's off today."

"That's fine." I sighed and straightened my shoulders. "Let's get this over with. I want these people out of my office."

He opened the door. Red turned, and our eyes met. I nodded, and he led the two detectives in as Erik slipped back out. Gabby Henson would just have to wait.

Although Mike Raleigh had caught the call the night before, Lisa Pedrovsky seemed determined to take over the case. I held my tongue, answering her staccato questions with patience and honesty. At one point, she insisted that she wanted to go through our files—ostensibly to see if they might provide a lead. I looked at her in amazement for a moment, then reached for the phone.

"What are you doing?" she'd snapped.

"Calling my attorney. She can explain to you that these are confidential work product, and you have no right to them. Unless a judge gives you a subpoena, which I'm pretty sure isn't going to happen with what you've got so far."

"You're right, of course, Mrs. Tanner." Raleigh, though at least a decade younger than Pedrovsky, seemed to be the more mature one of the pair. "We're only trying to establish a motive that might lead us to the intruder." He'd paused then. "You'll let us know if you discover anything missing that might bear on the case."

It wasn't a question, but I nodded anyway.

A few minutes later, they left, having parted with no information about the results of the fingerprint tests or anything else I might have found useful. For the first time, I regretted Red's having quit the department.

The cops left the door to my office open, and I could hear Red and Gabby Henson chattering away, her raucous laugh more irritating than usual. I was glad someone was having a good time.

"Gabby?" I called, and she turned. "You've got five minutes. Make them count."

Her notebook was already filled with illegible scribbling when she plopped into the chair in front of my desk, and I wondered how much she'd managed to pry out of my husband.

"You have the specifics?" I asked before she could get cranked up.

"Yeah, got all that from the duty officer at the substation. What I want is background. Your handsome husband says you were meeting a client here last night. Want to expand on that?"

"No. Here's what you need to know: I didn't see my attacker. He struck me from behind just as I unlocked the door. I was out for maybe twenty minutes. When I came to, I found the office trashed. I haven't yet determined what, if anything, was taken."

I leaned back in my chair and steepled my fingers under my chin. I had no hope that the reporter would thank me and be on her way. She didn't disappoint me.

"So which case do you think brought this on? Whose toes have you stepped on recently?"

"I don't know for certain that it had anything to do with one of our cases. And you know damn well I'm not talking to you about them anyway." I paused while she scribbled. "It could just have been some punk looking for something to steal. For drugs or whatever."

Her snort would have done the Judge proud. "Come on, Tanner. I haven't fallen off the back of any cabbage trucks lately. Unless you've started hoarding hundred-dollar bills or stashing hot diamonds around here, what else could it be about? You're in the information business, right? And someone wanted to know what you know."

I refused to be baited. I'd spent too much time around Gabby not to be way too familiar with her tactics. "Thanks for coming. If I come across anything you can use, I'll give you a call."

She must have sensed I wasn't going to be bullied. Or cajoled. "As if I haven't heard that song before," she said, rising. When she spoke again, much of the bantering tone had left her voice. "If I can help, Bay, let me know. I don't like people beating up on my friends."

"Thanks, Gabby. I'll tell you what I can, when I can."

"Good enough." At the door, she paused and turned back. "Try to stay off the floor," she offered a moment before she disappeared outside.

We retrieved Cokes from the mini-fridge and convened around my desk. Erik gave us a more detailed report of the results of his scan of my hard drive, but the bottom line remained that nothing had been accessed.

"Okay," I said, "here's the game plan. We still have a business to run. The detectives have a better chance at finding out who did this, so I don't want us to get distracted. Let's leave them to it. Erik, I think you should get all the information from the women's shelter recorded, but don't put anything on paper. Do whatever you have to do to make sure the data's secure, and don't transfer it to my machine. You take your laptop with you every night, so that should keep it safe."

"That was my idea, too."

"Good. Now, at some point I'd like to be brought up to date on how you plan to handle that case, but for now it's your baby. Do what you think is right, and I'll be here if you want to run anything by me."

"Thanks," my partner said. "So where do we stand on Blaine and Chambers? Did Nick Potter say if he still wants to go forward?"

I glanced at Red, who relaxed back in his chair, one long leg hitched across the other knee. For once he hadn't bristled at the mention of Nick's name.

"He does. I didn't have much chance to fill him in on everything last night, but he did say that he thinks it's more important than ever to get his grandfather out of Blaine's clutches. As for Dalton Chambers, we've lost our one good source at the bank."

I swallowed hard, and we all took a moment to remember why that was. I felt more than ever convinced that the death of Cecelia Dobbs was connected to the scam and the Castlemains, but—for now—the living took precedence. I still held out hope that the coroner would eventually rule it a homicide, although I had no idea how long that decision might take. For now, I would pursue the other side of the equation and hope to unearth information that might lead me to a killer.

"Red, do you think you can find out if they've located Cecelia's car yet? Maybe Mike Raleigh could clue you in. He seems like a decent guy."

"He is," my husband said. "He just got promoted, so he's a little touchy about not screwing up, but I've always had a good relationship with him." He stood. "I'll see if I can take him out for coffee."

"Good. Call me if he has anything we can use." He hesitated in the doorway. "What?" I asked.

"I may have to run up to Walterboro this afternoon. Joe Pickens called while you were in here with the detectives." His gaze slid away from mine. "I may have to start earlier than we thought." He paused, his shoulders hunched as if expecting me to throw something at him.

I let my head drop into my hands and massaged my temples. I reached to rub a smudge of fingerprint powder that still lingered on the edge of my desk, and suddenly jerked upright.

"I'm an idiot!" I said, refraining from smacking myself in the forehead in deference to the dull, lingering pain there.

Red and Erik exchanged a look. I ignored them and reached for my purse. I rummaged around for a moment before I pulled the wrinkled plastic bag from its depths. The bill in its crisp white sleeve lay nestled inside.

"Gabby said she didn't believe someone would have been ransacking the office for hundred-dollar bills. I should have picked up on that the minute she said it."

Red got it immediately. "Chambers' fingerprints. I should have thought of it, too."

"So we can give this to Detective Raleigh for comparison?" Erik reached for the bag and took it by the corner, passing it along to Red.

"I don't think so," my husband said.

"What do you mean? If they match any that came from here, we'll have our guy." I lowered my voice. "Chambers has never been inside this office for any legitimate reason."

"There's no chain of custody. They only have our word that any prints on here belong to Chambers."

"Why the hell would we lie about it?"

Red retained his calm in the face of my mounting anger. "That's not the point, honey. Even if they found a match, it would be totally inadmissible in a court of law."

"Then the law is useless! When the criminals have more rights than the people they bash over the head, the whole damn system's a sham."

I dropped my head back into my hands, fully aware I was being unreasonable. It felt good. If I couldn't get my hands on the piece of pond scum that attacked me, I could at least vent my frustration.

I felt Red's hand drop gently onto my shoulder. "Why don't you go home and lie down? Erik can handle things here."

I drew a long, calming breath and got my temper under control. "I'll be fine. You go do what you have to do."

"Tell you what," my husband said. "Why don't I take this with me up to Walterboro? I can probably get Joe to run it for me, as a courtesy. It won't help with nailing Chambers for the attack, but maybe we can get a handle on who he really is."

"Thank you," I said, my anger receding under Red's calm voice. "I'm sorry about—"

He kissed the top of my head. "No problem. I'll talk to you soon."

He turned and disappeared out the door.

"I can be such a bitch," I said, mostly to myself, but Erik's laugh broke the tension.

"I think you're entitled, under the circumstances."

We both looked up as the outer door opened, and Ben Wyler's daughter stepped into the reception area. She must have passed Red on his way out. In a flash, Erik crossed the carpet. I could tell he wanted to hug her, but he wasn't sure if this was the right time. Or place. His obvious discomfort made me smile.

"Hey, Stephanie. How are you?"

They walked hand in hand toward me, and I could see the shine of their happiness, almost like an aura around them.

"Hello, Bay." She'd begun to pick up a little Southern drawl that softened the harsher New York accent her father had never lost. "I'm sorry about what happened to you. Are you sure you're all right?"

"I'm fine. Thanks for coming in. Erik can show you what needs done."

She had a sweet smile. Her dark hair had been pulled up into a ponytail. Slim and athletic, her head came just to Erik's shoulder. For a moment I pictured her as I'd first seen her, standing in front of Starbucks, her father's arm draped casually across her shoulder. So much had happened—

"Then let's get to work. Where do we start?" Her bright words cut off my gloomy thoughts, and not a moment too soon.

"I'd set out the empty folders in some kind of order, then sort the papers into them." I checked myself. "But you guys figure out whatever system works for you." I pulled my bag onto my shoulder. "I'm going to bail on you for a while, but I'll be back, hopefully by lunchtime."

Erik didn't ask, but he had a right to know.

"I have an appointment with Nick Potter. At Canaan's Gate."

CHAPTER
THIRTY-TWO

*T*HE PASS WAS WAITING FOR ME AT THE WEXFORD
security gate, just off the roundabout that also led to the complex of buildings housing the Town of Hilton Head offices. I'd once
served jury duty on a domestic dispute case in the municipal court
there. I smiled to myself, remembering that I'd ended up wishing both
parties could have been thrown in the slammer until they grew up.

As I wound through the lush landscape of the most exclusive en-
clave on the island, I tried to remember the last time I'd had occasion
to enter this bastion of wealth and privilege. It might have been some
sort of charity fundraiser at the beautiful clubhouse overlooking the
harbor, something Bitsy had probably roped me into attending.

I'd been told or read somewhere that the original developers of
Wexford had been aiming for the ambiance of Bermuda in the British
colonial days, and the first homes I passed seemed to have fulfilled the
dream. Stately mansions in pastel stucco sported gleaming white columns and porticoes standing watch over rolling lawns and subtropical
landscaping. Farther in, I encountered some deviations from the theme:
Williamsburg brick and the occasional French chateau, all screened
from their neighbors by walls of shrubbery, live oaks, and royal palms.

Following Nick's directions, I made a couple of turns and located the Castlemain estate at the end of a cul-de-sac. The huge wrought-iron gates that apparently gave the house its name were flung open to a short drive that ended in a circle surrounding a classic fountain. Beyond lay another, smaller gate. Through it I could see a courtyard riotous with flowers. The house itself, looking as if it had been airlifted from the rolling hills of Tuscany and dropped down intact in the heart of Hilton Head, rose in two stories of creamy stone that glistened in the late morning sunlight.

There were no other cars in the drive, and I hoped Kendra Blaine had been sent off on some errand. Through the screening trees I could see a smaller version of the magnificent villa, probably a guesthouse. Maybe that's where she stayed. I admired the bougainvillea spreading next to the walkway as I pushed through the small gate. I pressed the doorbell and heard its chimes ringing deep in the house.

I breathed a sigh of relief when the door opened, not on Kendra Blaine, but on a trim black woman in nurse's whites. She smiled when she saw me.

"Mrs. Tanner?" She seemed surprised to encounter me on the doorstep of Canaan's Gate, but she recovered quickly. "Please, come in. It's good to see you again."

Cady Proffit stepped aside a moment before Nick Potter came trotting down a spectacular stone staircase that swept upward in a long, graceful curve.

"You, too, Mrs. Proffit," I said, shaking her slender hand. "How is Kimmie Eastman doing?"

The two of us had met when she'd been hired to care for a client's daughter, a teenager with a rare form of leukemia.

"Still in remission and back at school, last I heard," the woman said with an even wider smile. "Playing tennis again, too."

"That's wonderful. Hello, Nick."

He stood behind Cady Proffit, who apparently hadn't heard his approach. When no one spoke, she got the message and slipped discreetly away.

"Bay. Come on in. Welcome to Canaan's Gate."

While he ushered me across the wide entryway, I darted quick glances around. The whole area was flooded with light, the walls hung with Impressionist paintings in soft pastels of lavender and pink, their color matching the veins in the gleaming marble floors. As we passed an open doorway, a voice halted us.

"Nicky? Who's at the door?"

Beside me, I felt Nick Potter stiffen. He hurried me into a beautiful sitting room with an antique writing desk almost identical to the one my mother had used for her correspondence. An escritoire, she'd called it, if I remembered correctly. The windows looked out on a smooth expanse of lawn with another fountain glistening in the sunlight.

"Have a seat. I'll be right back."

Nick left me to roam among the treasures in what must have been his grandmother's domain, to judge by the delicacy of the furniture and the abundance of bibelots and small porcelain figurines. The silver laptop computer, open on the desk, looked entirely out of place. I meandered, my fingers brushing the folds of a pale yellow cashmere throw arranged carelessly on the back of the empire love seat. On a low, spindly legged table, a pair of wire-rim glasses lay next to an open book.

I looked up as Nick came back into the room.

"Sorry about that. I thought Granddad was still upstairs. He doesn't usually come down until lunch." He flipped his hand toward the love seat, and I sat.

"I assume you don't want him to know why I'm here."

"I told him you work for the appraisers."

That startled me. "Appraisers? Surely you're not thinking of selling any of this?"

Nick ran a hand through his thick hair before joining me on the narrow sofa. "I don't know what we're going to do. My grandfather certainly can't stay here alone. Grandma was the one who held it all together. He'll be utterly lost here without her." He paused for a beat. "And I'm sure as hell not leaving Kendra Blaine in charge."

"Where is she?"

"I sent her out to get Granddad's prescriptions refilled. I've taken charge of them. Well, actually Mrs. Proffit has. She's going to go over everything with his doctors and make sure he's not being given something he doesn't need. Or that might harm him."

He jumped at the sound of hard-soled shoes on the steps of the marble staircase. He rose quickly and shut the door.

"One of my uncles," he said by way of explanation. "They were all supposed to be gone this morning, but Wendell and his bitch of a wife are having a hard time tearing themselves away."

His face darkened as he rejoined me on the love seat, and I leaned away from him a little. He noticed, and visibly relaxed his shoulders.

"Sorry about that," he said, his devastating smile once again lighting the room.

"What is it you wanted to show me?" I asked, glancing pointedly at my watch. It seemed as if we would have no opportunity for a long, detailed examination of the Castlemain finances, something I'd been itching to get my hands on and what Nick had promised me in our hastily made plans the night before. If I had their bank statements and broker's reports, I might be well on my way to proving the validity of Cecelia's suspicions. And perhaps to finding out who killed her.

Nick rose and crossed the faded Aubusson carpet to the dainty desk. From the center drawer, he pulled a small silver oblong of metal and held it out to me. Thanks to Erik, I actually knew what it was.

"Flash drive? You've downloaded the records?"

"No, they were all on here to begin with. There's nothing on the hard drive except e-mails. Apparently my grandmother didn't trust . . . Anyway, she liked to keep this with her."

I stood and took it from him. "I'm surprised your grandparents were . . . are so tech-savvy."

"My grandmother was the one who loved all these gadgets. She hired a man to come in and teach her all about them. I wasn't able to access any of the files—they're passworded—but I thought maybe your partner would have better luck. Granddad is completely ignorant about any of this, and I certainly don't want to ask Kendra any more about it. She's the one who told me that the financial records were all stored on that drive."

It was better than nothing, I decided, a link between Blaine and the Castlemains' finances, but I'd been hoping for something more. Maybe the flash drive would give me the answers. "Can you come to the office this afternoon? There's a lot we have to discuss, and it doesn't look as if doing it here is going to work out. It shouldn't take Erik long to crack the passwords."

"Sorry about that. I thought we'd have the house pretty much to ourselves."

I shrugged. "Can't be helped. Will one thirty work for you?"

"I'll make it work," he said, his easy charm once again exerting itself. "Unless you'll let me buy you lunch? As I said before, the club is spectacular. You know, they have a system of locks here that allows the boats to go in and out at low tide, and the dining room overlooks the harbor. It's a beautiful setting."

I moved around him to the door, slipping the flash drive into my pocket. "Maybe another time."

As my hand closed around the knob, he reached from behind, crowding me up against the panel. His fingers covered mine. I could feel his breath in my hair. Once again, his proximity sent my heart rate climbing.

"Sorry." He leaned past me through the open doorway. "Just checking to make sure the coast is clear."

I could hear the laughter in his voice, and I cursed myself for the flush I could feel staining my cheeks. *Get a grip, Tanner.* Nicholas Potter was a handsome, charming, apparently wealthy man who spent his time among the political elite. Or so I assumed. He was probably used to having women swoon into his arms at the slightest hint of invitation. Like most male animals, he was constantly on the prowl. I ordered myself not to react, although I felt sure he could sense the heat of my embarrassment radiating off me in waves.

Business, I told myself, *it's just business.* If I wanted to help his grandfather escape Kendra Blaine's clutches, I had to view Nick as a necessary distraction.

I had taken only a couple of steps when the voice once again drifted from the open door on my left. "Nicky? Bring your guest in here."

I glanced back to see annoyance flicker in Nick Potter's eyes. Then he shrugged and smiled. I stepped away from his hand, warm on the small of my back, and into what could only have been the library, its dark furniture bathed in that same soft light so prevalent in the other rooms. Two walls, from floor to ceiling, held hundreds of books, many in cracked leather bindings. I itched for a chance to examine them, but Nick urged me forward to where his grandfather sat, his thin frame all but swallowed up by the leather wing chair.

"Hello, Mr. Castlemain, I'm Bay Tanner. We met at the memorial service on Friday."

"How nice to see you again," he said, his voice sounding much stronger than it had in the fellowship hall of the church.

"No, please, sir. Don't get up."

He subsided back into the deep leather chair. "Old bones," he said with an endearing smile. "The curse of aging. Won't you sit down?"

Nick pulled up a smaller club chair, and I nodded my thanks.

"May I offer you something to drink?" Thomas Castlemain asked. "Coffee, perhaps?" Before I could demur, he said, "Iced tea, I think. Go see to it, Nicky."

Nick hesitated, seeming unsure of whether or not he should leave me alone with his grandfather, but the old man's stare didn't offer him much choice. He spun on his heel and nearly trotted from the room.

"So. You're with the appraisers. I'm not sure what it is Nicky thinks I'm going to get rid of." He sighed. "Rebecca loved this house. She chose everything, right down to the linens. I can't think about changing anything right now."

As a rebuke, it was pretty mild, but I could tell that there was some steel left beneath the crepey, mottled skin. A man didn't become a multimillionaire by letting other people make his decisions for him, even a man weighed down by age and grief. It made me wonder, for the first time, if Cecelia Dobbs had seriously underestimated Thomas Castlemain. And if I had, as well.

"There's no rush," I said, trying to adopt what I thought would be the right attitude for someone who might be seeing a fat, juicy commission about to go up in smoke. "This is just preliminary."

"Miss Blaine, my assistant, will be happy to discuss it with you. Unfortunately, she's not in at the moment. You'll be dealing with her, if I decide to sell anything." He looked up as Nick came back into the room bearing a tray with three tall glasses balanced on it. "My grandson will be leaving soon."

Nick faltered, the tray tipping precariously before he managed to right it. He set it on the low table in front of his grandfather.

"I thought I'd stick around for a few more days, Granddad. I told you that."

A look passed between them as Nick handed me the glass of tea, and I wondered if this man Bitsy had described as his grandparents' favorite had somehow managed to alienate Mr. Castlemain. Lots of undercurrents here I didn't quite understand. Yet.

"So how do you like our home, Mrs. Tanner?" the old man asked.

"It's magnificent," I said without hesitation. "I can't believe how much light there is everywhere."

Thomas smiled. "That's Becky's doing. She saw a villa like this when we were in Tuscany, many years ago. When we decided to move here to the island, nothing would do but that she reproduced it almost exactly." His soft chuckle made me smile. "Becky was a wonder. Drove the architect totally mad until he had every detail precisely the way she wanted it." He sighed. "I miss her."

The simple statement brought tears to my eyes, and I sipped tea to cover my emotion. I set the glass back on the tray. "Where did the name come from?"

"I hate to rush you, Bay, but it's almost time for Granddad's lunch." Perched on the edge of his chair, Nick now seemed eager to move me along.

"Don't be rude, Nicky. Our guest asked me a question." He turned back toward me. "Becky came up with it. The villa she so admired in Italy had gates like these. The story went that they'd been salvaged from some temple in the Middle East. Persia or perhaps Azerbaijan. I don't recall exactly. She had them especially made and shipped all the way over here. We had them on our house in Virginia. When we sold it, she replaced them with some inexpensive replicas and brought the originals with us." He chuckled again. "You can't imagine how much it costs to have them carted all over the world."

Once again, Nick stirred in his chair. The old man's eyes drooped a little, and I took both as my cue. "Thank you so much for your hospitality," I said, rising, "but I'm afraid I have another appointment."

He forced himself back into wakefulness. "My pleasure, young woman. You come back again. Any time."

I held out my hand, and he took it briefly. "Thank you, sir."

Nick Potter urged me toward the front door, again with the pressure of his hand in the small of my back. "I'll see you at one thirty," he said a moment before the door closed firmly behind me.

I stood for a while, staring at the deeply carved panel, before I turned and made my way through the small gates back to the car. I fingered the flash drive in my pocket. It had been a strange encounter but worth it, if for nothing else than to see Thomas Castlemain in his own element. He wasn't quite the doddering old fool both Cecelia Dobbs and his grandson had made him out to be. I wondered if the addition of Cady Proffit to the permanent household staff had cut down on the pills the old man was being fed. That could have a lot to do with the gleam of intelligence I'd just seen in his faded eyes. I wished I could have met Uncle Wendell, too. Maybe another perspective besides Nick's would be helpful.

I turned the ignition in the Jaguar and followed the curve of the driveway around to the gates. I slowed to study the intricate swirls of wrought iron, towering at least fifteen feet in the air, and imagined the originals clanging shut against Roman or Greek or Carthaginian invaders. Spiked heavily at the top, they certainly looked capable of repelling attack. Images of legions of helmeted soldiers, marching in phalanx on some remote religious compound, occupied my thoughts until the phone buzzed.

I shook my head and dug it out of my bag. "Bay Tanner."

"Honey, it's me." Red sounded subdued. "Where are you?"

"Just coming out of Wexford. I had a meeting with Nick and Mr. Castlemain. What's the matter?"

I waited, about to repeat myself when he finally spoke.

"They've found Cecelia's car."

CHAPTER
THIRTY-THREE

WE RENDEZVOUSED AT THE OFFICE. RED BROUGHT lunch in the form of deli sandwiches, and we spread them out on my desk. Discussion of business had to be put on hold while Stephanie joined us for the impromptu meal. After we gathered up all the oil-and-vinegar-stained wrappers, Erik and his fiancée carried them out to the Dumpster. He paused at the door, and we made eye contact. When he returned, he was alone.

"Sorry about that," I said to my partner, pulling a legal pad from the center drawer of my desk.

"She understands." Erik had his laptop arranged on his knees, his fingers already typing. "If she comes to work for us, she'll be covered by the confidentiality agreement."

"Stephanie's coming to work here?" Red's eyebrows had drawn his face into a frown.

"Maybe. Erik and I have been talking about it. So did you find anything missing?" I asked, turning to my partner. Most of the paper had disappeared from on top of the filing cabinets, and the place looked almost back to normal. "I can't believe how much you got done."

"Almost all of it. Steph's a whiz when she gets rolling. I paid special attention to the folders dealing with Cecelia and the Castlemains. It seems to me that's the only case we're working on—besides the shelter—that might have been of interest to someone."

"Like who? You mean Blaine and Chambers?"

"Or Potter," my husband said.

I glanced up to find he had slumped in his chair, his arms crossed in front of his chest. His belligerent stance. I knew it well.

"Why would Nick Potter break in? I was about to share it all with him last night."

"Maybe he didn't trust you to tell him everything."

I opened my mouth to continue the argument, then realized how pointless it was. I turned my attention back to Erik.

"Anything else?"

"The only thing I didn't know about for sure was if there were any handwritten notes you might have stuck in there. I left the folders out so you could take a run through them yourself."

"Well, that's a relief." I directed the next question to my scowling husband. "What can you tell us about Cecelia's car?"

"They found it in a back corner of the parking lot at the Marriott. Actually, one of their security guys found it. He was doing his regular patrol and noticed that it hadn't moved for a couple of nights. He'd read the stories in the paper, got curious, and called the sheriff to see if it might be the one they were looking for."

I'd managed to contain myself until he'd finished. "The Marriott? Was it in the lot at the bottom of the hill, off to the right when you come in?"

"Yes. Why?"

"I checked that lot on Monday. I drove up and down every last damn row, including way in the back. That car was not there."

Both Erik and Red sat up straighter. "Are you sure?" my husband asked.

"Positive. I paid special attention to silver cars of any type, and I remember there was a Honda in that same area. It looks a lot like a Toyota, so I double-checked the license plate. Cecelia was already dead by then, right?" No one answered me. "Right?"

Red nodded. "It looks that way. TOD was probably between ten Sunday night and two the next morning."

That made my head snap up. "The coroner's report is in?"

"Preliminary. Cause of death was drowning, but she had a few unexplained bruises on her back. Didn't show up until they'd cut away her clothes. They're asking for help from SLED. It'll take a couple of days."

The State Law Enforcement Division was South Carolina's equivalent of the FBI. They had the best resources, both in investigative tools and laboratory facilities. They were often called in when a case rose above the expertise or capacity of local police and sheriff's offices. They'd recently spearheaded the statewide search for a North Carolina parolee who'd gone on a killing spree up near Gaffney.

"Any word on what kind of water was in her lungs?" I asked.

Red shook his head. "If so, they weren't sharing the information. Mike Raleigh said he thought we had a right to know, so I'm pretty sure he gave me everything he had."

"Did they find a note? Or anything else that indicated suicide?" Erik asked.

"Not that Mike knew of."

"You know what this means, right?" I studied my husband's face. "I mean, not only is her car found miles away from where her body was discovered, but it had to have been placed there after she was already dead."

Red nodded slowly. "You're right. I don't see any way they can hold on to the suicide scenario. Unless she had help. But it's most likely Cecelia Dobbs was murdered."

It didn't give me any satisfaction to have been proved right. I certainly didn't expect Detective Lisa Pedrovsky to come knocking on my door with an apology, but I had to admit to a certain feeling of smugness that I'd called it long before the *real* cops got around to it.

"So where do we go from here?" As usual, Erik cut right to the heart of it.

"I don't know." I looked at Red. "This opens us up to having to share our information with Pedrovsky, doesn't it."

It wasn't really a question because I already knew the answer. I didn't like it, but I couldn't see how cooperation could be avoided.

To my surprise, Red smiled, a brief lifting of the corners of his mouth, but a smile nonetheless. "You could always claim that you haven't been able to get your files back in order. That might hold them off for a while."

I grinned back. "I suggest you get your thinking back on track, Sergeant. You're about to start playing for the other team again."

That made him jerk upright and check his watch. "Damn it! I'm supposed to meet with Joe Pickens in less than an hour."

"You'd better get on your horse then," I said as he bolted from the chair. "And you're paying for your own speeding tickets," I hollered at his back.

"Love you," he called over his shoulder.

The door slammed behind him, and Erik and I exchanged a look.

"I'm glad you two ended up together," my partner said.

I hesitated a moment, then smiled. "Me, too." I drew in a long breath and let it out slowly. "Nick Potter will be here in a few minutes. We got interrupted this morning."

I gave him a quick rundown on my morning's activities, then reached in my pocket for the flash drive I'd completely forgotten about in the aftermath of Red's revelations about Cecelia Dobbs.

"Rebecca Castlemain's financials. The files are passworded," I said as I handed it over. "Nick and I were going to discuss them this morning, but he couldn't get access. See what you can do with it."

"You're going to let him into his grandparents' financial stuff?"

"Yes. Why not? I mean, if we're going to try to track down this scam Cecelia talked about, we're going to have to look at their records."

Erik glanced over his shoulder, and the look on his face when he turned back around made a little shiver run up my spine.

"What?"

"Things have been happening so fast around here, I never gave you the report on Potter."

I looked blankly at him. "Report?"

"You asked me to check him out, remember?"

"Right. So what did you find out?"

He tapped on the keyboard of his laptop. "Nothing earth-shattering, but a couple of interesting items. He's a lobbyist for the aerospace industry. Got a law degree from the University of Virginia and worked for a while in his grandfather's company. When Mr. Castle-main sold out, Nick left, too. No way to tell if it was his choice or not. He joined this firm in D.C. about five years ago. Lots of pictures floating around of him hobnobbing with senators and congressmen. Parties, receptions, that kind of thing. Never been married, although his name has been linked with a few celebrities. A couple of rock stars and one or two actresses." He paused and looked up at me. "He seems to enjoy his bachelor life."

"I can believe that." I looked away so he couldn't read my face. "Anything criminal? Or shady?"

"A few hints that some of his lobbying activities might have skirted pretty close to the edge, ethics-wise, but nothing concrete. He's a big supporter of the Boys' and Girls' Club and the Police Athletic League in McLean where he lives. In a pretty pricey neighborhood, by the way."

"So he's not hurting for money." I checked my watch. Nick Potter was running late. Again.

"Well, it doesn't look that way. But there's a couple of things that sent up red flags."

"Like what?"

"Well, he spends a lot of time in Vegas and Atlantic City. And in a couple of those casinos on Indian reservations. That's where some of those pictures were taken, the ones with the celebrities."

That got my attention. "You think he's a gambler?"

"Probably. But I didn't run across anything that points to him being in over his head. I didn't try to crack his bank accounts or anything like that."

I didn't know why that made me feel better, but it did. "You said a couple of things. What else?"

"Just out of curiosity, I checked the MLS listings, to see what houses in his area were going for. Mostly to get a handle on what his place might be worth." He paused. "He just listed his house for sale."

"Really? When?"

"Three days before his grandmother died."

I had only a few seconds to digest exactly what that might mean when the outside door opened, and Nick Potter walked into my office.

CHAPTER
THIRTY-FOUR

ORRY I'M LATE. GRANDDAD AND I HAD A LOT TO DIS-
cuss, and the time sort of got away from me."

I stared at the striking figure in my doorway, his black shorts revealing well-muscled legs and his white polo shirt setting off his dark
hair and tanned arms.

"Nick Potter," he said, holding out his hand to Erik.

I shook myself. "This is my partner, Erik Whiteside."

Erik set the laptop on my desk and rose to take Nick's hand.
"Pleased to meet you. I'm sorry for your loss," he added.

"Thanks. Some of the shock is beginning to wear off, but I'll be a
long time getting used to the idea that she's gone."

They both turned toward me, and I felt myself suddenly at a loss for
words. Some of Erik's revelations about Nick had been disquieting, and
I hadn't had time to wrap my head around what exactly it all meant. I
stalled, indicating with a flick of my hand that Nick should take the
seat Red had vacated a few minutes before.

"Any luck with those files?" Nick asked as he seated himself grace-
fully.

"There hasn't been time," I said, finding my footing at last. "Erik was just about to start on them."

My partner got the message and gathered up his computer. "I'll get on it now," he said, moving out to his desk in the reception area.

"There have been some developments," I said, leaning back in my chair. I fastened my gaze on his face, ready to judge his reaction to my next words. "The woman I told you about, the one who works . . . worked at the bank?"

"The one who killed herself?" he asked without a flicker of emotion.

"That was the assumption. It turns out now that she was most likely murdered."

Nick Potter didn't flinch, but his eyes narrowed. "Really? That's terrible. Do they know who did it?"

"No. The coroner's report just came down a couple of hours ago. And it's still preliminary. They're bringing in SLED."

"State guys?" he asked.

"Right."

He mulled that over for a few seconds. "Do you think her death had anything to do with Granddad? I mean, is Kendra involved somehow?"

I wasn't sure what to make of that leap of logic. Of course, it was the same one Red and Erik and I had made, but still . . .

"Why would you assume that?"

"I'm not assuming, just asking. You've got this poor girl from the bank accusing Kendra and this teller guy of trying to rip off my grand-parents, and then she ends up dead. I can't believe she's capable of any-thing like that—Kendra, I mean—but don't you think it's too much of a coincidence?"

He had me there, but I wasn't about to admit it. "It's early times yet. But what should most concern you is that I'm going to have to hand over my files to the sheriff's detective who's heading the murder investigation. I just want you to know that up front."

I could almost read the calculations going on behind his eyes.

"But I have no connection to this girl's death. I hired you on a completely different matter."

"True. But both cases involve Kendra Blaine and a possible theft. I don't see how I can separate them."

He rose abruptly. "Then I think I need to sever our relationship. I won't have my grandfather's name associated with something as sordid as a murder. Send me a bill, and I'll see that you're paid immediately."

I'd expected some resistance, but I hadn't anticipated our getting fired. By the time I recovered, he was already standing in front of Erik's desk.

"I'd like that flash drive, please." He held out his hand.

Erik looked to where I stood in the doorway, and I nodded. "Give it to him."

"You need to destroy any copies you've made. I'll wait."

"No need," my partner said evenly. "I haven't had a chance to get to it yet." He reached in his pocket and handed the drive to Nick. "Sorry things didn't work out," he said with a smile.

Nick turned back toward me. "I'm sorry if I seem abrupt, Bay, but I know you understand. I have to protect my grandfather's interests. I can't have him dragged into a murder investigation. I'll just have to convince him to terminate Kendra Blaine some other way." The charm machine cranked back up. "I really appreciate everything you've done. It was a pleasure to meet you both." At the outer door, he paused one more time. "Maybe we'll meet again, Bay. I'll look forward to it."

I spent the rest of the afternoon trying to concentrate on the information Erik had provided about the battered women's shelter. After a brief discussion, we'd decided to put everything on a CD that I could take home at night and lock in my floor safe. It made me wonder if maybe we should have something like that installed in the office. I'd never given much thought to how vulnerable our records were to a casual burglar. We didn't have an alarm system, either. I scribbled myself a note on the desk pad, a reminder to check with my own provider and see how much a setup here would cost, when my eyes fastened on another few lines I'd jotted and then completely ignored: *Call B Stokes re SPIG*.

Bob Stokes was my broker, and Southern Preferred Investment Group was the firm Cecelia Dobbs had been sure was the conduit for the money Blaine and Chambers were scamming from the Castle-mains. I leaned back in the chair and wished for a cigarette. To call or not to call. The bottom line was that we no longer had a dog in this fight. Nick Potter had just fired us, and Cecelia was dead. We had no client. I glanced at my computer screen. The shelter was a real problem, one that could put already traumatized women at even greater risk. And their kids. I should let the Castlemain thing go. Nick seemed perfectly capable of protecting his grandfather, and there was not the first indication that Rebecca's death had been anything but natural. As far as I knew. I grabbed up the phone.

Harley Coffin, my father's old friend and physician, answered on the second ring.

"Hello there, Bay, darlin'."

"Hey, Harley. Listen, I wonder if I could ask you something, and I need to tell you up front that I can't say why."

"Honey, I've learned over the last few years not to get too upset when you go all mysterious on us." His low chuckle reminded me of the Judge. "Fire away."

"Have you heard anything more about Rebecca Castlemain's death?"

"Like what?"

"Is anyone questioning the cause? I mean, you seemed surprised that it would have been heart failure." I paused, but he didn't reply. I let out a long breath. "Is there any indication that it may not have been natural causes?"

"You're suggestin' that someone murdered her?"

I could hear the tremor in his scratchy voice, and I could have kicked myself. "No, Harley. Well, not exactly. It's just that I've come across some information that leads me to believe . . . Oh, hell, I don't know. I thought maybe you might have heard some scuttlebutt around town or at the hospital. Humor me."

He took a long time to answer. "There have been a few rumors floating around, but that's just . . . You know how small towns are."

"What kind of rumors?"

"I don't hold with that, Bay, and you damn well know it. Careers and reputations have been seriously damaged by that kind of vicious gossip."

He didn't mention any names, but I didn't have to look too far from home to understand exactly what he meant.

"They didn't autopsy her, did they? Isn't that unusual?"

"Not for a physician-attended death. She was pronounced in the ER."

"So why would there be rumors?" I felt ashamed for badgering the old man, but I needed to know. Not just to satisfy my own morbid curiosity, but because it might be important. Especially to Thomas Castlemain.

"Because some folks got nothing better to do."

I waited. It was an old trick of the Judge's, and it worked more times than not.

"Okay. They're sayin' that there were some marks on her chest when she got to the funeral home. Little red dots. But it probably doesn't mean anything. They shocked her a few times in the ER. Defibrillator, tryin' to bring her back. That probably caused it."

I felt myself slumping in the chair. "And that's it? I don't understand why that would generate rumors."

Harley really didn't want to tell me. I wasn't buying his disdain-for-gossip story. My late father's cronies had been like a bunch of old hens around the poker table. I would bet the good doctor and his pals engaged in their own brand of genteel character assassination when they gathered for coffee at the back of the bookstore. No, it was undoubtedly some misplaced fear that he might be leading me into trouble.

When he spoke, his voice had dropped almost to a whisper. "You aren't going to leave it alone, are you?"

"No, sir," I said softly.

Again Harley sighed. His words, delivered in his cracked, septuagenarian's voice, sounded too bizarre to be real. "Ever see the marks a Taser leaves?"

"A Taser? No. What kind of marks?"

"Little red dots."

CHAPTER
THIRTY-FIVE

*A*FTER I HUNG UP, I SAT FOR A MOMENT TRYING TO order my thoughts, then turned to the computer. I saved the women's shelter file onto the CD, and brought up Google. For the next twenty minutes, I scrolled through more than a dozen Web sites related to stun guns, their effects, and availability: Apparently legal for civilians in South Carolina. Readily for sale online with few restrictions. Cited by coroners in dozens of cases across the country as at least a contributing factor in deaths involving police use. Most likely adverse effect—heart failure.

Rebecca Castlemain had been around eighty years old. How much would it have taken to stop her heart? Who would know that? I sure as hell hadn't. Someone with medical knowledge? With police training? Or almost anyone who invested a few minutes on the Internet—as I had just done?

Kendra Blaine could have applied a stun gun to Rebecca while she slept. She had access. According to Cecelia Dobbs, she had motive. With his wife out of the picture, Thomas Castlemain would be a sitting duck. Or Blaine might have designs on marrying him. So much simpler to control his money when she had legitimate access. And then what?

Would Thomas, too, suffer a fatal heart attack? Who would look twice at it in a man of his age, especially if Blaine had the sense to wait a year or so?

I could feel the sweat pooling between my breasts, my breath coming in short little gasps. I stood and peeled off my jacket. "Erik!"

He stood in the doorway, his face a mask of concern. "What's the matter?"

I dropped into my chair. "I think I know how they killed Rebecca."

I wished Red were there. His reasoned, just-the-facts-ma'am approach had more than once reined in some of my wilder speculations, forcing me to apply the cool logic of the accountant I had been. Erik did his best, but it wasn't the same.

I doodled on a legal pad while we hashed it out. I made few notes, still uneasy about the vulnerability of our files. Erik, however, typed steadily.

"Okay. Try this out," I said. "The scheme to transfer the Castlemains' funds was running along smoothly. Then Cecelia stuck her nose in."

"Wait," Erik said, looking up. "How did they know? About Cecelia, I mean. She came to us . . . what? A week ago today, right? Wednesday?"

"Yes."

"And Mrs. Castlemain died sometime that night or Thursday morning. There's no way they could have known Cecelia was onto them."

He had a point. Unless . . . "They didn't necessarily have to be aware that she'd hired us. Remember how fidgety she was? And how you asked after she left if she was a woman scorned? What if she'd been angling for something with Dalton Chambers and been rebuffed?" I hated it, but it had to be said. "She wasn't the most attractive girl on the planet. And can you honestly see her snooping around the bank's files without someone's noticing? I was there. It's a pretty small place. Maybe she gave off bad vibes, and Chambers picked up on it. Maybe she even threatened him before she came to us. Who knows?"

"That's just the problem, Bay—who knows? Cecelia is definitely unavailable for answers. Do we know of anyone she might have confided in? Maybe a girlfriend or someone at the bank? Or her parents?"

I hadn't considered that possibility, but it was a good one. I immediately wrote off her father, the haughty Dr. Emerson Dobbs. It was clear that, although he undoubtedly loved his daughter, he didn't hold her in high regard. I just couldn't picture Cecelia spilling her guts to him. But maybe her mother? I'd never even spoken to the woman, and this didn't seem like the best time to make an approach. Still, if she had information that could lead to her daughter's murderer, wouldn't she want to help? I made a note to see if someone could get me an entrée into the Dobbs house. Maybe Alexandra Finch. Or Bitsy.

I hadn't heard from my oldest friend since we'd attended Rebecca Castlemain's memorial service. That in and of itself wasn't unusual as our lives tended to run on different tracks, converging occasionally as they had on Friday. I'd intended to kick her butt about sharing my personal phone number with Nick Potter, not to mention telling him I was a PI, but she wasn't returning my calls. Avoiding me? One of those annoying little bells jingled in the back of my head, and I could feel my face pulling into a frown of concentration.

"Something wrong?" Erik asked, and it was gone.

"Not exactly. I've been assuming that Bitsy Elliott ratted me out to Nick. About being an investigator. But I've never confirmed that."

"Is it important?"

"I don't know. Maybe." I ran both hands through my mass of hair and squeezed my scalp. The remnants of the bump on the back of my head tingled a little, but the pain was pretty much gone. "There's too much going on."

"You need one of your famous lists."

That made me smile. "Later. Okay. Back to our speculations. Let's assume for now that Blaine and Chambers somehow got wind of what Cecelia was up to. But they kill Mrs. Castlemain. Why not just eliminate the outside threat and go on as before?"

"Good question. Unless something else happened that spooked them."

"Like what?"

"Maybe Mrs. Castlemain got wise to what was going on. They had to get rid of her before she blew the whistle."

"I don't know," I said, leaning back in the chair. "It was a hell of a risk, especially if they used a stun gun. Someone at the ER could have recognized the burn marks on her chest. It would have been a lot easier to give her an overdose of something. If she died peacefully in her sleep, no one would even think to raise a question."

"If she already suspected Kendra Blaine, Mrs. Castlemain would have been on the alert for something like that. She'd have been doubly careful about accepting medication or anything like that from her. I wonder what Mrs. Castlemain planned to do with the information, if she really had tumbled to the theft."

"I guess we'll never know. One thing I'm pretty certain of—she didn't tell her husband. He doesn't strike me as someone who cared all that much about the trappings of wealth. He's got more money than he'll ever be able to spend, at least to judge by the mansion he lives in. But Thomas would be shouting down the walls of Canaan's Gate if he had any inkling someone had a motive to kill his wife."

"So where does that leave us?"

I flipped to a fresh page on the legal pad. "I'll try to talk to Mrs. Dobbs, today if I can manage it, ask her if Cecelia ever mentioned anything about shady dealings at the bank. Or if she ever did anything about her crush on Dalton Chambers." I dropped my pen on the desk. "Damn it, I wish we'd had a chance to look at those financial records Nick took back."

When Erik didn't reply, I looked up to find him smiling.

"What? You said you didn't make any copies."

"I didn't. But it just occurred to me that I might have accidentally given him back the wrong flash drive." He reached into his pocket and took out one of the little oblongs of silver. "I was going to update my fantasy football league picks this afternoon, and I might have gotten the two drives mixed up."

I struggled to hold on to my look of stern disapproval, but I couldn't manage it. "And I called you *upstanding* just a few days ago. I'm shocked."

"Stuff happens," he said, grinning back. "Want to see what's on here? Just to be sure I'm right?"

"Not here. Wait until you get home, when you can discover your 'mistake.' You can confess your ineptitude tomorrow. Then I'll notify Nick. In the meantime, check their bank statements for those transfers Cecelia told us about. And see if there's a file for their portfolio. I want to know if Rebecca was aware of Southern Preferred Investment Group."

"Got it." He dropped the drive back into his pocket. "What do you want me to do now?"

"We can't go anywhere with this mess until we have more information. I expect Pedrovsky or Mike Raleigh to come waltzing in here any minute and demand our files. I'll hold out for a subpoena, which should keep them at bay for maybe twenty-four hours, but that's about it."

Erik stood and walked to the door, then looked back. "We could just let the sheriff's office handle this. I mean, technically, we don't have a client."

He was right, of course, and I fumbled in my head for some justification to keep pursuing the investigation. I told myself it had nothing to do with besting Red's—and my—nemesis, Lisa Pedrovsky. I told myself I owed it to Cecelia to complete the task she'd set for us which, one way or another, I felt certain had contributed to her death. I told myself I just wanted to make things right for Thomas Castlemain.

We stared at each other for a long time before he nodded once and turned toward his desk. Erik understood, even though I wasn't sure I did myself.

CHAPTER
THIRTY-SIX

BITSY DIDN'T ANSWER ON EITHER HER LAND OR CELL line, so I tried Alexandra Finch. My attorney was on her way out but took a few minutes to fill me in on what she knew about Millicent Davis Dobbs, wife of Emerson and mother of Cecelia.

"I'm not that close to her, you understand. Just a social acquaintance."

I could hear her breathing through the phone, and I pictured her striding down the hallway with that Bluetooth thingy stuck in her ear. Alex was a great one for multitasking.

"Her husband called her Millie," I said recalling the doctor's one brief mention of his wife.

"She hates that. She never said anything, at least not to me, but you can tell. She cringes every time he says it."

"Do you think she'd talk to me about Cecelia?"

I'd filled Alex in on some of the happenings of the past couple of days. She agreed with me that a homicide ruling was coming down and that sooner rather than later I'd be served with an order to produce my client records. She'd advised me not to hold out on anything but also not to consent to another interview without her present.

"Maybe. She must be devastated. Cecelia was her only child. And she's likely to be surrounded by family and friends. It might be tough getting through to her."

"Any suggestions?"

"Do you know Lily Middleton?"

The name rang a bell, but it took me a few moments to resurrect the reason from the back of my head. "She's connected to the Castlemains somehow. I know she was one of Rebecca's friends, and she was at the memorial service." The image of the tall, willowy blonde head-to-head with Nick Potter in the fellowship hall flashed into my mind. For some reason, it made my hand clench the receiver a little more tightly. "But I don't know her."

"Too bad. She and Millicent are close."

I heard outside noises then, birds and traffic, as Alex walked to her car.

"Tell you what. I'll call and try to pave the way for you." She paused. "You have their number?"

I fumbled through the Castlemain/Dobbs files once again stacked on the corner of my desk and recited Cecelia's home phone number.

"Give me about ten minutes. If I don't reach her, I'll call you back. Otherwise, try her in ten. Gotta run."

"Thanks," I managed before the line went dead.

Alex didn't call, but I gave it half an hour, just to be on the safe side. When a woman answered at the Dobbs house, I asked for Millicent.

"This is she. Is this Mrs. Tanner?"

"Yes, ma'am," I said softly, thankful my attorney had paved the way. "I'm so sorry about Cecelia."

"Thank you." Her voice, though a little husky, was firm. "Alexandra said you have some questions?"

"Yes. I wonder if I might speak to you in person."

"I'm afraid that's impossible. There's so much to do—" She broke off on a stifled sob and was a few moments getting herself back under control.

In the brief silence, I thought, as I had so many times before, of the term *steel magnolia*. I'd used it myself, just a few days before, in reference to Adelaide Boyce Hammond, my mother's old friend. The gentility and grace of our Southern heritage, the soft, cultured voices of our women masked the strength that had allowed us to keep our families and homes together through civil and foreign wars, deprivation, and loss. Underestimating a true Southern woman was always a mistake.

"I'm sorry," she said, quite unnecessarily.

"I understand," I said. "Perhaps you could tell me if your daughter confided in you about the concerns she brought to our agency. Regarding the bank."

"She tried. I mean, she told me there was some problem, and that she didn't know how to handle it, but only in general terms. I suggested she speak to her supervisor, but she said that wasn't possible. Maybe if I'd listened, if I'd paid more attention . . ." Her voice trailed away into silence.

"Did she ever talk to you about a teller, a young man she might have been interested in? Romantically?"

"I knew there was someone. . . . She seemed quite happy for a time, but I don't think it worked out. Cecelia and I—" Millicent Dobbs drew a shuddering breath. "We weren't as close as I would have liked."

I glanced down at my notes, convinced that Cecelia's mother would be of no help to us, when my eye caught on a few words from our discussion with Dr. Dobbs in the office.

"Do you know if your husband was able to get the records from your phone and Cecelia's cell? For that afternoon she . . . disappeared?"

She cleared her throat. "I saw some pages from the computer with numbers on them on his desk. Could that be it?"

I sat up straighter. "Yes, ma'am. Could I just stop by and pick those up? I promise not to disturb you or your family."

I had a fleeting thought that the cops might want them, too, but they could get them through regular channels. And if it came down to it, I'd just hand them over with the rest of the files.

"I suppose that would be all right. When?"

Their address was in Indigo Run, the plantation that sprawled between the office and Marshland Road.

"I'll need a pass, but I can be there in ten minutes."

"All right. I'll put the papers in an envelope for you and have someone call the gate. And Mrs. Tanner?"

"Yes, ma'am?"

"Thank you for trying to help my little girl," she said softly and hung up.

The woman who came to the door identified herself as Millicent's sister-in-law and handed over the envelope with a sad smile. I thanked her and offered my condolences. I would have liked to get a look at Cecelia's mother, for no other reason than to satisfy my own curiosity, but she was well guarded by her family.

Back at the office, I handed the landline records to Erik and took those from Cecelia's cell phone for myself. We both logged on to our reverse directory programs and began backtracking. Fifteen minutes in, Erik let out a whoop. I jumped up and bolted toward his desk.

"What have you got?"

"The phone company sent everything since the first of September, but I started with last week first. I figured we were most interested in incoming calls, so I—"

"Cut the lecture, and tell me what you found," I said, a little more harshly than I'd intended.

"Sorry. From Saturday until Sunday, when she disappeared, there were three calls from a prepaid cell to the house. None of them longer than two minutes. No way to say if they were for her or not, but it is kind of strange."

"How do you know it was a prepaid?"

"The exchanges are different from regular cell phones. And there's no registered owner of the number."

I felt the anticipation drain away. "But what does that tell us?"

"Most people don't use prepaids unless they're too poor to afford a regular plan or they're trying to hide behind the anonymity of it."

"That's a big assumption." I stretched out my hand. "Let me have those numbers and see if they show up on her cell bill."

He used a yellow highlighter to mark the entries and followed me back into my office. I'd been working on the same set of criteria as Erik, who looked over my shoulder as I scanned the list. I found two records of calls to Cecelia's cell from the same number, both on the Saturday after she'd been in our office.

"And there's no way at all to trace that phone?" I asked, slumping back in my chair.

"Nope." I looked up into his grin. "But let's call it and see who answers."

"Let's finish with these first," I said, handing the sheets back to him. "Do you have a number for Dalton Chambers or Kendra Blaine?"

"Blaine, yes. Chambers' is unlisted."

"Can you get it anyway?"

"Not legally."

"I don't care. I want to know if he or Blaine called Cecelia. I'll keep working on these." I added his lists to my pile and turned to the keyboard as he walked back to his desk.

There weren't that many numbers to check on the cell, and I finished without finding a smoking gun. I slammed my pen down onto the desktop in frustration. I'd been certain these records would give us a clue as to what—or more importantly *who*—had lured Cecelia Dobbs to her death on Sunday night. Still, she'd received two calls on her last afternoon from a number I couldn't attach a name to. I wrote it on a scratch pad and rose from my chair a moment before Erik stepped into the room.

"Got it," he said, a hint of pride in his voice.

"Read it to me."

I stared at the note I'd made as my partner carefully enunciated each number in precisely the same order.

"Got you, you son of a bitch," I said and looked up to find Erik staring at me intently.

"Chambers called Cecelia?"

"Not long after she talked to me, and again about an hour later. I can guarantee they weren't discussing bank business on Sunday afternoon."

"You think he got Cecelia out of the house so he could murder her? The cops are going to want a lot more evidence than this."

"So do I. But it fits with what we were speculating about before." I paused, something once again nagging at me. "Doesn't it?"

Erik sat down in the client chair. "I'm not sure. I mean, why would she agree to meet a guy she thought was ripping off her bank's clients?"

I laid the printouts aside and tried to marshal my thoughts. "Because, in spite of everything, Cecelia still had a huge crush on him. We both saw that when she was here. She even suggested that he might just be a dupe, infatuated with Kendra Blaine and being used by her. I think she desperately wanted to believe that. Her mother even seemed to think that Chambers might have encouraged her at some point."

I picked up the lists of calls. "A typical young woman her age would have pages and pages of activity on her cell phone, chatting with friends and making dates. Hers are mostly to or from her parents and a couple of others that trace back to two apparently single women."

"So you think she'd jump at the chance to see Chambers, regardless of what she suspected he was capable of."

"Yes, I do. Maybe she thought she could talk him out of it." I shook my head. "She might even have wanted to warn him. About us, I mean."

"Stupid," Erik said, his voice heavy with scorn.

"You don't have any idea what it must have been like for her." I could feel the anger rising in my chest. "In this day and age, it's all about being skinny and beautiful. When you're not, life is like being on the outside looking in. It's lonely. And humiliating, sitting home with your parents when everyone else you know is out partying. I can understand why she'd jump at any indication that Dalton Chambers might be interested in her. It's sad, but it isn't something she should be condemned for."

"Sorry," my partner mumbled, his handsome face reddening under his summer tan.

"I know. It's just not something that men get, how devastating it is to be the ugly duckling. I don't care how much feminism has preached about not needing a man to make your life complete, it still hurts." I forced most of the anger out of my voice. "I know it was stupid of Cecelia to go out and meet this guy, but she certainly didn't deserve to die for it."

"You're right." He forced a thin smile. "I can't believe you ever had that experience, though."

"I was lucky," I said. "Good genes. That doesn't mean I didn't have friends who suffered the way Cecelia did."

"So what do we do now? Turn this over to Detective Raleigh?"

"Tomorrow," I said. "In the meantime, I'd like to have a little chat with Dalton Chambers."

"You think that's a good idea? I mean, we shouldn't do anything to spook him or screw up the case for the sheriff's guys." He stood and moved out of the line of fire he knew would be coming. "Maybe we should talk to Red about it."

I looked at my watch to find it was nearly five o'clock. "We can't catch this bastard at the bank. You go home and keep an eye on his place. Call me when he shows up."

"And then what?"

"Then we'll decide what to do. I'm not a complete idiot, Erik, and I know you're right about not messing up the case for the cops. Red should be back soon. I'll run it by him."

I could see the tension drain out of his neck and shoulders.

"Good, that's good."

"Give me everything you've been working on with the phone records, and I'll take it home and put it in the safe."

He nodded and turned back to his desk.

As I gathered together my own papers and stuffed them into my briefcase, I determined that somehow I'd have a crack at Dalton Chambers before his ass got hauled off to jail. Not just for my own satisfaction. But for Cecelia.

CHAPTER
THIRTY-SEVEN

RED CALLED A LITTLE AFTER SIX, JUST AS I WAS ABOUT to give up on him and order a pizza.

"Everything okay?" he asked.

"There've been some developments," I answered, "but I'm fine. Still a little bit of a headache, but it's manageable. When are you coming home?"

"Well, here's the thing."

He paused, and I knew he was about to tell me something he was afraid I wouldn't like. His predictability made me smile.

"You're going to be late?"

"Joe asked me to stick around. There's been this string of break-ins, and they've got a pretty good line on who's involved. A local gang of thugs, and one of them got picked up for possession with intent and dealt his buddies for a lesser charge. They've got a raid all set up, and Joe thought I might like to ride along. Just to get a feel for how they mount an operation."

"That's fine," I said and heard his sigh of relief.

"It could go late. Joe said I could crash in his guest room if I need to."

"I hope his wife is okay with that," I said, rifling through the menus on the desk in the kitchen for the one from Giuseppi's. "You're staying back, though, right? In this raid? I mean, you're still officially a civilian."

"I'm just an observer. Don't worry." His voice lost its undercurrent of excitement. "You sure you're okay with this? I mean, after last night? You're not going out anywhere, are you?"

I thought about Dalton Chambers, darkly handsome and mysterious, luring Cecelia Dobbs to her death, and my hand tightened around the phone. I chose silence over an outright lie.

"Did the chief agree to run Dalton's prints?" He didn't answer right away, and I felt a surge of excitement. "What did you find out? Red?"

His sigh rippled clearly down the phone lines. "Can't it wait until I get home?"

"No! They got a hit on them, didn't they?"

I heard the rustle of paper before he spoke. "Richard Charles Johnson. He has a juvie record in Columbia. That's sealed, of course, but there's an open warrant out on him in Myrtle Beach."

"For what? Was he running this con game up there?" It would make sense. Lots of wealthy retirees there, too, although maybe not of the financial caliber of the ones we got on Hilton Head. Or at least not as many. Still . . . I suddenly realized that my husband hadn't answered. "Red? What is he wanted for?"

"They think he beat the hell out of an old lady and cleaned out her place—jewelry and electronics—along with her bank accounts. He was some kind of paid companion, or so they think." Again he paused. "If a neighbor hadn't gotten concerned when she didn't see the woman for a day or so, the poor old thing would have died of her injuries. As it is, she's been in a coma ever since."

"The son of a bitch! So he's not a stranger to violence. Killing Cecelia would have been just a way to cover his tracks. He probably never gave it a thought."

"You're jumping to a lot of conclusions here, Bay. In the first place, he's not officially a suspect, just a person of interest. There were legitimate reasons for his prints to be in the house. If they had hard evidence, they would have pulled out all the stops to go after him. And you have nothing but a set of circumstances and your own gut reaction to tie him to the death of the girl. There's a little matter of presumption of innocence, remember?"

My mind was whirling in a dozen different directions, none of them involving Chambers/Johnson's innocence. More than ever I wanted a chance to confront him, to put him through the same misery he'd caused that old woman and Cecelia's parents, to—

"Bay? You stay away from this guy, do you hear me? Tomorrow we'll meet with Mike Raleigh and lay it all out for him. Don't do anything to spook this jerk, okay? The best way to handle it is to let the boys with the badges and the big guns take care of it. Are we clear?"

I bit down hard on my lip and forced the anger out of my voice. "Got it. What time do you think you'll be home tomorrow?"

"Mid-morning, I'm guessing. Look, Bay, I'm serious about this. Stay away from Chambers or Johnson or whatever the hell his real name is. I don't want to be worrying about you all night long." When I didn't reply, he said, "Maybe I should just skip the raid and come home right now."

"Don't be an idiot, Red. Give me a little credit. I'm going to order a pizza and try to collate all our information so we can hand it over to Mike tomorrow."

"That's good. Try to have a nice relaxing evening and go to bed early. Read some. Put all this out of your mind, and I'll see you in the morning."

"You be careful yourself," I said. "No playing hero."

Red laughed. "Too old for that," he said, then added, "Love you."

"Me, too," I replied and hung up.

Immediately I punched in the number for my favorite pizza restaurant and placed an order, then called in a pass at the gate. In the bedroom, I changed into shorts and a T-shirt and carried my briefcase into the office across the hall. I assembled all the notes and the phone call printouts into some semblance of order and slipped them into the appropriate files. The lines Erik had highlighted jumped out at me, the ones from the prepaid cell. I picked up the desk phone and entered the number before I could think too hard about what I'd do if someone answered. I needn't have worried. I let it ring more than a dozen times with no result.

I carried the papers and disks into the bedroom, pulled back the carpet on the far end of my closet, and placed everything in the safe. A moment later, the front doorbell pealed. I stopped in the entryway to pull the Seecamp from my bag and slide it into the pocket of my shorts before I opened the door. No use pretending Red's revelation about Dalton Chambers hadn't spooked me, just a little.

I paid for the pizza and carried it to the glass-topped table in the bay window of the kitchen. I flipped on the TV that hung beneath the cupboards and tried to pay attention to the news while I polished off three slices of mushroom and pepperoni. I had just turned off the depressing litany of world crises and catastrophes when the house phone rang. I wiped my hands on a paper napkin and picked up.

"Just reporting in," Erik said. "Nothing so far."

"He's not home yet?"

"His car's not there. That's about all I can say for certain."

I checked the clock over the sink. "It's almost eight o'clock. Where the hell is he?"

"Probably out barhopping. Or maybe he had a date." When I didn't reply, he said, "Did you have a chance to run this whole thing by Red?"

I gave a fleeting thought to keeping the information about Chambers to myself. Like my husband, my partner would absolutely refuse to give me a crack at the slimeball once he heard about his background.

"Not exactly. But I did talk to him." Briefly, I gave him the rundown on Richard Charles Johnson.

"Jesus! So he could be wanted for murder if it wasn't for that neighbor. Does the sheriff's office know?"

"Not yet. Red wants us to lay it all out for Mike Raleigh tomorrow." I sighed. "I guess we might as well call off the surveillance for tonight, although it would be good to know if he shows up. Just to make sure he hasn't already flown the coop."

"I don't know, Bay. I'm starting to look conspicuous. The neighbors might think I'm casing the joint and call the cops."

"Why don't you have Stephanie go? All she has to do is walk by and see if his car's there."

"No way. I don't want Steph involved in any of this."

His tone made me bristle. "If you want her to come to work for us, she's going to be rubbing elbows with a few shady characters from time to time. It comes with the territory. There's no danger involved."

"Seems to me I've heard that before."

I cringed at the sarcasm in his voice. Erik, too, had nearly died in that Florida marina when Ben Wyler charged to his rescue. I had no defense to offer.

"You're right. Let it ride for tonight. We'll let the cops handle it."

"I'll keep checking," my partner said, his voice sounding contrite. "Talk to you later."

I held the phone against my ear for a few beats before setting it back in the cradle. That might have been as close to a full-fledged argument as Erik and I had ever come. It was what I had worried about when he'd first suggested that his future wife join the agency. Having Red hovering around playing nursemaid had been difficult enough, and he and I had been down a lot of roads together. This thing with Erik and Stephanie was shiny and new. And vulnerable.

I wrapped the rest of the pizza in foil and set it in the refrigerator. Back in the great room, I perused the book shelves that flanked the fireplace. In keeping with my obsessive-compulsive accountant background, my collection was arranged alphabetically by author. I didn't have anything too new, my preference being for the old classics that I had read before. Nothing stirred my interest. Restless, I wandered out onto the deck, shivering a little in a sharp breeze off the ocean. September and October were generally two of our most spectacular months, with low humidity and moderate temperatures and about a tenth of the number of visitors the summer brought.

I leaned my elbows on the railing and stared out over the dune toward the ocean, its surface rippling with soft color from the last rays of the sun settling over the mainland. The sky on the eastern horizon had already darkened, although it looked as if some of that might be storm clouds. This first month of autumn was also the height of hurricane season. There hadn't been anything concrete on the news, just that small tropical depression near the Bahamas I'd taken note of earlier in the week, but we were always wary this time of year. Hilton Head hadn't taken a direct hit since 1893, but Hugo in the late eighties had been a near thing. I shivered and walked back into the house.

I locked up and set the alarm before flopping onto the sofa and picking up the remote. There was bound to be baseball or college football on at least one of the two hundred channels. I surfed a while, feeling my eyes growing drowsy, before I found a Cubs-Braves game just going into the third inning. I stretched out and promptly fell asleep.

I clawed my way up out of a dreamless void to hear my own voice from the answering machine. I staggered up to the kitchen and got it just before the beep.

"Hello?" I mumbled, shaking my head to try and clear the cobwebs. "Bay Tanner," I said when no one responded.

"Is this the private detective?" The voice was female and unfamiliar, the hoarse whisper reminding me of that first phone call I'd gotten from Cecelia Dobbs. Suddenly, I was completely awake.

"Yes," I said. "Who's this?"

"It's Kendra Blaine. I work for Mr. Castlemain."

I couldn't have been more shocked if the woman had identified herself as Hillary Clinton. I pulled out the chair and dropped into it.

"Yes. We met at the memorial service."

"I need help," she said without further preamble.

"What kind of help?"

The silence stretched out, punctuated only by the woman's raspy breathing. It sounded as if she'd been running.

"Miss Blaine? What kind of help? Where are you?"

"At Canaan's Gate. I'm by the guesthouse. Can you come?"

My mind whirled. Was this some kind of game? Or a trap? Why on earth would Kendra Blaine be calling *me* for help?

"I don't understand. What do you want from me?"

I heard a sharp intake of breath. "He's going to kill me."

"Who? Who's going to kill you?"

My question met only silence.

"Miss Blaine? Kendra! Talk to me." Again I waited. "If you're in danger, you need to hang up and call the sheriff. Kendra?"

I almost missed the frantic whisper. "I can't! You know that! They'll arrest—" Her voice stopped abruptly, but I could still hear her breathing. "Oh, God! Oh, God! Help me. Please, you have to—"

Silence.

I pressed the phone more tightly against my ear, straining to detect the slightest hint of voices or any kind of sound. Nothing. I laid the handset on the desk and sprinted for my bag on the console table in the foyer. I dug out my cell, hit speed-dial for Erik's number, and raced back to the desk. With a phone glued to each ear, I waited.

My partner picked up almost immediately. "Bay, what's up?"

In as few words as possible, I related the phone call.

"I've still got an open line to her, I think, but I can't hear a damn thing," I concluded. "Is Chambers there?"

"No. I'm just walking back in from the last pass. His house is dark."

"I'm going over there. To Canaan's Gate." I left the house phone on the desk and carried the cell with me into the bedroom. "I just need to get some shoes on."

"Bay, for God's sake, call the sheriff. You can't go blundering into something you don't—"

"You call them. Ask for Mike Raleigh and tell him what's going on. Tell him about Chambers. Say I'll meet him there."

"Bay, don't be stupid! We need deputies rolling on this."

"I know that. But if she really killed Rebecca Castlemain, she may be more afraid of the sheriff than she is of whoever's after her. For whatever reason, she called *me*. Not the cops. Me. I have to go, Erik. I have to."

I hung up before he had a chance to throw any more common sense at me. He was right. Absolutely right. With luck, the sheriff's men would arrive before I did, but I couldn't wait. I'd let Cecelia Dobbs down, and she was dead.

I wasn't about to let that happen again.

CHAPTER
THIRTY-EIGHT

RAFFIC WAS SPARSE THAT LATE ON A WEDNESDAY night, and I ran through a couple of red lights after checking the intersections. Despite all that, I slid into the turn for Wexford Plantation just behind a Beaufort County cruiser with lights flashing. He blew through the security gate, and I followed right on his tail. I think the poor woman in the gatehouse was too shocked even to notice.

We squealed to a stop in front of the massive gates, and I leaped from the Jaguar. The white Crown Victoria I'd noticed in the parking lot of my office was skewed off to one side, and Detective Mike Raleigh stood in the open door talking into his cell phone.

Before the deputy could bar my way, I was standing at Raleigh's shoulder. He glanced at me briefly, apparently not surprised to find me in the middle of his operation.

"I understand that, ma'am," he was saying, "and I don't have any intention of disturbing Mr. Castlemain. We just need to check the grounds. We'll be discreet. Please unlock the gate and turn on the outside lights."

I looked around at the quiet neighborhood, its scattered houses concealed behind screening hedges, a gap in the trees where it looked as if some kind of construction was going on. The lights of the cruiser flickered across their facades in a pulsing rhythm like a heartbeat. Discretion was already out the window, I thought a moment before the sound of a motor broke the stillness. I watched the massive gates swing inward.

"Cut the light bars," Mike Raleigh said to one of the two deputies hovering beside their cars.

There was only a moment of darkness before the courtyard was turned almost to day by well-hidden floodlights. Only then did the detective acknowledge my presence.

"Give it to me again," he said without greeting or preamble. "What exactly did this woman say?"

I related it as best I could, considering I'd been wakened from a deep sleep and had been shocked by both the caller and her words. As I spoke, he began walking, through the gates and up the drive, and I trailed along in his wake. By the time we stepped through into the inner courtyard, Cady Proffit stood in the open doorway.

She had on her nurse's face, stern and defiant, prepared to protect her patient at any cost. I craned my neck, expecting to find Nicholas Potter looming behind her, but the vast entryway stood otherwise empty.

Mike Raleigh spoke softly. "I'm sorry to disturb you, ma'am, but as I said on the phone, we've had a report of someone in trouble here."

"Who?" Nurse Proffit nearly barked the question.

I knew enough to stay out of it. My head swiveled toward the guesthouse, which nestled in the trees to the right of the main building. I itched to get over there, but I knew the deputies flanking me would be having none of that.

"A Kendra Blaine." Raleigh nodded in my direction. "She called Mrs. Tanner here half an hour ago and asked for help."

"Miss Blaine isn't here," Cady said. "She left about seven thirty."

"For where?" Raleigh asked.

"Home, I expect. Mr. Potter told . . . asked her not to stay over in the house while he's here." She pulled herself up and straightened her shoulders. "Besides, I'm a trained LPN. I'm perfectly capable of seeing to Mr. Castlemain's needs."

"I understood Miss Blaine often stayed in the guesthouse," Mike Raleigh said, inclining his head in that direction.

"Sometimes," Cady Proffit replied. "But not tonight."

Come on, come on, I urged silently. I took a tentative step toward the smaller building and ran smack up against the rock-hard shoulder of one of the deputies. He didn't even flinch.

"We're going to check out the grounds. First," Raleigh added in a firm voice. His implication wasn't lost on the nurse. "With your permission, of course. Unless you'd prefer I speak to your employer?"

Cady Proffit held her ground, but she also knew when she was outnumbered. "That won't be necessary. I'll check around inside, but I can guarantee you she isn't here. I just got Mr. Castlemain settled in for the night, and I won't have you disturbing him." Her chin came back up. "I know my rights."

"Is Nick here?" I asked, and the detective turned to scowl at me.

"No, he's not. But I'll try to reach him." She relaxed her shoulders a little and spoke again, this time in a less belligerent tone. "I know you're just doin' your job, but I have to do mine, too. You look around outside all you want, but please do it quietly. Mr. Castlemain just lost his wife. The man deserves a little peace."

"Thank you, Mrs. Proffit. We'll do our best not to disturb him." He paused and held her gaze. "If I need anything else, I'll call."

He spun on his heel and nearly ran me down. "Stay here, Mrs. Tanner. Sanchez, Miles, you're with me."

I hadn't paid much attention to the deputies, but I recognized both their names. Rudy Sanchez had been to my house in answer to my alarm system a couple of times the past winter, in the middle of the whole mess surrounding Dolores and her son Bobby. And Ted

Miles I'd met at the crime scene where they'd pulled Cecelia's body from the lagoon. I suppressed a shudder.

"Detective, wait! If she's hiding out there, she isn't going to show herself to you or the deputies."

"Why not?"

I didn't want to get into a lengthy explanation of Kendra Blaine's reasons for avoiding the police. That could wait until after we found her. "She called *me*, remember?" I said. "Not the sheriff. Let me come along. I promise I'll keep out of your way."

"And what if this Chambers guy is out there with a gun or something? What if this isn't just some stupid prank?"

"Then I'm safer with you."

He thought about it for a moment, then jerked his head. "Okay. Just stay back."

I trailed behind him and the deputies across the acre of concrete, past the three-car garage on the side of the villa, and down a walkway that led to the guesthouse. All the windows were dark, the door locked when he rattled the handle. Although the floods cast a dim light against the front of the cottage, they didn't reach into the thick shrubbery surrounding it. Both men clicked on their flashlights.

"Sanchez, you stay here. Miles, take the right," the detective said and moved off in the other direction.

I swiveled my head between the two of them and headed left.

"Kendra," I called softly, and Raleigh turned to look at me. "If she's hiding from someone, we have to let her know we're not the bad guys," I said, ignoring his frown. "Kendra, it's Bay Tanner. No one's going to hurt you. Come on out."

Raleigh worked the light back and forth, but there wasn't much to see besides neat beds of hibiscus spread with pine straw and low bushes that couldn't conceal anything bigger than a raccoon. In a very short time, we met up with Miles at the rear of the house.

"Anything?" the detective asked, and the deputy shook his head.

"Looks normal to me," he replied. "No broken windows or any sign of a struggle."

Raleigh pointed his flashlight at the ground. His face was almost invisible, but I could hear the disbelief in his voice. "You're sure she said she was here?"

"Positive. And I'm convinced she'd been running." I looked over at the small bungalow. "She was definitely outside."

"And she said someone was trying to kill her."

I stifled my rising anger. "She said, 'He's going to kill me.' Not *trying*." I sighed and forced myself to speak more calmly. "Maybe she got away."

"Detective! Over here!"

Raleigh and I turned in unison. Deputy Miles had moved farther away from the house, into the trees that bordered the next property, and was waving his flashlight back and forth. We both sprinted in his direction.

Raleigh got there first. "What have you got?"

We looked down at the circle of light illuminating a few dead leaves and some broken twigs. And a bright red cell phone lying open on the ground.

"Hold this." Mike Raleigh thrust his flashlight into my hand, and I took it without thinking. He reached into his jacket pocket and extracted a pair of latex gloves.

I held the light steady as he snapped on the gloves and reached for the phone.

"Ever see this before?"

It took me a moment to realize he was talking to me. "No. But I never saw Kendra use her cell, so that doesn't mean anything."

Raleigh picked it up gingerly between his thumb and index finger. With the motion, the hibernating screen light powered up, and we both stared at the number stacked across the tiny square.

"Recognize it?" Raleigh asked, and I nodded.

"It's mine."

"Go get an evidence bag," he said, and Deputy Miles trotted off.

I still held the detective's flashlight, and I pointed it toward the line of bushes a few feet away. "Look at that," I said.

Raleigh followed the beam to where a gap had been forced into the otherwise unbroken line of shrubbery. He took the light with his left hand, the cell phone still dangling from his right, and held it on the narrow break.

"Somebody went through there all right," he said, almost to himself.

I followed him as he skirted a direct path, coming up on the area from the side, to avoid contaminating the scene, I assumed. I tried to follow where he stepped as exactly as I could. The broken twigs lay mostly on the opposite side of the break, which meant whoever had forced their way through had come from this side. He played the light slowly over the ground.

We both saw it at the same time. A white sandal, one strap ripped loose. Mike Raleigh stepped closer, working the Maglite in an arc out from the shoe. It wavered when I gasped, then settled steadily on the pale foot, its nails glowing bright pink against the dull brown of the pine straw.

CHAPTER
THIRTY-NINE

*S*HE WASN'T DEAD. AND SHE WASN'T KENDRA BLAINE.

I sat behind the wheel of the Jaguar, effectively blocked in by three more cruisers and, up until a few minutes ago, a fire department emergency response vehicle. The EMTs had loaded up a gurney and screamed off to the hospital with a hysterical mother hovering in the back over her dazed teenaged daughter.

I'd already called Erik and reported in. Of course he wanted to come charging to my rescue, but I talked him down. Raleigh had ordered me to stick around, and I knew our next discussion would be a lot more intense and probably conducted across a table in an interview room at the sheriff's office. I didn't have a problem with that. Things had gone too far for me to hold out on him, especially now that innocent bystanders were being drawn into the violence. I felt almost relieved to be handing things off to the quiet-spoken detective, just as Red and I had planned.

"Did Chambers ever show up?" I asked once Erik and I had made our joint decision to turn everything over to the sheriff.

"Nope." He hesitated. "You think he's involved in this?"

"Don't you? It sounds to me like the classic falling-out among thieves. Maybe Dalton decided he didn't want to share anymore. Or Kendra could have wanted out. We won't know until they catch up to them." I paused to watch Mike Raleigh move into huddled conference with his two deputies in the brightly lit courtyard. I'd given him everything Red had told me about Johnson alias Chambers and a general description of his car so they could get it out on the wire. *Wanted for questioning* was how Raleigh had put it when he called it in. Hopefully, they'd pick up both of them soon. I didn't want to think about Kendra lying facedown in another slimy lagoon. "Do you have everything downloaded off your computer?"

"Yeah. Say the word, and I'll bring it wherever you need. It all fit on one flash drive, so—"

"Wait! Did you get a chance to look at the drive you . . . accidentally kept from Nick Potter?"

Raleigh was walking toward me as Erik spoke. "Just a quick run through the files. The new program I've got cracked the passwords in less than five minutes. You know I'm not really up on all this financial stuff. That's more your area, but I can tell you this—those people have got more money than God. And there's something—"

"Hold that thought. Raleigh wants me. I'll call you about where to bring the drive." In a rush, I added, "But stash the one from Nick. It's not part of our— Yes, Detective?" I slapped the phone closed and stuck my head out the open window. "How's the girl?"

Mike Raleigh rested a hand on the roof of the Jaguar and leaned down. "She'll be fine. Sprained wrist and a nasty bump on her forehead, but nothing too serious. She was only out for a couple of minutes."

"So we just missed Kendra," I said, more to myself than to him.

"Assuming she's the one."

"Who else would it have been? Isn't that her cell phone? And her shoe?"

"The phone, sure, especially with your number on there as the last one called. And you're right, that sandal didn't belong to the girl next door. She was barefoot." In the bright, floodlit driveway I could see his weary smile. "Out looking for her cat and ended up in the wrong place at the wrong time."

"Does she remember anything about it?"

"She's still a little groggy, but she says she heard someone running on the other side of the hedge. Then whoever it was burst through and just ran her down."

"Was it Kendra?"

"The girl didn't get a good look. It all happened too fast."

"So she *was* being chased."

"We don't know that for a fact."

I shut up, because he was right, and neither one of us spoke for a few moments. Finally Detective Mike Raleigh stood up straight and ran a hand over his face.

"Look, Mrs. Tanner—"

"Call me Bay," I said.

"All right. Bay. Here's the thing. I have a lot of respect for your husband. He was a damn fine officer, and a lot of us think he got a raw deal, getting passed over and all. We really hated to see him go. Walterboro is going to be lucky to have him."

I interrupted. "But that doesn't mean you can cut me any slack about this whole mess." When he didn't respond, I said, "Right?"

It took him a moment. "Right. I'm sorry, but that's how it is."

"I understand. If there's one thing Red's taught me it's that there comes a time when I just need to step away and leave it to you guys." I smiled. "Even when it kills me to admit it."

He smiled back. "I appreciate that. You know, you've got a good reputation around town. You're honest, and you don't try to muscle in on things we should be taking care of. Most of the time. But everyone in the department knows you're a straight shooter."

"Thank you. So now what? You want me down at the station?"

"Yeah. We'll need a formal statement. I've got one more thing to do here." He glanced over his shoulder to where Sanchez and Miles still stood sentinel in the driveway. He motioned them over, then turned back to me. "I'm going to do a room-by-room inside the house. Just to cover all the bases. We've already been over the cottage. I'm sure the nurse would tell me if anyone was hiding out in there, but it's a huge place. Can you wait here a while longer?"

"All the files you'll want to see are in my safe at the house. And my partner downloaded everything from our computers. Why don't I go grab all that and meet you at the station?"

His hesitation surprised me.

"It'd be better if you hang on here until I'm done. I'll follow you over."

I bristled. "You think I'm going to abscond with the evidence, Detective?"

"Of course not," he said as Miles and Sanchez joined him. "Chain of custody. It'll be better for the case if I take possession directly from your safe. And from your partner. When we catch up with whoever did this, I don't want some smart-ass lawyer getting the bastard off because we screwed up."

I sighed and leaned back in my seat. "Fine."

"Thanks," he said, as if I had some choice in the matter.

I watched the three of them approach the inner courtyard, then more light spill out onto the pavement as the door opened. A moment later, they all disappeared inside.

I leaned my head back against the seat and closed my eyes, going over in my mind all the jumbled pieces of the case. When it came time to make a statement, I wanted to be able to lay it all out, logically, so that Dalton Chambers—and Kendra Blaine—would be tied up with a bow. In the silence, I felt myself drifting off, an image of the Judge floating into my head. Not as he'd been in his later years, crippled by the strokes, tied to the wheelchair, and almost helpless without Lavinia, but as I'd seen him so many times, first as an attorney and finally behind the bench. On many of the scorching summer after-noons of my childhood, while my mother hobnobbed with her society friends over tea and cucumber sandwiches in some stuffy mansion on The Point, I'd sneaked away to huddle in the back of the courtroom, entranced by the formality and pomp of the law in action. Tall and straight, his hair just beginning to gray, my father had righted wrongs and meted out justice in a booming baritone that sounded to my child's ears like the voice of God.

I missed him so much it was a physical pain in my chest.

I jerked open the car door and stepped out into the night to find that the air had grown chilly. The house must be close to the water, I thought, the breeze carrying that unmistakable odor of pluff mud and the marshes that ringed the island. I breathed deeply and leaned against the fender of the Jaguar, lusting after a cigarette. Restless, I walked past the empty cruisers and Raleigh's unmarked car to the tall gates folded back at right angles against the pillars. I ran my hands over the intricate scrollwork, tracing a pattern that, according to Mr. Castlemain, had first been conceived by artisans a couple of thousand years before. I wondered how they'd managed to construct something so delicate and yet so massive without modern tools. Was it like the pyramids, I wondered, picturing a thousand sweating slaves hauling the hundreds of pounds of iron onto a set of rollers and laboriously dragging it across a vast desert or up a mountainside—

I started to turn at what had sounded like a footfall behind me, but I never made it. Before I could even move my head, I felt the cold barrel of the gun pressed against my neck.

CHAPTER
FORTY

"**N**OT A SOUND."

It was a whisper, and I froze where I stood.

"Back up. Slowly."

A hand gripped my left arm, guiding me as I shuffled my feet, my eyes fastened on the door into Canaan's Gate. I didn't know whether to pray for it to open or stay firmly shut. Even if the three sheriff's men came bolting out at that exact moment, there was no way they'd be able to take him out. I made the perfect shield, and my captor knew it.

It took only a minute for us to reach my car, but we didn't stop there. In just a few steps we were out of the glare of the floodlights and into the half twilight of the street. So far I hadn't seen even the shape of his hand, the gun jammed into my neck making it impossible for me to move my head even a fraction. Taller than I, and strong. His fingers dug into my upper arm like talons, cutting off the blood. I could feel my left hand going numb. He breathed evenly, calmly.

I stumbled against the curb on the other side of the street, and he jerked me upright. He hadn't said a word since we'd begun moving. A moment later we were in the trees of the vacant lot opposite Canaan's

Gate, the darkness pressing in on me as he pulled me deeper into the sparse woods.

I tried to judge our direction and distance by keeping my eyes fixed on the dwindling light from the Castlemain house. Abruptly, we swung left and moments later came out into a clearing. I could feel loose dirt under my feet, and Canaan's Gate had disappeared completely from sight. It was lighter, too, and I could make out shapes—piles of lumber stacked nearby and lengths of plastic pipe. A construction site. I remembered then that slash in the trees. I spotted a foundation and rough framing rising from the cleared ground.

I still couldn't turn, and a wave of dizziness washed over me. My captor and I moved behind two towering stacks of bricks and finally stopped. Neither of us had said a word, although the unterrified part of my brain had been churning. Dalton Chambers had made a terrible mistake. Somehow or other I'd make that painfully clear to him. I just needed an opportunity.

"On the ground." Again that raspy whisper.

He jerked my left arm up behind me, forcing me to my knees. For the first time, I seriously considered that he might be going to shoot me right there.

"Okay. Take it easy," I managed to croak out.

I let myself slide forward until I lay facedown. The pistol in my pocket pressed against my thigh, but there was no way to get to it. Suddenly, the pressure was gone from my neck, and I tensed, ready to make a move. As quickly as the thought passed through my head, my right arm was wrenched behind me, and I felt some sort of twine being wrapped around my hands. I grunted at the pain. Work completed, he jerked me to my feet. Something silky, like a scarf, slipped over my eyes, and I felt panic beginning to rise in my throat.

"This is ridiculous, Dalton," I said, proud that my voice sounded almost steady, "or Richard or whatever the hell your real name is. Just tell me what you want."

Again the vicious grip on my arm steered me across the rough ground. A few moments later we stopped again. I heard locks click and the soft *whoosh* of a trunk lid or rear door sliding open on its hydraulic lifts.

"You don't have to do this." This time I could hear the terror quivering in my own words. "Please."

I'd never considered myself especially claustrophobic, but the thought of being stuffed into a trunk, bound and blindfolded, entirely helpless, made my whole body tremble in naked fear. I felt the gun again, this time pressed against my forehead, and forced myself to get control. The rational part of my brain kept arguing that he wouldn't risk a shot this close to Canaan's Gate, with Mike Raleigh and the two deputies liable to materialize at any moment. Still, this whole kidnapping thing had been the work of a madman to begin with, so why should I expect him to be thinking logically?

At least he hadn't gagged me. "Tell me what you want. This isn't going to work, Dalton. You know that."

"Shut up."

I gasped as his hands gripped my waist and hoisted me up. My face connected with the rough nap of a carpet. He swung my legs in, and I almost sobbed with relief to find myself in the back of a van or closed truck of some kind, not the cramped trunk of a Lexus sports car. I wondered if he'd stolen it. Regardless, I gave thanks for the feeling of space around me. I jerked when he grabbed my ankles. The same twine was wrapped around them as on my wrists. Then he pushed me forward, and I felt something soft, like a blanket, settle over me.

I heard the back door click shut, then the driver's. A moment later, we were moving.

I tried to brace myself, to keep from rolling around like a sack of potatoes, and finally managed to wedge my feet into a depression of some kind on the side panel. As the vehicle crept slowly across the uneven ground of the construction site, I flopped back and forth a little, my bare arms sliding painfully across the carpeted floor, but I managed to stay mostly stationary. Once out on the paved roads of Wexford, it got easier. I kept my head turned to the side so I had some room to breathe between my face and the smothering blanket.

I forced my mind to concentrate on where we were going, but I wasn't sure I was getting it right until the combination of a marked slowing, followed by a gentle curve, right, then left, told me we'd come out of the plantation and into the small roundabout just past its entrance. Then a long stop—for the traffic light at Route 278. We turned left onto the highway.

Dalton Chambers drove slowly. Getting pulled over for speeding would definitely ruin his plans. The next light was at Palmetto Dunes. But if it was green, as it was likely to be at this time of night, that wouldn't give me another marker as to our destination. The idea of my not surviving this nightmare never crossed my mind. I'd find a way.

For a while I tried to memorize the stops and turns, but eventually I lost all concept of time and distance, and the constant humming of the tires and the total absence of light combined to lull me into a state of numbed acceptance. I'd know where we were when we got there. Instead of trying to track our route, I gave myself up to visions of what I would do to this incredible moron when I finally got my hands on him. I pictured him as I'd glimpsed him in the bank, handsome and smiling, his head cocked to one side in rapt attention to the woman who stood at his teller window. Until Red had unearthed his previous record, I hadn't been sure he was the one responsible for poor Cecelia's body being abandoned in the mucky lagoon off Pope Avenue. It could just as well have been Kendra who had actually done the dirty work. She was the one with opportunity, the only one who could have pressed a stun gun through the bedclothes against the sagging skin of Rebecca Castlemain's chest. I'd seen Chambers as the brains, Kendra the muscle.

But I'd obviously been wrong. I wondered where she'd run to, how she'd managed to get away. I told myself she might call the sheriff, once she'd put some distance between herself and her former partner, but it was a slim hope. If she'd managed to escape Dalton's attempt on her life, she'd more than likely just keep on running. I couldn't picture Kendra Blaine giving a damn about what happened to me now that I'd served my purpose.

Suddenly, I felt us slow, then a stomping of the brakes and a violent turn to the left ripped my feet free of their precarious hold and rolled me all the way across the floor of the vehicle. My nose banged painfully as we bumped across uneven ground, and I was flung over onto my other side. My knees came to rest on something solid, but it wasn't a metal or upholstered side panel. The bare skin of my legs brushed up against something slick and scratchy, like heavy plastic. The implication of it barely had time to register before the vehicle stopped.

I held my breath and scooted as best I could away from whatever lay next to me. I heard the front door open and close. When the rear door lifted, I could hear the ocean, and fear gripped me. Trussed up like a Thanksgiving turkey, I wouldn't last a minute. I'd heard drowning wasn't a bad way to go, like drifting off to sleep. But how did anybody really know that? Cecelia could have told me, except— My mind cannonaded from one wild thought to another. I twisted at the twine that held my wrists behind me, and the pain finally broke through my panic.

While I was still alive, I had a chance. While I was still alive . . .

He pulled me almost gently from the back of the vehicle and set me on my feet. I could smell the water now, too, and the rustle beneath my shoes was definitely sand.

"Throwing me in there isn't going to solve anything. There are records. And a lot of people besides me know all about your little scheme. You won't be able to kill them all."

I heard a sharp click and thought, *Knife!* But why bother when the ocean—

A moment later my ankles were free, and a few seconds after that, my arms. I shook my hands, hoping to return enough circulation to them to make a grab for the Seecamp in my pocket.

"Please don't try anything, Bay. There's no point."

I gasped. No, I had to be wrong. Slowly, I raised my hands and slipped the blindfold from my eyes. The moon had risen, and I blinked even in that dim light. I shook my head and looked up into the barrel of a handgun.

And the scowling face of Nicholas Potter.

CHAPTER
FORTY-ONE

I FOUND MYSELF UNABLE TO UTTER A SINGLE WORD.
Amazingly, Potter smiled.

"Not even a hint it was me? Maybe I gave you too much credit all
the way around. I figured you had it all nailed down when you switched
flash drives on me."

I swallowed and procrastinated, still trying to get the feeling back
in my hands. "That was a mistake. They got mixed up by accident."

"Come on, Bay. If that's true, why didn't you call and tell me?"

I flexed my knees slightly, pleased to find myself steady on my feet.
"Erik just told me tonight. I would have let you know in the morning."

"Kendra said the same thing, but I'm not buying it. I want that
drive. And the passwords. I'm sure your genius partner has cracked
them by now."

I couldn't suppress a shudder at what probably lay wrapped in the
sheath of plastic in the open hatch of Nick Potter's SUV. I folded my
arms across my chest and glanced briefly over my shoulder. "Is that
Kendra?"

He ignored the question. "Where is the drive?"

I almost told him it was in my bag in the Jaguar and probably in the hands of the sheriff by now. Just in time, though, I realized it was my one bargaining chip. And I sure as hell wasn't giving up Erik. "At home," I lied with not a quiver in my voice. "In my safe."

"Then we'll need to hurry. I have plans for later this evening."

He said it as if he had a dinner date. He was either the coolest murderer I'd ever heard of or completely out of his mind. Neither one boded well for my getting out of this in one piece. But he needed me alive and conscious—and unbound—to get him inside the gates of Port Royal Plantation. And supposedly into the safe in my bedroom closet.

I turned toward the SUV. "So let's go." I used the motion to cover easing my right hand into my pocket. *Empty!* I almost gasped in frustration. The little pistol must have slid out during that last turn that had sent me rolling across the floor. If he saw it there, my best chance would be gone.

"Not so fast. We have a little work to do first."

Again I shuddered as he shoved the gun into my back and urged me forward.

"Take the legs."

I whipped my head around. His face, lit dimly by a glint of moonlight off the water, looked perfectly calm, as if he'd just made a comment about the weather.

"No."

The gun barrel bored into my spine, and I couldn't prevent a grunt of pain.

"If I shoot you right now, no one will hear."

"If you shoot me right now, you won't get the flash drive."

"I'll find another way. Besides, I've learned a little over the past few days about how your mind works. Your clever little brain is racing, trying to come up with a way out of this. Who knows, you might even manage to outsmart me. But not if you're dead. Your call."

Again he pushed me forward. He was right. I reached for the plastic bundle.

"Good girl. Just haul it out."

I didn't see any alternative. I held my breath, wrapped my hands around the ankles, and pulled. Potter stepped back to give me room, and I jerked with all my strength. I winced when the head bounced off the rear bumper, but Kendra Blaine was beyond feeling. I hadn't been able to save her any more than I had Cecelia. The effort and the pain of my failures left me breathless, and I leaned over, gasping for air. I let a whimper escape and dropped to my knees.

"No games, Bay. I know this isn't the first dead body you've run across." He took a step toward me.

"Okay. Just give me a second." I braced myself against the sand, my probing fingers finally closing around the pistol. I prayed he hadn't seen it slide out from under the body and onto the ground. I feigned using the back of the SUV to lever myself to my feet and dropped the gun in my pocket as I turned. Even if I'd managed to raise the pistol and get off a shot, he'd still have time to put one right into my forehead. We were too close together. I forced myself to stay calm. My chance would come.

"Now into the water."

I could see the white froth of the surf breaking just a couple of yards from my feet. "Why didn't you just leave me tied up and do the dirty work yourself? It would have been faster."

"But not nearly so satisfying. I've decided I don't like you, Bay. You're too arrogant, too sure of yourself. Pretty much everything I despise in a woman. Pity, too. You're quite attractive, in an Amazon sort of way."

"So are you. In an oily, gigolo sort of way."

The backhand came out of nowhere and staggered me. I stumbled up against the back of the SUV.

"Enough! Get him in the water."

Tears blurred my eyes, and I could feel the welt already rising on my cheek. I reached for the plastic and began tugging it the few feet toward the lapping of the waves when his words registered.

"Him?"

"Move!"

I heaved again, the muscles of my shoulders screaming in protest. In a few moments, I stood, breathing hard, calf-deep in the ocean.

"You said 'him.' This isn't Kendra?"

He laughed. "You actually fell for that damsel-in-distress business? She said you would. Frankly, I was surprised you'd be so gullible." His face clouded for a moment. "The cops were an annoyance we hadn't planned on. I felt sure you'd come riding to the rescue all on your own. But then everything eventually worked out." The half sneer, half smile was back. "She's a terrific little actress, isn't she?"

"You're not so bad yourself."

"Years of practice, hanging out with politicians. Kissing their asses and greasing their palms. You've never met a greedier bunch of con men in your life."

An idea had begun to form, but I needed him distracted. "You must have felt right at home."

"If I shoot you now, I won't even have to drag your body into the water."

"What would be the fun in that? Where's Kendra?"

"Cleaning up a few last-minute details. That's far enough."

As we talked, I'd been steadily hauling my burden farther out into the wash of the tide. Without landmarks, I had no idea where we were along the shoreline of the island, except that we had to be on the north end. That first turn at the light had been a left, then a series of turns, and the hard left before we bounced out onto the beach. We couldn't be in one of the plantations. Potter wouldn't have a pass. And besides, I hadn't heard any conversation between him and a security guard. I was guessing somewhere in the area of Mitchellville, maybe the end of Beach City Road or behind Barker Field.

"I said that's enough." His voice rose, and he moved closer to the water.

For the first time, I noticed he wore long pants and dress shoes, his white shirt almost a beacon in the moonlight. If the Seecamp had any range, I would have taken a chance right then and there. Maybe I'd have to investigate a bigger weapon. If I lived long enough.

"Unwrap the plastic," he called more softly, and I saw the glint of the gun in his hand as he raised it higher, aiming right at my heart.

I scrabbled to find the edge, then began tugging on it. The gruesome package unraveled, and its contents splashed into the surf. A wave washed over it, spraying the legs of my shorts and causing the body to turn slowly, faceup.

I was not the least surprised now to find myself looking into the still, handsome face of Richard Charles Johnson, alias Dalton Chambers.

I didn't have to exaggerate my jump back as the body bumped up against my leg. Even in the wavering light I could see the hole in his forehead, the edges crusted with blood that had stopped flowing hours ago.

I forced away the nausea and did a quick check on either side of me. To the left, I thought I could make out a boardwalk or jetty, just a darker outline against the moonlit night. My eyes still on the stiffening corpse, I slowly worked the sneakers off my feet.

"Get in here," Nick Potter called, motioning with the hand that held the pistol. I drew in a deep breath and held it a moment before I spun on my toes and flung myself backward into the surf.

CHAPTER
FORTY-TWO

SWIMMING UNDERWATER—IN THE OCEAN, IN THE dark—is completely disorienting. I'd dived to my left and back, into deeper water, where I hoped my silhouette wouldn't make me an easy target. I waited for the report of the gun, but if it ever came, I never heard it. I used up every last molecule of oxygen before I rose, gasping, and nearly ran face-first into a piling of the boardwalk jutting out from the shore. I wrapped my arms around a slimy post and moved behind it.

Though I scanned the beach back in the direction I'd come from, I couldn't make out either Nick Potter or his SUV. I strained to hear over the soft lapping of the waves against the pilings, but my own harsh breathing overrode almost every other sound. I began counting, slowly, until I'd reached enough seconds for a full five minutes. I ducked back beneath the rolling surf and stroked out into deeper water, trying to gain some perspective about exactly where I was. I couldn't see any point of reference except the structure I had taken refuge behind.

No boat dock at the end, so it must have been strictly for pedestrians. A walkout we called them, a place, perhaps with benches, to sit and revel in the beauty of the sea and the beach. The Spa! Finally far enough out, I could see the faint outline of the condominium complex, its security lights casting a glow against the canopy of trees surrounding the several buildings. I had been right. Potter must have taken us in at the new park at Mitchellville. He'd driven right down the wide access path onto the beach.

I treaded water and looked to my left. Port Royal Plantation lay in that direction. *Home.* I pondered whether or not I had it in me to swim that far, or whether I should chance the beach. I couldn't remember any other access in this direction that didn't come through a gated plantation until you got close to the Westin. Running would be faster.

In a few strokes I hit the shallow water and walked up onto the tightly packed sand. I dropped down and sat for a moment, catching my breath, before rising and breaking into a sprint.

I knew better than to leave a spare key in some obvious place, like under the welcome mat or a flowerpot on the front porch. My hiding place of choice was on a string tied to the base of the third hibiscus plant from the corner of the house, the key itself pushed down into the sandy soil. It took me only a moment to retrieve it, and in seconds I was inside, shivering, but safe. I fumbled in my code and immediately reset the alarm.

I slid down onto the hardwood floor in the foyer and let my head drop onto my knees. Though my clothes had dried during my frantic run down the beach from Mitchellville, I felt as cold as if I'd taken a plunge into some icy lake in the middle of January. Finally, I forced myself to my feet. Tracking sand behind me, I stumbled into the hallway toward my bedroom. In a moment, I had my crusty, filthy shorts, T-shirt, and ruined underwear wadded up in a ball and the blessed familiar warmth of my old chenille robe wrapped tightly around me.

More than anything I wanted a shower, but it would have to wait. I curled up on the bed and, with shaking hands, picked up the phone.

"Beaufort County Sheriff's Office. Do you have an emergency?"

I almost laughed. Tough question. "Detective Mike Raleigh, please. Bay Tanner calling. It's urgent."

"Did you say 'Tanner'?"

"Yes, ma'am."

"One moment."

It took a little longer than that, but not much.

"Bay? Where are you? Are you all right?"

"I'm home. And yes, I'm fine. Now."

"What the hell happened? Where did you go? I came out and—"

"Detective, listen. We can talk about all that later. You need to find Nicholas Potter. He killed Dalton Chambers."

"What?! What are you saying?"

"He grabbed me from in front of Canaan's Gate while you were inside. He made me help him dump Chambers' body in the ocean, somewhere around Mitchellville Park. Get someone over there before it gets carried out to sea. Potter's driving a black Expedition, fairly new. You saw it that night at my office. I don't know if it's a rental or he owns it. He and Kendra Blaine are in it together. They probably killed Cecelia Dobbs and Rebecca Castlemain as well. And if they've got an ounce of sense, they're running."

"Slow down, Bay. How do you know all this? You're saying he *kidnapped* you? How did you—?"

"Remember that little speech you gave me tonight? The one about how everyone at the sheriff's office knows I'm a straight shooter? If you meant that, then trust me, for a little while at least, and get the information out on his vehicle. I'll explain everything then."

The silence seemed to go on for a long time. "Okay," he finally said. "I'll get it in motion and call you right back."

"I'll be here."

"Are you in any danger? Should I send someone?"

I glanced at the Seecamp on the bedside table, unsure of whether or not it would function after its dunking in the ocean. But I had its twin stashed in an old, empty VHS tape box next to the fireplace in the great room. And there was the alarm.

"I'm fine, but I'll be a lot better when you have Potter and Blaine handcuffed to chairs in an interview room."

"I'm going to send a couple of guys over to park themselves in your driveway just in case. I'll be over myself as soon as I can. Don't let anyone in unless you verify their ID."

I bit back a retort and simply said, "Of course," before hanging up and immediately speed-dialing Erik.

By the few seconds it took him to pick up, I knew he'd been sitting with his cell phone clutched in his hand.

"Bay! Where the hell have you been? Did they arrest you or something? I've been trying—"

"I'm fine, Erik. Take it easy. I'm sitting at home, and I can't talk long. I expect Mike Raleigh to be calling me back in just a couple of minutes. Listen now, and don't interrupt. I'll give you all the details later."

In a few, brief sentences, I told him what had transpired since we'd last spoken.

"So hopefully Raleigh will pick them up and that'll be the end of it," I concluded. "But Potter risked a lot to get that flash drive back. As I said, he thinks it's here in my safe, but that doesn't mean he might not have figured out I was lying. He could come after you. I'll ask Mike to send a cruiser over there to keep an eye on things."

"We're all locked up here. Don't worry about us."

"You don't have a weapon there, do you?"

Erik had never been a big fan of firearms, although I'd tried on several occasions to convince him that our line of work often made going armed the smart thing to do. I didn't like the idea of the two of them sitting in his condo unprotected by either firepower or an alarm system with Nicholas Potter on the loose.

"Stephanie keeps a gun here."

The revelation surprised me. "Really? You never said anything."

"Ben taught her how to use it. I'm not crazy about the idea, but it makes her feel better."

"Me, too. Tell her to keep it handy. Just in case."

"Potter wouldn't be stupid enough to try something like that. You're right—he's on the run now."

"I wouldn't have thought he was crazy enough to kidnap me right out from under the nose of three sheriff's officers either, but he managed to pull it off."

"But I don't get it about the drive. I mean, he's the one who gave it to us in the first place. If it was so damn important, why did he—?"

My phone beeped. "Incoming call. Gotta go. I'll get back to you as soon as I know anything."

I pushed buttons. "Bay Tanner."

"Mike Raleigh. We've got an APB out on the Expedition. Are the deputies there yet?"

"I don't know. I'm in the back of the house. Hold on." I carried the phone with me down the hallway and through the dining room. All the lights were off, except for the one over the sink in the kitchen, and all the drapes were pulled. I twitched aside the one overlooking the driveway. The security lights bathed the whole area. "Not yet," I said, staring at the empty concrete pad in front of the garage.

"Damn it! Let me get them on the horn. Listen, I'm on my way, too. I'm about five, ten minutes out."

He hung up before I could reply.

I looked down at my robe and realized I was completely naked underneath. I dropped the phone on the dining table and hurried back to the bedroom. I dug clean underwear and a pair of sweats out of the bureau and pulled them on. In spite of the warmth of the heavy material, I still felt chilled all the way to my bones. In the adjoining bathroom, I wet a cloth and wiped the worst of the salt off my face and the mud from my feet. Emerging back into the bedroom, I glanced at the clock, congratulating myself that I'd managed it all in three minutes flat. Smiling, I headed for the kitchen to put the kettle on but skidded to a stop just short of the great room.

I couldn't have said what primal instinct had sent the warning signal stabbing deep into my brain. I only knew, suddenly, that I was in danger. Something in the air—a current? A smell? Long ago—and in a very painful way—I'd learned to trust the hairs on the back of my neck, even when logic told me they had to be wrong.

Very slowly, I slid my feet backward, silently, across the hardwood floor. At the doorway to my bedroom, I darted inside and eased the door shut, engaging the lock. After my very first encounter with an intruder in my house, I'd had all the wood doors, inside and out, re-placed with steel ones. It would require a tank to take them out. I raced to the nightstand, stunned to realize I'd left the phone out on the din-ing room table. *Idiot!* The Seecamp lay next to the empty phone cradle, and I picked it up. It felt dry, but who knew if it would work?

I turned toward the windows. Once before, I'd crawled out into the night to save myself. I could do it again. Before I could make a move, his voice cut through the silence.

"I want that flash drive, Bay. Give it to me, or I'll burn the damn house down around you."

CHAPTER
FORTY-THREE

I DOUSED THE LIGHT BESIDE THE BED AND CREPT TO-
ward the window. Smashing it would set off the alarm, though
I had yet to figure out how Nicholas Potter had managed to get
around it in the first place. Had I left a door unlocked somewhere? A
window not closed tightly? That should have triggered an alert on the
panel. Maybe it had, and, in my panic to reset it, I'd missed the warning. Or maybe it had malfunctioned. It wouldn't be the first time.
Electronics had taken over our lives, and we put such faith in all the
gadgetry that we never stopped to think how easily it could all go
wrong. Until it did.

I moved away from the window, just in case Kendra Blaine was
outside waiting for me to show myself. Where in the hell was Mike
Raleigh? And his deputies?

"Why is it so important to you?" I hollered, stalling for time.
Surely reinforcements couldn't be more than minutes—or seconds—
away. "Why did you give it to me in the first place if you're willing to
go through all this to get it back?"

"You're wasting time. You've got one minute to come out with it."

I could hear him turning the knob, testing the door. I strained to detect the smell of gasoline or some other kind of accelerant. I didn't believe he'd be stupid enough to burn up his one chance to get the drive, but he hadn't been exactly rational in the past few hours. Although the contents of my safe would probably survive a fire, that wouldn't bring him any closer to getting his hands on what he sought, even if it had been in there.

The doorbell, sounding faint and far away through the reinforced door, made me jump. The cavalry had arrived. I raced to the closet and grabbed up one of Red's heavy boots and flung it straight at the window, turning at the last moment to throw my hands over my face.

The alarm didn't go off, but in a moment the whole world erupted. From outside, I could hear someone calling my name. I edged closer to the broken pane.

"He's in the house!" I shouted.

"Stay down!" I thought it was Mike Raleigh's voice, but I couldn't be sure.

A moment later, I heard more glass shattering, car doors slamming, and a lot of yelling. Footsteps pounded on the hardwood floor—whose, I couldn't tell. I clutched the Seecamp to my chest and waited.

Then, from just below my broken window, I heard someone holler, "Over here! By the dune. He's running!" followed by Mike Raleigh's "Go! Go! Go!"

A shot! Then two more, in rapid succession.

"He's down! He's down!"

It felt like listening to an old radio program from back in the forties, the kind the Judge used to talk about, where sound effects and dialogue had allowed the listener to fill in the visuals himself. In the darkness of my bedroom, my imagination followed Mike Raleigh and the deputies as they raced up to stand, breathing heavily with exertion and adrenaline, over the fallen body of Nicholas Potter.

Dead? I wondered. I hoped not. I still didn't understand the tangled threads, all the violence that had erupted since the day, barely a week before, when Cecelia Dobbs had made her first, tentative call to my office. And I wanted to understand, to be able to tell her parents why she'd died. And to be able to tell myself it hadn't been my fault.

Everything outside had gone quiet. I reached out and turned on the lamp on the nightstand. The bed was covered with splinters of glass, although most of it had fallen outside. I leaned into the closet and pulled out my old Birkenstocks, slipping my feet into them in case some of the shards might have ended up on the floor. I gripped the Seecamp and moved to the door. I stood for a few moments, listening, then swiveled the lock. Slowly, I eased it open, the gun held against my shoulder. *Never lead with your weapon.* One of Red's many lessons when he first taught me how to shoot.

The hallway was empty, and I let out the breath I hadn't realized I'd been holding. I dropped the gun in my pocket so that if I encountered one of the deputies he wouldn't mistake me for a bad guy. I had already passed the guest bathroom across the hall, when it registered that the door was closed. Tightly. It hadn't been like that before. *Had it?* I slid my hand into my pocket and had just turned back when the door suddenly flew open. Before I could react, Kendra Blaine stepped into the hallway, and for the second time that night, I found myself staring into the barrel of a gun.

"Get the drive," she said without preamble.

"I don't have it."

She took a step toward me, the gun wavering a little in her hand. She looked confused, her eyes flicking from side to side. It made me wonder, for a brief second, if she really was the stone killer I'd labeled her, at least in my mind. Maybe it had all been Potter. He'd completely snowed me with his good looks and easy charm. Later, hopefully, I'd have time to examine why I'd been so easy to fool. And what that said about me . . . about a lot of things.

"It's not worth it, Kendra," I said softly. "*He's* not worth it." I waited a beat. "He left you here and ran."

"Shut up!" A few seconds passed before she said, "Is he . . . ?"

"Dead? I don't know. But they definitely have him. It's only a matter of time before they come to check on me. Put the gun down."

"It's my fault," she said, more to herself than to me, I thought. "I let him down."

"It doesn't matter now. It's over."

"No!" The gun came up, steadier now. "I can still disappear. But I need the money. Get that damn drive, or I swear I'll kill you!"

"I told you, it's not here."

"You're lying! Nicky said—"

We both heard the pounding on the door at the same time, followed a moment later by Mike Raleigh's voice.

"Bay? It's me. Raleigh. We've got him. Let me in."

I watched her eyes grow round with surprise, and her gaze shifted briefly to the hallway behind me. Without any conscious thought or plan, I lowered my head and lunged at her, staying beneath her gun hand and aiming directly for her midsection. We fell together onto the hardwood floor, and I heard the breath rush out of her lungs in one long *whoosh,* followed a nanosecond later by the deafening report of the gun.

And the terrifyingly familiar sound of a bullet whizzing past my ear.

CHAPTER
FORTY-FOUR

GRAY DAWN HAD JUST BEGUN TO STREAK THE SKY out over the ocean when I finally walked out of the sheriff's substation off Pope Avenue. My Jaguar, delivered by a couple of off-duty deputies, sat across the parking lot next to Erik's Expedition. He'd been waiting for me. He stepped down onto the blacktop and raised a hand as I walked over to join him. His statement had taken a lot less time than mine, once he'd handed over Rebecca Castlemain's flash drive and the passwords he'd teased out of it.

I forced a smile. The look of exhaustion on his face pretty much mirrored how I felt. Without a word, I held out my arms and enclosed him in a hug. It wasn't something we normally did, but it seemed appropriate for the occasion. After a brief hesitation, he squeezed me back.

"You okay?" he asked, holding me away from him.

I disengaged and leaned against the side of his SUV. "Yeah. You?"

"Glad this is all over, more than anything. Is Blaine talking?"

"Nonstop. Mike told me they can't shut her up."

We stood for a while without speaking before Erik said, "You hungry?"

"Famished. How about Sunrise Café? I think they open at six."

"You sure you're all right? You look a little . . ."

"Like I had a run-in with a bus? That's exactly how I feel, but I'll be okay. I'll meet you at Palmetto Bay."

Ten minutes later I wheeled into the parking lot beside the marina. The air off the water was cool, but I took a table outside. The other few scattered early birds had opted for indoors, so we had the raised patio to ourselves. I asked for hot tea for myself and coffee for Erik, who joined me a moment later.

We sat in silence until the drinks had been delivered and both of us had ingested a sufficient quantity of caffeine to reactivate a few brain cells. We ordered enough food for four people before finding ourselves again alone.

"You want to talk about it?" Erik asked.

"Sure. Although we should do a formal debriefing back at the office so we can get it all down for the record. Mike said we'd have our files back as soon as they copy everything."

"Potter's going to make it?"

"Yeah, so they say. Either one of the deputies is a crackerjack shot, or he got lucky. Got him dead center on the right thigh. Shattered bone. He went down and stayed there."

"Is he talking?"

"Not yet. They sedated him at the hospital so they could dig out the bullet and set his leg. Mike has a deputy stationed there to let him know when Nick wakes up."

I looked up to find the waitress bearing plates. I inhaled the fragrance of the eggs Benedict and double order of hash browns a moment before I attacked them. When I came up for air, I said, "Kendra says they never intended to kill Rebecca Castlemain."

"Are they buying that?" Erik spoke around a mouthful of pancakes.

"She says the plan was just to get her into the hospital and out of the house so Nick could get access to her financial stuff on the computer. He figured she'd give him the passwords under the guise of taking care of things for her while she was laid up. Judging by what everyone says about Rebecca, I'm not sure she would have bought into it, but that's what Blaine's claiming."

"Does she say why they abandoned the scheme with Dalton Chambers? Seems to me that was working pretty well."

I dragged the last of my English muffin through the egg yolk on the plate. "Potter and Blaine set that up, but then things went bad, and he couldn't wait. He'd gotten himself in so deep with the gambling, he had to have a lot of money, fast. All those pictures you found of him in Vegas and Atlantic City should have set off my alarm bells, but they didn't."

Erik sat back as the waitress approached and refilled his coffee. When she'd moved back inside, he said, "Why is Blaine being so cooperative? I thought she'd probably lawyer up and keep her mouth shut."

"I don't think she quite trusts Potter. My guess is that she's getting her version in before he wakes up and decides to toss her under the bus. He's the one with the connections. She could never afford the kind of high-priced legal talent he's going to have access to."

"Maybe not, if he was broke enough to resort to murder in order to get his hands on his grandparents' money. And I sure can't see Mr. Castlemain helping him out, can you? I mean, they killed his wife whether they meant to or not."

"I guarantee Potter has an ironclad alibi for that night. He'll put that on Kendra. And maybe he can swing some cock-and-bull story about self-defense with Chambers." I shrugged. "He's slick. I wouldn't want to bet against his coming out of this a lot better than she does."

"But the kidnapping charge isn't going away," Erik said. "That should keep him out of circulation for a while."

I shuddered, telling myself it was the cool wind off the water. "True."

"I wonder if he knew about Rebecca's will. The one I found on the flash drive," Erik said, almost to himself.

"I think he did. That's why I'm inclined to believe they didn't mean to kill Rebecca. Getting his hands on the access codes to her accounts would have been a lot easier than waiting for a will to be probated, even if he would have come into a lot of money on her death."

"You're probably right. It was always about the gambling. He was selling his house, probably getting ready to run. There are lots of very nice places without extradition treaties with the U.S. Two birds with one stone. He gets all his grandparents' cash and escapes the guys he owes money to."

After our plates had been cleared and I'd settled up the bill, we walked around the side of the building and over to the marina. A couple of early rising fishermen loaded supplies into a sleek powerboat at the end of the dock, but few others had yet ventured out of the condos that ringed the small harbor. We leaned against the railing and watched a weak sun struggle to burn away the thin layer of mist hovering over the water. Farther out, over the ocean, the sky seemed darker than it had at dawn. Maybe a storm brewing.

"I still don't get why Potter gave you that flash drive in the first place, then was ready to kill to get it back," Erik said softly. "I mean, if he wanted us to crack the passwords for him, he could just have waited a couple of hours."

"I told him that Cecelia's death was being ruled a homicide, and I'd have to turn over all the records to the sheriff—including his. I think he panicked. All along it was meant to look like a suicide, which would have given them enough time to loot the accounts and get out of the country. Chambers—or whichever one of them it was that killed Cecelia—screwed that up by leaving the car in a place we'd already checked. If not for that, they might have gotten away with it."

"But why did they have to kill Cecelia?" Erik spoke without turning his head, his voice quiet against the cool morning air.

"All Mike Raleigh would say was that Blaine claims it was Nick's idea." I had to swallow around the hard knot of guilt in my chest. "Nick told them someone from the bank was onto the scam, and they needed to take care of it. Supposedly Chambers knew immediately who it had to be. He lured Cecelia out to a meeting on Sunday night and got it out of her. Blaine swears she doesn't know any more than that."

"And Chambers is conveniently dead. Was that Potter?"

"Kendra says yes. Ballistics will have to match the bullet in his brain with Nick's weapon, but I don't have reason to doubt her. I saw how she handled the gun she was waving around at me. If I'd thought she had any experience with it, I never would have taken the chance of charging her. I don't see her being capable of it."

"How did she get in your house?"

"She says Nick stopped and picked her up. They left his car at the Westin and walked in from the beach. Found one of the back windows open. They planned to locate the drive and take off. They didn't count on my having made it out of the water alive."

"Well, since it looks as if they've basically turned on each other, we'll probably get the whole story eventually." Erik turned and rested his elbows on the railing. "Do you think Potter would have taken her out, too?"

"Who knows? I wouldn't have trusted him, if I were Kendra."

He took a long time to respond. When he did, he turned his face away, out toward the water. "You did, though, sort of. Trust him, I mean. Didn't you?"

Yes, I replied, inside my head, but I couldn't make the word come out. I wanted to defend myself, to insist it hadn't been the glint of desire in his steel blue eyes—eyes that reminded me so much of Alain Darnay's. That I hadn't been flattered by his dogged pursuit of me, the innuendo that floated just below the surface of our verbal exchanges. The truth was I'd been shocked just a few hours before by his obvious disdain for me as a woman. Shocked not only at his words but by my own lack of perception. I prided myself on being able to read people, and he had single-handedly destroyed my faith in my own ability to tell the good guys from the bad ones. I'd be a long time getting that back.

"Bay?"

I sighed and turned to face him. "Yes, I did. I'd like to think I would have tumbled to his game sooner or later, but I may just be kidding myself."

"I didn't pick up on his vibe, either, so maybe we can just concede that he was a damn good con man."

"He pretty much said the same thing last night. He said it came from hanging out with politicians all those years."

"I can believe that." I could feel him relax a little. "Anything else we should talk about? I need to get home to Stephanie. She's been sitting up all night waiting for me."

My heart leaped in my chest. For the first time in way too many hours, I thought about Red, tucked up in the guest room, I assumed, at Joe Pickens' house in Walterboro. Through everything that had happened, it had never once crossed my mind to wonder if he'd tried to call me and might be worried when I didn't answer. Or that I should reach out to him for comfort. Suddenly, the reason for all those middle-of-the-night wanderings, the sleeplessness that had plagued me, came into focus. I jerked away from the railing and walked briskly up the dock. I didn't want to think about it. I *wouldn't* think about it. Too much stress. Too many things to feel guilty about. On top of everything else, I couldn't deal with the idea that I might have made a mistake. A life-altering mistake.

"Bay! Wait up!"

Erik's voice bounced off my back as I broke into a trot.

CHAPTER FORTY-FIVE

J SLEPT FOR NEARLY TWELVE HOURS AND WOKE TO complete darkness and the sound of rain beating on the roof. I rolled over out of my cocoon of sheets and blankets to find that every muscle in my body was screaming. The expanse of king-size bed beside me lay empty. I stretched and watched the numbers on the clock roll over to 11:21.

I felt leaden, a heavy, dull headache pressing against the inside of my skull. I had just forced myself upright and pulled on my robe when the bedroom door slid open.

"Oh. You're awake."

Red stood in the doorway, the light from the hall casting his face into shadow. I could feel the tension radiating from his body, sense the wariness in those three words.

Our reunion hadn't been exactly pleasant.

"I'm going to take a shower," I said, skirting by him on my way to the bathroom.

Neither of us made a move toward touching the other.

"I'll make some tea. You hungry?"

I had to think about it. "Yes."

"Dolores left some chicken soup. She said to make you eat it when you woke up."

That made me smile. Dear Dolores. I wondered where my Hispanic housekeeper and friend had learned the Jewish tradition of chicken soup as the cure for all ills, both mental and physical.

"That sounds good. Give me fifteen minutes," I said and closed the bathroom door behind me.

It took closer to twenty, and I spent the time under the blessed steaming spray to get my head—and maybe my life—back together.

I towel-dried my hair and got clean sweats from the dresser. The face that stared back at me from the mirror looked haggard, but I couldn't be bothered to worry about it. I paused in the hallway, hesitant to confront Red in a way I'd never felt in all the long years I'd known him. I sucked in a breath and squared my shoulders.

Red had set the table in the alcove by the bay window in the kitchen. Almost every light was on, beating back the stormy darkness that pressed against the house on all sides. He turned from the stove when I came slowly up the three steps. Wordlessly, he ladled soup into a wide bowl and carried it over as I slid into my chair.

"You want crackers? Or bread? Dolores left a loaf of that sour-dough you like."

How formal we're being, I thought. *How careful.*

"Bread would be good. Thanks."

I didn't wait but began spooning up the broth, rich with chicken and thick, wide noodles. Red slid a plate with three slices of buttered bread onto the table and dropped heavily into the chair across from me.

"I got the broken windows all boarded up. I'll call the glass people tomorrow."

I didn't answer. If he wanted to make small talk, that was fine by me.

"And I had the alarm company here. They aren't sure exactly what happened, maybe a circuit shorted out. But it's all tested and working now. They'll rewire the new windows once they're in."

"I should sue them," I said, slurping noodles.

"You really want to do that?"

When I didn't respond, he let it rest. Then, for a long time, he just sat and watched me eat. By the time I'd taken the sharp edge off my hunger, I couldn't stand the strained silence any longer.

"I have to call Bitsy."

His raised eyebrows told me my words had surprised him. "Bitsy? Why?"

The realization had come to me in those few floating moments between sleeping and waking, when your conscious mind hasn't quite regained control. And it came in the wavering image of Nick Potter, his head bent conspiratorially next to Lily Middleton's at his grandmother's memorial service. And a lot of things clicked into place.

I looked up at my husband. "Because I need to get this damn thing straight in my head. I know she wouldn't knowingly hurt anything or anybody. Hell, she can't bring herself to kill bugs. But I need to know exactly what she said to Lily Middleton. I know as sure as I'm sitting here that she told her about my interest in Kendra Blaine. She must have. And Middleton told Potter. He was onto me before he ever laid eyes on me." I sighed. "Bitsy couldn't keep her mouth shut. That's where the chain started."

And ended with Cecelia Dobbs facedown in a slimy lagoon.

I could hear Red choosing his words carefully. "But what's the point? You said yourself it wasn't intentional. There's no way Bitsy could have known what would happen. Can't you just leave it alone? Are you prepared to ruin a lifelong friendship by calling her on it? What would that accomplish?"

"I confided in Bitsy. I trusted her. And Cecelia Dobbs is dead."

"You didn't kill her, Bay. When they finish with her car, they'll know which one of them was with her. If it wasn't Chambers, then Potter or Blaine will go down for it. Someone will pay."

I pushed the empty bowl away and finished off the last slice of bread. "I don't want to argue anymore, Red. But you have to understand that I'll carry the guilt of that around with me like a tumor for the rest of my life. And Bitsy needs to know her part in it. She needs to know what violating my trust cost that poor, silly girl."

I could see him struggling to control his frustration. We'd both lost our tempers during the long shouting match we'd had when he came home to find Dolores and me sweeping up glass from two broken windows. He'd trotted up the steps from the garage, buoyant from his participation in the successful raid in Walterboro the night before, and I'd had to crush him with my tale of kidnapping, home invasion, and gunfire.

His first reactions had been fear and relief, and he'd alternated between hugging and shaking me until I ordered him to back off. Then anger, his efforts to control it finally unsuccessful. Why hadn't I called him? Why had I let him walk into this nightmare totally ignorant of everything? What the hell had I been thinking to leave him sleeping a hundred miles away while I was being threatened and attacked in our own damn house?

Dolores had grabbed up her handbag, murmured something about the shopping, and beat a hasty retreat out the door to the garage.

I'd let him rant, then made him sit beside me on the far end of the sofa in the great room while I laid it all out for him as best I could: Rebecca Castlemain's death, then Cecelia's. The flash drive. Kendra's phony call and my wild ride in the back of Potter's SUV. The escape and the two confrontations. I'd tried to be logical and succinct, downplaying my own personal danger, but I could tell he wasn't buying it. He didn't get the whole thing, he said. I wasn't sure I did myself, not completely. At one point, he'd held up a hand to stop my rambling explanation.

"Who attacked you at the office?"

I'd almost laughed. After everything else that had gone down, that seemed like the most trivial of incidents. "I don't know," I said. "Mike said neither of them is copping to it. Erik's theory that it might have been connected to the case with the battered women's shelter is probably as good as any."

"My money's on Potter," my husband had said. "The bastard showed up early for your meeting, whacked you, and rifled the office. Then he left and came back to 'discover' you when he didn't find what he came for."

It could have been that way. I remembered there'd been a bottle of wine, wrapped in a brown paper bag, in his car that night. Maybe he'd used that to club me in the back of the head.

Red's voice jerked me back to the present. "You have to get past this, Bay. You were trying to help the Dobbs girl. *She* came to *you*. You didn't go seeking her out." He ran a hand through his short hair in that typical Tanner fashion that always reminded me of Rob. He forced himself to speak softly. "You can't take responsibility for everything that goes wrong in the world, honey. You always try to do what's right. Sometimes it just doesn't work out the way you want it to."

I was sure Red had no idea he'd just pretty much described my life. And our marriage. I swallowed hard against the pain of it. The question was, what the hell was I going to do about it? I watched the love radiate from his tired eyes, love that I felt desperately unworthy of. I wanted so much to reach across the table and take his hand. Tell him it would be all right, that we'd figure things out. But would we? *Could* we?

I wondered if he'd been able to read all that in my face when he rose abruptly and crossed to the stove. I dropped my head into my hands, too beaten down from the horrible events of the past week to think rationally anymore. I looked up when he set the mug of tea in front of me. Before I could reach for it, Red captured my hands in both of his.

"It'll be okay, honey. We'll talk some more tomorrow. Drink your tea."

I forced a smile. I didn't deserve his understanding, his patience. I didn't deserve *him*. I'd let a deathbed promise to my father lead me into a hasty decision that could ultimately ruin two lives. I cared for Red. Deeply. I just wasn't sure if I—

"I'm not taking the job."

I stared at him. "What?"

"I called Joe and told him to find someone else."

"Red, you can't do that! It's perfect for you. You want— No, I won't let you give up your career because you think you need to baby-sit me. Call him back. Tell him you changed your mind."

My husband stared steadily into my eyes, his own calm, with not a flicker of regret I could discern. "It's a done deal, sweetheart. And it's not about not trusting you on your own. I hardly slept last night. I kept thinking about all the nights it would be like that. Without you. And I decided it's not worth it."

I felt the tears rolling down my cheeks, and Red reached up a hand to wipe them away.

"It'll be okay. I know things . . . aren't exactly the way I'd like them to be between us. But we'll work on it, okay? If you're willing. I'll be here, and we'll just work on it. I love you so much."

The phone rang, shrill in the nighttime stillness. I jerked back, and Red rose to answer, his last words hanging in the air between us.

"Lavinia," I heard him say, "what's wrong?"

I jumped up. The clock over the sink had ticked past midnight. Only bad news came this late. In a few steps I crossed the kitchen and jerked the phone out of Red's hand.

"What's the matter?"

"Bay? I know it's late, but I was just asking Redmond if you've been watching the TV."

"Watching TV? What the hell are you talking about?" I could feel my pulse jumping in the side of my head where the phone was pressed.

"Language, Bay," she said automatically. Then, "We've been glued to it almost all evening long. What are you going to do?"

I felt as if I'd fallen down Alice's rabbit hole into Wonderland. "What are you talking about? Do about what?"

"There's a hurricane on its way," she said. "And we're dead in its path. They could order mandatory evacuations by tomorrow morning."

"Are you sure?" I asked stupidly. "Turn on the Weather Channel," I whispered to Red, who was hovering at my shoulder. "Hurricane warnings."

In a moment, I could see the big red and orange blob that filled the screen, rotating menacingly off the east coast of Florida.

"Of course I'm sure," Lavinia snapped. "Where have you been all day?"

I almost laughed at that. She really didn't want to know. I watched the feeder bands of rain and thunderstorms streaming off the main body of the hurricane drifting right over top of us. And I could hear them pounding on the roof and rattling the palmettos and oaks that surrounded the house. It must have come out of nowhere. Usually we had at least a few days' warning.

"I've . . . been busy with work." Feeble, but nonetheless true.

"Well, Lizzie and I have decided to stay put, at least for now. Julia is having a hard time dealing with all the noise and fuss. If we do have to get out in a hurry, I'll need some help."

"Of course," I said. "Let me get the details on what's happening, and I'll call you back. Will you be up?"

"I don't think anyone will be getting much sleep tonight," she said, her voice quivering a little.

"Red and I will batten down the hatches here and be there in a couple of hours. Try to keep everyone calm."

"You be careful," she said and hung up.

I turned to Red, who was standing in the middle of the kitchen, his attention riveted on the image of the swirling mass of potential catastrophe.

"This could be bad," he said. "It's already a Category Two and strengthening. It was supposed to swing out to sea, but it's suddenly taken a tick to the west. We're right in the path of the northwest quadrant. Worst possible scenario."

He held out his arm. Without thinking, I moved into the comfort and warmth of his embrace.

"We need to get to Presqu'isle," I said. "They won't be able to handle things there on their own."

"We'll get the rest of our windows boarded up, grab the essentials, and head out," he said, planting a soft kiss on the side of my head. "Don't worry."

I turned my face toward his and met his steady gaze, full of strength and love.

"Lots of storms to weather," he said, "but we'll get through them."

I smiled and let my head drop briefly onto his shoulder.